LIFE
After
DEATH

The Extraordinary Life of JC Merrick

Book One

Emory D. Lynn

ISBN 978-1-63784-317-8 (paperback)
ISBN 978-1-63784-318-5 (digital)

Copyright © 2024 by Emory D. Lynn

All rights reserved. No part of this publication may be reproduced, distributed, or transmitted in any form or by any means, including photocopying, recording, or other electronic or mechanical methods without the prior written permission of the publisher. For permission requests, solicit the publisher via the address below.

Hawes & Jenkins Publishing
16427 N Scottsdale Road Suite 410
Scottsdale, AZ 85254
www.hawesjenkins.com

This book is a work of fiction. Names, characters, locations, businesses, events, incidents, and dialogue in this novel are either the products of the author's imagination, or are used fictitiously, or are cases where much literary license has been taken.

Any resemblance to real persons, businesses, conversations, events, or characters, living or dead, is purely coincidental.

Printed in the United States of America

EPIGRAPH

"I have counted the hairs on your head before your were born. The fullness of your journey was known before your creation. All that you are and will become I have planned and foretold."

The Illuminated Book of Life

Preface

Writing is a collaborative effort. Blessed or cursed, with a fertile and wicked imagination, I've sought to incorporate true life experiences with flights of fancy. Countless people have encouraged me to write. Observing human nature has given me a wealth of information and ideas to pursue and include in my writings. Most of you know who you are. Nonetheless, I'd like to thank Charlie, David, Don, Helen, Bobbi, Dan, Steve, and Jack, among others too numerous to count. Most of all, I'm dedicating this book to Lucienne and Kip, the two loves in my life. And of course, this book is dedicated to all readers everywhere. After all, where would writers be without their readers and fans? May we all live long and prosper.

I hope you enjoy this book as much as I've enjoyed creating it.

Cheers,
Emory D. Lynn

CHAPTER 1

Say what you want about my life. It is not anything close to normal. I'm an orphan. And I'm dead. Well, I was dead. I'm alive now, but different. Not nearly the same and about as far from normal as you can get. Confused? Hey, stand in my shoes for an hour. You'll think you're going nuts too.

The significant events in my life began about a year ago. First thing, both my parents died in a car wreck. So did nine other people. Just one of those freak things that happens. Semi blows two rear tires as my parents were right next to those rear duals. The force slammed my parents' BMW into oncoming traffic, and seconds later, eighteen vehicles were wrecked, and nine people were dead, including Jonah and Catherine Merrick, my mom and dad.

I was sixteen when it happened. Didn't turn seventeen until March 14 of '94. It's hard, freaking hard, going from being a member of a loving family one minute, and in the blink of an eye, I'm an orphan. But the wreck happened, and there is not one single thing I can do about it. You think time heals all wounds? Huh. Think again. The best I've been able to do so far is grow a scab over it. Still picking that scab. Still bleeds. Counseling? Sure. For the first six months I attended more talk therapy sessions than you could count. I prayed more in those first six months than all the other times put together. Did prayer help? It did. But talk therapy? Not so much.

At first, I was an emotional wreck. I think only God's grace held me together. Being a wreck lasted about two weeks. Then I felt more alone than anybody in the history of the universe has felt or will ever feel. Not lonely, mind you, just alone. Kip probably saved my life. He's been my constant companion since I was about fourteen. Kip's my Goldendoodle, a mix of poodle and golden retriever. Deep-green eyes, pure, unconditional love, and hugs forever. Kip's genetics must have been off somewhere. He's the only dog I've ever seen or read about that has green eyes. Sure, some huskies have startling blue eyes. But I've never heard of a green-eyed dog. Go figure.

I've come to realize Kip is my gift from God. He really is. I know it sounds very strange, even unbelievable. But I swear I can sometimes see the Holy Spirit in Kip when he looks at me. Most of the time, he's just a lovable fur ball. But there are times…

Kip's a handful sometimes but has the sweetest and goofiest personality ever. And intuitive. Kip knew something was up the night I got the knock on our front door, telling me what happened. That was late Wednesday evening, September 8, 1993. I will never ever forget that date.

Both my parents were as loving, kind, nurturing, and supportive as any kid could ask. They listened to me, encouraged me, supported me, guided me, challenged me, and made me think. In short, my first sixteen years were idyllic. They taught me right from wrong, what it is to be a moral person, and helped me build a solid foundation through my faith in God. Then with a knock on the door, they were gone.

My schooling helped. Kings Academy teaches boys and girls to become productive young ladies and gentlemen. Proper manners may sound stuffy, but a "Please" and "Thank you" are never ever out of style. Holding a door open for somebody entering or leaving an establishment, whether they're eight or eighty-eight years of age, man, woman, boy or girl, is just plain polite. The world is in need of a serious dose of polite.

LIFE AFTER DEATH

Then I died. Seventeen. Drown during a scuba diving accident or what I thought was an accident at the time. What a lousy life event, dying at seventeen. The docs told me I was gone about a half hour. Now I'm back, I think. Go ahead, look it up. I did. Nobody dies for a half hour, then wakes back up. No detected brain waves for thirty minutes. Sheet-over-your-head dead. You figure it out. Only one person has come back from that, and He walked on water. Trust me, I am not that guy.

It was Saturday. Late May, Memorial Day weekend, in fact. About eight months after Mom and Dad died. I was still sometimes feeling lost, lonely, and pissed. A group from school was going scuba diving out of Sunrise Beach Park. They invited me, and I'd thought, *What the hey, the distraction might do me some good*, so I went along. I figured it might even be fun.

Everything was great. We were all enjoying ourselves until it wasn't and we weren't. The scuba gear rental outfit and the police investigated. The best they could figure, something was wrong with my air tank mixture. I'm told I blacked out. Next thing I knew, I was being hustled down a hallway filled with bright lights. My sense was it was a hospital, but I don't really know. I remember feeling disconnected, not in touch with my body in any way whatsoever. Like it didn't matter, wasn't important. And that was it. Lights-out. No more anything. I guess that's when I died. Clinically dead for a full half hour. Sheet-over-my-head dead.

Anyhow, the team of docs who worked on me when I drowned were still in the room when I came back. Nobody had a clue. Even my longtime doctor, Phyllis Church, was there and just as clueless.

Then I was in a coma for a month. I guess I caused some chaos when the sheet covering me moved. Maybe it wasn't a coma exactly. Nobody grows when they're bedridden or comatose. Nobody gets smarter when they're out. Nobody attains a deeper understanding of life when they're unconscious. Except me apparently.

Nobody knew anything, and they were loath to use the m-word. But after spending countless hours trying to explain events, exploring every available theory, all you're left with is either "I have no idea" or "It's a Miracle" (yes, with a capital *M*). For me, it was a God

Wink. You've heard of God Winks, yes? If not, they're instances in life that you can ascribe to coincidence or luck or being in the right place at the right time. I'm a firm believer in God Winks. That's when God intervenes in your life, sometimes subtly, sometimes far more powerfully. My life has never been this strange, and it's getting more so almost by the week. I wonder what Mom and Dad would have thought about all this.

During the month I was unconscious, I grew two inches taller. I gained fifteen pounds of bone and muscle. From IV fluids? My muscles did not atrophy. I got stronger. None of this is supposed to happen. Ever. No way, no shape, no matter or form. Impossible. Yet, here I am. Taller, heavier, more muscle and better tone and living proof of the impossible. So luck? Nope. A happy coincidence? No way. A God Wink? There is no other explanation, at least not for me. Not even the docs were able to explain it. So God Wink it was.

I was pronounced healthy and released from the hospital on Thursday, June 30, 1994. Felt like I imagined it would feel when you get out of prison. Hospitals are wonderful institutions when you need them, right? But I was out and really jazzed. I could go where I wanted when I wanted. Eat what I wanted when I wanted, and it didn't taste like, well, hospital food. The little things in life, ya know? Wow!

Being thoughtful in expression always pays dividends. Kind words can heal where a thoughtless comment can devastate. My folks taught me that well. When Mom and Dad died, I was a junior at Kings and had years of academy manners and comportment to help guide me, including the strong foundation built by my folks. Not everybody has the benefit of that guidance and love. Some have the benefit but choose to ignore it. I was, and am, smart enough to pay attention. Most of the time. Now I'm stuck in the "anger" step of healing. Mostly. That part has been getting a bit better, maybe.

Mom was a world-class geneticist, involved in cutting-edge technology and theory. Holds… Held multiple patents. Suppose I hold 'em now. Dad cofounded a boutique investment firm a few years out of college and became very successful. Only after they died did I learn just how financially successful they both were.

LIFE AFTER DEATH

I was the beneficiary of their insurance policies, to the tune of $23 million. When they died, I became an instant multimillionaire. Big deal. I'd take my parents over the money every single time.

What does all that tell you? The character, Sherlock Holmes, supposedly once famously said, "Once you eliminate the possible, only the impossible remains," or something like that. That's me, Mr. Impossible. And I'm not even to the freaky stuff yet. I promise you, this gets interestinger and interestinger. I apologize, I'm getting ahead of myself.

It's been a rough ride during the last nine months since Mom and Dad died. Friends at school have helped, at least some of 'em. Mateo, Mat, has been a rock for me. We're the same age, born about a month apart, but our backgrounds couldn't be more different. He and his two sisters are being raised by his mom. Mat said he doesn't remember his dad, and I've never pried. It was pretty clear when we met all those years ago that his mom cares and does her best for all her kids. He's here at Kings Academy, and that says a lot about his family. Mat drives an old Honda. Takes care of it like it has to last a hundred years. Who knows? Maybe it will.

He's here on a full-ride scholarship. Kings Academy is a private school and not cheap. But Mat is as bright a guy as I've ever known, yet soft-spoken, down-to-earth, and somebody I've known and trusted since third grade. I love him like the blood brother I never had. Maybe more.

Mateo Betancourt has friendly golden-brown eyes and grins a lot. You can see he's always thinking. Mat is a little awkward. Kinda gangly. Hasn't grown into his legs or arms or feet for that matter. Hands that easily palm a basketball. Kid has massive feet! He's a bit shorter than my six-foot frame and has medium-length, wild dark-brown hair that always looks like he just came in from riding a tornado.

He's incredible with this computer stuff. It seems like those electronic bits are hardwired directly in his brain. Seriously, Mat's a computer genius, and he doesn't realize just how really good he is. It's like the electronics and code that make a computer a, well, computer, are the easiest thing in the world for him. He sees code like you and I see words on a page. He's just fully fluent. Has a real gift for those things, a bona fide full-on geek.

Kyle Follard is a year older, turned eighteen this past January. An only child, like me. A deep thinker and serious guy, Kyle is going places. No idea in which direction, but he'll definitely get there, wherever there is. We've known each other five or six years now. Long enough to become close. He's bigger, a bit over six feet tall, built for football but doesn't play. Brown eyes, light-brown hair, almost dark blond. Still battles acne some and has a few scars to show for it. Overall, he's a good-looking guy. Girls at the Academy are interested, so Kyle has more than a couple friends but nobody serious. He's said he's way too young to get involved in any serious romance. Like I said, smart guy.

I don't know much about his folks. I've met 'em. Been over to his house a few times. They seem normal, I guess. I know they both work. Don't know if Kyle is on a scholarship here or what. He drives an older VW bug, so he's not getting spoiled. Guy has a real good moral compass and good character. Superstrong academics. Always making honors and lists, and I know he works for his grades. Like I said, good family, good upbringing.

Kyle's an excellent listener, encouraging, and doesn't judge or preach. That's huge for me. Pretty quiet guy. But watch his eyes. He doesn't miss anything. In class or out. When he opens his mouth, something interesting, sometimes profound, comes out. That's Kyle. He's another anchor in my life right now.

Lucienne Abreo is seriously funny. We all need one of those in our circle of friends, right? Lu, to her friends, is younger but only by about six months. Drives an older Toyota. Has dual citizenship with Canada and here. Incredibly smart without an inflated ego. She's never gotten a grade lower than a 98 percent in her years at Kings. I think that's a record. She loves the hard sciences and is scary good at math. She's already put advanced statistics behind her. Gifted that way, but humble, ya know? She even keeps her instructors on their toes. What a hoot!

Lu was the one who took care of Kip while I was in my coma and hospitalized. What a blessing to be counted among her friends.

Besides that, she's a knockout at five feet, six inches, slender, startling blue eyes, naturally blonde hair with some curl, and definite curves where God intended. A figure that can stop traffic, and she's not even aware. She turns seventeen on August 9. Mischievous that one. A smile brighter than the sun. She's a runner. Her daily routine, in any weather, is a forty-five-minute run. She told me she's down to a mid-six average and wants to be in low sixes before winter. So the math genius that I'm not, it means she runs nearly eight miles a day. And there's just something about her, some quality or something I've not been able to identify that's drawn me to her. Physical attraction? Of course. I'm not dead, am I? But this is something else, something different. Something more. She is so out of my league. Nuts.

Mr. Crenshaw was my counselor at Kings. We've worked together for the last four years. He's kinda old, probably sixty or more. I know he's been at Kings quite a while, and he's smart. He's been a great guide and excellent resource, especially during these last months. Mr. C listens and sometimes suggests. Mostly he asks really introspective questions, nudging me toward figuring out my own stuff. Oddly enough, or maybe not, it works.

That's my circle. Oh, except Angus Dunbar. He's my attorney. Older than Mr. Crenshaw, probably seventy-ish. He's tall, several inches over six feet. Very slender. Long arms and legs. Bald on top without any evidence of a stupid comb-over. Always dresses well. I've never seen him in jeans, or as he calls 'em, dungarees. Easy to talk to, which has been a real blessing these past months. Incredibly intelligent. I can tell when we're together. He's looking at and listening to everything. I've always thought Mr. Dunbar doesn't suffer fools. I think he spent some time in England. Was born there maybe. Some of that culture is still in him, I think. I like it.

Every seventeen-year-old kid needs an attorney, right? Mr. Dunbar was my folks' attorney and counselor since before I was born. He's the executor of my estate. God! That sounds so snobbish, "my estate."

Where Kyle is quiet, Mr. Dunbar is reserved, you know? But maybe reserved like a volcano. He has an incredible command of the English language. I doubt he's ever really cussed in his life. And

I believe him to be very capable of reducing a courtroom opponent to a blubbering mess. Between his eyes and command of the English language, anybody engaging in a battle of wits with Mr. Dunbar would die the death of a thousand cuts, and his eyes would likely melt them on the spot. I've always respected Mr. Dunbar, and found him a bit intimidating. Then again, I'm seventeen. Haven't grown completely into myself yet.

Mr. Dunbar insists I call him by his first name, Angus. He looks out for my well-being, financial and otherwise. He's already been a huge help keeping me grounded. Makes sure I don't get all cocky and spoiled or do anything blindingly stupid. That would be sooo easy. How many seventeen-year-old kids do you know who are worth something north of $280 million? Not so many, I think. And my inheritance is growing faster than my trust allows me to spend it. Then again, my values aren't surrounded by dollar signs. My folks taught me that.

The way it's set up, I inherited my parents' life insurance policies. That's a hefty $23 million. I don't have ready access to my inheritance other than the life insurance proceeds. Angus has some control of my access to the stocks and bonds left by my parents until I'm twenty-one. As I said, when they died, that amount was right at $280 million. I really don't know what it's worth now. As far as I'm concerned, I'm already set for life from the life insurance benefits.

Angus doesn't have control of my inheritance; he just has some control of the "why" I can access my portfolio monies. Dad inherited stock from his family. Walmart, Berkshire Hathaway, and Home Depot in his inherited portfolio. Mom and Dad bought stock in Microsoft's initial offering. Dad had told me a couple of years ago all those stocks were purchased at their initial offering, and they've all split a time or three along the way. Looks like I need to become more informed about stocks and the stock market. Probably good to get to know some of those folks. Maybe I'll start with Dad's partner. See what I can learn from him.

Then there's the income from Mom's patents. She held, and now I hold, several patents on processes and technology related to

DNA sequencing, some of the DNA itself. I'll never understand how anybody can patent DNA, but I guess they can.

Anyhow, I own seventy-three patents and am leasing the rights to nine of them. Even Angus had to bone up on current law and regulations regarding Mom's patents and how we can allow others to benefit from what she discovered and invented. Well, there was a way, and Angus found it. Together, Angus and I set up licensing agreements for everything. Nine patents are now licensed to fifteen entities all over the planet. I think Angus told me the active licenses were generating around $75 million a year. Those funds go into a separate portfolio account. I don't need the money, at least not now. I've no idea what I'll end up doing with it. Whatever it is, it'll honor Mom and Dad.

My folks told me often money's just a tool. Like a hammer or a drill. Great to have when you need it, but nobody walks around bragging about their hammer or drill, right? Same with money. It's a tool, and like any tool, it is to be used well, and that's it. Enough said.

Angus has convinced me of the wisdom of keeping my wealth well under the radar. The interest alone on the combined insurance payouts is a bit over $110,000 a month. What seventeen-year-old kid needs to spend $110,000 a month? Not so very many, I think. That includes me. Because my inheritance had no debt attached, I spend less than a thousand dollars a month. That just means the rest keeps on earning interest, and the balance keeps increasing. But its only money, like I said.

Besides, for now, I'm only beginning to figure out my life, what I'm going to do with my finances, and how I'm going to use my inheritance. Damned if I'm going to become some spoiled rich kid. No way. That's not how I was raised. If I'm going to do anything good in this life, and I am, I intend doing it to honor my parents. After all, I'm their legacy. I intend to respect that gift and use all my talents in the service of others. Haven't figured out yet what all that means, but it feels and sounds right so far.

Like I've said before, I pay attention. My financial wealth is yet another gift from God. Nobody deserves what I've been given. We don't earn our way into heaven. But we're all responsible for ourselves and our actions and choices while we're here on earth. I'm determined to do good works because I want to, because I can, because it's the right thing to do. It honors my parents and acknowledges God's good in this world.

I also plan to live my life quietly. I don't need or want any fame, notoriety, or praise. I've done nothing to earn the gifts I've been given. They are mine to give freely and anonymously. And I will. Maybe in this way, I can be a God Wink for somebody else. Kinda like paying it forward.

The first thing I decided after riding my own personal emotional roller coaster for a few months was to petition the court to become an emancipated minor. I'd be eighteen in about a year anyway, but why wait? Now I'm legally considered an adult; can't legally drink or vote, but I get to be held accountable like a regular adult. Yikes!

It didn't make sense to become a ward of the state for a year. It seemed stupid. Angus agreed, so we did it. Lots of forms and legal maneuvering, gathering sworn statements from supporters and demonstrating a level of maturity beyond my biological age. Most of it was easy, if sometimes frustrating. We got through it. The court listened, reviewed our petition, sent me to court-appointed shrinks (at least I think they were shrinks), banged a gavel, and that was that. Declared an adult at age seventeen. Now I'm supposed to act like one, at least most of the time.

The second thing Angus and I tackled was to challenge all my senior-year coursework at Kings Academy. First finding was that it had never been done at Kings. Tradition said I should avail myself of my senior year studies because, well, everyone else did it that way. It was the law (maybe), and it was their tradition.

Angus looked for instances where others had challenged coursework in other schools, both public and private. Short version, it's been done. Not a lot, but there's precedence. After seemingly endless meetings and negotiations, we agreed on a series of tests proctored by academy staff. No grading curve because, well, they'd never done it before. So straight-up pass or fail. Fail just one test or interview, any of the tests or interviews, and I'd spend nine more months in school. Pass 'em all, and I'd graduate a year ahead of myself. Hmmm.

Two weeks of tests and interviews later, a full sixty hours of intense grilling, and I graduated. I am sooo glad to have that behind me. Now I get to focus on the rest of my life. Already know I've a ton of thinking to do. I have excellent resources and access to more if or when I need. Life may be looking up.

CHAPTER 2

Then there's the freaky side of my life. All the stuff I've shared with you so far is kinda normal, some of it in a strange way, but only on the unusual side of normal. However, this is where my life really goes off the rails. Nobody, but nobody, knows this yet. Not Mr. Dunbar, Lu, Mat, Mr. Crenshaw, or Kyle. I mean nobody. They'd lock me up and use me as a lab rat until I died. Not my idea of a life. What's so freaky? I'm just beginning to figure it out.

I have this ability. Maybe more like it came to me. I didn't go out and buy it. Didn't train for it. Things were mostly normal all my life, and then this…ability showed up. Or blossomed. Or announced itself. Another God Wink? I have absolutely no idea. But how can this be anything else? It sure isn't me, not in a million years.

Maybe I have more than one ability blossoming…maybe. I don't know. Probably. More than one. It is, or they are, for lack of a better way to explain, growing. Maturing, right? I mean this stuff keeps me up at night. I've not had a normal night's sleep since I died. Maybe I'll never get another good night's sleep as long as I live. Who knows?

First thing happened shortly after I got out of the hospital from drowning and dying. I was home. It was a great mid-July day. I was in the sunroom, cum atrium of our home, my home, studying. It's a glassed-in room, well lit with natural sunlight during the day. Dozens of plants inside, some semitropical in nature. It really is an excellent place to study and think.

I heard a *thunk* against a pane of glass and a robin lying on the ground, not moving. I went outside to see what happened. Looked to me like the bird just flew into the glass and broke its neck. I mean, even a bird's neck can't rotate that far without something happening, right? Well, I went back inside to get a couple of paper towels to pick up the bird. My thumbs were touching it gently so it wouldn't fall from the paper towels. What did I know? Maybe it wasn't dead.

As soon as I picked it up, I swear to you, it blinked its eye. Not my imagination. Freaked me out, and I almost dropped the thing! A few seconds passed, and it righted its neck, looked at me, and calmly as you please got up and flew away. I figured it was just my imagination. I didn't feel anything special when it happened. Nothing at all. But it, whatever "it" is happened. Bird wasn't really dead, just stunned. Except, when you turn an animal's neck around that far, it does some damage. Has to. Broken neck kills 'em, right? So this was just a case of mistaken mortality until the next freaky thing happened.

The next event was a couple of days later. We live—that is, I live—in a wooded area just outside Gig Harbor, Washington. Neighbors are spaced apart by a bit, not crammed next to one another like in Seattle or Tacoma proper. Our... (dammit!) My home sits on a bit over twenty acres of woodland forest and grass. It's about as idyllic as you can imagine. Mom and Dad built our home when I was young. It isn't a mansion or anything, but it's pretty nice. All sorts of wildlife consider our acreage a recreational park and visit often day and night.

I'd walked from our deck into our backyard and saw a fox just lying there. Three baby foxes were there too, likely her kits. All of them as still as death. First thing flashed in my mind was the robin. I walked up to the adult fox and saw some blood on her coat by her neck. Looked at the three kits and saw the same. But no obvious point of injury on any of them, just some blood, but not a lot. No idea what happened. They weren't mauled or anything, but somehow they died. By the looks of things and the blood, it wasn't by a natural cause unless death by predator is natural.

Thinking of the robin, I knelt down and stroked the fur of the adult fox. After a couple minutes of doing this, I saw her stir. Next thing, ignoring me completely, she used her snout to gently nudge each of her kits, and they, too, began to move. Meanwhile, I'm kneeling there, still petting the momma, and she's just taking it in. Not frightened or aggressive, not protective or anything. I don't know how long this went on, maybe seconds, maybe minutes. Time just seemed to suspend. Same thing as with the robin. I didn't feel any different, not in any way. But the same result as with the robin. I admit to being more curious than anything, but it kinda freaked me out, ya know? All I knew was that something very special and powerful was happening in my life.

Then the momma and her kits got up and sauntered into the trees as calm and cool, as though nothing out of the ordinary had just happened. At the edge of entering the woods, momma looked back at me for a brief moment, then turned around and sauntered away, kits in tow. Coincidence? No way. Spooky? Damn skippy! Spooky or not, freaky or not, I didn't sense having any particular power. What I did get a sense of was responsibility. Heavy responsibility. I'll get to that in a bit.

I thought about those two events for hours. I came up with a theory to test. I'll admit I was spooked, yet curious, ya know? There'd been a recent story in the newspaper and on TV. A twelve-year-old girl was in a Seattle hospital fighting a losing battle with primary cardiac tumors, cancerous. Maybe one or two cases reported worldwide each year. Incredibly rare. Even with surgical intervention, the five-year survival rate is about 17 percent. According to the news stories, the docs had tried everything except exorcism, and nothing's worked. This quiet small voice in my head kept telling me to visit her. That inner voice has been much more active of late.

Karen is her name, Karen Danvers. Seems like a sweet kid. Her folks, John and Betty, had been interviewed on TV. What form of hell must they be going through watching their child wither away, unable to do anything to even slow the progression of her deadly disease? I'm just beginning to come to terms with maybe being on the other side of that situation. Different circumstances, sure. But kinda the same in a way. Given what I suspected, I couldn't just ignore their situation or my quiet inner voice, could I? Would you? Hmmm.

Mom and Dad brought me up to believe in God. The good folks at Kings Academy encourage us to practice our own faith, that in God's Kingdom there are many mansions. They were there to guide us when we had questions on faith, but they were certainly not preachy. I always liked that. I got my faith, spiritual beliefs, sense of duty, and knowing right from wrong and that there are consequences for our choices and actions from my parents. They were steadfast in their guidance, and I was given a very strong moral compass. Some of the most important lessons life can teach, right? Having faith and a strong moral compass.

By the third day of hearing the story of young Karen Danvers, I knew I had a mission. My intuition told me not to talk about it with anybody. And I knew I probably needed to be invisible in carrying it out. Hospitals are quiet in the evenings, almost deserted at night. Almost. Getting to Karen's floor unobserved wasn't difficult. I just needed to be patient and was.

Getting into her room wasn't much more of a challenge. Again, patience was needed and given. Looking down at Karen, so small in that hospital bed, swallowed up really. Poor coloring. Deep-purple bruising under her eyes. Tubes and wires everywhere. Shallow breaths. Monitors blinking and beeping. Bags hanging from poles delivering God only knew what to her weakened, disease-ravaged body. Karen was in the fight of her life, and by the looks of things, she wasn't likely to win.

Softly, gently, quietly, I knelt down and reached out, laying my right palm on her feverish forehead, looking directly at her, eyes level between us. Her forehead was about the only exposed flesh on her body that wasn't invaded with some disease-fighting insult or other. She stirred a bit and opened her lackluster eyes expressing a question without voice or alarm. "Hi, Karen. I'm Michael. Just checking on you. Go back to sleep, sweetheart. I think you're going to get better now." Her eyes closed. I stood, and quietly I left her room and the hospital.

Held my breath all the way home. In that moment with Karen, when her eyes opened, my words just flowed. I hadn't rehearsed what I'd say if she was awake or woke up. Hadn't thought about it at all. You couldn't even call what I said spontaneous. It was like somebody speaking through me. Freaked me out! No idea where the name Michael came from. It was just there, then out my mouth. Thinking about it after, probably a good idea to not use my own name. Doing that could make staying anonymous complicated, right?

Almost a week later, John and Betty Danvers held a news conference in their daughter's hospital room. Strangely, or maybe not so much, there was no beeping, no visible monitors, only one IV in evidence. Karen looked like a different person than the girl I'd visited only a few short days earlier.

"Betty and I are here today," said John, "to thank all of you for your prayers and support. The doctors tell us our daughter is beating the cancer she's been fighting. They're telling us they have no idea what's happened, but against all odds and logic, Karen is recovering. They don't know what else to call it. They've told us for weeks the type of cancer Karen had doesn't go into remission. Betty, Karen, and I are calling it a miracle." Lifting his eyes to the ceiling, I could see John whisper, "Thank you, God."

I could see a huge smile on Karen's face and tears in her parents' eyes. So now I knew. Or at least I knew something. It was awesome, and it scared seven kinds of hell right out of me.

CHAPTER 3

You tell me. What in the world am I supposed to do with this knowledge, this ability, this gift? Think about it. That's all I've been doing for the last couple of weeks. My brain is in knots already. First, I'm an orphan. And I'm dead. And emancipated. And a diploma'd high school student. And a millionaire a few hundred times over. And I can heal the sick by the laying on of my hands. Apparently.

Trust me. I am not Him. But exactly what am I? Just how many more ands are coming my way anyhow? What's happened? So far, I'm feeling elated, alone, and scared shitless all at the same time and to the same degree. Kip is comforting, but I am not comfortable with what's happening, not comfortable at all.

Look. I know I'm smart, okay? Kings Academy doesn't enroll or teach average. They let us take intelligence tests if we want, and I was curious. Three batteries of tests later, my supposed IQ averaged 165. Huh. That doesn't mean much without common sense attached, and I think I've a fair dose of that.

Like I've already said, my folks were hands-on. They actively parented me. Challenged me. Encouraged me. Believed in me. We're not born with a whole lot of knowledge, maybe just the capacity to learn to some degree or other. My folks invested their time, patience, and intellects in me. I'm beyond grateful and will always be a better person for it. I know a lot of kids, and adults too, who were not nearly so blessed and fortunate. So to some degree, I have privileges. Then again, to whom much is given, much is expected, right?

I'm no snob about being smart, and I'm not about to belittle or look down on anybody. We all have gifts and burdens. I'd trade my privileges for having my parents back quicker'n a heartbeat. But. One of my privileges is being blessed with a pretty good brain. I had nothing to do with that. Having it, it seems important to use it properly. My parents taught me that lesson, and I bought into it completely. Now I also have this gift or ability or whatever it is to heal people and animals. Maybe. But let's not count that yet, okay? Smart as the tests say I am, I'm still not able to figure out what happened. And to be painfully honest, I'm not even sure I like it.

Mat is way smarter than me. Lu as well. Kyle too, probably. He's not a brainiac, but he has scary good insights. I figure Kyle and I are about equal in the gray matter area. I think Kyle has a lot hiding under his bushel, if you know what I mean. Angus has the advantage of decades of experience. I suspect he sometimes looks at me and is just shaking his head and laughing his ass off. Cut me some slack already, okay? Remember, I'm seventeen. Seventeen going on fifty.

Back to my situation. Smart as I am, supposedly, this is new territory. Really new territory. I've a wickedly fertile imagination. Sometimes it gives me inspiration. Now it's giving me perspiration and agitation. Think of it this way. Imagine you're old, sick, wealthy, and a not nice person. Imagine you learn of somebody with my, hmmm, ability. If you were that person, would you knock on my door and ask nicely for my help? Or would you sneak up on me, throw a bag over my head, take me to some undisclosed location, and use me against my will? See what I mean? Scares the snot right out of me. See what I mean by heavy responsibility? A weight I'm not so sure I want to carry. Then again, God doesn't give us anything we can't manage.

All those platitudes: "What doesn't kill you makes you stronger," "It's God's way of bringing His glory to the world, "This is a God Wink," "Reveal His glory to others." That's all well and good. But I'm seventeen years old for crying out loud. Seventeen, not forty or fifty. I'm just figuring out my life. I've not had dozens of years' experience, have I? I don't yet have the benefit of having lived decades of life experience, right? Then again, maybe that's part of why God has brought this into my life. But I could think about this gift or ability for years, and still I'd arrive at the same realization… It just is. It'll be with me for as long as it is and not a minute longer. I'll do the best I can and pray for His guidance, ask Him to lead me down the correct path. Then I have to learn to trust Him in all things. I am, as we all are, a work in progress. In my case, a young work in progress…asking Him to mold me as He wishes.

Suppose you were the Danvers. Perfectly good people with a child dying. To what lengths would you go to heal your child to prevent her death? Realistically, how could they be blamed for going to dark places in order to save their child? No sane parent wants their child or any child to suffer, especially when there is a cure, a way out. What steps would you willingly take in order to save your child, most especially when you knew, *knew* they could be healed? I think you'd justify a lot of dark things to heal your child, right? Welcome to my paranoia.

Imagine you're just John Q. Public, and you hear about a guy who has the ability to heal others. A bona fide miracle worker. How many people do you think would seek that person? In just one day, a week, a year, thousands of seekers, probably more. Every hour of every day and night. Relentless. Unending. Are you beginning to understand? Not good. In point of fact, pretty scary.

Then there's my side of this *gift* or mess. Take your pick. If I can help, and it sure seems that I can, is it a moral imperative that I do so? I am not the savior of mankind or the animal kingdom. I am very clear on this. I also know this ability I now have is to be used, employed, shared, entrusted in the service of others.

That's all well and good, except, except, except… How do I pick and choose? How do I approach one person and help them while walking past another who has just as great a need, perhaps greater, and not help? You're so smart. You figure it out because I'm honestly totally and completely lost on this one. My days of easy choices are a universe behind me. Besides, I'm seventeen years old! Nuts!

So here I am. Home. Tuesday? Huh. Wednesday. I'll have to check. Sitting in the atrium, staring toward the woods, but not really. I think they call it a thousand-yard stare, and I'm doing it. No idea how long I've been here staring. I think I originally was going to eat breakfast. Looking down, two congealed eggs stare back untouched. Stale toast and warm orange juice for companionship. Yuck. The clock says it's 3:30 p.m. Hmmm. Not the first time and not good. Time to fix this.

"Angus, JC here. Have I caught you at a good time?"

"JC! Good to hear from you! How are you, Lad?"

"I think I'm headed toward the dark side. Lately, I'm catching myself staring into the distance for hours. I forgot to eat today. Breakfast on the table, then it was half past three. I need to fix this. This is a big house, too big for me really. But I love it. So I'm thinking about hiring. Butler sounds stuffy and snobbish. Maid sounds worse. Think I would go mad. Any ideas?"

"Sounds to me you're thinking this through. Taking it seriously, I agree, isn't healthy, especially right now to be there alone with all your memories and idle days. I know Kip is a comfort, but still. Difficult to dialogue, yes? Seems a splendid idea, human companionship. Formal, but familiar. Of course, nobody can replace your mum and dad. That's not what you're seeking, I know. But somebody competent to quiet the rattles day or night, right? Somebody to provide occasional, gentle distractions. Maybe something like a minder. Certainly not a nanny! Good God no. You're too bright, too far beyond, don't you see?"

"My thinking as well, Angus. Anybody come to mind? Some service or other where I could poach a good fit?"

"Well, you've the funds. Hate to say it that way, but we must think on that, mustn't we? You've been very frugal with your insurance inheritance. Haven't touched any of the rest. Better than I think most others your age would behave. You know your insurance payments went into a money market account, right? You've really not touched that money in any significant way. Your monthly income from the interest alone is now a hundred eleven thousand. You've the funds to hire a couple people, pay them well, and still be quite comfortable. I checked your investments just yesterday, and they're doing nicely as well. The value of your inherited portfolio now stands at just over $300 million.

"Your patent portfolio is now at $57 million and counting. It looks like you're about to have another five licenses issued on two of your patents, so that portfolio will see a nice increase in the coming quarter and beyond. My advice to you is to let these two portfolios continue to grow. Anyhow, it sounds like you're thinking right in looking for qualified staff members.

"Building trust takes time, and I'll not be with you forever. JC, we all need a circle of those we can trust completely. I know you've your friends from Academy, but I think you'd benefit from some age. Not like me. Good heavens no, I'm a regular dinosaur. I'm thinking thirties somewhere, perhaps a bit more. Young enough to not remind you of your folks, old enough to have some experience, if you see what I mean."

"Exactly what I'm thinking as well, Angus. I've been writing lists of qualities I think I'd like this person to have, but I'm getting bogged in detail."

"Are you thinking long term on this? Sum it up for me, JC. What's your focus? And remember, we don't have to stop with one. There could be full- and part-time. Occasional or seasonal. It's your life, Lad. Now's the time to build your foundation. And we can always change focus and shift things around. Main thing is to make it strong, durable. Worthy. Then you can grow from there in whatever direction you wish."

"Is it possible or even reasonable to think one person could fill the role of a live-in mentor, minder, chef, and housekeeper? I'm getting involved in something that looks like it'll take up a good part of my days and weeks. I'm not ready to talk about it yet. But I can see I'm starting to neglect the house and grounds already. Lord knows my diet lately isn't altogether healthy. And I'm beginning to consider my personal security. There's just too much for me alone. If I'm going to build my foundation to last, I think I need a core of compatriots. More than casual friends. Deeper. More secure. Doesn't mean I'm tossing Mat, Kyle, or Lu. Lord no. Or you. You're all essential to me. Vital. As you said, I think we would all benefit from somebody or a few somebodies with some age and experience behind them, yes?"

"Has something happened? Have you seen or heard a prowler?"

"Nothing like that. It's complicated. I'm not ready to share it yet. But with the press from Mom and Dad's death, my inheritance now public along with my emancipation, it makes sense to me to take some proactive steps, wouldn't you think? Right now, I feel like I've a target painted on my back." I had no intention of telling Angus about this healing others thing. At least not yet. That time would come, but I had some figuring out to do first.

"I suppose you're right. Have you given any thought to man or woman? Perhaps a married couple? No children obviously. More distraction than you'd want at this stage and age, yes?"

"Agreed, no kids. Let's start with one. What do you think? See how many boxes get checked and go from there."

"Good. Done. I'll make some calls and arrange interviews. You'd like to do them here, I'm assuming. Be a bit mysterious about your home location until we've found our candidate. No sense in advertising what we're working to avoid."

"Yes. Just let me know when you've candidates. Let's do deep background checks on our selection before we interview. Make sure we're dealing with honest folks. I'm available anytime, as you know. This might sound strange, but I want to be exposed to them before they know who I am. See if I can get any sort of feeling about them before they have their interview face on. Does that make sense? I don't really know how to create that situation. It just sounds like a good idea to me. What do you think?

"I miss the academy. They were kind enough to allow me to test out on all my senior-year work. So school is behind me. And I'm in semiregular contact with Lu, Kyle, and of course, Mat. But not every day like in school. Even Mr. Crenshaw checks in now and again. Still, I used to see him almost daily. That changed when I left Kings. I'm not likely to become a hermit, but I don't want to grow in that direction either."

"Leave it to me, JC. Give me a week, and we'll have some folks worth chatting up."

"Deal. Thanks, Angus. Talk with you next week." And that's how it started.

CHAPTER 4

Nothing unusual happened the rest of the week. Tuesday morning, 8:00 a.m., Angus called. "JC! I've rounded up some possibles for us to look at."

"Have you done any background on 'em yet?"

"Not yet, just gathered some interesting characters for us to look at."

"Okay. Send me what you have. I'll get hold of Mat. He really loves this stuff. I'll have him dig into their backgrounds. See if everything makes sense, then we can go from there. Can you give me 'til the end of the week?"

"Sounds good. Catch me when you're ready, and we'll go over their quals. See you, then," and the line went dead.

Time to give Mat a call. "Mat! How ya doin'? It's been a bit, yea?"

"JC! Good to hear your voice. What cha been up to? Adjusting to life? Haven't seen you around for a bit."

"Getting better, man. Getting better. You know how it is some days, just one foot in front of the other. The alone part gets to me sometimes. Still, God is being very good to me. Part of the reason I'm calling. You up to doing some serious background checking on a few folks? I'm considering hiring one or two. Don't know what to call 'em yet. Maybe a minder type and somebody to do cooking, cleaning, and some groundskeeping. This place is a lot of real estate for one person. Or maybe it's just me. I'm feeling overwhelmed, and the edges are getting a bit dodgy if you get my meaning."

"Oh yeah. I get it. Mom still gets on me about my room. Forget about a house and that forest you live in. So what kind of background are you looking for? Anything interesting?"

"Maybe. You know about my inheritance, right? That's a lot of temptation for bad actors. Like flies to fresh poop. I want to avoid fortune hunters, anybody sketchy. My family worked for generations to create this. I'm not about to get stupid or lazy with it. I know you like sniffing in the underground, and I'm thinking you've some unusual and quiet skills. Am I right?"

"Uh-huh. On all counts. So let's change the subject a bit. How many are we looking at?"

"I've an initial list of seven candidates. Ages are from thirty to fifty-six. Men and women mixed. Some with interesting backgrounds on paper, some not so much. I don't want to assume anything with anybody. At the end of the search, I only want squeaky clean. Top-notch moral compass, folks who can't be bought, good history, and solid integrity. Loyalty is huge. And it'll be good to know their economic status, how they're fixed financially. Heavy debt load or gambling habits. Drugs. You know, the bad stuff. How they grew up. That sort of thing. Is that something you'll be able to dig out?"

"Some of it. Maybe a lot of it. But I think you're also going to need eyes on, you know? Check with friends and neighbors. Look 'em in the eye and see how they respond to questions. See what kind of signals they give off. Body language. Know what I mean? Anybody can fool a piece of paper, right? Fooling a person can be a bit more challenging."

"Definitely. Got it. Okay. I'll send these names and info to you via email using that encryption stuff you wrote. I really don't want this floating around out there. This is a paying gig for you, and don't argue. I've no idea what you'd charge a normal for something like this. Check your email in a couple days, and watch your regular mail for my check. You know the mail service between here and your home? Close, but not. If the amount needs adjusting, man up and tell me. Deal?"

"Come on, dude! You should know better. We're friends, yes? It'd not be right charging you. I sure as hell know you'd not charge me if our roles were reversed."

"Maybe. But you're still in school. You have bills, yea? And highly marketable skills, which you employ and for which you get paid, yes? And it's not like I can't afford it, right? Besides, I'd not trust anybody else with this stuff, you know? No argument, okay? Besides, maybe someday I'll be able to bill you for something!"

"Okay. Give me a few days. I'll get back to you."

"Thanks, Mat. Talk with you then." And that was that. I wrote him a check for $2,000 and got it in the mail. If his digging helped me avoid one bad decision, it would be the best money I ever spent. And I felt good about helping him. This was a business deal, right? I'd no idea what he would charge a local business, but I also knew he had some serious skills. So in my mind, the money was well invested. Next step, coordinate with Angus to do some in-person background investigation.

As it happened, it was the following day, Wednesday, late morning before I got back with Angus. "Angus, JC here. Do you have a free minute?"

"Certainly. That was quick. What do you think?"

"I think we need to back up our background checks with some personal investigation of friends and neighbors. References. Paper is fine, and electronic digging helps. I'm also thinking some belly-to-belly visits will give us insights we'd not otherwise get, at least not as easily or quickly. What do you think?"

"Agreed. I've been thinking along the same lines. I know a firm. A group of men and women who were military and law enforcement. They set up their own private-sector shop. I've contracted with them in the past. They've always produced. I'd be comfortable employing them with this as well. They're discrete and thorough. Let's use them for both personal and digital background checks, see if they find anything Mat may miss. No worries, I've known about Mat's abilities for a while. Part of my job looking out for you. It will also help us gauge Mat's skill set. Knowing his strengths and areas needing improvement helps everybody, right? Give my guys a couple weeks. We should have good information by then. Okay?"

"Thanks, Angus. Have them get after it. Until then, I'll focus on getting this place more presentable. Besides, I need the distraction and manual labor. One more thing, Angus. How is my account with you? I know we agreed on an annual retainer. I want to be sure we're good with the number."

"You're fine, JC. Your retainer with me is more than generous. I already told you you're well above my hourly rate. You've a respectable credit balance with me. Unless there are some significant events coming that neither of us have anticipated, we'll be carrying a sizable credit balance forward."

"That's okay, Angus. I don't want to end up in any negative territory with my account. I expect you to tell me if or when my account is getting close to a drawdown. It's important to me that you're always fully compensated with me, okay? Regarding the reference checks, I'll wait for your call." And that was the end of that, for now.

The next eight days were a whirlwind. First, I cleaned the house. Every room, top to bottom. Three days later, I thought the inside of my home was presentable. Not ready for the cover of *House Beautiful*, but you couldn't write your name on any dust either. Next was the garage area.

That was the hardest part for me. Dad's domain. I'd not been in the garage since before their deaths. I'd just always kept my pickup in the driveway. After the accident, I couldn't bring myself to go in there, at least until now. Standing in the driveway, I took a deep breath and pressed the remote to open the double-car garage door. I'd forgotten just how big our…my garage was.

I'd never measured it but thought I could park at least six normal cars or pickups inside without having to walk sideways or crunch Sheetrock or a fender. The concrete floor was heated and sealed with about an eighth inch of epoxy. Looking at it now, I remembered the two weeks everything had to be kept out of the garage while Dad laid down I don't know how many coats of epoxy. I remember each layer had to cure for days before another layer could be put down. And I remember Mom being less than thrilled as those days wore on. Funny what you remember, the odd little details of life. I also remember and was witnessing it now how Dad kept the entire space spotless. I could see a thin film of dust on everything, but all the doors here had been closed for nearly a year, so no real debris anywhere.

I didn't know what I expected exactly, but what I was seeing certainly wasn't it. Mom and Dad's Series 7 BMW had been totaled and scrapped courtesy of their wreck. Not in the garage obviously. What was left of it was probably turned into cans for Coke or Pepsi. What I was looking at in the garage back in the corner furthest from the house was, I think, a '67 Mustang, a Shelby GT 500, that I'd not noticed before.

Walking toward it, I could see it was fully badged and looked like it was just about finished with a full restoration. My eyes nearly fell out of my head! It looked like all that remained was to put the hood on, install the headliner, and reinstall the twin bucket seats. Everything was there. Just needed installing.

The car next to it, at least I think it was a car, was under a canvas tarp. I'd never before noticed any of this stuff. I'd been in and through the garage countless times, obviously not paying much attention. Talk about being otherwise absorbed! Maybe it's true that teenagers lived in a world all their own. I didn't realize it until that very minute, but I'd obviously been otherwise focused. Argh! How long had these two cars been hiding in plain sight?

Fully covered, I couldn't tell what was under the tarp, but it was smaller than the Mustang. Shorter, closer to the ground. I walked over and pulled the tarp off, and my eyes did fall out my head. I was staring at a 1966 Shelby AC Cobra. As far as I could tell, it was an original, not a kit. It even smelled new! I stuck my head in the cockpit and saw the odometer showed 1,367 miles. Original dark blue with the white stripes. Not a mark or scratch on it.

I'd never seen Mom or Dad drive this car. Never saw it in the driveway or here in the garage. And it's here, all quiet and covered under a tarp. I think I died again and went to heaven. And that's when I saw the envelope sitting on the driver's seat on top of the owner's manual, my name in Mom's flowing script on the envelope. I know I stopped breathing. Felt like hours later I could feel tears running down my face. With trembling fingers, scarcely willing to breathe, I reached down, picked up the envelope, and opened it.

Dear son, we are both so very proud of you. We've watched you grow and mature. We've watched you blossom at Kings Academy and become a young man right before our eyes. We can both clearly see God in your life. You are such a gift to us both. Can't imagine having a better son than you.

We hope you enjoy your graduation gifts. The Cobra is all yours as is the Mustang. Our thoughts are that the Cobra is an investment that will only grow in value as the years go by. Someday you might want to donate it to a museum. Until then, enjoy it.

The Mustang is altogether different. It's your driver. Perhaps your date-night car. We know there is nothing wrong with your pickup. You've always taken good care of your things. We also know you weren't expecting either of these presents. That's what makes it so deliciously fun giving them to you.

You are a good man, JC Merrick. We are both bursting with pride and excited to watch the man and leader you become. We ask God every day to watch over you, to bless you, and to keep you close in His heart. We see so very much good in you, JC. We're so very blessed that you are our son.

All our love always,
Mom and Dad

I sat down and bawled for an hour, or it seemed like it. Mom and Dad had no idea when they bought those cars, when they wrote that beautiful note, they'd not live to give either to me. They'd not see the joy on my face, my astonishment, my sheer exuberance at receiving such an overwhelming note or gifts. Now they're dead. I was alone. The cars sat here, and I'd cried enough for it to look like I peed my pants. Time for a few deep breaths and pulling myself back together.

The last car in the garage was pretty ordinary but only by comparison. It was a 1989 Lexus LS 400. Mom loved that car, drove it everywhere all the time. Even so, when I peeked at the odometer, it showed only 67,531 miles.

My ride, on the other hand, suited me just fine. It's reliable, invisible, comfortable, and very utilitarian. It's a 1990 Ford F-150 pickup extended cab with a short box. I picked the extended cab so Kip could ride along stretched out if he wished, although he generally preferred to ride in the front passenger seat, sitting up, taking in the view, nose out the window when weather permitted.

No dents or dings. Paint looked new, and to me it sounded like a pickup should sound, mellow with a little snarl. It had a four-speed manual transmission and four-wheel drive. V-8 engine that ran sweet. It's practical, mostly. Not known for gas mileage, but that had never been a thing I worried about. Most important to me, it got me where I wanted to go when I wanted to go, and I didn't have to worry about it breaking down. That's huge.

Looking around the inside of the garage again, I tried to figure out where to start. Looked to me like this space just needed a good dusting and vacuuming. All Dad's tools were well organized in tool chests and on wall shelving and pegboard. Dad was many good things. One of 'em was highly organized. This entire garage was testament his organizational skills.

Seemed like I was getting over my case of the willies being in the garage. I didn't have to move any of the cars. There was plenty of room for me to start parking my pickup inside. Get back to paying respect to my chunk of Dearborn steel. I decided to do just that after I gave the area a thorough dusting.

By the end of Thursday, the garage was clean. And again, I'd forgotten to eat. Maybe I needed to check in with our family doc, my doc, just to make sure I wasn't ruining my health with my lousy eating habits. I'd been behaving like this for more weeks than I'd care to admit.

Next day, Friday, I called my doc, Dr. Phyllis Church to make an appointment. Dr. Church had been our family doc since before I was born. Knew all our family history. I hadn't seen her since my death by drowning thing. Time to check in.

I called, and we set the appointment for the coming Wednesday, 9:00 a.m. Perfect. Dr. Church's office was in a medical complex located near downtown Tacoma. Close enough to be convenient to downtown, far enough away to not have any real parking issues. She's a family physician and certified internal medicine specialist, interesting combination. And she knew her stuff. Didn't pull any punches, no BS, but still compassionate, ya know? How's that for a winning combination. If that wasn't enough, she had style. She might wear the white lab coat docs wore, but every time I'd seen her, she's wearing a very colorful and figure-flattering dress. Like I said, style.

I was only in the waiting area about five minutes before I was called back to one of the exam rooms. Say what you want about doctors, needles, and the state of medical care in general. We'd the best care in the world and some of the best docs. Dr. Phyllis Church was at the top of her game, as was her partner, Dr. Walt Meihoff. I'd trust either of them with my life. Come to think of it, I had.

"Good morning, JC! To what do I owe the pleasure of your visit?" Dr. Church said, walking into the exam room wearing a striking dress with large lavender flowers. Really accentuated her almost violet eyes.

"Hi, Doc. Thought it might be a good idea to touch base. It seems I might be developing some habits I don't like much. But I'm not sure what, if anything, to do about them. I don't know if it's time for some pharmaceutical intervention or if this stuff will just work itself out."

"You have my attention, JC. What's going on?"

"I've not been sleeping well. No nightmares, at least not that I remember. Just restless all night long. I wake up several times a night. Get up, prowl the house for no reason at all…no odd noises or anything like that, just restless. I go back to bed, fall asleep for a bit, wake up again, and rinse and repeat."

"When did this start?"

"I'm not sure. Seems like it's been developing or evolving for a few months. One of those things I didn't notice until I did. And by then, it was in full bloom. And I'm forgetting to eat. No appetite to prompt me. I get busy doing something, anything really, or nothing at all, and the next thing I know, it's dark, and I'm still not hungry. So the first person I thought of was you, and here I am."

"And your appetite has followed the same type pattern as your sleep? Maybe they started around the same time?"

"Hadn't thought of that. Hmmm. Maybe." I paused for a moment, then, "I think so, now that you ask the question."

"Any other signs of anything? Headaches, generally feeling upset, or depressed? Angry? Unusually moody?"

"Not really. I was angry after Mom and Dad died. You already know about all that. But that seems to be working itself out, at least mostly. I'm not really depressed, at least I don't think so. I cleaned the house and garage these past few days. Did a top-to-bottom thing. That brought back some memories. Made me sad for a while, but it passed. I think I've mostly made my peace with my folks and their deaths, at least as much as I'm able right now. Feels like I'll always have this hole inside me, ya know?"

"JC, I don't know. Both my parents are still living, as are my husband's. I can only begin to imagine. You've gone through something that, at your age, should never have happened. But it did, and you are. And so you know, I think you are doing remarkably well, given the past year and what you've had to handle."

Huh. Dr. Church and I had been talking for only a few minutes, and I had this strong intuition, knowing with absolute certainty, that Dr. Church was being honest and truthful. It startled me a bit. Was this just my imagination or something else?

"Are you okay, JC? You look a little distracted."

"Huh? Oh. I'm okay, Doc. Just a flash of memory."

"Is this part of what's going on? You were flushed there for a minute. Now your color is back to normal."

"Hmm? Oh, I'm fine. Just the sleeping and eating thing, I think."

"As your doctor and your friend, I think stress and recovery are what's going on in your life. I think your new reality is settling in. I think you're feeling some overwhelmed. Maybe more than a little bit. Who are in your support circle now?"

"Well, you know Angus. We are in regular contact, though usually by phone. Mat and I are in regular contact, just spoke with him this past Monday, in fact. Again, usually by phone. He's busy with his last year in academy, so he is pretty tied up most of the time. Kyle and I have drifted but only a bit. Think we connected by phone within the last few weeks. Kinda the same with Lucienne. Lu and I have drifted a bit. She's deep in school too, really keeps her moving. That's about it."

"I'm hearing you're not getting out socially. No dates, not attending any events, nobody over for burgers or dogs. Sounds like you're becoming socially isolated. Do you attend church regularly?"

"No on attending church. I mean, I go but not weekly, like I did before Mom and Dad died. You know I was a mess for a bit. When that was going on, all my routines just fell apart. I have attended, had a few conversations with Rev. Miller. He's helped some. I'm still picking up the pieces if you know what I mean. I'd not realized I've become socially isolated, didn't really think of that. Angus and I did decide it might be a good idea to hire one or two people to help out a bit. Remind me to eat, cook a bit, help keep up the house and grounds, maybe somebody to be a kind of minder. I'm feeling a bit vulnerable, and I'm not liking it at all."

"Knew I liked Angus. Great idea for you having others around. I'm assuming you're taking proper care in selecting the right fit?"

"Absolutely. We're doing deep backgrounds before we make contact. Seven candidates so far. We'll see where they get us, then do whatever needs doing. "

"Sounds to me like you are doing the right thing, JC. Just add some social time in there. Make a point of getting out with at least one of your friends once or twice a month at a minimum. Okay? Humans are social animals. Most of us don't do well isolated, and you're isolating yourself. Make sure you're not brooding. Stay busy mentally and physically. Think about taking up some form of martial arts. Many of them are great for building mental discipline, though I don't think you're lacking there. They teach focus as well. Could help you sleep better and build back an interest in eating. Deal?"

"Thanks, Doc. You've given me a lot to think over and work on. I always appreciate your insights and wisdom."

"You're very welcome, JC. Just do more than think about it. Right now, you need some activity and socialization. It's your life. It's completely in your hands. Now get out of here and start living again!" And with that she was gone. What was all that about intuiting she was honest and caring? My imagination seemed to be in overdrive.

Chapter 5

"Hey, Lu! JC Merrick calling." I'd left Dr. Church's office earlier in the day. Now late afternoon, academy classes were over, and I figured Lu would be home. So I'd taken a deep, calming breath and picked up my phone.

"Like I'd not recognize your voice! It's good to finally hear from you, Mr. Merrick! What's up?"

"The Mariners are playing this Friday night. I have two tickets. Interested in an at-home ball game?"

"Why, JC Merrick, are you asking me on a date?"

"Um, sure, I guess?"

"You guess? Make up your mind, Sailor. Clock's ticking, and you, kind sir, are about out of time."

"Of course I'm asking you out on a date, Lu. It'll be fun!"

"Better. Much better. And about time too. When does the game start?"

"With traffic, we should probably get there by five. Home games get stupid busy. So how about I come get you at 4:00 p.m.? That should give us plenty of time."

"Deal. I'll be ready!"

And that is how I started the first date of my entire life. I was nervous, I admit it. Who wouldn't be? Lucienne is wicked smart, easy to be around, a very companionable personality, and incredibly attractive both inside and out. She'd just turned seventeen on the ninth, yesterday. I'd have to remember that during our date. And like I've said earlier, there is just something about her that draws me in. Then again, I'm seventeen, so maybe hormones? I figured it'd work itself out, whatever it was, given time.

I'd met her folks several times, and looking at her mom, Gabrielle, I knew Lucienne would mature into a gorgeous, very intelligent, accomplished woman. Just being around her, I knew she was well on her way in every respect. And with Lu as my companion for the game, I knew we would have a terrific time. And we did.

I thought about driving Mom's car or the Cobra to the game. But I knew Lu wasn't one to be impressed with stupid stuff. And I was being stupid. I wasn't trying to impress her. Okay, maybe a little. Everybody wants to be liked, right? But my folks started teaching me early on to be comfortable in my own skin. Dad explained that meant living my life on my terms. Being true to myself and my values. Not being influenced by the masses or the public opinion of the day. Not really caring what other people thought or said or did. Being true to me. Honoring my parents and my faith. Holding tight to my moral compass. Being kind and thoughtful to everybody, friend and stranger alike. Being completely at ease being me. I'd been taught that living a life to please others would be miserable because there are so many different opinions and values everywhere. If I lived to please others, I'd end up losing myself and my values. No thank you.

The interesting part is that I'm still discovering who I am. After all, I'm still seventeen, still figuring out life. But I knew my faith and foundation were solid. No issues there at all. So why go around being all ego stupid about anything? I did wash and wax my pickup before getting Lu. Spiffed it up all shiny-like. Want to honor Lu too, and a dirty ride was not my way to go, especially with Lu. Hmmm. That got me to thinking.

Lu's one of those people who seems you've known 'em forever. I suppose she came to Kings Academy somewhere around sixth grade. About there anyhow. She was cute even then. Several guys, especially those a couple of years older, tried to mark her as theirs.

Funny as hell. She shut 'em up and shut 'em down, sometimes with just a look.

Have you ever seen the look? Well, Lu had it then and now. She had a mouth on her right from the beginning. Nothing crude or vulgar, simply an incredible command of the English language, especially for someone her age. I suspect she had that same command in French too, but I've enough trouble with English. Maybe it was because English was her second language. Whatever she said back then, and she only had to say it once and soft enough that nobody but rude boy heard, oh, man, did he hear. Red ears. Red face. Turned around and was scarce for days. I liked her instantly. Over that first year, we became friends and have stayed that. Now maybe something more? We'll see. I'm certainly not in any rush. My life is complicated enough right now. Last thing I need is to start obsessing about girls.

Lu has this glow about her. Really. Almost like she's walking in Light. I don't know how to explain or express it. I've not said anything to her. I'm too shy, I guess. But she has this inner light, and she just glows! I've expected to see halos of light above her head! None are there, of course, but I still expected 'em. I've seen lightning in her eyes too! Flickers of lightning bolts sometimes. Not in anger, although I suspect they'd be there if she ever got really angry. Just these lightning bolts of life living inside her. Eyes are supposed to be windows to the soul or some such. Sure seems to be true with Lu Abreo.

Anyhow, the game was great. Lu was great. We both had an incredible time. We went to a nearby Starbucks after and just hung out. Got to know a little bit more about each other. I was tempted to tell her about my healing-by-touch thing but chickened out. Probably a good thing. While we were in Starbucks, that other thing happened. I realized that Lu was trustworthy. I mean, without question, trustworthy. Very strong in who she is. Like with Dr. Church, I figured this might be my imagination or wishful thinking or simply just wandering thoughts. But the same sort of thing twice now. I needed to pay closer attention.

"Hey, are you okay? You went away for a bit." Lu was looking at me, I mean really looking, paying attention.

Argh! Gotta learn to hide this better. "Yeah. I'm fine. Just over-swallowed my latte. Still kinda hot. Think I toasted my tonsils a bit."

"Well, Sailor, sip. That isn't a big gulp, after all." Lu has a terrific laugh. Throaty. Sexy as anything. Almost a belly laugh but way classier. When she laughs, her whole body lights up, and there's playful sparkle in her eyes. I could get lost forever in those twin blue oceans of life.

"Gotcha." We continued with some more small talk. School, some of her classwork, what she's thinking of for a future. Things from her life in Canada. Stuff like that. We stayed away from my parents' death and me dying. I avoided mentioning my new gift. But I sensed she wouldn't freak out if I told her. I'm just not comfortable sharing that ability yet, ya know?

By the time I got Lu home, it was pushing eleven at night. Her parents knew games could run long, and they trusted us both to not do anything stupid. I intended honoring them by honoring their daughter. I certainly knew enough to not run around like a crazed hormone looking for anyplace to land. Nope. My parents taught me to respect myself and others. Acting stupid, making dumb choices even in the heat of the moment is inexcusable. Choices, actions, have consequences, good and bad. Life's full of 'em.

Except, I did experience my first kiss.

"Hey, Sailor, don't I even get a good-night kiss?" Those twin green oceans again. What's a guy to do?

"Uh," was as far as I got before her lips met mine. This was my first kiss! I didn't have any technique at all. But I have to tell you, I was in the arms of an expert. I don't know how many boys, men, guys, whatever, she's kissed, but her kiss was perfect. Took my breath away. Made my heart flutter. I'll remember that kiss for the rest of my life.

I guess I did okay, though. "Nice tonsils, Sailor." She gave me a huge smile, said, "Good night," opened the door to her home, and went inside. I do not remember my drive home, but I sure do remember that kiss.

Chapter 6

The weekend. Looks like I might have another puzzle to solve or a theory to test. I had two new experiences in the last week. First with Dr. Church, then with Lu. Kind of like my intuition lit up. Not mind reading really but definitely getting a sense of others, how they are as people. Strong, intuitive knowledge maybe. For now, that's about as good as I can describe it.

Nothing like that happened at the ball game. Lu and I were surrounded by dozens of people, thousands in the stadium. Nothing. No intuition about anybody while we were there. Zip. Hmmm.

Nothing in Dr. Church's waiting room. Several people waiting for whichever doc, but I sensed nothing. No intuition about anything until Dr. Church and I were in the exam room. Double hmmm.

It's Saturday. Think I'll go to the mall and see what happens. Southgate is as good a mall as any to test whatever is going on in my head. Besides, it's busy, reasonably close, and huge, yet enough distance from home that I'll not likely run into somebody I know. That could be awkward. What am I doing here? Oh, nothing much. Just seeing if I can, you know, read your mind, get a sense of who you are as a person. The straitjacket guys would haul me away!

Anyhow, the drive to the mall was uneventful. Parked near Nordstrom and walked to about the middle of the main concourse.

Found an empty seat on a nearby bench and sat and waited. And waited. Nothing in two hours of butt-numbing boredom.

Maybe something closer to the crowd? I went to the food court. Found a vendor selling soft drinks and soft pretzels. Ordered a small Coke with extra ice and a soft pretzel with butter and salt, found an empty two-top table, and sat. Looked like a husband-wife pair directly behind me and four high school or early college girls directly across from me. Maybe I'd get some sort of reading or spark or whatever sitting here.

In my peripheral vision, I could see one of the girls glancing my way, but nothing. I guessed if I wasn't picking up anything from anybody, it was still something.

It was weird. I got an impression, feeling, or whatever you want to call it from Dr. Church. Same with Lu. Very similar feeling from them both. Now nothing. I was thinking my earlier impressions were just the product of my fertile imagination. I was just about to get up and get back home when it happened again, only this time, different.

A couple of guys walked up to the girls. Obviously, they all knew one another. Right away I could feel one of the guy's hostility. From the corner of my eye, I could see him glaring at me. Not a happy guy at all. Anger was practically dripping off him. This guy and I had not even made eye contact, and I could feel his hate building.

In fact, I'd not made eye contact with anyone in that group. Weird, and I was feeling a definite air of hostility floating around. Time for me to move on. I very casually picked up my Coke and, with my back to that group, made my way onto the main concourse and down the walkway.

Wow! More information than I think I wanted to learn. But good to know. Another God Wink? Now I knew more about this newest ability/gift/curse. It was not gender-specific. It involved only the folks who were actively thinking about me, or so it seemed. What I read or intuited or whatever involved both positive and negative thoughts and/or emotions. And maybe, this gift/ability/curse was growing in capability? Then again, today was the first time I'd been among a larger group of folks, so maybe that suggested something as well.

Except the ball game. There were thousands of people at the Mariners game. Lu and I were together, and nothing happened at the game, from Lu or anybody else. Maybe nobody was thinking about me during the game. Or maybe it was because I was focused on the game and Lu. How weird does that sound? My connection with Lu was at Starbucks after the game. Nuts! What in the world was going on? Maybe I was going crazy after all.

Maybe this was a heightened intuition. We all get those hunches, right? Maybe this was the same thing, only more so. Another God Wink. This newest ability or whatever seemed less complicated, more easily explained. Some people will call them lucky breaks. Others say you're just in the right place at the right time. Or the opposite, that so-and-so "Just can't catch a break." I don't think it's that at all. Now that I'm paying closer attention and thinking about it. I've always thought we make our own luck and are either tuned in or not. I think being tuned in is being aware of God's blessings and guidance throughout our lives.

I think most everybody goes through life completely unaware of the miracles that surround them, just waiting to be noticed. I believe most of us have that extra sense of danger or opportunity or whatever. Some say to trust your gut, believing our gut is our second brain. There's even a bit of quiet research on it. I believe we're tapping into that portion of God that lives in us all. It's that spark that gives us life and our humanity. It seems mine is in the process of waking up, maybe. However you looked at it, this was going to take some serious brainpower to figure out if that was even possible.

I realized it was going to take more than just me to figure out this mess. Who was I going to trust with this information? Seemed to me I needed to do some very serious, time-consuming thinking before I picked anybody. At or near the top of my selection list is a pretty sobering qualifier. I need to pick a person or people who wouldn't be freaked out by the knowledge and who could handle the stress this knowledge might impart. Argh! Time to ask God to guide me, ask Him for His help. I need to remember to seek His guidance in all things. I was pretty good at it before my folks died. Need to actively regain that perspective and guidance.

LIFE AFTER DEATH

I spent Sunday with Kip. Just the two of us. That's been our usual routine. But before now, I've been mentally distant with him, at least most of the time. Kip didn't seem to mind. Moreover, he seemed to understand. He was going through loss too. We used to be a family of four. Now we're a family of two. Time I started appreciating Kip and expressing in dog language just how much he means to me.

Made a point of making myself a good Sunday morning breakfast and eating it. Egg whites, dry wheat toast, bacon, cranberry juice. A special treat for Kip. I made him cooked turkey burger mixed with steamed brown rice, diced fresh apple, and just a sprinkling of cheddar cheese. Talk about spoiling my pup!

Kip isn't like most dogs in many ways. He doesn't inhale his food. Really. He eats it thoughtfully. He'll take a few bites, then pause and lift his head. Then he'll drink some of his water. Then go back for more of his food. Only dog I've ever seen or heard of eating like that. However, not this Sunday morning. Nope. He went straight to his food, muzzle buried deep, and ate until it was gone. Not gulping but not pausing either. I think he liked breakfast!

Once we were both finished and I'd cleaned up and loaded dirty dishes in the dishwasher, Kip and I went into the backyard. I had his two most favorite toys in hand. A tennis ball that was completely disgusting. New, it had been a bright lime green; now it was brown with lots of pinholes in it. Kip loves to play fetch. Most of the time. On occasion he enjoys watching me play fetch for his amusement. He'll just sit and wait for me to retrieve the ball in which he's lost all interest. He doesn't do this often, but when he does, I think it's how he expresses his humor. I like to think he just sits there laughing his butt off as I play fetch for him.

His other favorite toy is a large braided rope with loops at both ends. It lets him really get a good bite on one of the ends while I pull the other. He loves the game of rope pull. Usually.

This day was full-on for my furry companion. We played dog fetch, where he did the fetching for a solid hour. Of course, treats were involved every now and then. Keeps him focused and motivated, ya know? Then we moved to rope pull. Kip loves rope pull.

He's a big dog for his breed. He's a hundred and thirty lean pounds of fur, teeth, muscle, bone, and personality. At four years, he's still not grown into his paws. They're huge! He runs like a colt, a gangly gallop that's hilarious to watch. His head is nearly as tall as the top of my jeans. Long legs, large body, that's my pup.

Kip's mouth is very soft. What I mean is, he doesn't chomp down with bone-crushing force when you hand-feed him. When I've fed him from my fingers, he is very gentle about using his front teeth, using only enough pressure to grasp the treat I'm feeding him. Most dogs will chomp onto the treat, and if your fingers are in the way, they figure it's more treat for them.

When he was younger, Kip loved to eat deer and rabbit poop. Go figure. I think it really is a dog thing. Some dogs like to eat their own poop. Thankfully, Kip doesn't. Just deer and bunny pellets. It's taken me nearly three years, but I think we're past ingesting those morsels. Or maybe Kip is just sneakier about it. At this point, I prefer to not know.

There's a sort of trail along the perimeter of our land. It measures about a quarter mile for a full circuit. Perfect running trail. Cushion of leaves and pine needles, soft, loamy ground. Just wide enough for both Kip and me side by side. It isn't a beaten path but a faint trail we both use with some frequency. Today he and I did eight laps, so about two miles. It was great exercise for us both. That was one of our shorter runs, only about fifteen minutes. By the end of the last lap, I could tell Kip was getting tired. After all, a hundred and thirty pounds of dog is practically a force of nature to move.

All in all, we'd both been playing and active for nearly three hours. We were both needing some quiet time, so back in the house we went. I sat in the recliner, an oversized model that is super comfortable. Used to be one of Dad's favorite spots to relax. Now when I sit there, Kip becomes a lapdog. I kid you not. As soon as I snuggle in and get comfortable, Kip climbs in my lap, wiggles his butt to the side of the chair, and lays his front paws, chest, and head on my stomach. He then usually proceeds to talk to me with his soft grunts and groans. Telling me all about his day, or so I imagine. He really is quite expressive with his voice. I sure wish I understood dog talk. I know he's doing his best to communicate. I'm just a lousy interpreter.

But we did talk, at least I talked, and Kip listened. Really. I think he understands far more words and intentions than anybody realizes. Looking down at his head, I said, "Kip, I've got a problem, and I just don't know the best way to solve it."

A soft groan from the furball.

"I want and need to share this weird stuff with somebody who can help me figure it out. Somebody who can help me understand what's happening. Somebody who can help me navigate the weirdness and moral implications involved. Do you understand? Of course, you don't. You're a dog."

That's when Kip decided to wiggle and redistribute his considerable self. Then a sigh of contentment. From both of us.

"What do you think, buddy? Should I tell Lu? Kyle? Mat? Angus? All of 'em? Just a couple? I'm really stumped with this one. You're a smart dog, right? What's best to do with this?"

Another soft groan from Kip, almost like a cat purring.

The weirdest thing, I really felt like Kip understood me, like he was thinking about what I'd just said and was considering his answer. Kinda gave me goose bumps.

So I just sat there, relaxed. Lay my head back in the chair, closed my eyes, and stroked Kip's muzzle and ears. Thought about who to tell, what to say, and whether or not it was anything close to a good idea. Thought about the implications of sharing with somebody else. The possible dangers and the benefits.

I realized the benefits were almost exclusively mine, and the dangers moved directly to those with whom I shared the knowledge of these "gifts." Maybe. Sharing didn't seem to lessen my danger in any way. In fact, I'd be more vulnerable to outside pressure, intended or otherwise. Hmmm. Whomever I told couldn't employ my abilities, nor would they receive any direct benefit. On the other hand, some of the weight of this burden I'm carrying would doubtlessly lessen for me but transfer an unequal share of the danger and burden to them. Plus, I would open the door for bad actors to get to me through threatening others. Not good.

Then again, any average or worse bad actor would attempt to get to me through others anyway if they thought that kind of leverage would benefit them in their pursuit of whatever they were after. Bad folks make bad decisions and do bad things regardless. So there was that. Seemed like my friends, those with whom I was close, were at risk, whether they knew what was going on or not. What a mess.

The question became, Do I tell my friends what's going on and make them aware so they can make informed decisions? Or do I keep them ignorant so they have true deniability? Plus, they couldn't help me puzzle out any of this stuff if they were unaware, and I was really needing help with this puzzle. My brain felt like it was tied in knots. There were advantages to sharing and not sharing. Hmm. Time to ask God for some guidance.

That decision made, I felt better, lighter somehow. I could hear and feel Kip snoring. So soft and gentle, it really was soothing. Then I must have dozed some.

Chapter 7

Kip's barking woke me, and it was dark outside. Startled the hell out of me, really. He only barks at the mail truck, UPS, and the FedEx folks. Even then, those barks are pretty half-hearted. Today's Sunday, it's late evening, so those folks are not around. And Kip's barking was full throttle. He was completely focused on the forest and more agitated than I'd seen him in ages. What the...

From where I was sitting—okay, reclining—I could see outside through the front window and view part of the forest of trees around us. Kip's attention seemed to be focused in that direction. His growl was now full throated, and his hackles were straight up. Neat trick for a curly-haired dog. He'd long ago given up barking at our forest friends. What on earth? Had to be something unusual, right? Kip was really wound up.

Staring directly into the forest, right at the edge of my peripheral vision, I noticed a quick movement in the undergrowth. Whatever it was, it was larger than a rabbit or fox. More like a deer or something hunched over. There one second and gone just as quickly. A deliberate movement. Quiet. Sneaky. The hairs on the back of my neck were standing straight up too. Clear as a bell and from Kip no less, "Danger."

Oddly, it didn't startle me. I knew very clearly Kip communicated with me. Pushing that revelation aside for now, it was time to move. Acting very normally, I got up, walked a few short steps, and grabbed Dad's shotgun. Since I got home from hospital after dying and coming back, I've kept that shotgun loaded and leaning in the corner formed by where the outer wall meets the fireplace, within quick and easy reach. I thought it odd at the time, keeping the shotgun loaded and handy. But I didn't really question it then or now.

It was loaded with #00 buckshot and would do some very nasty work at twenty yards or less and was still effective at about double that distance. When I was younger and Dad took me to gun school, I learned that engaging an adversary at less than twenty feet can be extremely dangerous. Several tests had proven conclusively that a person armed with a knife can kill you even if you shoot them when the separating distance is twenty or fewer feet.

That really surprised me. It was drilled into me by my instructor and Dad that if you are armed with a firearm, you never ever let any threat break the twenty-foot barrier. To do so can easily cost you your life. Regardless, Dad's shotgun was a Mossberg 500, a 12-gauge bird gun, and held five shells. Definitely not a home-defense or tactical shotgun.

Regarding defending myself with deadly force, and the Mossberg is most definitely deadly force, "One is none, two is one, three is better," my instructor drummed into me, meaning shooting a bad guy once doesn't count. Hitting him or her twice is really only hitting them once, and hitting them three times is better. Better to neutralize the threat than to guess.

The Mossberg was, in that moment, what I had to work with. A bird gun. I had one shell in the chamber and four more in the tube. I was one shell light. Maybe. Dad taught me how to shoot when I was young. Sort of a father-son bonding-type activity, and we did it often, usually weekly, always more than monthly. Accurate shooting is a fairly perishable skill. I'm no professional shooter, but I'm not a novice either. When Dad and I shot together, we used our shotgun, Dad's rifle, and both of our pistols. Dad's pistol of choice was a

Glock model 23, full frame. Mine was and is a Beretta 92F with a modified grip.

Right now, in hand, I had our Mossberg. My Beretta was in my bedroom on the nightstand. Stupid. Isn't hindsight a wonderful thing? Completely useless. Without taking my eyes from the outside forest, I stepped back until I was at the far end of the living area. Including the front porch, I now had about a thirty-foot or ten-yard safety zone.

Shooting is one of the few activities I've kept up after Mom and Dad died. It's been one way to manage my anger and frustration. There is something immensely satisfying about making a suspended metal disc ping and dance every time you pull a trigger. As a result, the shotgun was familiar, even felt comfortable in my hands. Unfortunately, my Beretta was in my bedroom. Oops.

I wasn't nervous, at least not in those moments. I'd not really seen an intruder either. I seriously think shooting a human is a far different proposition than shooting at some metal disc or piece of paper. But if it came to it, I'd shoot before they could shoot me. Self-preservation can be a powerful motivator, and in this moment, I was feeling extremely motivated. I was not put here to be a soft target for anybody.

All the doors and windows were closed and locked. It was a habit I'd begun right after Mom and Dad died. Part of how I figured I could keep myself safe. At that time, I had no idea why I believed I needed to lock all the doors and windows and how that could possibly keep myself safe. But I had recognized the need and developed the habit anyhow. Now I figured those locked doors and windows were my alarm system. Anybody breaking in through a window or knocking down a door would surely be my advanced warning system. I knew it wasn't much, but it was something. And something is better than nothing, right?

To make myself less of a target, I moved to the light switches and turned off the kitchen lights, dining area lights, and the lights to the living area. Now the entire main living area of my home was dark. Next, I flipped the two light switches that controlled the front porch lights and the lights that ran under the eaves along the sides of our house. That gave me a slight advantage. Figured I'd see an intruder before they saw me. And I flipped the switch that controlled the lights on our back patio and deck. Now the exterior of my home was lit up, and the interior was dark or in shadow. Much better for Kip and me.

Kip had stopped barking but was still in a very aggressive posture, facing the front door and that portion of our yard and forest. His hackles were still raised, and he didn't appear to have relaxed in any way. I'd seen no additional movement in the trees. And I didn't hear anything unusual, but that really didn't mean a lot. It was only by happenstance that I'd seen anything at all. No idea if our creeper was still there or gone. Whoever or whatever was outside, they'd evidently walked into our property. I never heard any car sound at all. And I'd not heard any noise other than Kip's barking.

It took Kip over an hour to settle. He whined, stared through the front window near the door, sat, and stood countless times. Finally, he seemed to relax some. Needless to say, neither Kip nor I got any sleep that night. Nothing else happened, at least nothing we noticed. Kip and I were both thankful to God for keeping us safe.

That didn't mean we lowered our guard. We didn't. I knew neither of us could continue living like this, not knowing if or when some spooky person would sneak up on us. It was time to get proactive again.

At eight on the dot the following morning, Monday, I picked up the phone and called Angus. "Good morning, Angus, JC here."

"Good morning, Lad. What can I do for you this fine morning?"

"I need some advice. Do you know of a good alarm company? I need a good security system."

"Why? Has something happened?" I could hear the concern in his voice.

"Kip and I had a visitor last night. About 11:00 p.m., maybe a bit later. I only got the briefest glimpse of something creeping through our trees. Whoever or whatever it was, they were very good at staying hidden. No idea of an intent. They were very quiet and sneaky. I know it wasn't my imagination. Kip sensed someone as well, barked his head off for over a half hour, stared a hole through our front door and into the trees and undergrowth. It was well past midnight before either of us was willing to begin to relax.

"I figured Kip was my early warning system. I had Dad's shotgun chambered and at hand. But nothing else came of it. Seems to me I'm in need of a good alarm system. Figured you might be able to recommend somebody particularly competent."

"You certainly lead an interesting life, JC. Just when I thought you were settling a bit, getting comfortable, a new situation pops up. You are right, of course. An alarm system is appropriate, given last night. Really, it's appropriate given your overall situation, you know. Your age, wealth, and comparative isolation out there. A security system is an excellent idea.

"As it happens, I do know someone. Runs his own shop, not affiliated with a local or national alarm company. That said, he uses only the latest technology and only after it satisfies his standards. He also employs a staff of personal security specialists. As far as I know, those folks are all former military, usually from some special operations group or other or former law enforcement.

"I know Jack has military connections to do deep background checks on all his staff. I've heard he also does that regularly to verify his team is still his team, not infiltrated by a higher bidder if you get my meaning. He requires both loyalty and discretion from all his team. And I've heard that client safety comes first. His company is who I've contacted to do our deep background checks on your potential staff.

"I know from someone involved that one of Jack's specialists took a bullet for a client. That, my son, is loyalty that you cannot buy. I also know that particular assignment ended well for all concerned. I've heard he compensates all his team well above average. And I know he's done some high-profile security work for some national and international dignitaries that have visited our area in the past.

"I can tell you Jack is expensive. I believe he is worth every dollar you'll pay him. He is also particular about his clients. To the best of my knowledge, he only does electronics and security for legitimate individuals and companies. He has also done some work with our military and federal people. He does all the electronics work in-house, doesn't sub out anything. He has a monitoring staff that has been with him since the beginning. If he takes you as a client, and I think he will, you'll be in the best care any security company can provide.

"I'll get in touch with him straight away. Give him the particulars without using your name. If he's interested, I'll get the two of you together as soon as he can be available. How does that sound?"

"Sounds exactly what I'm looking for, Angus. Sooner is better for Kip and me. I don't think either of us really slept last night and probably won't again tonight. I think the longer I drag this out, the less ready both of us will be if some uninvited guest comes calling."

"Okay. I'll make the call as soon as we hang up. Call you back as soon as I have something. Expect today, perhaps before noon." And with that, Angus was gone.

Putting my phone down, I turned my attention to Kip. "Whaddaya say, curly one? Let's have breakfast!" Kip stood up, and his nose and tail twitched in agreement.

Breakfast was an easy one. First, I asked God for His protection and guidance, then began breakfast prep. Kip got his favorite kibble with some moist, cooked ground turkey and brown rice mixed in. I also cooked a piece of bacon as a treat for us both. I made oatmeal and wheat toast for my meal. Kip was finished eating before my oatmeal was cooked. Sat his furry butt right beside me and watched intently for any accidental spillage.

As I ate my breakfast, Kip was again at attention. He knew I'd share my bacon with him, and I didn't disappoint. In reality, Kip always gets way more bacon than me. Only minutes later, with breakfast gone, Kip had eaten well over half a rasher of bacon. I'd managed two nibbles. I just can't deny Kip his breakfast treat. But I draw the line at overfeeding him. I microwave the bacon in paper towels, so there ends up having far less bacon fat than if it was fried or even baked. Kip and I both like our bacon crispy and slightly overcooked. Microwaved bacon is crispy, our favorite way to enjoy it.

I've often wondered if Kip has noticed he gets less kibble in exchange for his daily bacon treats. All I know is that his weight stays right at 130 pounds, and the vet has never scolded me for Kip being overweight. Dr. Soux, our vet, often says Kip is in great shape, that if all her furry patients were as healthy as Kip, she'd be out of business. So I figure Kip's bacon treats aren't doing much harm. Besides, the bacon is so thinly sliced before cooking you can practically see through each piece.

With breakfast over and everything cleaned up, it was time for Kip and me to do a little nearby exploring. We stepped out the front door, across the porch and grass, and entered the trees and underbrush. Gotta get a handle on this undergrowth. Some of this tangled mess is pretty unavoidable, but this really is too much. Another item to add to the list for a gardener to clean up.

Standing there, I was reminded of God's best work. He created the universe, but I think His finest creation was right before my eyes. Our home sat on twenty acres of wooded forest, combined with a lush green lawn surrounding our home. I looked over the trees, shrubs, undergrowth, and flowers, marveling at how He can create such beauty.

I know most kids my age aren't introspective, but I've always been that way. I've often looked at Kip, watched him doing whatever, and marveled at how he is so joyous and carefree. Well, except for last night. I think God looks in on me through Kip. It sounds strange, I know. But I'm convinced. I see that look in Kip's eyes, and I'm convinced there is divine light there. Even with all that's gone on in my life, I am so very blessed.

Kip and I were pretty careful how and where we walked, looking for evidence of last night's creeper if, indeed, there was one. Kip's the tracker, not me. I mean, I'm observant and all, and I know intuitively what to look for. However, until now, I've never had cause to pay such close attention to my immediate surroundings. Maybe I'd benefit from some of that training. Hmmm.

Kip practically lives in the woods around our property. He's smelled every critter that's ever strolled through the area. And like I said earlier, he has an acquired taste for deer and bunny poop. Absolutely disgusting. But Dr. Soux, our vet, says it's pretty normal for a dog and generally doesn't harm them. Go figure.

I was looking around, seeing and finding absolutely nothing at all, when I noticed Kip paying attention to one particular spot. His nose was right at the ground and moving within a small area. I looked up and noticed where Kip was investigating was near the spot where I'd seen the movement last night. I walked up to Kip and looked down. There was a faint impression in the dirt, pine needles, and leaves.

Kneeling down for a closer look, still being careful to not disturb that small area, I gave it a more intense look. I could clearly make out a footprint, but no detail. Didn't see any tread marks, just the outline of a shoe or boot and a pretty shallow impression at that. Maybe some lightweight body? The depth of the tread or lack of depth suggested lighter rather than heavier weight. However, it hadn't rained in a few days, making the ground fairly firm, not soft, so not prone to make easy footprint impressions.

Looking around to find another print, Kip was way ahead of me. Just a couple feet away was another similar print. Same as the first one. Shallow, no tread marks, no distinct heel print, and no foot or heel dragging between steps. The only thing that made this print different were the two snapped bush branches beside it. This particular piece of underbrush would be going dormant. I tested a branch on its neighboring bush, and it easily snapped between my fingers. Quite fragile. Maybe this is where our creeper squatted to look into our house? Looking that way, it seemed about the right angle and distance. Certainly, the right amount of underbrush to obscure the creeper even in daylight. At night, it was a miracle I'd seen anything at all.

Kip and I looked all around for three hours. All either of us found were those two impressions and the snapped branches. Nothing leading to them, nothing leading from them. The prints themselves suggested the creeper was traveling from the direction of our entry drive and toward the bedroom side of our home. We couldn't find any prints out of the trees and closer to the house, but we sure did look. Practically went all around our house on my hands and knees. Kip had kept his nose to the ground during this entire time and didn't alert to anything else, so he and I figured our creeper left somehow without giving us any additional clues.

Kip has a nose like a bloodhound. How does somebody sneak through my woods without leaving any scent? Did they wrap up in plastic or Tyvek before coming on the property? Kip's nose is about a hundred thousand times more sensitive than mine, no joke! He can scent almost anything. Maybe it was that "almost" that kept him from finding anything more about our forest creeper. Huh, maybe the creeper left those two prints on purpose. How else would they be the only two prints in the area? Made me kind of wonder about the whole thing.

Time to go back inside and give this some serious thought.

CHAPTER 8

Kip and I thought about the whole Sunday night event and finding two footprints earlier today. We came up without any additional information, hunches, or insight. Bothered me that there were only two prints. It was like whoever made the prints magically appeared, then just as magically disappeared. I really don't believe in magic. But then not so very long ago, I wasn't completely convinced about miracles either. Miracles happened to somebody who knew somebody, who…you get the idea. They were never first person until they were. Apparently. So what did this mean about two footprints without any nearby companions? This was beyond Kip's and my ability to reason out. God certainly knew what was going on, but He wasn't giving any hints. At least not yet.

Then the phone rang. "JC. Angus here. Tried to call you a while ago. You must have been out."

"Yeah. Kip and I were exploring our yard and forest looking for creeper footprints or sign."

"Did you find anything of note?"

"We found two light footprints about two feet apart. Faint, but definitely there. Couldn't see any tread, just the outline of a boot or shoe. No heal marks, no scuffing. Just two prints coming from the direction of our entry drive and heading toward the bedroom side of the house. We checked the perimeter of the house for anything. Kip and I found nothing else. It's like somebody landed, made two prints, then flew away. Impossible, I know, but that's what we found. The print location lines up with what I thought I glimpsed last night."

"Interesting. I got hold of Jack. He's going to come to your house today. Expect him there about four thirty half an hour from now."

"Okay. How will I recognize him? What's he driving? What does he look like?"

"You'll know him. Shaved head, a bit taller than you by an inch or two. Outweighs you by fifty pounds or more. No fat. And he walks like a panther. Black as midnight and drives a new pickup, maroon-red Ford."

"See what you mean. Hard to mistake what you've described. I'll watch for him. Thanks, Angus." And with that, there was a dial tone in my ear. This sounded interesting. Oddly, I was looking forward to meeting Jack.

It was 4:25 p.m. when a maroon-red Ford pickup pulled into our driveway. The guy who climbed out was a small mountain with legs. It looked like God used a railroad tie for his shoulders. He was huge! Bald, no fat, and he did, in fact, walk like a jungle cat. I didn't know whether to crap my pants right then and there or be delighted to have this guy on my side. Whatever my side was.

Kip was just lying there taking it all in. Not excited in the least. What was up with my dog? Maybe he senses people too?

Front doorbell rang, and I walked over and opened the door. "Mr. Merrick? I'm Jack. Angus said you needed some security work done?"

"Hi. Uh, do I just call you Jack?" I said as we shook hands.

"Yup. All my friends do."

"Did Angus fill you in on what's going on?"

"Mr. Dunbar gave me enough background to get me here. Why don't you give me the full picture from the beginning?"

"Sure." Taking a deep breath, I began at the beginning. "My parents died almost a year ago, last September 8. They were killed in a traffic accident on I-5 at night. Eighteen vehicles were involved.

Nine people died, including my folks. I was sixteen when that happened. I've known, my whole family has known, Angus Dunbar since before I was born. He's been our family attorney since that time. He's now my attorney, confidant, and sometimes counselor and mentor.

"When my folks died, they left me a substantial inheritance. All this was in the news at the time, but not in great detail. Working with Angus, I petitioned the court and was granted an emancipated minor status. We also worked with Kings Academy and successfully challenged all my senior year coursework. I've earned and received my high school diploma. I'm only mentioning this so you know I no longer attend school. Right now, I'm in the rattling-around phase of my young-ish life.

"I don't have complete control over my inheritance. I was the sole beneficiary of my folks' life insurance policies. The insurance policies alone have left me fairly wealthy. My inheritance is significantly more and separate. When my folks died, their estate was placed in a trust for my benefit. I'll not gain control of my trust until I'm twenty-one but have full control of the life insurance payouts. And as I've already said, the size of my inheritance is substantial. That's the quick background stuff.

"Last night, about 11:00 p.m., Kip, the guard dog lying across your feet, alerted to something in the forest. He was rigid, barking like he's never barked in his life. We'd both been dozing in the recliner there when this happened. Kip was staring holes through our front door and through the window into the nearby trees. I got up to see what the fuss was all about.

"In my peripheral vision, I noticed a very brief movement in the underbrush at the edge of the tree line. I grabbed our shotgun and moved to the rear of this room. From there I shut off all the interior lights and lit up the front and side porches and the patio. Kip and I waited, sitting with our backs to the kitchen island, looking at the front door and windows. We sat like that for over an hour. Kip didn't bark again, nor did I hear anything. Neither of us slept last night.

"This morning, Kip and I went out to the tree line and started looking for some indication of somebody having been there last night. Kip found a footprint, and we found a second print about two feet away. Just those two prints. Nothing leading to them. Nothing after them. Oh, a bush by the second print had two small branches broken. They're dry this time of year and easily damaged.

"We looked closer to the house, practically crawled around the house on my hands and knees. Neither Kip nor I found anything else. That brings you up to date on what happened."

Through all that, Jack didn't interrupt or ask questions. However, I could tell by how he watched me he was paying very close attention. Maybe he'd thought this was a prank or hoax or some such. If it were, Kip and I had nothing to do with it.

"Mr. Merrick. You are very observant, seemingly intelligent, a bit brave, and foolish."

"Huh? Wha—"

"You are observant in that you found two footprints and the broken bush branches. Brave because you didn't go hide under the bed last night but sought to protect yourself. Somewhat intelligent because you had the good sense to turn off the interior lights, then turn on the exterior lights. Foolish because you went traipsing into the woods this morning heedless of the risk that your visitor could have lain in wait until then to kidnap you or do you bodily harm. Now while we've still decent light, why don't you show me those two prints you found?"

That said, we walked out the front door, across the porch and lawn, and into the underbrush near the two footprints. Stopping nearby, I squatted down and pointed out the nearer print to Jack.

"Hmm. And there's the second print, yes? Ah, I see the two snapped twigs you described. I don't like this at all. Is there anything else you can remember?"

"I don't think so. I mean, I didn't go into excruciating detail, didn't and don't think you need to hear that I was scared silly for a time. Or that I was completely comfortable with my dad's shotgun in my lap, loaded and ready to go. I really don't know of any motive for this whole thing." I was not going to tell him about my two abilities, at least not yet.

"I suppose this could be some nut ball, but I don't think so. What bothers me are the two foot impressions. They most assuredly are not genuine. They were planted deliberately. The two twigs were likewise broken on purpose. Like you said earlier, I find nothing leading to or from those two prints. Has Kip, as you said, not alerted to anything else?"

"No. Nothing."

"I can tell you two things, Mr. Merrick. First, somebody was absolutely here watching you last night. What we do not know is how long they were here observing you. Nor do we know what, if anything, they were doing while observing you. Kip gives us some idea. As you've said, he barked for about a half hour. Had your intruder stayed longer, I think Kip would have continued barking. The glimpse you saw was certainly not somebody out for a late-night stroll across your property.

"Second, whoever visited you has certain skills. From what you've described and what I've seen here, those skills are significant. Not necessarily in the class of any of my team but skillful nonetheless. I will be back here in the morning, 7:00 a.m. I'll have two of my team with me and introduce you to both. At least one will be with you every hour of every day until your electronic system is installed and functioning. With the size of your acreage, we can set up a very effective, defensive perimeter.

"There is one thing I need to make absolutely clear to you, Mr. Merrick. Every security system in the world can be defeated. Nothing is foolproof. The systems I design and install are reliable and work without mechanical flaw. They can, however, be defeated. The two members I'm assigning you can be defeated as well. But in order to defeat any of my team, your enemy will have to kill them. This is not dramatics or theatrics. This is life and death. Our purpose is to protect you to the extent that getting to you is simply more expensive to them than they are willing to pay. We aggressively encourage bad actors to seek easier prey. Make sense?

"And one more thing. You left out the part of you drowning and being pronounced legally dead. That, too, is significant, yes? I grant that it likely has nothing to do with your security, but it is a significant life event, isn't it?"

What on God's green earth had happened to my life? "Sure. I understand. But look, I'm seventeen, okay? I've had a lot on my plate for the past year. I'm not a Green Beret wannabe. Well, maybe I wannabe, but in brutal honesty, I'm not. Okay? Not even close."

"Of course. Our job is to keep you safe. I want you completely aware of the absolutely worst case scenario. It is highly unlikely anything like that will happen. It is highly likely nobody is going to point a weapon in your direction and pull the trigger. In my line of work, we anticipate and plan for the worst. That way, we're not surprised. If any of my team are surprised, we've already lost. Our job is simple: do all the hard, demanding work on the front end. We hone our skills right to the razor's edge, then we sharpen that edge. In that way, we don't get surprised, and we don't lose. Ever."

"Jack, I don't even know your last name or the name of your company. Feels like I should be calling you Mr. Whatever-is-your-last-name. Anyhow. To me, this whole thing feels like an overreaction. Yes, somebody prowled my property last night. Yes, Kip barked, and I was spooked to the point of grabbing Dad's shotgun. But no harm, no foul, you know? Aren't we getting ahead of ourselves just a bit?"

"Mr. Merrick. If you were some ego-crazed, spoiled rich kid running around with a sketchy crowd, I'd not be here. If you worked at Burger Barn or Pizza World and lived in a small rental with mates, I'd not be here. I do not yet know you in depth. That will come with time or if and when you decide it's time to trust me. That said, I know a bit more about you than you think. I've not snooped you out completely, but I do get background on potential clients before we ever meet. I know you are smart. I know you are industrious. I know you are not some snot-nosed rich kid. I do know you are quiet and wealthy. The exact degree of your wealth is not important to me or my team. Suffice to say I know you can afford my services. And I know there is more going on in your life than you are telling me.

"Mr. Merrick, I live my life by being careful and cautious. I only take well-calculated risks and then only after I've done my due diligence on my employer. You, young Merrick, are about to become my employer.

"What you have lived through, losing both your parents so early in life and the degree to which you have handled it, is quite remarkable. There is nothing average or typical about you. At least not yet, and I suspect that is how you will continue to live your entire life, well beyond average and very untypical. My job is to see you get that opportunity. Only when you're ready, I encourage you to tell me about what you're holding back. I suspect with time that particular secret will become an ever heavier burden. It may grow to cause you to lose focus of the important things in life.

"One final item, son. All my local team members are on other assignments until tomorrow, as am I. After hearing from Mr. Dunbar, I took a short leave from my current client. As I said, that assignment ends at midnight tonight. I'll be here as soon after the end of my current assignment as possible. I expect it might be as late as 2:00 a.m., more likely about 1:00 a.m., this coming morning. I'd rather you were less secluded until I get back and can arrange solid coverage. Have you given any thought to going to a hotel for the night?"

"No. I really do think Kip and I will be just fine. Frankly, I'm a bit embarrassed by all this attention and caution. I'm not exactly the danger-seeking type, but this does feel like overkill."

"Mr. Merrick, my team and I have never lost a client. We vowed from the beginning to take every reasonable and perhaps some unreasonable precautions in protecting our clients. I do not use my last name because you and every one of our clients, past, present, and future, have no real need to know. The important thing for you to know is we operate as a tier one company. Worldwide, very few agencies like ours exist. We are not singular in our profession, but you could count our peer groups on the fingers of one hand.

"We do not have a company name. As a company or outfit or organization, we simply do not exist. Our clients come to us exclusively through word-of-mouth recommendation. Mr. Dunbar referred me to you. I've known that gentleman for a good many years. I respect him and trust him. Mr. Dunbar is a known quantity to us. There are few people today who cannot be bought, compromised, or muzzled in one manner or another. Mr. Dunbar is one such individual. If I'm reading you correctly, you will grow to be another. You, young Merrick, are rare on several levels."

"How big is your company, Jack? How many folks do you have on staff? You sound like a pretty good-sized company."

Jack, chuckling, said, "We have as many operators as we need. And now I must leave you. I want you to do as you did last evening. Turn on all your outside lights. Keep your inside lights to a minimum. Make certain you are not backlit at any time. Make sure your shotgun is at hand with one load chambered and the safety off. Do not leave it in one room while you go into another. Take it and Kip with you even when you go to the bathroom. Are we clear?

"I will call you as I'm leaving my current assignment tonight. Twenty minutes later, I'll be on your property. Expect my call at some point between 1:00 a.m. and 2:00 a.m. You won't see or hear me when I arrive. The whole idea is to not advertise my presence in case you have a prowler on-site. If they are here when I arrive, I'll take care of them, then let the law step in. Do we have an agreeable understanding of each other?"

"Yes. I'm sure Kip and I will be just fine. I do have to admit we'll both feel better once you are back here. You have me just a little bit spooked. There is one thing, sir. If I'm to call you Jack, will you please call me JC? Mr. Merrick is my dad…was my dad. Is that okay?"

"Certainly, JC. If I didn't think you'd be just fine, I'd make other arrangements to have someone here now. I believe there is no imminent threat, but I do not tempt fate. I will be in touch with you later tonight."

Saying that, Jack walked back to his pickup, climbed in, turned around, and drove out our driveway. It was later now, getting on toward dusk. Time for Kip and me to make supper and unwind.

By the time we'd cooked (Kip is a very attentive watcher of all things food related), eaten, and cleaned up the mess I'd created, it was full-on dark outside, nearly 10:00 p.m.

Kip and I relaxed for a while. I was still a bit wound up from last night and didn't want to go to bed until I'd relaxed some. Otherwise, all I'd do in bed is toss and turn and not get a minute of rest.

It was nearly midnight by the time I felt like I'd be able to sleep. Finally, it was time to turn on the outside lights, turn off most of the inside lights, and head to bed. I'd checked all the doors and windows before supper, so all was about to be safe and secure.

CHAPTER 9

I'd just turned on the outside lights and was reaching for the light switches controlling most of our living area lights when I heard glass break followed by the sound of a very loud firecracker. Momentarily stunned, I looked to the front door and saw the window next to the door cracked with a hole in it. What the? Somebody just shot at us! My shotgun was about four feet away.

Kip was barking like crazy. I could hardly think with how loud he was barking. Just as I crouched and began to move toward the shotgun, another loud sound and glass breaking, and I dove for the shotgun.

"Kip! Kip, get over here!" I yelled as my hands grabbed the shotgun and aimed at the front door. I'd managed to turn off all the indoor lights. Thankfully, all our exterior lights were on. I saw nothing moving outside as I laid on my belly and peeked around the corner.

Just then I heard two more shots that hit our front door. It looked like our intruder had shot out the deadbolt lock and door handle. However, the door was still closed, though I didn't think there was anything to resist just nudging the door open and walking in.

I reached for Kip and held him by his collar as I lay on the floor. He got the idea and lay there with me, barking and growling, hackles straight up. I had the shotgun tight against my shoulder, pointed it directly at doorknob height slightly to the right of middle, so if somebody was stupid enough to crash through the door, it would swing away from where I had the barrel pointed, allowing me a clear shot at whoever was barging in.

Neither Kip nor I was making a sound now, though I believed they could hear my heart pounding all the way to the Canadian border. After what felt like hours later but was probably only seconds, the front door started to slowly swing open. Somebody, maybe more than one somebody, was going to walk through the front door! Three thoughts flashed through my brain at that same instant.

Maybe this front door was a feint thing, intended to get me to move or give away my position. Second, maybe somebody was sneaking through the back door right now. And third, maybe there were more than just one or two idiots out there, and they'd come in both doors at the same time.

Nuts! All I had was a shotgun with a total of five shells. The rest of the box of shells might as well had been in the garage for all the good they would do me right now. No other firearms present. Double nuts!

Thoughts raced through my brain. First shot would be if or when somebody came through the front door or if I heard or Kip alerted that somebody was making a play through the back kitchen door. I'd not wait for the back door to open. It wasn't a solid core door like the front, just two thin sheets of aluminum with a Styrofoam-like center. Great for keeping heat and cold out and keeping warmth in. Not so great at defeating intruders. I didn't think anybody would come through a window. Shoot through one maybe. But we weren't exposed to anybody looking through a window. Breaching a window would be very noisy, so that was third on my list of threats.

Kip and I slowly scooted a bit, giving me better reaction to a backdoor entry without sacrificing my aim at the front door. It felt like we'd been there waiting, anticipating, and thinking for an hour. It was likely no longer than several seconds, probably less than even that. But that's where the outside guy, gal, or people made their mistake. They shouldn't have given us any time to think or prepare.

I watched as the barrel of some rifle or other prodded the front door open a bit more. Kip's head jerked to the back door, alerting me somebody was indeed there. I heard a crash from the back door just as I had moved the shotgun in that direction. Without hesitation, and with the barrel pointed directly next to the doorknob, I pulled the trigger. A hole about six inches in diameter appeared in the door, and I heard a thud on the deck.

As quickly as I fired that first shot, I pumped another shell in the chamber and swung the barrel to see a second intruder three steps into our living area about twelve feet from me. Pulling the trigger a second time, the intruder was pushed back by the force of the blast. I pulled the trigger again, and he crumpled to the floor. I kept my shotgun trained on the person lying there as I tried to control my breathing.

I waited, maybe a minute, but nothing else happened. That's when I reached up for our phone and dialed 911.

"911. What is your emergency?"

"My name is JC Merrick. I'm seventeen years old, white, wearing a navy tee shirt and blue jeans. I'm inside my home. I've just shot two intruders. I live at 413 Cove Road. The outside lights are on. I've left the interior lights off. I do not know the status of the intruder who opened my back door. I shot him through the door as it was opening. The intruder on the floor in my living area is dead, I think. There's some sort of rifle beside him. There may be more people outside. I'm not sure. I'll put my shotgun on the floor and show my empty hands as soon as I see blue and red lights flashing and officers opening the doors of their patrol vehicles."

"Sir? Stay on the line with me until officers arrive."

"Ma'am, I'm going to hang up and call my attorney, Angus Dunbar. I expect he will be here in about twenty minutes. When your officers arrive, they will see my hands empty, held up in the air in full view." With that I hung up and called Angus.

Two rings later… "Angus? JC here. I've just shot two intruders. I've called the police, and they are on the way. At least one intruder is dead. I don't know about the person on the other side of our back door. I'd like you here quick as you are able. I'm hanging up now in case the police call back before arriving." And I hung up.

The phone rang immediately. "Is this JC Merrick?" It was a voice of a man.

"Yes. This is JC Merrick. Who is this?"

"This is Detective Archibald Winslow, Pierce County sheriff's department. You've called in a shooting, is that correct?"

"Yes. One intruder is dead, lying on the floor in my living area. A second person is likely lying just outside our back door that enters onto our backyard deck."

"Why did you hang up on our 911 operator? She told you to stay on the line."

"I called my attorney, Angus Dunbar, to advise him of what happened. He is on his way here now."

"Deputies are on their way to you. They should arrive in the next five minutes. I strongly suggest you do as you are told by the sheriff's department deputies. Are we clear?"

"Look, Winslow. I am seventeen years old. I've just called you telling you I've shot two individuals who had first shot at me. I was in fear of my life. I don't know if there are remaining bad guys on my property or not. I am not trying to be uncooperative with you or anybody. But I will look after my best interests, and calling my attorney was in my best interest at this time.

"Further, I will cooperate with you and your staff at all times so long as it is in my best interest to do so. In fact, I'm seeing two patrol cars driving up the driveway with their light bars lit right now. Do you want me to get off the phone now so I can show them my raised empty hands? Or do you want me to continue hanging on this phone and have them wonder whether I'm a home invader with something questionable in my hand?"

"Merrick, get off the phone and raise your hands now!"

I hung up and did exactly that, while I hit every light switch in reach. Made the house interior well lit and placed my empty hands up and in full view of the approaching deputies.

"Keep your hands up where we can see 'em and don't move!" This from the deputy closest to what used to be my front door. Three more deputies accompanied him.

"What's your name, and what are you doing here?" It was the same officer. Big guy. Looked like a gym rat.

"Deputy, my name is JC Merrick. I live here."

"Merrick, what happened here?"

"I shot the dead guy on the floor in front of you. He had some sort of long gun. You can see it beside him. Loud as hell. His first shot went through the front window. Kip, my dog, alerted just before the first shot. I grabbed my shotgun, moved to the light switches here beside me. Just then, the intruder put two shots through the front door, ruining the locking mechanism. At about that same time, Kip alerted to the back door. I moved so I had some safety from either door but was still able to view both. Kip and I lay down right here." I pointed to where he and I had lain down.

"Somebody outside started to enter the back door as the dead guy here slammed through the front door. I put one shot through the back door. You can see it clearly. I turned to the living area and saw the dead guy there on the floor moving toward me with his weapon raised, his finger on the trigger, looking for exactly where Kip and I were located. I was in fear for my life and Kip's. I shot him in self-defense."

Just then another sheriff's deputy, dressed in plain clothes this time, walked in and approached the uniformed deputy I'd just been talking to. They moved away a bit and started talking back and forth in whispers. This went on for a few minutes, then the plain clothes deputy, detective maybe, approached.

"What's your name?"

"As I told the 911 operator, the sheriff that called back, and the deputies you were just whispering with, my name is JC Merrick."

"Tell me exactly what happened here and how you came to be in this house."

I was upset, getting shaky from my body having dumped about a gallon of adrenaline into my system, and I didn't like the attitude this guy was radiating. "Respectfully, I'm done talking until my attorney gets here. His name is Angus Dunbar. He should be here any minute. Once he arrives, I will cooperate fully with his guidance. I'm going to go sit on that sofa until Mr. Dunbar arrives."

I moved toward the sofa furthest away from the dead guy. That sofa and immediate area were not affected by what had happened, so I figured I was not messing up any part of the crime scene, and frankly my legs were feeling like if I didn't sit down, I'd end up on the floor on my butt.

The plainclothes guy reached and grabbed my upper arm, and Kip let loose with a loud, deep growl, hackles raised again. It was immediately obvious he was not happy that some stranger was going to grab me. The deputy gave my dog a dirty look but did remove his hand.

I went and sat on the sofa. Kip walked over, hopped up on the sofa with me, and sat with his back to the back of the sofa, his eyes staring at all the strangers in the room. His body was tense, hackles up, and ready to defend his home and me if he thought it was necessary.

Kip and I sat like that for only a couple minutes before another vehicle drove up the driveway, stopped, and parked. I could hear feet crunching on the driveway and pause, then Angus walked through what used to be my front door.

Chapter 10

"What's going on here?" asked Angus in full-on attorney mode. "My name is Angus Dunbar, and I am Mr. Merrick's attorney in all matters. If you intend asking him any questions, you ask them through me. Are we clear?"

The plainclothes guy did not look happy. Maybe he thought I was just some kid who shot people for fun. Who knows what was going on in his brain? "I was asking this kid what happened—"

"This 'kid,' as you call him, is JC Merrick. He is an adult in all matters, legal and otherwise. You are standing in his home. By now, he has likely told you the basics of what happened. Am I correct?"

"He told me a version of events, yes. However, there is a lot going on here that I do not yet know, and I intend to get to the bottom of these shootings."

By now it was just after 1:00 a.m., and I was getting tired. The adrenaline had nearly worn off, I had the shakes from all the chemicals my body had dumped in me, and all I wanted to do was go to bed and probably have nightmares for a month.

"I am going to take Mr. Merrick to hospital to get looked after. As you can see quite plainly, if you'd have bothered looking, Mr. Merrick has been shot."

Wait. What? Shot? Only then did I notice that my left arm hurt like crazy. I looked down, seeing a bloody furrow plowed from just above my wrist to my elbow. I was leaking blood, more than a bit by the looks of things. But it didn't look like I was in any immediate danger of bleeding to death. Still... Son of a...

"You have not sent for an ambulance, have you, Detective? And as much as both Mr. Merrick and I have introduced ourselves to you and your officers here, you've yet to tell us exactly who you are."

"I am Pierce County sheriff's deputy, Detective Archibald Winslow."

Then I heard and saw another three vehicles pull up the driveway. I noticed one was a coroner's van. The second was a crime-scene truck sort of thing. The third was a red pickup. Oh, good. More mayhem coming to visit, except for Jack. In all this mess, I'd forgotten all about his coming back tonight.

Jack was the first one through the front door. "What the hell happened here? I was able to get here earlier than expected, but it seems not nearly early enough. I called about fifteen minutes ago, but there wasn't any answer. Mr. Merrick, JC, are you alright? Hi, Angus. Good. You're here."

"I'm just taking Mr. Merrick to hospital. Seems he's been a bit shot. I'll get him seen to and fixed, then go from there."

"Mr. Merrick, I'm calling two of my team to get here as quickly as possible. The sheriff's department will do their investigation, and we'll do ours. We'll stay out of their way but make certain everything necessary is attended to. I strongly suspect we'll find things they'll miss. They're good, but not good enough for something like this." This was all said in the presence of Sheriff's Detective Archie, whom I didn't like much at all.

"Detective Winslow," said Angus, "Mr. Merrick and I will be at your office at 10:00 a.m. tomorrow morning for you to discuss this investigation. Will that be convenient for you?" Angus was still in attorney mode.

"I can work with that, Dunbar."

Angus gave him a sour look, turned to me, and gestured for us to leave. By now my arm was throbbing in time with my heartbeat and still leaking a fair amount. I walked to the kitchen, opened a drawer, and grabbed a dish-drying towel. Wrapped it around my arm to try to prevent leaking any more than necessary.

"Mr. Merrick, I'll be here the rest of tonight and until you return in the morning. You are now my client, and my team will take very good care of you. I imagine you're not feeling so good right now, but it will pass in the next day. In my career, I've not seen anyone your age so composed, focused, and determined. I'm proud of you, JC. Take care. We'll catch up in the morning." Saying that, Jack turned and grabbed his cell phone as he started taking in the crime scene.

Angus and I walked to his car, a very nice Lincoln land yacht. Talk about room! Angus drove us to the Tacoma Medical Center Hospital. We walked into the emergency room, all bright, white, and shiny even at this hour. I noticed I'd gotten blood on my tee shirt and pants, and the dish towel I'd wrapped around my left arm had blood leaking through it. One look from the nurse at the front desk and we were taken directly to an exam room. I was told to lie down on the provided gurney-like bed, which I was more than happy to do. It was only a minute or two later that an ER doc came in.

"Well, what do we have here? I'm Dr. William Swensen by the way. Looks like you've been shot," he said as he looked at my bloody arm.

Over the course of the next ninety or so minutes, my arm was examined, x-rayed, anesthetized, cauterized, cleaned, slathered with antibacterial solution, then stitched. The last thing was a technician putting goop along my arm and then doing an ultrasound along the length and sides of my wound/stitches.

I'd watched as they picked pieces of whatever out of my arm for twenty minutes (big clock on the wall above the entry door). They'd put my arm on the top of a table-like affair, looking through a large, bright magnifying lens. I couldn't see what they saw, couldn't identify any of the bits and pieces, but there was a pretty good pile of goo in the stainless-steel tray when they were finished.

Doc Swensen gave me a scrip for antibiotics and four white tablets for pain. He explained the pain pills were particularly strong and to take them only every twelve hours with food, beginning when

I got back home. He warned me about staying "ahead" of the pain and the consequences of taking the meds on an empty stomach (diarrhea, vomiting, all the lovely consequences). "You're not to sign any legal documents while taking this medication, nor are you to drive. Your mental faculties will be reduced to the point that you're not likely to make good decisions, and your reflexes, as far as driving is concerned, will be completely unreliable."

Saying all that and after wrapping my stitches with cotton gauze and an Ace bandage, Dr. Swensen was ready to send us on our way.

"Dr. Swensen, thank you for everything. I appreciate your thoroughness, explanations, and skills. Angus drove me here. He'll drive me home. I'll mind regarding these pain tablets. I suspect I'll be seeing Dr. Phyllis Church at some point tomorrow. Thank you again." And Angus and I got up and left.

We walked to Angus's land yacht, and I climbed in. I was now so tired and wrung out I could have slept on a pile of rocks. However, there wasn't time yet. I still had to deal with the mess at home, at least some of it.

"How are you holding up, JC? Your coloring is off, and your eyes look stressed and tired."

"Well, that's exactly what I'm feeling. Wiped out, stressed, and more tired than I can remember. This has not been one of my better nights. Then again, I could be the guy lying dead in the living room. So all things considered, I think I'm doing okay. Not great, but okay. What a mess. Thank you for coming tonight, Angus, or is it last night now? For taking over with the sheriff's deputies. That detective was a jerk."

"I only know Detective Winslow by reputation. Meeting him in person tonight, I'd say he has earned his reputation for being rude and obnoxious and a bit of a pompous ass. One of those folks who, when given a modicum of power or authority, think they've become a god, small *g*. We'll manage him just fine. If necessary, I'll school him on manners during the coming days. Whether he learns anything or not is up to him. Never fear, he will not talk with you or approach you without my being present.

"As soon as we get you home, I'll call police headquarters and tell them we will not be attending our interview later today. Your medication will have you mentally compromised for the next few days. They dare not interview you when you are influenced by a prescribed controlled substance. I want you to see Phyllis Church and follow her instructions for care and medication. Make her aware... No, wait. I'll take you to Dr. Church directly. Can't have you driving around under the influence.

"No. I'll have Jack or one of his team take you. You certainly don't need me with you when you see your doctor, but you need to be driven anywhere you go, and I want you accompanied until we get this whole episode sorted. Is that agreeable to you?"

"If Jack's available or one of his team, I'm fine with that. Dr. Swensen really pushed on the effects of the tablets he gave me. You know, I've never gotten drunk or high in any way. Closest I came was having my wisdom teeth pulled. That was just before, you know, Mom and Dad. I was asleep for that, coulda cheerfully strangled that doc. I looked like a chipmunk for two weeks and hurt like crazy for the first week. Best I had for that pain was aspirin. Never went back to him either. Like my dentist now, Dr. Bradley Kriskonovich. His group are super. Sorry, I'm beginning to rattle."

Angus was smiling. "No worries, JC. You've been through a lot. Not only tonight but the past year. You look to be holding up well, but I know you better than you might think. I suspect inside you have all manner of emotions and thoughts bouncing around. I'm here, JC. Not just as your attorney but as your friend too. Don't ever hesitate to get in touch with me if you feel the need to talk, vent, or, as you say, rattle. Alright?"

We were pulling into our...my driveway. Coroner's van was gone. Crime-scene truck was gone. All the sheriffs cars were gone. All that remained in my driveway was Jack's red pickup, an older Corvette, and a newer Jeep Wrangler. Angus and I got out of his car and walked to the house and through what used to be our...my front door. It was nearly 4:00 a.m.

Chapter 11

Jack was there with two people I'd not yet met. Guy was white, thirty-ish, about five feet nine inches, very thick body but didn't look like a gym rat. He had short light-brown hair. Not military cut but nearly. It looked like he could go outside and tuck the Jeep under his arm and walk down to the county road.

The other person was a woman, Japanese or some sort of Asian, mixed heritage, I thought. No idea on her age. She was slender and tall. At least five feet, ten inches, maybe closer to six feet. Very striking. Mid-back-length dark hair worn in a tight ponytail. Deep-blue eyes that get noticed at a distance. Killer smile.

Jack walked over to us. "How'd it go, Mr. Merrick? Looks like you're bandaged up, at least for tonight. How ya doing? Hell of a thing you've just been through. But I know you've been through worse. Sometimes it seems stuff just piles on and on. Tell me how you're coping. Oops. Forgive my manners. The short guy who looks like a sumo wrestler without the fat is Paul. Whatever it is, if Paul can't handle it, it can't be handled. He is top shelf in every way. You're in the best of hands with Paul. His partner here is Kim. She's every bit as accomplished as Paul but with a better sense of humor. Now tell us how you're really doing."

Both Paul and Kim nodded when Jack introduced them. I noticed Jack, Paul, and Kim were all wearing light jackets covering dark tee shirts, jeans, and wearing some sort of what looked to be heavy black tactical boots. I also noticed each of them seemed to be carrying a concealed pistol of some sort, holstered on the inside of their jeans, mostly hidden by the jackets they were wearing.

"I'm okay. Physically, my left arm has some damage and is beginning to thaw. They shot my arm with lidocaine before working on it. Gave me four strong pain meds. I'll take the first one in the next little bit. There is some muscle damage. Bullet cut a groove almost a half-inch wide and quarter-inch deep the full length of my arm just above my wrist to my elbow. No bone damage. Fair amount of nerve and muscle damage. I'll likely be purple from trauma from shoulder to fingertips. I'll learn more when I can get in to see my regular doc and they scan my arm. I need to call my regular doc first thing when their office opens in a few hours, then go from there."

Kim had gone into the kitchen and returned with a glass of water. "For the pain med you're about to take," she said, handing me the glass of water.

I dug one of the pills out of the little white paper envelope Dr. Swensen had given me, tossed the pill in my mouth, and took a couple swallows of water. "Thank you, Kim. The ER doc warned me to stay ahead of the pain or suffer the consequences. Don't think of myself as a wuss, but I'm not keen to learn my level of pain tolerance, at least not tonight."

"Jack," Angus asked, "do you think either Paul or Kim could take JC to see Dr. Phyllis Church for his appointment? He's not to drive under the influence of the pain med he just took. As his young body hasn't yet been exposed to opioids, I expect he is going to crash and burn in the next few minutes. JC, you need to get some food in your stomach, or you'll throw up. Your choice."

Once again, Kim went into the kitchen, grabbed a loaf of sliced bread, and gave it to me. I ate three slices, washed 'em down with the rest of the water, then felt like I was going to fall asleep right then and there. I walked to the sofa I'd sat on when the police were here, tipped over on my side, and went to sleep with my left arm tucked under me. Looked like I was staying ahead of any pain issues for the time being at least. Why else would I have tucked my injured arm under me while falling asleep?

It seemed only moments later I was being gently prodded awake by Paul. "Hey, JC. How are you feeling?"

I noticed there was a blanket draped over me and a pillow under my head. I must have really been zonked out. "I'm feeling fuzzy, a little disoriented, and still sleepy. What time is it?"

Grinning, Paul said, "That's your pain medication doing its job. It's just past 10:00 a.m. You have an appointment with Dr. Church at eleven thirty this morning. Just enough time to get cleaned up, eat a bit, then I'll take you to your appointment."

"Wow. I really was out of it. Thanks. How'd I get the blanket and pillow?"

"Well, you looked pretty uncomfortable all tipped over on that sofa," Paul said. "Kim rummaged around and found the blanket and pillow. She and I just moved the sofa side cushion, lifted your head a bit, and scooted the pillow under. Then Kim draped the blanket over you. Easy as that. Kip was guarding you the entire time. Would not leave your side. He's been dozing a bit right below you on the floor. Good dog, Kip."

"Yea, Kip and I have been through it these past several months. Don't know what I'd do without him. And I'm sure he saved me last night when whoever it was started coming in the back door."

"I've no doubt of it. What breed is he? I've never seen a dog like him before, certainly not one with green eyes. What's with his eyes?"

"Kip's a Goldendoodle. Big, even for his breed. He's right at 130 pounds of bone, muscle, hair, and personality. His dad's a large standard poodle named Buck. Buck is big for a standard, weighs about eighty-five lean pounds. Standards are normally around sixty to seventy pounds thereabouts. Kip's mom, Puddin, is half standard poodle, half golden retriever, and big for her breed. The result is Kip. Best dog ever and goofier than any dog you'll probably meet. No idea on his green eyes. I've never heard of it before. I think his eye color is one of a kind. No idea where or how. Kip's too smart for his own good. He's more lover than fighter. But his protective side really came out last night. Without his awesome instincts, neither of us would likely be here this morning.

"Give me a few minutes to get cleaned up and changed. Then I'll grab a bite, and we can head to see Dr. Church. Is that okay?"

"Sounds perfect." Saying that, Paul moved to the kitchen and through the door to our…my patio.

I went down the hall to my bathroom and washed my hands and face, brushed my teeth, and looked at myself in the mirror. Think I was a little pale with puffy eyes and unusually messy hair. Worked with my hair until I gave up with nothing accomplished. Went to my bedroom and changed into clean sneakers, jeans, and a Moody Blues tee shirt.

Back downstairs, I raided the fridge. All I found was some cheese, a partial loaf of bread, a roll of summer sausage, and milk. Other stuff there but not for a quick breakfast. I threw a sandwich together from two slices of bread, two thin slices of cheese, and four slices of summer sausage. Poured myself a glass of milk, and breakfast was ready. A few minutes later, it was gone, and I was ready to go.

Making sure I had the little envelope of pain meds Dr. Swensen gave me, I went to the backyard and found Paul. "I'm ready to go whenever you are."

CHAPTER 12

"Kim's going to drive you to the doc, JC. I'm going to stay here and take a good look around. I'll be picking locations for your security system as well as looking for signs of your visitors last night. Kim and I have already been looking around some. The police were back here while you were sleeping. They walked around a bit. I didn't see them noticing anything. They were far more interested in the inside of your home, the damage, and how that damage happened. When you get back, you, Kim, and I will walk around and look around outside, a good, thorough look. Then we'll discuss what measures we're going to take to prevent something like this happening again. Okay?"

"Sounds good to me. Thank you, Paul, for all you've done. I appreciate you, Kim, and Jack being here. It means a lot to me."

"No worries, JC. Make sure you tell your doc everything. Stuff you're holding in, how you're feeling physically and mentally. This is a load for anybody, especially someone your age. You're handling it remarkably well, but still, there's stuff you'll need to deal with. Either now or later. Please believe me when I tell you dealing is much better done earlier. Dealing later can bite when you least need or expect it."

With that, Paul led me back through the house and out the front door to find Kim. She was standing just outside on our front porch. With her back to me as I walked out, she seemed to be studying the trees and woodland just beyond our front yard. I noticed she'd changed into stylish jeans, another dark tee shirt, and was now wearing a blazer-type jacket. I assumed she was still armed but saw no evidence of anything showing.

As I walked up to her and with a twinkle in her eye, Kim looked down at my now slightly bloody arm and said, "Hey, Merrick, ready for a good time? Let's go see your doc." With that, she led me to what was evidently her car, a classic Corvette, a split-window '63. "Climb in and buckle up, Cowboy. Time to drive." And we were off like a shot.

"Nice car! First time I've ridden in a Vette. This is killer! Do you like it?"

"It took me a while to get used to the split rear window, but I do like it. Saved for years to afford this thing, but it's worth every penny. And don't kid me, JC. I've seen what's stashed in your garage. You've a fine eye for Michigan metal."

"Yeah. But those two are my dad's. I mean, I inherited them, but I've not driven either one yet. Still feels like I need permission, like I'd be sneaking out with them without asking my folks. Stupid, I know, but there it is."

"Hey. I understand, JC. Jack filled us in a bit. You've had a rough year. Losing your parents, drowning, well, dying, I heard. And now this? You'd probably be safer joining the spec ops community!" said with a grin.

It seemed like only minutes later when we arrived at Dr. Church's office. Kim parked her Vette away from the other cars in the lot. Took up two spaces but was considerate enough to be distant from the entrance. We got out of the car, and she locked up.

"I notice you're careful where you park," I said as we walked toward the front door to Dr. Church's practice.

"Yeah. You know how much it costs to fix door dings on a fiberglass body? Besides, parking away from the front doors gives me time to check our surroundings, make sure things look right."

I'd not thought about that. Until last night, no reason to.

Approaching the front door, I moved to grab the handle and open the door. Kim interrupted me, "No. Remember, JC, I'm not just accompanying you. I'm your bodyguard. Whoever is with you needs to get the first look inside any building. We won't ever be obvious about it, but we can scan for immediate threats in a split second. We're trained in this sort of thing. I appreciate your manners, okay? But this is part of my job, protecting you in every setting."

Saying this, Kim reached for the front door, opened it, and walked through with me trailing behind. Like she said, smooth. No interruption, nothing noticeable to my inexperienced eyes, but I now knew she had already checked the few folks in the waiting area.

I walked up to the receptionist. Her nametag said Kathy. "Hi, Kathy. I'm JC Merrick for an eleven thirty with Dr. Church."

She glanced at her appointment book. "I see you here, Mr. Merrick. Have a seat. Dr. Church will be with you in a few moments."

Kim had already taken a seat, where she had a view of the front door and doorway to the exam rooms. I sat to her left, placing her between the front door and myself. "You learn quickly, JC. Keep it up. We'll make you an operator yet," she said, grinning, with that same twinkle in her eyes.

LeAnne, Dr. Church's longtime nurse, came through the door leading to the exam rooms. She walked up to me. "JC, Dr. Church is ready for you. If you'll follow me."

"Sure, LeAnne. This is Kim. She's kind enough to be my driver today. They gave me serious pain meds last night in the ER. Kim's just making sure I don't do something dumb, like try to drive."

"Thank you, Kim," LeAnne said. "We think the world of JC and appreciate you helping." Turning, LeAnne led me through the door and to an exam room.

"Dr. Church will be right in. You can get ready by removing your tee shirt. Dr. Church will want to examine your entire left arm." She left the room, and I awkwardly removed my tee shirt, this one a dark-blue Moody Blues tee, given to me by my dad.

It seemed only seconds later that Dr. Church knocked on the door, opened it, and walked in. "You had quite an adventure last night, JC. What in the world happened? Tell me as I examine your arm."

Saying this, she reached to the Ace wrap clipped to my forearm and began unwinding it. As she did, I told her only that I'd been shot during a home invasion.

Exposing the stitches, she began looking at them. "I read the report from Dr. Swensen when I got in this morning. So far, your injury looks good. Your ultrasound images from last night don't give me all the detail I want. I'm going to send you next door, to Tacoma Imaging, for a scan. Your arm has moderate swelling, about as much as I'd expect to see from a wound like yours. I do want an MRI scan to get a look at your muscle damage. See what we need to do to regain full function.

"TI is right next door. I had a hunch when you called this morning. They're expecting you. It seemed good practice to have them prepped for your arrival. What I saw on your ultrasound didn't satisfy me. As soon as TI is finished, I want you back here so we can follow up. Their report usually takes a few days. However, I've made arrangements with them to read your scan right away and walk the report to me. I expect to see the scan results and you in less than an hour. Okay?"

"Sure. Thank you, Doc."

"JC. Before you go, what's your pain level right now?"

"Right now, I'm feeling a bit fuzzy and goofy. My pain is about a four."

"No throbbing or shooting pain?"

"No. Nothing like that. Just a deep ache that doesn't go away, but isn't horrible."

"Okay. Get over to Imaging, then come right back, okay?"

"You bet. Thanks, Doc." I awkwardly put my tee shirt back on. Dr. Church had left the Ace wrap off my arm, so I did as well. With my tee shirt back on, I walked back to the waiting area and Kim.

"Well, what'd your doc say, JC?" Then she noticed my left arm. "Wow! That'll be a nasty scar. Make the girls swoon and want to mother you. When it's healed, it'll look really sexy!"

I rolled my eyes at her. "We go next door to Tacoma Imaging so they can take an MRI scan of my arm. Soon as they finish, we come right back here to see Dr. Church again. She said less than an hour before I see her again. Then she'll read the images and go from there."

"Okay, let's go." Saying that, Kim stood and walked to the front door, opened it, and walked through to the sidewalk with me right behind her. I noticed when Kim walked through a door, she did not hold it open for whoever was behind her. I assumed she wanted both arms and hands free as much as possible. I realized not holding a door open wasn't Kim being rude. It was Kim being vigilant and ready.

Oddly enough, the events of last night either hadn't hit home yet or I was already completely at ease being in Kim's protection. I had a fleeting reminder of all the good God had brought into my life, how He had always taken care of me. While I could have dwelled on the negatives in my life, and there were a few, I was raised to see the sunshine, not the clouds. I'd certainly experienced a terrible loss, but I could have died twice and stayed dead. I'd count my outcome as sunshine or more clearly said, "son-shine."

We walked down the sidewalk, a short distance to Tacoma Imaging. Again, I noticed Kim walking on the outside of the sidewalk, something I would normally do. I'd learned at academy that men walking on the outside of any walkway, when accompanying a woman, had its origins a very long time ago. Chivalry had it that a man walking on the outside protected the woman in his company from being splattered with mud from passing horses, carriages, wagons, and the like. Odd what you could learn about manners and their beginnings. Anyhow, I noticed it.

There certainly wasn't any mud on the asphalt, but Kim's body was definitely shielding me from whatever might come at us from the parking area, at least as much as was practical. It was only about 150 feet to the entry of Tacoma Imaging, and we arrived in about a minute.

Again, Kim went through the door first, and I followed close behind. I walked up to the reception desk. Before I could even open my mouth, the receptionist said, "Mr. Merrick? I'll take you back for your scan."

I looked at Kim. She nodded and sat, again facing the entry door.

The receptionist must have been told to expect a young guy coming in with stitches the length of his left forearm. Anyhow, she took me through the patient door. Down the hall, four side doors later, we came to the end of the hall and walked through the door straight in front of us. She held the door for me, and we entered. It was a large room with a huge piece of equipment in the center. Off to the right was another room with glass all along the front, facing what I assumed was their MRI machine.

"Mr. Merrick, we're going to be scanning your left arm today. We'll need you lying on the bed you see in front. There's a gown on the chair here. Please remove your tee shirt, jeans, and shoes. You can leave your shorts and socks on. The gown opens in the back. The technicians will be with you in just a couple minutes and get you situated and as comfortable as possible. Your scan will only take a few minutes once we get you situated. MRI's take a bit longer than a CT scan, but your doctor wants as complete a view of the damage to your arm as we can get.

"It's very important you keep your left arm as still as possible. They'll brace it to get and keep it in as comfortable a position as they are able. If you have any questions, the techs will answer them for you before they begin." Saying that, she left and closed the door behind her. No name tag, so I'd no idea of her name. She had been cordial and efficient. I got undressed and had just put the huge gown on when two techs walked in.

"Mr. Merrick?"

"Yes. I'm JC Merrick."

"Hi, JC. I'm Brad. This is Don. We'll be doing your MRI. I understand Dr. Church is waiting for the results of this scan. Is that correct?"

"Yes. That's my understanding. I'll go right back to her office as soon as we're done here."

"Okay. To speed things for you just a bit, if you'll wait in our reception area after we're finished, we'll have Dr. Goodman read your scan, write his findings, and give you the films and report to take back with you. Is that okay with you?"

"Sure. Works for me."

"Okay. Let's get you on the table and situated. Have you ever had an MRI or CT scan?"

"No. This is my first."

"It might seem odd, running your entire body in this machine to just look at your arm. However, we can't just shove your arm in and get a full picture. Your stitches look very new. It looks like your left arm sustained some serious trauma and a good bit of damage. It's already bruising from that trauma. Take heart, we've seen much worse, even with patients somewhat younger than you. So let's look at the bright side, okay?"

"Absolutely. I came out of this much better than the other guy."

"Oh?"

Oops. I broke eye contact and kept my mouth shut. Thankfully, neither Brad nor Don asked any more questions.

"Okay. Hop up on the table, and we'll get you situated."

Hearing that, I stepped on the small stool positioned alongside the table and climbed up, then lay on my back, my head toward the scanner opening.

Brad and Don worked for a few minutes getting me both comfortable and my left arm positioned and braced for the scan.

"Remember, don't move while we're scanning. Lie as still on the table as you are able. We've some headphones to give you so you can listen to music while we take your scans. Are you claustrophobic at all?"

"Not that I know of, but I've not climbed in any tunnels either. I think I'll be fine."

"Okay. Focus on your breathing. Nice slow breaths in and out. What kind of music do you like?"

"Do you have any Pearl Jam or Radiohead?"

"I think we can get you there. Okay, headphones on, and remember, we can hear you if you need to let us know anything. If you start feeling claustrophobic, just say so. We'll be as quick as we can, but we want to get good images. Ready?"

Headphones covering my ears, everything positioned, and not moving, I said, "Ready." And the techs went to their glass booth. Just seconds later, with my eyes closed, I felt the table begin to move me into the tunnel. The table and I reached our destination quickly. Curious, I opened my eyes. Big mistake! My nose was about an inch from the top of the tube! Holy crap! I snapped my eyes closed fast.

"You okay in there, Mr. Merrick? We're about to begin."

"I'm dandy."

Music was coming through my headphones. The machine made enough noise that I could barely hear the music, but it did help distract me. I focused on my breathing and listened to the headphones as best as I could.

"You're doing great, JC. We're over halfway there. Just a little longer."

Wow. This thing was quick. Seemed like I'd only listened to a couple songs. So not bad at all so far.

It seemed only a minute or two later I could feel the scanner bed begin to move back toward the opening. I opened my eyes again and watched as the tube slid along with me very nearly rubbing my nose against it the full journey. Then I was out in the bright lights.

Brad helped me sit up. I removed the headphones and stepped down to the floor.

"You did great. Dr. Goodman is already reading your scans. Just get dressed and go back to our waiting area. You can find it, okay?"

"Sure. Through the door and straight ahead, yes?"

"Yup. Just leave your gown on the chair."

"Thank you, Brad. And Don too. You both made this process easy and painless."

"You're welcome. Sorry about the noise. That was the magnets doing their magic for you. We got great imaging. Your doc will go over the results with you." Brad turned and left the room.

It was only a minute later I was walking back into the waiting area and sat beside Kim, again placing her closer to the front entry. "They asked us to wait. Their doc is reading the images and writing his report now. Soon as he's finished, they'll give the scans and report to me. Then we can go back to Dr. Church's office and give her or whomever the images and report. They said it wouldn't be long, but I don't know what long means to them either."

"That's okay. We've no other set destination or time commitment. I've called Paul and let him know what's going on. How are you doing? Pain manageable?"

"Yeah. I'm doing okay. It's been almost nine hours since I took a pain pill, so I'm good for another three hours at least. I expect we'll be home well before then."

It was another twenty or so minutes before we were approached by a man, who looked like a doc. "You're Mr. Merrick?"

"Yes."

"I'm Dr. Goodman." He handed me the large envelope. "I've reviewed your scans and written my report. Everything you need is inside. I understand you're going right back to Dr. Church, that she's waiting for my report?"

"Yes. We'll be going right back over. Thank you, Dr. Goodman, for getting this done so quickly. I don't imagine this is the typical time frame for something like this. I appreciate your accommodation."

"You're quite right, this is not our normal speed. Phyllis asked if we could speed things up, and we were delighted to be able to. You've a nasty arm, Mr. Merrick. However, it could have been much, much worse. I'll let Phyllis give you all the detail. You're in very good hands with her. Please let her know we were delighted to work with her." Saying that, Dr. Goodman turned and went back through the patient door.

Kim and I stood and made our way through the front door and back toward Dr. Church's office. As usual, Kim led and walked on the outside of the sidewalk. All went smoothly, and a moment later we were once again in Dr. Church's reception area.

I walked back up to Kathy with the envelope containing the scan images and Dr. Goodman's report. "Hi, Kathy. These are the scans and report from Dr. Goodman for Dr. Church. She's expecting them."

"Thank you, JC. I'll get them to LeAnne right now. She'll get them to Dr. Church as soon as she's finished with her patient."

Handing the envelope to Kathy, I returned to Kim, who was sitting in the same chair as last time. I sat, again with Kim between me and the entry door. "Now we wait for Dr. Church. She's with a patient. Soon as she's finished, she'll read Dr. Goodman's report, look at the scans, then see me. Shouldn't be more than fifteen or so minutes." Kim nodded. We waited.

Twenty minutes later, LeAnne came and got me, and we headed to an exam room. This time I didn't need to take off my tee shirt. So I sat and waited but only for less than a minute.

Dr. Church rapped on the door once, opened it, and walked in, MRI scan envelope in hand. She walked to the light boxes, where you viewed x-rays, and popped four scan images into the clips that held the scans for viewing. With Dr. Goodman's report in hand, she gestured over to the light boxes.

Pointing to the second scan, Dr Church said, "See this area, JC? It's swollen with some inflammation, but you can clearly see you've had muscle destruction. Here, and again in this area," pointing to two areas of the scan. "Dr. Swensen did a very good job stitching you up. I'm not seeing anything beyond what I'd expect from a wound track like yours. You're on a heavy dose of medication to fight any infection, so I don't expect any surprises. You have three choices, JC. We can get you to an orthopedic surgeon right now for a consult. Liz Cantor is the best for your damage. She specializes in this type of muscle loss and its repair. She's my favorite arm specialist.

"Option two is to give your wound time to fully heal, then see what kind of loss of function you have. I know you'll have some. The bullet that hit your arm destroyed over twenty percent of the muscle along your arm. That's significant muscle loss. Once you're healed, we can put you through some tests to determine loss of strength, range of motion, and your hand and finger functionality. Based on the results of those tests, we can discuss best options and still get a consult from Dr. Cantor. Your third option, which I do not recommend, is to let your injury heal and be done with it. Just live with whatever the result."

"If this was your arm, Dr. Church, what would you do?"

"JC, I'd take a conservative approach. I'd let my arm heal for the next couple months, then assess the results. I'd start some gentle physical therapy in a couple weeks. I know Kellie Kress. She owns and runs Tacoma Physical Therapy. I've sent patients to her for over ten years, and patient feedback has always been positive. There is no magic bullet here, JC. Bad pun, I know. But there is nothing short of surgical intervention that is going to return your arm, hand, and fingers to full function. There's just too much damage. That said, I'd like to see how much function you regain before we go digging around, grafting tendon and muscle.

"I've always been clear with my patients, JC. You've significant damage to your arm, but it can be fixed. With a good surgeon, you'll likely regain better than 90 percent of your original function, perhaps full capabilities. If you opt to just let it heal, you'll probably lose at least 30 percent function in your hand and fingers. I'd not be surprised at a 50 percent loss of function. And the strength in your left forearm will always be similarly compromised.

"However, surgery is going to hurt for a time, much like what you're experiencing now. Your arm can take up to a year with physical therapy before you're fully healed and as functional as it will get. What you have, whatever your choice, is not a quick and painless fix. Your choice really boils down to an inconvenient year of lessening discomfort attended with regular physical therapy. The end result is most likely a return to near normal function. Or do nothing and you'll be pain free in a few weeks but have lifelong weakness and reduced function."

"That makes my choice pretty easy, doesn't it? Not fun and not convenient but a pretty easy choice nonetheless."

"I think you've made the right decision. Now let's talk about your pain medication. How are you tolerating what Dr. Swensen gave you?"

"Well, I'm remembering to put some food on my stomach before I take one of the tablets. I've taken one so far and have three left. Next one is about 4:00 p.m. today."

"I'm going to take you off those, JC. They are, as you've already noticed, very strong. I'm writing you a prescription for hydrocodone, 5 mg with 500 mg of acetaminophen. Begin this tomorrow morning.

"I'm writing your prescription for thirty tablets. The instructions will say to take one every eight hours. If after about an hour of taking one your pain has not subsided to a tolerable level, take a second one. You might need to do that for a day or two, but I expect in a week you'll not need any at all. I want you to take only the minimum necessary and stop taking them as quickly as possible. Don't take one just because your arm is uncomfortable. These are for pain. Tylenol and ibuprofen are for discomfort.

"Let your body tell you when to reduce the frequency of this medication. If you take one in the morning and you're fine until evening, then don't take one until a half hour before bedtime. But if your arm starts to really hurt after four hours, take another one. These can become physically and emotionally addictive but not quickly, especially if you follow my instructions, which I know you will do, right?"

"Yup. You're my doc, Doc. I've always followed your advice. Even had my first date, thanks to your gentle nudging."

"That's great! Do I know the lucky girl?"

"I think you've heard me mention her, Lucienne, or Lu, Abreo. We went to the Mariners ball game last Friday night. Had a great time!"

"Does she know about last night's adventure?"

"No. I've not contacted her since our date. Need to take care of that yet today. Not the adventure but letting her know I enjoyed our first date and ask for another."

"You're a wise man, JC Merrick. It is so very interesting watching you mature. I don't want you driving until you're only taking hydrocodone at bedtime. Until then, have Kim or somebody else drive you. The prescription I've written you are opioids, JC. They will affect your judgement, though not as remarkably as the tablets given you by Dr. Swensen. And these aren't so upsetting to your system. Take your second one this evening. Do you have them with you?"

"I do."

"Why don't you give two of them to me? I will dispose of them for you. We don't want them in the water supply, so no flushing down the toilet. We'll dispose of them properly. This way, you won't need to worry about remembering to dispose of them."

I dug the small envelope out of one of my jeans pockets and handed two to Dr. Church.

"Thank you, JC. Just remember to take your last one when you get home. Then start your hydrocodone tomorrow morning. Remember to take them with food as well, and no driving until you're down to one hydrocodone at bedtime. No signing legal documents while you're taking these caplets in any dosage without Angus present. Okay?

"If you notice an increase in tenderness or soreness or if your wound gets inflamed or starts to discharge blood or pus, get over here. Don't make an appointment, just get here. I'll work you in." Saying that, Dr. Church had LeAnne rewrap my arm to protect the gauze pads now covering my stitches.

"Change this dressing every day, JC. No showers for five days. Don't get your stitches wet, but do apply this antibiotic ointment with every daily bandage change until Monday, the twenty-second. Rub it in, but be gentle. Your arm is going to be tender for a while. After five days, you can shower and get your arm wet. Wash it daily, thoroughly, but no scrubbing. Put on a thin layer of petroleum jelly after every shower. Keep those stitches moist as much as you can. We'll get you back in here on Friday, the twenty-sixth, so LeAnne can remove your stitches. The more moist you keep your stitches, the less pulling when she removes them. Okay? And the petroleum jelly will help keep the scarring supple."

"Sounds good to me," I replied as LeAnne put an antibiotic cream along my stitches and began applying a dressing and wrapping my forearm with a new Ace bandage.

"JC," said Dr. Church, "I've spoken with Angus. He and I have known each other since before you were in diapers. As your friend, he told me what happened. There is more going on here than just the trauma and damage to your left arm. How are you doing emotionally? Taking a human life is traumatic for anybody, especially someone your age. Add to it the loss of your parents and drowning and I can only imagine what's going on inside you right now."

"Well, Doc, I'm a little numb. Emotionally. In my head, I know I did what I had to do or die. There was no time to think or ponder the consequences. I knew in an instant that if I didn't do something, I'd be dead. I knew I couldn't run. They'd just shoot me in the back or run me down. I had no idea how many were involved, if more were waiting outside or not. Talking about it with you now, it's really odd. I knew in that moment I had to fight back. Had to fight for my life and Kip's. My head was clear. I don't remember being nervous at all. I've never been in a situation like that. I don't even play computer games, where I'm a good or bad guy and shoot other people or aliens, whatever. Never had an interest in that stuff.

"I remember knowing that adrenaline was dumping through my system, but I wasn't nervous. I remember thinking they could probably hear my heart beating all the way to Canada. I remember asking God for His help. In the moment, it was like time just slowed down, like everything was happening in slow motion, and then it was over. I got light-headed. My stomach felt like I was gonna throw up, and I started to shake. I blamed it on the adrenaline working through my system, not from shock. But maybe, I don't know.

"I don't feel any particular remorse. I know I took two human lives. I know I'll live with that forever to some degree. I also know, in those moments, my choices were to defend myself or die. Easy decision. And I know the only thing I could have done to change the outcome would have been to die. I've already done that once. Figured once was enough until God decides to take me home. Does that make any sense at all?"

"It does. You are a singularly remarkable young man, JC Merrick. I've watched you since you came into this world, more so since the passing of your parents. Frankly, you surprise me in a very good way. You are mature beyond your years. Don't get all full of yourself. But then again, that's never been you, has it? You've certainly had several opportunities to exploit your wealth, make stupid and destructive decisions, or act out badly from anger or frustration. Or become a conceited, arrogant young man. Yet you haven't. You've grieved the loss of your parents in a healthy way and worked through their tragic loss. You didn't get stuck in your grief, as some do. You didn't turn to drugs or alcohol. You've kept your head, sought good counsel, and listened.

"I like nearly all my patients, JC. Doctors aren't supposed to have favorites when it comes to patients. We're supposed to maintain a professional view and emotional distance. Caring too deeply could influence how we might treat a patient's particular disease or injury. Emotions can interfere with good judgement.

"I've also learned, if we're to care, truly care, for those we treat and help, we need a certain level of involvement. It can help us work harder to heal that person. Without getting all maudlin, I'm saying that as well as your physician, JC, I'm your friend. I'm enjoying watching you grow even in this clinical setting. If you ever find yourself needing an ear to bend, call me." Saying this, she picked up one of her business cards and wrote on it.

"Keep this handy. My personal phone number is on the back. Don't be afraid or hesitant to call at any time. I'll have LeAnne come in and set up your next appointment for two months from now. She'll give you the contact information for Kellie Kress. I'll write you a prescription for physical therapy, and LeAnne will have that as well as your prescription for hydrocodone. Give us just a few minutes."

Saying that, Dr. Church was out the door and down the hall. Just a couple minutes later, LeAnne came in with several pieces of paper. "Here you go, Mr. Merrick. Here's a scrip for PT with Kellie Kress and for your hydrocodone. And instructions and timeline for taking your med. I've set your next scheduled appointment for two months out. How does Tuesday, October 18, 9:00 a.m. work for you?"

"Should be fine, LeAnne. I've not planned my life that far in advance yet. Probably a good time to start, especially with something like this."

"Okay. I'll send you a reminder in the mail about a week in advance. I've also set you up for a week from this Friday to get your stitches out. It'll take only a few minutes. There's no particular time of day. Just come in and let reception know. We'll work you in, and you'll have this behind you. Until then, take care of yourself. Okay?" Saying that, LeAnne opened the exam room door and left.

CHAPTER 13

I followed LeAnne out the door and back to the reception area, walked up to Kim, and told her we needed to come back a week from Friday and that we could leave. Kim stood, and we walked to and through the front door, Kim still taking the street side of the sidewalk. "Is there anything we need to pick up before we head back?" Kim asked as we approached her Corvette.

"Yup. I've a prescription to fill and need to stock up on gauze bandages. Dr. Church gave me an antibacterial ointment to use for the next five days. No showering until next Monday. Baths only. Yuck. That's like stewing in my own juice. I hate baths!"

"Look at it this way, JC. Would you rather take a daily bath or not shower or bathe at all until next Monday?"

"Gross! Maybe baths aren't so bad after all."

"There you go. That's a more positive attitude, yes?"

"Sure. Point taken." Settling in and buckling up, I was ready for our ride to my regular drugstore, Walgreens, nearby.

A very few minutes later, we'd arrived at Walgreens, and I got my prescription and all the necessary supplies. Back in Kim's Corvette, we pulled into traffic and headed toward home.

We'd only gone a couple blocks when I noticed Kim paying very close attention to her rearview mirrors. She was spending more time looking at them than she was to immediate traffic. "JC, don't turn around. I think we've picked up a tail. It's a white Chevy sedan, keeps about five to seven cars behind us. I'm going to see if they're really on our tail or if this is simply a coincidence. I'm not a believer in coincidence, so hang on, okay?"

Hanging on with my left hand was a joke, so I grabbed hold of the door armrest with my right hand and tightened my grip just in case. Kim drove casually but made four useless turns just to see what would happen. I could tell from the expression on her face we still had company. "Hang on," was the only warning I got.

Kim hit the gas, and we skidded around the next corner, a hard right. The Vette surged to the next intersection, and Kim took the next left, accelerating through it. I glanced in my side mirror and didn't see any sort of white car behind us. At the next six intersections, we turned in random directions. Seems we lost our tail. Why would anybody want to follow me or Kim?

"Well, that was interesting. We lost them way too easily. Even more strange, the car following us had no front license plate, which is required by Washington state law. I was able to see two people in the front seats. Wasn't able to see in the back, whether or not anybody was there."

We were about a mile from the bridge connecting Tacoma with Gig Harbor, the Tacoma Narrows Bridge. I noticed Kim was watching her mirrors again just as intently. "JC, we may have another tail. This one looks like a Chevy Suburban or something similar. Black. Same lane, about six cars back. Can you see it in your mirror?"

I looked through my side mirror without turning my head around. "I can see a larger Suburban or similar, uhhh, yup. Six cars back. Are you sure they're following us?"

"It looks like it. Sorry, but hang on again," she said as she hammered the Vette around the first right turn, hit the gas hard, and swung us left at the next intersection. Now we're at some crazy speed for in-town driving. Looked and felt like fifty or sixty miles an hour, and we were still accelerating, hard. A couple more quick turns and we were back on the street we'd just left, just eight blocks further from the bridge. Kim took another right and pulled to the side in front of a large high-cube delivery truck. She parked and kept the motor running. I gave her a questioning look.

"I'm tired of being the mouse. I much prefer the role of cat." Now she was really on her mirrors, waiting for a dark Suburban to drive by. It seemed only seconds later, and Kim pounced. A dark Suburban drove right by us, headed in the direction we were pointed. They couldn't see us because of the delivery truck was unknowingly hiding us. As the Suburban drove by, Kim pulled out and was right on their tail.

"Keep hanging on, this could be fun!"

The Suburban driver noticed us right away. They'd done some sort of modifications to the Suburban. The rear tires started smoking as it accelerated away or attempted to.

"See what I mean by fun? There aren't many cars able to keep up with mine, and a Suburban sure as hell ain't one of 'em."

Say what you will about women drivers, I gained a whole new respect for the fairer sex behind the wheel. The Suburban was no match for Kim's Corvette. They gave it a pretty good try but lost. Spectacularly. That was until the passenger lowered his window and started shooting at us.

Corvettes have astonishingly good brakes. Did you know that? At least Kim's did. She slowed us from around eighty or ninety miles an hour or better to take the next available left without losing control or much tire rubber. Maybe she'd give me some driving lessons?

"Okay. This is now officially pissing me off! We need to get you home, JC. I need to let Jack and Paul know, and we need to figure out what's going on."

Moments later, we were going across the Tacoma Narrows Bridge, headed to Gig Harbor area and home. We didn't see anybody following.

We were back home minutes later and parked at what used to be my front door, hopefully would be again soon. For now, a piece of thick plywood was fastened across the doorway with a handle attached. Attractive? It was not. Functional? I suppose.

As Kim and I walked inside, I noticed the "door" was an inch-thick plywood attached to the inside frame with four heavy-looking hinges. There were two sets of thick L brackets fastened to both sides of doorframe, sturdy looking and beefy enough for each set to hold two-inch-by-four-inch lumber laid on the four-inch side. I noticed the back door to the deck had the same set up. Each L bracket on both doors was fastened by three heavy lag screws. I assumed each lag screw was tight and deep into the inner frame of each door. Nobody was kicking in these doors any time soon.

We met Paul in the main living area. He was hunched over a laptop computer doing who knew what. He looked up at our entry. "Hey, guys. How'd your appointment go, JC?"

"Oh, the docs were fine. Saw my doc, had an MRI scan of my arm. I change medications as of tomorrow morning. Baths only for the next five days. No driving for about that long or until I'm taking only one hydrocodone at bedtime. That's about it other than the drive back here."

Chapter 14

"Oh? What was so interesting about the drive back?" Paul asked, eyeing Kim.

"We picked up two different tails, Paul. First one was easy to ditch. White Chevy sedan, maybe a '92. No front plate. Second one was a full-sized Suburban, probably an '89. Heavily modified engine, again no front plate. We went from mouse to cat in about a minute. They didn't like it and started shooting at us. I boogied, and here we are."

"What the hell?" Paul had pulled a very puzzled face.

"I've no idea," said Kim. "The drive to the clinic was normal, no issues. Nothing while we were there. We even walked from the docs to JC's scan. No more than 150 feet, door to door, but still. Nothing odd. Those two cars were not in the lot while we were there. The white Chevy showed up just after we pulled out of the Walgreens parking lot after getting JC's prescription, bandages, and dressings. That's when we picked up our first tail. Or at least the first one I saw. Maybe the Suburban was further behind the sedan."

"Okay. I think it's time to get Jack updated and involved. It's 4:00 p.m. I'll call him and see if he's available for a supper meeting. JC, you okay with that?" Paul asked.

"Sure. But we need to go to a grocery store. I'd intended doing that, well, today. But I've been a bit preoccupied."

"No worries. We'll go to a restaurant. I'll have Jack bring our team rig. Room for everybody and sufficient protection." Paul stepped away and began punching buttons on his cell. I'd just now noticed his cell phone. It looked different from mine and those I'd seen around. A little thicker, maybe a bit longer, and not a flip. Looked anything but normal or fragile. Maybe a military version? I didn't know, but I did notice.

I could only hear Paul's side of the conversation. "That's right. Tailed twice and shot at. No, no injuries, and Kim swears nobody followed her across the Narrows Bridge. "Yeah. We're both here now with JC. Thinking you could bring larger wheels, and we'd go get something. Work things out over supper." Paul listened some more. "Sure. Sounds good. See you then." With that, Paul disconnected and walked back.

"Okay. Jack's on board. He'll be here about 6:00 p.m., maybe a bit later. Everybody likes Chinese, yes?"

Kim nodded in approval.

"Sure, I love Chinese food. But then I'm hungry in two hours," I said.

Kim and Paul roared with laughter. "How right you are," they both said in unison.

"However," Paul continued, "we're going to Jack's favorite Chinese restaurant in Seattle's International District. They have some seriously great food. Guarantee you'll leave pleasantly stuffed and happy."

"Looks like we've about two hours until Jack gets here. JC, do you want to relax, maybe catch a short nap to rest until he's here?"

"I've never been a nap kinda guy. But right now, it sounds perfect. First, I'm going to call Lu and see if we can get together this weekend. Then I'm going to coax Kip to join me on the sofa."

I picked up my phone and called Lu. She answered on the third ring. "Hey, JC! Thought I'd have heard from you before now. You okay?"

"Uh, I'm fine. Had an interesting couple days. I called, wondering if you had some free time this weekend."

"Sure. I always have time for you, JC. What's up?"

"Well, there's a story to tell, and I'd rather tell you in person. I know your folks might not be so keen on you spending time alone with me in my home, and I don't want to pretend anything. So what do you think?"

"Now my curiosity is up. I'll ask my folks about Saturday afternoon and tell 'em I'll be home before dark. Will that work for you?"

"Works for me just fine. I'm going out with new friends for a while. Wanna call me back tomorrow, whenever works for you? And let your folks know we'll have two adults here with us. Your folks are welcome to call at any time to chat with my company or even stop by if they'd rather. You'll meet and also be with Jack, Paul, and Kim, any two of the three."

"Wow! You sure know how to build suspense! Sure. I'll call around lunchtime tomorrow, okay?"

"Perfect." And we both disconnected.

At the front door, I called, "Kip! Wanna cuddle?" I'd raised my voice so my dog could hear me, wherever he happened to be. It wasn't a minute later that Kip came bounding through our front door. He looked at me, then jumped on the sofa. I joined him. We both got comfortable, and I was out like a candle in a hurricane.

It seemed like only minutes later that Paul was nudging my shoulder to wake me up. Kip's eyes were open, looking at our temporary front entrance. Jack had arrived.

"Everybody ready for some great food? JC, you're looking a bit better. Coloring's improved. How you feeling?"

"Think I'm still feeling medication effects. I'll take my last one during supper."

"Okay. Let's saddle up. It's a longer drive than I'd like but more than worth the time. I've called ahead so we're sure to have a table when we get there," Jack said.

"Nobody else seems to be saying, so I'm asking. Where are we going for supper?" I asked.

"You are in for a treat, JC. We're eating at *Tai Tung*, the oldest Chinese restaurant in Seattle. It opened in 1935, now on South King Street. It was Bruce Lee's favorite Seattle restaurant back in the day."

We all walked toward the front door. I let Kip outside again. "Kip, you get to stay here. Watch our home, okay? Bark if you hear a stranger, but run and hide if it feels unsafe. I know you understand me. We'll be back after dark, so go snuggle or hunt in the forest, okay?

"Seems to me like he'll be safer where he can run away if needed. I don't want him feeling trapped in the house if we have visitors again tonight."

Saying that, we all went outside, and I got my first glimpse of a huge vehicle. It was a Hummer H1, first generation. Large and in charge. I was impressed.

CHAPTER 15

"This is not your standard H1, JC. It's been heavily modified throughout. The seats are more comfortable. The glass is bullet resistant (no glass out there is bulletproof). The glass will withstand at least three rounds of .50 caliber to the same spot. After that, all bets are off. All body panels are hardened to withstand similar caliber ammunition strikes, including the engine compartment. This Hummer can be driven with all four tires shot out. The engine is a 6.5 L turbo diesel and has been heavily modified for more speed, greater torque, and improved stability at higher speeds. It won't keep up with Kim's Corvette but not much can. Even with all the wind resistance and huge run-flat tires, this beast can top 125 miles an hour.

"It has twin modified and armored fuel cells, each holding fifty gallons of diesel. Each tank has its own on/off toggle switch mounted on the dash. In the unlikely event one tank gets punctured, we can switch to the second tank. Because this thing runs on diesel, there is less chance of any sort of explosion. All that said, this Hummer gets horrible mileage, around 5 mpg. It's other saving grace, however, is that we can drive it under hostile conditions in any weather—well, maybe not into the eye of a tornado—and it goes uphill like a goat." I could tell Jack really loved his Hummer H1!

"Alright. Let's get in and get going!" Jack, of course, was in the driver's seat and buckling up as the rest of us were climbing in.

"Oh," Paul said. "While everybody was away, I took the liberty to set up some motion-sensor infrared cameras. If anybody comes prowling around your house tonight, JC, these cameras will likely capture their infrared image and time/date stamp each frame. That way, we'll know if any creepers come to call."

"Cool! I'm feeling a bit more safe and secure by the minute. Now if we could just figure out what's causing all this because quite frankly, I do not have one clue."

The drive to Seattle was without incident. We were all lost in our own thoughts most of the time. Just a nice ride to Seattle and the big city lights.

Jack easily found the *Tai Tung*. Because this was a weeknight and after 7:00 p.m., we were able to find a parking spot on the same block, and near the restaurant.

We all climbed out of the Hummer and made our way to the *Tai Tung*. It was obvious upon opening the door, this restaurant had a ton of history and stories to tell. We were greeted and seated at a round table capable of easily holding eight adults. I was certain we'd use all the available room quite effectively.

After everybody had ordered and our beverages were delivered, Jack started our supper meeting. "Thanks for being flexible and agreeing to meet here. This is my favorite Chinese restaurant outside China itself. First, JC, we've designed your security system. The three of us will go over it with you tomorrow, Wednesday morning. See if you have any suggestions or see something we've missed or overstressed.

"It'll take us about two and a half days to get your system installed and operating. I think we've struck the right balance between robust security combined with proper defense, protection, and reliability. As I said to you in the very beginning, JC, any security system can be defeated. The trick is to make your system robust enough to deter an intruder to the point they either move on to an easier target or give you and our monitoring staff enough warning to have the police on scene. That's our goal. We plan to begin installation as soon as you've had time to review and discuss our design and are satisfied with it. Then we'll move forward with the installation."

"Jack, I don't think any of you have met Mat, Mateo Betancourt. He's a kid, like me, but he's a serious computer geek and has some mad skills. I think he'd love to see your design of my system. What do you think about having him along for the review? I'm not nearly as tech savvy as y'all or Mat. Maybe another set of eyes would help? Mostly, I know he'd love to see the stuff you use."

"JC, if you want him there, we can arrange it. He's still in school, right?"

"Yes. However, he can miss one afternoon. His heavy load is in the mornings, so any time after noon will probably work for him. Does that help?"

"It does. Why don't you give him a quick call and see if he's available tomorrow, say, 1:00 p.m.?"

Hearing that, I got on my cell phone and called Mat. Once he heard what was going on, he couldn't wait for tomorrow. I knew he'd be excited to be part of this process. He had questions, but I put them off until tomorrow. I'd forgotten none of my friends even knew I'd been invaded or shot! How time flies when you're living life. Jack heard my end of the conversation, so he knew Mat would be joining us right after lunch tomorrow.

Jack then continued, "Next, I've done some digging since you were invaded, JC. Tried to find out the who and why of things. Unfortunately, I've not learned much, but that in itself is a bit telling. First, your two home invaders don't exist, at least not in any of the files and records we normally check. I've had our back-of-the-house folks check your invaders' fingerprints against every available database. That includes the NCIC, FBI, CIA, and Interpol. Those two guys have no trail. That in itself is telling.

"While it's possible they have no prior arrests, it doesn't feel right. There was a reason you had a creeper who left only two footprints and two broken stems on one bush. I'm convinced that was deliberate on somebody's part. It's the why that leaves me unsatisfied. Obviously, your home invasion was deliberate. Same folks involved? Who knows? But it's too far a reach to say both events were random and unconnected. Something is going on. Know I've asked you this earlier, JC. Can you think of any person or reason for your recent events?"

"I've not had a lot of time to devote to your question, Jack. However, I have thought about it. Doesn't make any sense to me. I may not be a typical teenager by a couple measures, but I'm not that unique either. My wealth could certainly be a magnet for trouble, and I've thought about that. But the bulk of my wealth isn't liquid, and I'm not in control of it.

"Could somebody kidnap me for a ransom? I can see the possibility. What they don't know, like I just said, I'm not in control of my inheritance. And the two guys I shot didn't seem interested in capturing me. Front door guy tried to shoot me in the face while he was still outside. It looked like backdoor guy had a pistol in his hands as he was opening the back door. The investigation didn't turn up any bag to throw over my head, nothing to restrain my hands or feet. So if kidnapping was their idea, they were completely unprepared and ill-equipped to pull it off.

"Remembering back and in those few seconds, I knew they were trying to kill me. My reaction to the assault wasn't a fight-or-flight response, and it wasn't reflex. Either of those two things should have had me running for my life. Running through the back door straight into backdoor guy, whatever. I don't think I responded in a typical way. Nobody's said anything or suggested anything, including you three, Angus, or the sheriff's deputies. But I believe my response was anything but typical. I know, looking back on it, I wasn't surprised by my response. However, in hindsight, I know only a trained and aware person would have logically done what I did. I know this doesn't make any sense at all, but I really knew exactly what to do in those moments even though I've had zero training in any situation like what I went through. To me, that's as odd as the assault itself. Maybe more so."

As I said all this, I could see all the others at the table were paying particular attention. "You're right, JC," said Jack. "That's been one of my concerns. You handled the situation like somebody who had specific training in self-defense, particularly small-arms weapon systems. Your particular shotgun is not made for self-defense. It's for bird hunting. While you did manage to put down two bad actors, you did it with a fair degree of professionalism without benefit of that sort of training. Your shotgun is not a tactical weapon, nor is it a practical weapon for self-defense. However, you used it as one and effectively.

"You didn't waste any shots. And you didn't miss any. You didn't panic. I would expect anything except your level of performance. Understand me, JC. I don't think I'm being unduly critical, certainly not in a negative manner. Frankly, I'm surprised. Pleasantly, mind you, but surprised nonetheless."

Paul was next. "What surprised me most was your level of composure after you were shot. Most people in your position, even had they not been shot, would have been a nervous wreck after having survived a home invasion. You weren't. Granted, your wound was not life-threatening, but my point stands. While you were more intense than if you'd just won a friendly game of checkers, you were in control. I can tell you from more than a few years' experience, there are uncounted thousands of professional soldiers who would not have been as composed as you in the same situation. I've seen it. What I'm telling you is not a compliment or a criticism. What it is is odd. Damn odd."

Kim finished. "JC, we don't know each other. We met the night you were shot when Angus brought you home from the hospital. We spent some time together when you saw your doc, and we were being chased and chasing. And being shot at. That brief history doesn't give me deep, inner insights, but it does give me a sense of you, the person. I know your background. I know what you've gone through with the loss of your parents and everything that followed. Like Paul, I've seen enough action to last normal people a lifetime or two. Yes, even at my young and tender age. Paul, just shut it," she said with a grin.

"I don't know what makes you tick, how somebody your age can be so calm and cool under pressure. Your behavior might be what they'd write for the hero's part in some movie, but this is real life. People your age, with your lack of experience and training, people who lost what you've lost, experienced what you experienced, they wouldn't act like you're acting.

"I'm not saying you are or were acting per se. I know this is your normal. What I'm saying is, in the breadth of the 'normal' scale, you are coloring way outside the lines. My concern is, what are we missing? I don't believe you're hiding anything, certainly not deliberately. But something, I think a few somethings, are going on that we don't know yet, much less understand. Those unknown things could get you killed. They sure as hell hamper us from doing our jobs as effectively as we want. They somewhat limit our ability to act in your best interest. What I'm saying is, you are a nondeliberate mystery that we need to solve. Sooner is better than later. For you and for us, solving the mystery of JC Merrick is a priority, as important as keeping you safe. I think when we solve the mystery of you, we'll solve the mystery of why you were attacked."

Jack's turn again. "Understand us, JC. We're not being cruelly critical. We're not piling on. You've hired us to protect you and design, set up, and monitor a whole-property security system for you. We've accepted. Then at the very beginning of our working relationship, you are attacked, very seriously I might add. We're not backing away. We're certainly willing to continue. I'm assuming you want us to continue as well?"

"Of course," was my immediate reply. "If I had any idea at all what was going on, I'd have told you and Angus already. And while I appreciate what I think were a few compliments given me in your feedback, critique, whatever, I'm just as clueless as the three of you. I can assure you, on the inside I've been much more nervous than you seem to have seen. Certainly feels that way to me. While it's true I didn't faint, pass out, puke, or pee myself, I was nervous. Wait. That's not exactly accurate.

"While I was being attacked, I wasn't nervous. Looking back, I felt calm and in control. I'm reasonably self-aware and know I had no right to be as calm or collected as I was in those moments. However, a part of me was just an observer, like part of me had stepped out of myself and was watching. I know that sounds nuts. But that's the best I can describe what was going on.

"Same thing when Kim and I were being followed, chased, and shot at. In those moments, I wasn't nervous. I knew I was safe. Kim, a lot of that was due to you and how you handled the situation as it developed. But there was more to it inside me. I knew everything was okay. In those moments with Kim, it was the same as when I was being shot at. I knew everything was going to be okay.

"You could think I was being blindingly naïve in those moments. I'd disagree. I am young and don't have the benefit of decades of experience and life to use as a reference. At the same time, I've not lived a sheltered or pampered life. Yes, my folks had money. But it's not like we had servants or minders. We didn't live in a castle, protected by high walls and a moat filled with hungry alligators. My folks taught me to be responsible, to view and live life by acceptable standards of conduct.

"I was taught to be independent, to not rely on others. I was taught strong moral values. I was taught, and firmly believe, that God is the highest power in the universe. From a very early age, I was taught the difference between right and wrong in countless ways. I was taught and learned the whys of right and wrong. My values, morals, and faith were instilled from practical and impractical applications.

"My folks constantly engaged me in no-win scenarios, made me defend whatever impossible position I selected, made me defend the why of my choice. Scenarios like both my parents are in mortal and immediate danger. If I don't act, they will both die, but I only have time and resources to save one. Which one do I save and why?

"That kind of impossible choice. There are no good answers. Each one is worse than the other. But in life, we have to make choices. Our choices define us. Big and little choices. Daily choices and life-altering choices. If my life is defined by my choices, and it is, I'd better be very certain of the choices I make. Even when I have only the smallest part of a split second to make a choice. I have to live with whatever consequences result from my choice every time. That was part of the environment in which I've lived.

"Now looking back, I can see my parents were constantly preparing me for my life. They parented an adult, not a child. So no,

I wasn't sheltered. But I was loved. Immensely. They showed their love for me every day in countless ways. I know there is a world of people less fortunate than me. I know I had and have advantages that countless others do not. There are responsibilities that come with my advantages. Responsibilities I am obligated to take on. On the one hand, I'm a kid, no better or worse than any other, just a kid. On the other hand, much has been given me, both material and non-material. I am obligated, and I have decided after very much thought and introspection to dedicate my life to honoring my obligations, accepting my responsibilities, and doing what I am able to be of service to others.

"I don't know what that fully means yet. I suspect I'll travel many roads during my life. I don't think my life will be defined by one thing. I'm no Einstein or Edison. Think my life will be more involved in one-on-one and small group events and acts. I'm not a seeker of the grandiose. I've no need for the spotlight, preferring others stand in that light while I do my work in the background. Not secretive, just not a glory hound.

"How does all that help us in the here and now? I have no clue. Probably doesn't. It might help you with perspective. Maybe. But none of it addresses the why of being attacked and Kim and I being shot at. In those things I'm likely more clueless than the three of you."

Jack looked at me with an intense gaze. "There has to be more going on here. The two footprints at the edge of your lawn, the two intruders, Kim getting tailed then shot at, none of that makes sense in a random-event scenario. There is something somewhere, and we're missing it. Has anything odd or unusual happened at all? Anything in the last year or more recently?"

"Of course! My parents died! I died! I became an emancipated minor. I inherited millions of dollars! All of that is unusual, don't cha think? I mean, there doesn't seem to be a particular start to this mess. Altogether, it's more than one person would expect to experience in a very long lifetime. I'm seventeen! I haven't really started to live, ya know? None of this makes any sense to me. It's like a damn gordian knot! No beginning. No end. It just is. If you're getting frustrated, welcome to my world."

"Okay." Jack grinned. "Guess I had that coming. Even this early in our working relationship, it's too easy to forget you're seventeen. I'm already seeing you as a mature adult, JC. I think anybody around you for an hour comes away the same, seeing and relating to you as a mature adult. However we look at you or however you appear or sound to us, you're not a mature adult, at least not fully. Perhaps we all need to keep that in mind. It still remains, we're missing something somewhere. Besides, our food's here. Let's dig in!"

Platters and baskets covered our table. Over the next half hour, I think we all ate more than our share of delicious food. Served family style, we each helped ourselves to each dish and basket until nothing but empty platters and baskets remained.

"Thank you, Jack! That was a feast." I wasn't sure my legs would support the extra weight of all the food I just ate! But I'd probably be hungry right after we got back to my place. Hey, I've an idea." Everybody looked at me expectantly. "Why don't you all come over this coming Saturday? We've a huge outdoor grill. Somebody can figure out how to cook on it. I'll do a grocery run for steaks and chicken. I'll invite Angus, Mat, Kyle, and Lu. It'll give you a chance to meet my close friends and for them to meet you. I need to make an effort to be more social, and this is a perfect way to start the process. Whaddaya think?"

"Sure," Paul said. "I'm in. What can I bring?"

"I dunno. Whaddaya think? Green salad? Fruit? Dessert? Rolls of some sort?"

Kim was bouncing on her chair. "I'll bring *taho*. It's a specialty dessert from the Philippines, made with soft tofu, doused in *arnibal syrup*, and has sago pearls sprinkled on top. It really is one of my favorites."

Paul jumped in, "I'll make a green garden salad. That means it'll have every seasonal salad ingredient in it. If you don't like one of the ingredients, pick it out. You'll not hurt my feelings! And I'll cover the fruit too. There's a bunch in season right now, so I'll bring a variety."

Jack was next. "I'll do beverages, okay? Might even bring beer besides soft drinks. I'm imagining you and your friends have had beer in the past, yes? My group will make sure nobody gets more than they can handle."

"Okay. I'll cover the chicken and steak. There's a small local bakery that makes outstanding dinner rolls. Mom and Dad were practically addicted to 'em. I love 'em too. I'll make sure there's enough for everybody to take some home. They are really a treat! I think all our bases are covered for Saturday."

Jack rose from his chair. "Looks like we've done all the damage we can do here. Let's head out and get back to your place, JC." Saying that, we all trooped out of the restaurant and returned to the H1 for our drive home.

CHAPTER 16

The drive back was uneventful. We were all quiet and pleasantly full of delicious food. It gave me time once again to marvel at God, at how He worked His will throughout the fabric of each of our lives. Beauty surrounded us all if we're deliberately aware. For this brief time, I was calm and at peace. It seemed I'd made some new friends and was the better for it. I was reminded to always be aware and grateful even of the little things in life, like a good meal shared among friends.

We arrived back at the house right at 9:00 p.m. Everything looked peaceful and undisturbed. Kip heard us drive up and ran from the forest to the driveway, wagging his tail so hard his whole butt wiggled.

Jack and Paul walked the entire house perimeter. We didn't expect any trouble, but I noticed both had their pistols out and in the low-ready position.

I raised the double garage doors. All the garage lights came on as the door lifted. Kim had her pistol out, also in low ready. I stayed back a bit and let her do her thing. Kim entered the house from the garage. All was as it was supposed to be, so I lowered the garage door and entered behind Kim and walked into the house from the garage and turned on the main area, kitchen, and exterior lights.

Kim had a clear view of most of the living area from that garage doorway. I moved to the kitchen area and opened the back patio door to let Jack and Paul inside. They all trooped throughout the house and verified there were no nasty surprises.

When they were finished, we all met back in the front living area. Paul and Kim would be staying. Paul had first watch until 2:00 a.m. Then Kim would take over until Kip and I were up usually by 7:00 a.m. or so. Then we'd all rattle or whatever until Jack and Mat arrived around 1:00 p.m.

The night passed uneventfully. No banging on windows or doors. No gunshots. Kip didn't alert, and everybody got some sleep. When Kip and I got up, Kim had already retreated for a nap. Paul had coffee going in the kitchen.

"Are you a coffee drinker, JC? I swear, my entire life would grind to a halt without coffee. Somebody ought to put this stuff in a can and sell it by the six-pack or twelve-pack. Hot, cold, or room temperature. Who cares! It's coffee!"

"Well, I'm not as passionate about coffee as you obviously. But I do enjoy it. Gets me going, same as Coke and Pepsi. Caffeine, in any of its forms. Some form of caffeine was necessary for most upperclassmen at Kings. Someday somebody will concoct an energy beverage so we can guzzle 'em during the day, something with more than just caffeine in it. Vitamins, minerals, different flavors. Somebody'll come up with that stuff. Until then, coffee, Coke, Mountain Dew, and Pepsi rule.

"Paul, I need to call Angus. I've completely forgotten about the interviews we're supposed to schedule. Do you know anything about the background checks your folks are doing on our candidates for hiring?"

"JC, I don't. Let me give Jack a call and see where our folks are on that." Saying that, Paul pulled out his cell phone and called Jack. I could only hear one side of the conversation. It sounded like we had some activity on our candidates. "Okay. Jack says he's bringing information on the candidates with him. You and he can go over that stuff once he's here and we've gone over your security system." Paul was already on his second cup of coffee.

"You bet. I need to call Mat, Kyle, and Lu, invite them for Saturday. I'd also like to include Angus and Dr. Church." Then I got on the phone and started calling.

Chapter 17

Mat was first. "Hey, Mat. I know you're coming over in a few hours later today. I'm inviting everybody over for an afternoon of grilled food and relaxation this Saturday. Can you make it? Say, be here around 1:00 p.m. or so until dark or a bit later?"

"You bet! Sounds like fun. Will your security folks be there too?"

"Yeah. I want you guys to meet them and for them to meet you. Look, I still need to call Kyle, Lu, Angus, and Dr. Church. We can visit when you get here this afternoon. Cool?"

"See you then." And Mat was gone.

My next call was to Lu. She picked up on the first ring. "Hey, Sailor. What's up?"

"Hi, Lu. I know I invited you to come over Saturday. I've kinda changed plans a bit. I want you to meet some folks that'll also be here Saturday. I'm planning a casual dinner-barbeque thing using our outdoor grill. The folks you'll be meeting are bringing some of the food. I'm getting the rest. Somebody with more skill than I have needs to tend the grill for steaks and chicken. We'll gather about 1:00 p.m. and end it around dusk or so. Whaddaya think? Should have asked you before now, I know. This thing just hatched last night. Is it okay with you?"

"Of course! Sounds like fun. Is there anything you need? Anything I can bring?"

"We have all the major food groups covered: salads, rolls, steaks and chicken, beverages, fruit, and dessert. Am I missing anything? I know I need somebody to grill the chicken and steaks. I'll watch and learn, but I don't imagine anybody would appreciate my burnt offerings as a main course."

"It'll be fine. So Saturday, around 1:00 p.m., right?"

"Yup. That works, Lu. See you then!" She disconnected, and I was on my phone to Kyle.

Three rings later... "Hey, Kyle. JC here. Are you free this Saturday afternoon and evening? I'm planning a small gathering and want you to be here if you're available. Lotsa food and some folks I'd like to introduce you to and them to you. Will that work for you?"

"Sure. Sounds great! We haven't connected for a bit. I was going to get in touch, but you know how it is. Life just gets in the way sometimes."

"Hey, man, I understand. This promises to be fun and interesting. There's some stuff I want to bring you and Lu up to speed on, stuff that's been going on."

"What? Are you okay? You didn't die again, did you?" he said with a smile in his voice.

"No, nothing that dramatic. Just some stuff I'm working on and through. Part of it is I only want to have to tell this story once, you know? All is well, so no worries. We're getting together about 1:00 p.m. and going until anybody wants to go back home or until dark, whichever comes first. You'll be here?"

"Absolutely. Anything you'd like me to bring?"

"Not unless you can channel your inner grill master. I need to learn how to use our grill. I'm hoping one of the folks you'll be meeting can take over on the grill and teach me a hundred tricks on how to not burn stuff. See you Saturday!" And that was finished.

I heard Kim walking toward us in the kitchen. "Good morning! Thank you for staying last night, and you too, Paul. Kip and I got a decent night's sleep for a change. We both appreciate you two, and of course, Jack."

"You're welcome. Did I just hear you on the phone planning our get-together?"

"Yup. Everybody's on board. Oops. Not everybody yet. I forgot Angus! Jeez, don't say anything to him! Calling him right now." And I picked up my phone.

Two rings later… "Angus? JC Merrick. Do you have a quick minute?"

"I do, JC."

"Jack, Paul, Kim, and I are planning a Saturday get-together. Starts about 1:00 p.m. and goes until whenever. Lotsa food. Kyle, Mat, and Lu will be here as well. Thought I'd share my recent adventure, or misadventure, with everybody once instead of telling it over and over and give everybody a chance to meet everybody. Can you make it?"

"Most certainly. However, probably not until around 3:00 p.m. or so. Will that work?"

"Of course. No worries at all. There is some stuff I want to share with everybody that nobody knows about. Stuff I've been trying to figure out. Haven't made any progress yet and am thinking this might require more brains than I have to get it settled."

"As usual, JC, you have me intrigued. I'll be there. What can I bring?"

"Hey, if you can figure out our grill and teach me a few things about it, I'll be forever in your debt. Steaks and chicken, salads, fruit, dessert, and those great rolls from *Olsen's Bakery*. Please tell me you are a master griller."

"I think everybody is in good hands, JC. Are you inviting Phyllis?"

"Phyllis?"

"Your Dr. Church."

"She's next on my list, my last call actually."

"Excellent. I'll see you Saturday." And a dial tone was in my ear.

Next call was to my doc. Third ring… "Tacoma Medical, this is Kathy."

"Hi, Kathy. This is JC Merrick. Is Dr. Church available for a quick call? Less than a minute, I promise!"

"Hi, JC. Let me put you on hold and find out." And I was listening to canned music.

"Hi, JC. What can I do for you?" I always liked Dr. Church's voice.

"Dr. Church. Thanks for taking my call. Purely social. I'm having a barbeque this Saturday. Starts at 1:00 p.m. I'd like you and your husband to come if you're able."

"I'd be delighted, JC! What can I bring?"

"Everything's covered. Just bring yourselves. You know where I am?"

"I do. Haven't been to your house in ages, but I do remember the way. See you Saturday!" And we disconnected. Excellent!

Kim and Paul were consuming more caffeine, and I needed to get some food. "Angus is in. And my doctor, Phyllis Church! Everybody'll be here around 1:00 p.m., except Angus. He'll be here around 3:00 p.m. Everybody has their food to bring." Now for breakfast.

I walked to the refrigerator and opened the door. There still wasn't much in food choices. I'd not gotten to the store to restock. I was rummaging around in the fridge when we all heard a very loud bang that shook the walls. "What the…"

"Kim, check the perimeter. I'm going to check all the locks and see if some asshole got in here and how. JC, don't touch anything yet. Stay here."

"No worries. I'll wait right here." Saying that, I moved to reach for my shotgun. I felt better with it in my hands.

CHAPTER 18

I watched as both Paul and Kim drew their pistols; Kim went outside, while Paul was examining every window and the doors from inside. A few minutes later, he was back, headed for the door from the house to our garage.

Paul knelt and used a small flashlight to shine on the door lock. He then opened that door and went to the garage side and examined it. It took only a minute, then he went to the man door at the front of the garage. Same thing, he looked closely at both sides of the lock and keyhole. It wasn't long, and he was at the man door leading to our backyard. Then he opened the door and shouted for Kim.

"Kim! Do you see anything outside? I'm coming out the back garage door. Where are you?" Hearing no reply from Kim, I watched as Paul cautiously moved toward the west side of the house.

It was only a moment later. "JC! Call 911, now! Kim's down!"

What in the world? I picked up my phone and called 911. "Hello, 911? This is JC Merrick. I live at 413 Cove Road. Send the police and an ambulance. One of my guests has been attacked and is hurt."

"What is your name, sir?"

"Are you listening? I told you all that. You have it on tape if you need listen again. Get that ambulance here now, okay? I'm going to hang up. I have others to call."

"But, sir—" And I was gone.

I called Jack. First ring... "Jack, this is JC—"

"I know. Paul called. I'm on the way. Be there in a few." And he was gone.

Angus was next. Second ring... "JC, What can I—"

"Angus, we were attacked again. Kim's injured. No idea how or how bad. I've called an ambulance maybe a minute ago. They should be here soon. Hung up on the 911 operator again. There'll be grief, I'm sure. Paul called Jack. He's on his way. Can you come? Police are on their way."

"I was moving as soon as I heard you say attacked. I'm on my way. Twenty minutes. If Winslow shows up, say nothing. Just tell him I'm on the way." And Angus was gone.

This should be interesting, especially if Detective Archibald Winslow showed up. Thinking this, I went outside to see what happened to Kim, to check on Paul, and to see if I could help. Around the west side of the house, about six feet from the southwest corner, I saw Paul kneeling beside Kim. She was lying on the ground. I could see Paul had removed his jacket, folded it, and placed it under Kim's head. Walking toward them, I didn't see any blood and hadn't heard any shots fired.

"Paul, how is she?"

"She's unconscious, JC. She's already got a goose egg on the side of her head, and it's already discoloring. Her heartbeat is strong and steady. I think someone hit her with something and knocked her out. I want you back in the house."

Paul had his back to the house looking at the trees pistol in hand and aimed in that general direction. As I moved away from him toward the man door at the front of our garage, I could hear sirens. Sounded like they were getting closer. Hmm, more than one.

I went into the garage and raised the primary double garage door as the first one and then a second sheriff's car plus an unmarked sedan and an ambulance came up our driveway. I moved toward the ambulance as Detective Archibald Winslow started climbing out of his unmarked sedan.

"Merrick! Where do you think you're going?"

"I'm going to tell the paramedics where Kim is! What did you think I was going to do, give 'em a plate of cookies?"

"You know, I've had just about enough of your—"

I walked up to the two ambulance paramedics, a man and a woman. I pointed. "Kim is around the west side of the house. She's still down. Big bruise and knot on the side of her head," I was saying this as we three hustled our way to where Kim was lying on the ground.

"Merrick!" I could hear Winslow bellowing all the way from our driveway to where Kim was lying. Okay. Paul would get 'em squared away. Time to get back to Mr. Detective.

Walking back toward the front of our house and the officers and Detective Winslow, I braced myself for his rant or tirade or whatever.

"Merrick. What's this all about? What's going on here?" Winslow demanded.

"We've had another prowler, or it seems like. Huge noise rattled the house. Paul and Kim went to investigate. Kim was attacked in some manner. I called 911. Then I called Kim and Paul's boss, Jack. He's on his way. I called Angus Dunbar. He's on his way. That's all I know. I have nothing more to add until Mr. Dunbar is here."

"Listen to me, you little shit. I ask the questions, you give the answers. Are we clear?"

I figured the best and most legal way to get at this guy was to not respond and get sucked into whatever game or drama he thought he could play with me. So I stood there, looking at him, saying exactly nothing. No smile or sneer, though I was mightily tempted. I deliberately schooled my face to neutral, no expression of any kind.

Winslow glared back at me, like if I was ice, his glare would melt me. Good luck with that. His little fit and my lack of responding went on for a couple minutes maybe. I could see his face getting redder and redder. Guy needed to be on blood pressure meds. Then again, maybe he was already.

I heard tires crunching along our driveway. Pretty sure I knew who had arrived. Broke my eye contact with Winslow to glance at the driveway. Jack was here. I began walking toward him as he hurried out of his truck.

"Jack, the paramedics are with Kim now. This way," I said as we both started a quick hustle toward where Kim lay. "Big bruise and knot on the side of her head. Paul said she has a good pulse." And we were there. I kept back as Jack walked up to Paul, giving the medics room to do their work.

"Have you heard 'em say anything, Paul?" I asked as we stood together.

"Her vitals are strong. They're loading her up to take her to emergency. She's a nasty gash on the side of her head. Jack will go with her. I'm on you until we know what's going on."

"Okay. Angus is on his way. I'm going to go stare at Mr. Winslow some more until Angus shows up. Don't think he likes that much, and it seems I'm happier when he's aggravated." I walked back toward the front of the house and Detective Winslow.

It didn't look like his red face had changed much. He glared at me as I walked up. "Merrick! What the hell's going on here? What's this all about? Why did you hang up on my operator again! What's all the emergency?"

That was when I heard another set of tires on our driveway. This time I knew who was driving up. I turned my head toward the driveway and began walking in that direction.

"Merrick! Don't you walk away from me! I ought to arrest you for obstruction!" And Angus got out of his car.

"He's in rare form, Angus. Threatened to arrest me for obstruction. But he's just standing there with his hands in his pockets, not looking around or asking anything except what's going on. I waited for you before answering his questions."

"Excellent. Now let's see what we can figure out. Where's Kim? What do you know?"

"Kim's on the southwest corner of the house with Paul and Jack. We were all in the kitchen when we heard a huge bang noise from outside. Paul and Kim went to check out all the doors and windows. Kim took outside, Paul inside. Paul finished, called to Kim from the back garage man door. She didn't answer. He went looking and found her out cold where she is now. Paul says she has a huge knot on the side of her head, bruising already. That's all I know right now. Oh, Kim's vitals are strong. Paul overheard the paramedics talking. That's it."

"Okay. Come with me while we check on Kim, Paul, and Jack. Then we'll deal with Detective Winslow." Saying that, we both started walking toward the west side of the house. This time, Winslow and his entourage of four started walking toward us. Just as we came to the corner, the medics came around with Kim loaded on and strapped to the gurney. She still looked unconscious. Jack and Paul were right with her.

"Jack. What can you tell us?"

"They're telling me she got a hell of a whack to the side of her head. They're taking her in to check for a fracture, concussion, and any other trauma. She's still unconscious. I'm going with her. Paul stays here. I'll be in touch when we know more."

Kim was loaded into the back of the ambulance as Jack turned his pickup around and got out of their way. Angus, Paul, and I turned our attention to the police.

Chapter 19

"Detective Archibald Winslow. How delightful to see you again. Why don't the four of us go inside and get some questions answered?" Saying this, Angus began walking toward the open garage door and inside our house, the rest of us following.

Angus, Paul, and Detective Winslow sat in the main area, while I went and closed the refrigerator door, left open since the earlier event. Returning, I sat alone, where I could watch, listen, and participate when necessary.

Naturally, Detective Winslow was first. "What's this all about? What's going on? What happened to the person on the gurney? Why was Jack here? Why is Paul here? Does this have something to do with our earlier investigation? Merrick hasn't yet come in for an interview. That needs to happen, Dunbar, and not at your convenience. Merrick hung up on my operator again. This place is getting to be a headquarters for mayhem and mischief. What's going on? Well?"

"I thought it would be rude to interrupt you, Detective Winslow. You seem to be in particularly fine form this morning. Frankly, you've started repeating yourself." Angus was at his absolute best. "Let's take this in turn, shall we?" Angus was about to hold court. I could tell from the look in his eyes. "JC, why don't you take Detective Winslow through the events of this morning?"

"Sure. Kim, Paul and I were in the kitchen having coffee when we all heard a very loud bang. Sounded like it came from the west side of the house. Paul went to check all the interior doors and windows. They were closed and locked last night when we all retired. Kim went outside at that same time to check the perimeter. Paul finished inside, having not found anything amiss, right, Paul?"

"Yes. All was as it should be. I checked the locks on all windows and doors. Everything checked out."

"When Paul finished checking inside, he walked to the man door in back of the garage, opened it, and called for Kim. She didn't answer. Paul went outside to find her and a few seconds later shouted for me to call 911, that Kim was injured. I called for paramedics and an ambulance. Hung up. Called Jack and learned Paul had already called him. Hung up and called Angus. He said he was on his way. We hung up, and I waited for the paramedics and apparently you. That's everything I know."

"Well, isn't that convenient? How is it you're getting into all this trouble? Why aren't you in school? What are you trying to pull with these stunts?"

"Detective Winslow." I could tell Angus was about at his limit. This could get interesting quickly! "What exactly are you trying to communicate? Please say what's on your mind. You've been upset with young Merrick since his home invasion. What exactly are you suggesting?"

"This, this *kid*, belongs in school. Why isn't he there? What kind of crap is he pulling by shooting and killing two people? What did he do to attract them to himself? Is he luring these people to him as some sort of sport? I don't like this. I don't like it at all. And his blatant disregard for authority is another thing. He has no respect for the police. He's insubordinate. You said the two of you would be in my office this past Tuesday, but you were both a no-show. I've a mind to haul the kid in for obstruction of justice."

"Are you quite finished, Detective Sergeant? First, your attitude, Detective, is appalling. Mr. Merrick is not accountable to you for his private and personal life. Second, I'll remind you, in our earlier conversation, I told you Mr. Merrick owns this home. It is his. Not the bank's, not the mortgage company's, his. Third, Mr. Merrick is an emancipated minor and is accorded all the rights, privileges, and responsibilities that distinction entails. Fourth, Mr. Merrick has graduated secondary education. With honors, I might add.

"I'll also remind you, Mr. Merrick was assaulted. He was the victim of attempted murder. His home was invaded, and he appropriately defended himself. He was shot and will need to undergo reconstructive surgery as a result of that home invasion. I'll remind you as well that Mr. Merrick has broken no laws. Finally, while JC Merrick does not have the advantage of decades of life, he does not suffer fools. You, Detective, are being an ass. You'll gain far more by treating Mr. Merrick as a law-abiding adult and getting rid of your aggressive attitude toward him. Are we clear? Or do I need to use smaller words?"

"I may have to take this from you, Dunbar, but I'll be damned..."

"I see. Very well. JC? You're not to speak with any police official without my being present. I am your attorney of record in all matters. As you are currently under the care of your personal physician and taking potent, prescribed opioid medications, you will not be available for any conversation with the authorities until you no longer need to take those prescribed medications. Do you understand?"

I looked at Angus and deliberately ignoring Detective Winslow. "I do."

"Good. I think you've had quite enough excitement for today. I want you to get something to eat and then do your best to relax. These police officers are leaving now to pursue whatever investigation they deem appropriate outside. Paul will do his investigating, while you rest, and Jack will contact us when he has an update on Kim.

"Detective, you are no longer welcome in this home or on the property. If you require an investigation in this matter, you will confine yourself to the area outside this home. If you find yourself in need of examining any area inside or outside this home and/or garage after today, I require a search warrant. Until I have a search warrant in my possession, you are dismissed." Saying that, Angus turned his back on Winslow and the officers and moved to Paul and me. With his voice lowered, he said, "JC, have you had anything for breakfast yet?"

"No. We were just starting when this mess happened. Both Paul and I have had coffee but not any food yet."

"Right." He turned to the two sheriff's deputies and Detective Winslow. "Gentlemen, you need to leave now. We're going out and must lock up. We'll be back at some point later today. I believe you have my contact information, Detective." And we headed toward the inner garage door after securing the front-door barricades.

Detective Winslow looked like his face would explode. It had grown from an indignant red to an impossible purple. The guy had serious anger management issues and likely needed stronger blood pressure medication. Seriously, he looked like he could stroke out any minute. Regardless, all the sheriff's deputies left for their cars as we walked toward Angus's Continental. Once they cleared the driveway, we made our way to Gig Harbor's best breakfast secret, *Hattie's*.

Chapter 20

Hattie Swensen only serves breakfast, and her menu is limited. But what she serves are works of art. Old-world oatmeal, waffles, true sourdough pancakes (each as big as a dinner plate), and French toast made with Hattie's special thick-sliced sourdough bread. Golden crisp hash browns, ham, site-cured bacon, and breakfast sausage. Eggs any way you like 'em and four-egg omelets. Coffee brewed in heaven, cinnamon rolls from heaven, and that's it. *Hattie's* is not where you eat if you're counting calories. We invaded, and we ordered. Mere minutes later, we were served. Everybody was hungry. It was only a short time later, and our plates were empty, and we were stuffed.

We left *Hattie's* satisfied and in better spirits. I knew we were all waiting for a call from Jack, anxious to learn Kim's condition. While Angus was driving us back home, Paul's cell phone began ringing. "What do you know?" Obviously, Jack on the other end of the call.

The call was quick, and Paul disconnected. He turned to us. "Jack says Kim's in surgery. She has swelling on her brain, and they need to relieve the pressure. Said they told him the surgery was pretty straightforward but not common. They've put her in an induced coma to help reduce brain trauma and swelling, letting her heal. She's in good hands. They're monitoring her closely, and he said the next twenty-four hours are critical."

Paul looked glum. None of us expected this turn of events. "Whoever got to Kim really knew what they were doing. She must have heard or sensed something just before she was attacked. Jack said they told him she'd evidently just started turning her head when she was hit. Absent Kim turning her head, even that little bit, the blow would most likely have been fatal. What in the world's going on here?"

"Paul, I don't know. All of this is outside my experience. None of it makes any sense to me. I just don't see how any of this is tied to me directly. Then again, it must be. They came at me in my home. They shot at me in my home. One guy had an assault rifle for the love of Mike! This all happened to me before we started working together. From that, I'd say this is definitely about me or something to do with me. Not from your past or Kim's or Jack's.

"It's not about Angus either. He's been in my life since I was born. Certainly more so since my folks died. But again, the attack or invasion, whatever, was my home, not Angus's. It wasn't a kidnapping attempt. We've already plowed that ground. Nothing useful in going through it again.

"They went after Kim and me after we left my doc's office. I suppose we could argue Kim being the target. Somebody did shoot at her and me, then successfully attacked her. But I have to go back to the initial assault. You three were unknown that night. Jack had been at my home but not before the planted footprints. That happened first. We could make a case of coincidence, but I just don't buy it. I believe my creeper was a prelude to the subsequent invasion and attempt on my life. Nothing else makes any sense, and even this is stretching my imagination to the limit. Paul, Angus, do either of you have any thoughts or ideas?"

"JC, I'm getting an idea." Paul looked deep in thought as he spoke. "It's not fully formed, and I want to talk with Jack first. Something he said last night planted a seed. I want to revisit it before bringing it up for our group. Quite honestly, I'm thinking more about Kim right now than anything. She and I have worked together for a decade, partners for nearly that long."

"JC, Paul, let's take this one step at a time. Right now, Kim is our focus. I'm sure Jack is already working alternate options. I expect we'll be hearing from him as soon as he knows more certainly before tomorrow. Until then, I want JC to think about every event since and including the death of his parents."

Angus continued, "JC, think about the days and weeks leading up to your folks' wreck. I know you've gone over it in your head most likely countless times. That's been from a loss and grieving process. Look at it, if you are able, from a different perspective. Dredge up your memories of the days and weeks prior to their passing. See if anything sticks out as odd or unusual. Anything at all. If you find something, however small, write it down. Frankly, I don't expect anything earth-shattering, but you never know." Angus was really in the flow and kept going.

"As we've all said, none of this makes sense to us. It makes sense to somebody, but not us, not yet. I'm confident something will trigger a memory, something to give us a hint of the root cause of these recent events.

"And, JC, remember, this isn't about fault. We can search for fault, but we'd never find it, for it simply isn't there. I am absolutely certain there is nothing you did or didn't do that has caused these events. Whatever is going on is doing so with you as the intended target, not the agent. I do not mean this cruelly at all, but Kim being attacked was a means toward whatever end our mystery aggressors have in mind for you, JC. I'm becoming convinced our aggressors are extremely focused on your demise. I'm equally convinced they will learn you are not the soft target they presumed you to be due in no small part to your association with Jack, Paul, Kim, and whomever else Jack believes is necessary to protect your well-being.

"No. We're looking for an event, a word, a hint of any sort. A phone call, a note, or letter in the mail. An offhand comment made by anybody about anything that now, in hindsight, doesn't quite fit. Paul, you'll have no information on this, but there is research to be done. With Jack's blessing, I'd like you to do some deep digging into the fatal accident that claimed Jonah and Catherine's lives. It might be an odd place to start, but we need to find the beginning of this, not the middle. I'm no longer satisfied with the official findings regarding that freeway wreck that took Jonah and Catherine from us. It may turn out no different at all, but I believe we can no longer take things at face value. We must reexamine everything from that wreck forward. Every piece of every account of that wreck needs to be reexamined.

"Paul, with Jack's endorsement, I want your operators to reinterview every person even remotely connected with that wreck. Survivors, police, insurance investigators, family, paramedics, tow-truck drivers and any of their helpers, hospital staff who treated the injured. Interview the coroner and their assistants. Look at the autopsies of every person who died in that pile-up. The truck driver, who is he? What's his story? Is he still around? How does he explain two simultaneous blowouts on the back of his trailer? Check with the NTSB. How often does an event like that happen? Where's the truck driver now?

"I think we need to suspect everything until we prove to our satisfaction otherwise. We cannot take anything at face value. Going forward, I believe JC needs permanent protection. Two people at all times, round the clock, every hour of every day. Same detail so nobody sneaks in and poses as a bodyguard when they're not. I know this is going to get expensive. I'll authorize whatever amount is necessary. JC needs this resolved so he can get back to leading a normal life.

"We can revisit this after JC has staff on-site but only after everybody is comfortable with their fitting in and their performance. Are we agreed?"

"Sure, Angus. I've not problems with anything you've said. Of course, Jack needs to know, and we need his buy-in before we move forward. You already know he makes his decisions quickly, and I'm certain he'll agree with everything you've said. This is especially true with Kim attacked. We've not had this situation in a protection assignment in several years. I know Jack will want to resolve the attack as a first priority, so I'm confident he's on board.

"I also suspect that at some point he will address the associated costs going forward. You already know Jack is very protective of all of us. My suspicion is he will assume some portion of the financial costs of this part of our service. Just how he is, especially with staff. That said, I can't and won't speak for him. But as I've said, you'll likely have your answer no later than tomorrow."

"Angus, you've given me a lot to think about. You're right, I've thought about Mom and Dad from the perspective of loss, not from anything else, up to now. Kip and I will take the time necessary to look at everything we're able, between that car wreck and today. I'll write down anything that seems odd or unusual. I still want to have our get-together this Saturday even if Kim is unable to attend. I'm going to ask Mat, Kyle, and Lu to help me think through the last year since Mom and Dad died. I can't imagine that wreck being any sort of beginning, but there is a whole list of things right now that I'd not have imagined even a short month ago.

"Are we good to go now? I know I need to deal with Winslow, but can we push that back to next Monday? I'll feel better about dealing with him after we know Kim is healing, and we've had our gathering on Saturday. Does that work for everybody?"

"Sure," from Paul.

"Yes," from Angus. "I'll leave you two now. Strange as it sounds, there are other clients in my life, and I need to take care of a few danglers." And he walked out and down the driveway toward his car.

Chapter 21

"Paul, can you take me to the grocer? I'm in serious need of a happy refrigerator, freezer, and pantry. They're all currently on a starvation diet. I need to fix that. You okay with going?"

"Sure. Jack can reach me on cell whenever he needs. Let's get you properly stocked up."

We headed to Paul's Jeep and drove to Finholm's Market on Harborview Drive. There, we loaded up on fresh everything, many cans of assorted things, frozen things, and bags of munchies. I went to the meat counter and asked Andy, the meat department manager, to select a dozen rib eye steaks and the same amount of chicken leg quarters for a Saturday morning pickup. Andy's a great guy. He's been their meat department manager longer than I've been alive and is always eager to accommodate. In a tough retail market, Andy's one of the reasons for the outstanding success of Finholm's. Loaded down with all our purchases, I wheeled a fully bagged grocery cart to Paul's Jeep. Even with all the crap going on, I remembered Paul needed both hands free, just in case.

Our drive back home proved uneventful. I was grateful for the lack of action. I hauled everything inside and restocked my pantry, reefer, and freezer. Then Paul and I sat with Kip jumping in my lap and snuggling in. Felt like it was time for some idle chat while we waited for Jack to give us an update on Kim.

Paul asked about Kings Academy, what it was like to go to school there. Courses, student population, instructors, the whole experience. I couldn't compare it with regular school as I'd never been. I did give him enough of an explanation that he could understand how Kings worked and how they justified their tuition. Most of us attending Kings were gifted, or maybe *advanced* was a better word, and how staff encouraged our individual talents. I'd never thought of myself in that manner, but I guess it fit.

I didn't think I had any particular standout talent. I thought of myself as well-rounded with an ability to figure things out. Talking with Paul, I came to realize I did have a gift of sorts. I had the ability to solve puzzles. Hmmm. Hadn't ever thought about that. Challenges to overcome, problems to solve, barriers to defeat. Huh, wonder why I'd never realized that before. Then Paul got more specific.

"JC, how did you not realize you had this talent or gift, if you prefer?"

"I never thought about it. I mean, questions require answers, right? A puzzle is just a question, isn't it? Solve a puzzle, answer a question, or the reverse. Same thing. Some are more or less obvious than others. Talking with you like this, I'm realizing this whole mess I'm in is a puzzle, isn't it? It's a classic whodunit, right? Certainly not classic in the sense of literature. And not a real classic because we're living it right now. But classic in the sense that somebody yet to be known, the whodunit to Kim and me so far. We know what they've done. Maybe. Angus may be onto something in going back to the wreck. I hope not. Still, answers would be nice probably. My life as an Agatha Christie mystery? Not hardly.

"Suppose we need to figure out a why to go with it, why they done it. We have a couple hows, how they done it. So we don't know who and we don't know why. We know a bit or more of the what they done, but likely not all of the what yet. We even have a bit of the when, when they done it. Most importantly, to me, is who they is or are. Is they a singular individual behind it all, or is they an organization with many folks involved, or is they several people without a true organization behind them? Just a bunch of individuals with a common interest in a 'what'? Huh.

"Paul, the more questions I ask, the fewer answers I have. Questions require answers, not more questions, right? Do we keep asking questions until there are no more to ask? Is that when the answers kick in? Hmmm. Not thought of anything in this manner. Life is more complicated than school, that's for sure. A lot.

"Are there nonsense questions to avoid asking? I don't think so. At least not yet. It may be that some questions and their attendant answers will not help solve the puzzle, but the end of their pursuit and value won't necessarily be known until the answers are discovered. Only then will the value of the question be able to be weighed.

"I suppose what we really need to do is drill down through all the questions to the questions those questions bring and keep doing that until we're at the bottom," JC reflected. "Then we can start filling in answers, right?"

"Are you always like this, JC?" asked Paul. "Do you get this deep on purpose? Regularly? I'm about half lost. I understand your thought process. I understood every word you said. I keep forgetting you are seventeen. You're swimming in deep water, my friend. Very deep water."

"Yea, and I drowned if you remember. Died. Maybe I'm not such a good swimmer after all. Maybe it's time to haul my butt into the shallows. But I think Angus is right. We have to question everything. Then answer every single question. Take back every assumption and prove it right or wrong. One question, one step, one answer. Eventually, we'll get there. It's for sure going to be interesting, probably uncomfortable, and frequently. I just don't see any other way. Do you?"

"No, I don't. I think we're at least moving in the right direction. I mean, we have to get to where this makes sense to us. I think…" And Paul's cell phone rang.

"Jack. Where are we? How's Kim?" I watched Paul's face for some suggestion of Kim's condition. The call lasted maybe three minutes, and Paul disconnected.

"Kim's in intensive care. The surgery to remove pressure on her brain was successful. Now they need to monitor her for a few days in the ICU. If all goes well, they'll bring her out of her coma either this Saturday or Sunday. Then she gets moved to a regular room for more days of observation. Then they'll release her. So far, she's doing as well as they would expect. Good news, all things considered. Jack will be here later. We'll go over Angus's plan then." I heard some relief in Paul's voice, so that was a good sign. "I imagine while Jack's here, he'll make arrangements to get you another operator. We'll see what he says."

Paul and I and, of course, Kip rattled around until Jack arrived. We just visited, got to know each other a bit more, but didn't further pursue or explore our current situation. We'd wait for Jack, then dive in and figure out what to do next. Jack arrived just after 5:00 p.m.

All three of us heard a vehicle pull up. Sounded like Jack's pickup. Must have been because Kip just raised his head a bit. After what we'd been through recently, he'd have raised a loud fuss if our new arrival had been a stranger. Amazing how quickly Kip learned friend from stranger or foe.

Just a minute later, Jack walked through our makeshift front door. "I'm glad you're both here. Everything okay?"

"Of course. What do you know about Kim? What's the latest word from the docs?" Paul was obviously anxious and concerned, hungry for current information.

"She's doing better. They have her on some heavy meds to manage her brain swelling. She's hooked up to multiple monitors. They want her quiet and not stressed. One person visiting but only briefly. She'll not be aware anybody's with her, at least for now. Pretty restricted at this point."

"You're feeling confident Kim's getting all the care she needs, yes?" I needed to know this. After all, Kim was attacked while working for me. That's a responsibility I could not and would not sidestep.

"Yeah. I don't have any worries about the level of her care." Jack appeared calm enough. I wanted to make sure he was justified in his thinking.

Chapter 22

"If you two will give me just a couple minutes, I need to make a call. I'll be right back." Saying this, I moved to the back patio and called Dr. Church at her office. No answer there, so I called her private number from the card she had given me earlier. She picked up on the second ring.

"Hi, Doc. JC Merrick here. Do you have a moment to talk?" Wanted to be sure she wasn't driving in heavy traffic.

"Good evening, JC. Yes, I'm fine to talk for a bit. What's up?"

"One of my bodyguards, Kim, was attacked this morning. She's at Tacoma Medical Center Hospital. No last name, but she's in ICU, likely the only Kim there. Can you check on the docs treating her? She was hurt while acting as one of my bodyguards. I'm feeling responsible, Doc. I want to be sure she's getting the care she needs."

"Of course. I understand. Give me no more than a half hour. I'll call you back and tell you what I found. Okay?"

"That works. Thank you, Doctor. I appreciate this more than you know." I disconnected and moved back inside. Time to update Jack and Paul.

"Okay. I just called my doc, Phyllis Church. She's a family doc, has been treating me and my folks since I was born. Longer for Mom and Dad. Anyhow, I asked her to check on the docs caring for Kim.

I'm feeling responsible here. Kim was guarding me when this happened. Feels like I need to be involved enough to be certain her care is appropriately high level.

"I'm not trying to butt in or take over. Those guys want to take a run at me, fine. Bring it. I've dealt with that piece of this situation. But coming after one of you? That's completely unacceptable. I badly want to get to the bottom of this. I have the resources and determination to become involved in this as something other than a victim. As Kim said yesterday, when we were being followed in Tacoma, I'm tired of being the mouse. Time to be the cat."

"JC, your plate is full enough. This is the part of our job that none of us like. This is part of our job description. Now you better understand what it means to fully guard and protect a client. We are, deliberately, in harm's way in the work we do. What I don't understand is how Kim was caught so unaware. She's better than that. Something happened outside a normal distraction. Something caused Kim to lose focus, if only for a piece of a second. That can be all it takes to compromise safety."

My cell phone rang. Dr. Church calling. "JC, Phyllis here. I've called Tacoma Medical. The doctors treating Kim have already consulted with the neurology head at University of Washington Medical Center. Dr. Oyama is staggeringly brilliant. He is not your doc if you want a warm and fuzzy doctor-patient relationship. However, when it comes to diagnosing and treating acquired brain injury, there is none better in this country and very few as good. Kim's docs are following Dr. Oyama's protocols. I have every confidence in Kim's treatment. Does this help relieve some anxiety?"

"Yes. Thank you, Dr. Church. This is the best news yet. Please accept my apology for disturbing your evening. I know your personal time is precious."

"JC, I'm glad you called. Helping, if only like this, is one of the reasons I gave you my private number. Do not hesitate to call. Okay?"

"Got it. Thank you again." And we disconnected. Now to update Jack and Paul.

"I've just had a call back from my doc. Kim is getting excellent care. Her docs have consulted with Dr. Oyama. He's the neurology department head at University of Washington Medical School. Doc Church says he has a lousy bedside manner, but he's the best in the country when it comes to diagnosing and treating acquired brain injury. Church said Kim's docs are following Oyama's protocols in treating Kim, so I think she's getting the best care available. I believe we can take this as very encouraging news."

"Wow. I really didn't know. I mean, I watched the care Kim was getting, the parade of doctors in and out of her area. I saw all the monitors she was hooked up to and all that. But still, thank you, JC. I think we can all feel a bit better now." Jack seemed to relax a bit as he took in the news regarding Kim.

"Thanks, JC." Paul, too, seemed more satisfied with Kim's care and our overall situation.

Crap! What was I thinking? Or more correctly, I wasn't thinking? How in the world…

CHAPTER 23

"Uh, guys? I need to go and see Kim. I know I really don't know her. But we connected, ya know? And I'm still feeling some responsible, justified or not. Whaddaya say? I just want to see her. I guarantee I won't feel any part of at ease with this until I can actually see her. So can we go?" I was still taking one hydrocodone in the morning and another when I went to bed. Meant I had no business driving, or I'd already be gone.

"Something to eat first?" Paul was practical.

"That can wait, right? I'll not starve in the next hour, I guarantee it...even if I am a teenager with a supposedly bottomless pit for a stomach." I moved to the kitchen and secured the back door. Then I walked toward the makeshift front door to do the same. For now, we were getting in and going out through the front man door in the garage.

"Why are you in such a hurry? Kim certainly isn't going anywhere. Why are you so fired up?" Jack, the ever curious one, didn't miss much.

"No particular reason. I just think, the sooner I'm able to see Kim, the sooner...well, the sooner we can get back and start to relax for the evening. That is, if relaxing is really on the menu. Somehow

I don't think any of us will get that far, but maybe we can unwind a bit and figure out what to do next."

"All right. Let's get loaded up. We'll be at the tail end of rush-hour traffic so the drive won't take long. Let's take my rig. Guess it did make sense to drive the Hummer here." Jack was first out the door walking toward his H1.

Paul followed, and I walked out with Kip. I secured the garage door and was ready to leave. "Kip, watch the house, okay? Stay in the woods and be safe. We'll not be gone long, and when we get back, I'll make you a special supper, okay?" Both Jack and Paul looked at me like I'd lost part of my mind. "What? Kip understands a lot more than any of us really know. I'm convinced of it. Spend enough time around him, and you'll think the same way."

We all loaded in the H1 and maneuvered out the driveway, Kip watching until we turned onto Cove Road. It was a quick twenty-minute drive to Tacoma Medical. Thank God for light traffic!

Jack found a parking spot in their primary lot. It was only a short walk to the north entrance to the hospital. Jack walked in first. I followed, and Paul was last in our little procession. As Jack knew where Kim was located, he continued to lead the way until we reached the third floor and ICU area.

Jack walked up to the reception area for the ICU and spoke to a nurse behind the counter. Paul and I were close enough, but I didn't hear what Jack said to the nurse.

"I'm sorry, sir. Visitors are limited to one person and only ten minutes. We're quite strict on this policy."

Time for me to chime in, "Hi. We certainly understand. Kim is in my employ, and I'm feeling responsible for her being here. All I want is a quick minute to see her, sort of ease my mind about the whole thing."

"Are you family? You don't look like family, if you don't mind me saying." Looked like the nurse was going to be difficult. Should have brought Angus too. Damn!

I thought quickly. "Family? No, not immediate family. But we are related if that helps." Maybe she'd buy it, maybe not. It was the only shot I had, and I was taking it. Besides, she'd likely seen Jack in and out, and I was with him. A white lie didn't seem unreasonable to me, and I was certain God wouldn't mind. Saying this to the nurse in front of Jack and Paul might just add enough credibility to be successful. Worth a shot, right?

Stink eye from the nurse. Jeez! Regardless, I forged ahead. "Kim's mother is my mother's aunt. I don't know what that makes me beyond a relative. Besides, Kim's mom is deceased, as is mine. So we're really closer than blood relations would indicate." Now to shut up and hold my breath.

"That's correct, Nurse," from Jack. This might work yet!

Eyeing me again, Nurse Ratched wasn't amused at all. Looked like she was ready to resist and fight regardless. Also looked like she'd enjoy it. "I really don't see any reason…"

Paul this time said, "If you'd like, we can get our attorney here to attest to the veracity of JC's right to visit as a relative of Kim. But is that really necessary? He only wants a few minutes with Kim. He's not here to upset anybody or cause any sort of fuss. However, if you won't abide by your own rules…you see where this can go, yes?"

The biggest sigh in the history of the universe was followed by a very serious stink eye aimed at me. "Very well. But I am limiting your visit to five minutes, young man. Five minutes only and not a second longer. I just don't see the importance of this at all. And just so you know, I'll be watching you and keeping an eye on all her monitors. You just behave yourself, you hear?"

Perfect. Five minutes was three more than I likely needed. I'd be in and out, and all would be well. "Thank you, nurse. Appreciate your accommodation." I started walking toward Kim's bed. Reaching her side, I squatted so my head was nearly at her eye level. My body obstructed the nurse from viewing my hand as I gently grasped Kim's fingers in the palm of my left hand.

"Hi, Kim. It's JC. It's still Wednesday evening now. You've given us quite a scare. You can relax. Everything is going to be fine. You'll be out of here in no time. You have great docs caring for you. I think your recovery will amaze even them. Nurse Ratched has only given me a couple minutes with you, so it's time for me to go. Jack's been here visiting and watching over you. Time for you to get some rest and heal. You'll feel ever so much better in the morning. I can almost guarantee it." *Thank you, God, for watching over Kim.* I let go of Kim's hand and moved toward the watchful eye of the nurse.

"Thank you, Nurse Ratc…excuse me, nurse. I feel so much better having seen Kim. She really is a remarkable person. I'm encouraged by her coloring. You saw for yourself that I didn't disturb her. No monitors alerted or started blaring. She didn't code when I was with her. All in all, must have been rather disappointing for you." Blame it on my youth, if you must, I just had to goad that cranky woman, if only a bit. She was a seriously not nice person.

"Jack, Paul, are you ready? I feel so much better having seen Kim. Feels like a weight really has been lifted, ya know?" Now I had to wait to see if my healing gift was an on-command thing or only worked somctimes. Guess one more sleepless night would tell the story. I was going to be nervous until tomorrow regardless.

We walked back to Jack's H1 and headed home. This was looking like one of the longer nights of my life so far. Good Lord! What was my life turning into?

CHAPTER 24

Later, Wednesday evening, we'd arrived back home, and I was feeling much better about Kim and her full recovery. I also suspected she would be able to attend our Saturday gathering, but we'd see what the next couple of days held.

Kip was excited for everybody to be back home. He'd obviously missed us as he followed me like a shadow until it was bedtime. Jack and Paul decided that Paul would remain with me exclusively, acting as my full-time bodyguard until we learned Kim's prognosis. We decided to take one day at a time, and I'd already promised Jack, Paul, and Angus that I'd exercise extra caution until we could get some better handle on what was going on.

Wednesday night proved unremarkable, far less complicated than I'd imagined earlier. Paul and I had an easy omelet supper: dicing onion, tomato, green pepper, ham, and cheese with jalapeno peppers. Together with wheat toast and coffee, it was perfect for our evening meal. I treated Kip to more cooked ground turkey mixed in his kibble. He'd had a hard day too and deserved some sort of treat.

Our evening was spent with Paul prowling outside, creeping in our forest and Kip relaxing with me in our favorite recliner. Kip and I went to bed about 11:00 p.m. right after Paul checked in and said he'd continue looking around outside for a while, then make his own sleeping arrangements.

I was pretty anxious for morning to get here. With any luck at all, Kim would show remarkable progress in her recovery, and I was looking forward to hearing good news in that regard. Kip, being his usual dog self, was taking every hour and day as they came, living life like a pampered and well-loved dog should: comfortable, secure in his home, and alert to opportunities and challenges. For the rest of the evening at least, there was much right with the world.

Kip and I woke at seven the next morning, Thursday. I figured we'd hear something from Jack by midmorning. And we still had to go over the security system for our forest and home. I thought we'd get into that at some point, probably earlier than later. First, we needed Kim on a fast track to a full recovery. I had high hopes of hearing very encouraging news.

Paul was sleeping on a sofa, a blanket over him. I noticed both doors were closed and barred. Nobody was getting in without making a good racket first. Paul's Beretta was sticking out just a bit from under his pillow just inches from his hand. Kip and I kept as quiet as we were able but still made some noise. Kip padded to where Paul was sleeping and lay down on the floor right beneath him. Hmmm. Guard dog guarding the guard. How often does that happen? I wondered.

I decided cooked oatmeal with raisins and pecans would make a great breakfast, so I started in. Evidently, I wasn't quiet enough as I saw Paul raise his head and look in my direction. "Good morning, Paul. How did you do last night?"

"All was quiet. No issues anywhere."

"Did you manage to get any decent sleep at all? I can't imagine you had a restful night."

"It was fine. We're pretty used to sleeping when and where we can. Just part of our normal work. Probably totaled about three or so hours, pretty standard."

"Well, if you're up for cooked oatmeal with raisins, pecans, dried cranberries, and brown sugar, it'll be ready in a few minutes. I'll make some toast as well if it sounds good to you."

"Sure! Give me a couple minutes to get cleaned up, and I'll be ready."

"Easy deal. It'll be ready in another five or so minutes, and I can keep it hot until you're ready. I'll start the coffee, and we'll be ready to go when you are. No hurry. Take the time you need."

Paul made his way to get ready for the day, while Kip and I continued making breakfast. It was only about five minutes later when Paul was back in the kitchen. He was bright-eyed and looked ready for whatever the day would bring. I noticed his Beretta was back in its holster on his right hip. Funny, I'd already become accustomed to seeing him, Kim, and Jack armed and ready. I'd not grown up in a home where Mom and Dad walked around wearing pistols, but it already seemed normal or at least my new version of normal for now.

I'd just finished filling Kip's food dish with more kibble and the rest of the cooked ground turkey and giving him fresh ice water (told you he was spoiled) when Paul's cell phone rang.

"Paul… Okay… That's great! Sure… See you then." It was a one-sided brief conversation between Paul and somebody.

"JC, that was Jack. He just heard from the hospital. Kim's been moved to a private room, no longer in ICU. She's out of her coma. Seems she made remarkable progress during the night. Her brain swelling is gone. She's fully aware of her surroundings, knows what happened, and is ready to be released. Jack talked with her docs. They don't really understand but have seen and heard of a few other instances of this sort of quick recovery. They're encouraged and optimistic. They intend running Kim through a few tests and scans today. If all goes well, they might release her tomorrow. They told Jack, when she's released, nothing strenuous for her for two weeks, then she can work back into normal activities."

"That's super! I'm so glad! She had us all worried. I know you and Jack more so because of your partnership and time together. This is great news!"

"It is. Jack said he'd be here around ten this morning. We'll go over your security system then, and he'll start designing it and pulling hardware together."

"Okay. Let's eat before it gets cold. I'm probably one of the only people on the planet who enjoys cold oatmeal. I sure don't want to subject you to it."

"Hey, you can't begin to imagine the things I've eaten while on the job. Cold oatmeal is a delicacy by comparison."

Hearing that, I finished putting out the oatmeal condiments, cold milk, butter, and toast. I poured us both a cup of coffee, and we helped ourselves to oatmeal and the rest, standing and eating at the kitchen island. One thing about oatmeal and toast, it's a quick breakfast. But like the Chinese food we'd had only a couple nights earlier, I'd be hungry in a couple hours. Oatmeal was great fuel. But for me, it burned hot and fast; didn't stick to my ribs as others claimed. Regardless, it was filling for a time, tasted good, and was healthy food. I hadn't learned to be a good cook yet, but I'd mastered the art of cooking oatmeal a while ago. With all the food we'd just stocked up on, we weren't in any danger of starving. Suffering through my cooking, very likely, but at least we wouldn't starve.

Chapter 25

Paul and I visited while we ate and then cleaned up after ourselves. He described some of the security systems they'd designed for other clients and their advantages and disadvantages, giving me some valuable information and definite food for thought. When it came to security systems, I didn't know anything about anything. I was at least smart enough to listen and ask questions. Time seemed to fly, and before we knew it, I saw Jack drive up.

Walking to our reinforced front "door," I removed the two wood crosspieces and opened the door for Jack. "Good morning, Jack. Great news about Kim! What a relief to hear she's doing so well."

"Thanks, JC. Yes. Kim is doing much better than anybody expected. She's got her full memory, no amnesia of any sort, and the swelling on her brain is gone. Even the area where they went in and relieved the pressure from swelling is further along the healing process than her docs expected.

"I visited with a couple of the docs this morning. They had told me earlier it would take a month for that incision to fully heal, longer for that area of her skull to knit. This morning they told me her incision has only a faint scar visible. The sutures look ready to remove, and they've only been in a day, not the ten days they are normally left in to knit and hold her scalp together. They said they asked Kim if this is how she normally heals. And they asked me. Thinking back, I've not known Kim to heal especially quickly. I mean, she's young, so she has the advantage of youth going for her. Otherwise, I've no idea.

"Paul," Jack continued, "Do you remember any of Kim's earlier injuries healing noticeably quicker than would be normal? I can't think of anything."

"No. I remember a couple times when Kim's gotten into a scrape or two. I remember a black eye…that seemed to take a couple weeks to resolve. I remember when she got shot in the leg. I remember that injury bled like crazy but was only a through-and-through flesh wound. Seems like that took a few weeks before she wasn't limping. No. I don't remember anything ultra quick in her healing."

I just sat there, keeping my mouth shut. I knew last night when I visited Kim that this would likely happen. I mean, I expected it. I also remembered when you expect a certain outcome, you are sometimes setting yourself up for disappointment. Then again, we tend to get what we expect in life events. Think positive, and positive things normally happen, not always but usually. Think negative, and that's generally the outcome of your life. Mom and Dad taught me that. So has life. So has my new ability or gift or whatever you want to call it.

It seemed Kim didn't remember me visiting her last night, another good thing. Maybe I was able to heal others, and they wouldn't remember me being there with them. That would sure be nice, and it would help me continue to be invisible when using this gift or ability or curse, whatever. I was still getting used to having it, using it, and figuring out the morality and responsibility of it. Like I've said before, my life is getting interestinger and interestinger.

"Paul, have you and JC discussed any ideas or wants regarding JC's security system? We need to move forward with that. Sooner, I think, is much better in this case than later."

"No, we haven't yet. I did tell JC about some of our earlier systems. Went over some of the advantages and disadvantages of the ones I described to him. But I've not suggested anything specific to him outside those examples."

"JC, do you have any particular concerns or features in mind?"

"I don't. I know we were going to have Mat here when we went over the design. He's not due here until about one this afternoon or as soon as his latest class ends. I know he's pretty excited to be involved. I can call him and see if he can be here sooner. I don't want to hold you up or cause any delays. Let me call him."

Saying that, I picked up my phone. It was almost 10:30 a.m. Mat would likely be right in the middle of his last class for the day. If I remembered right, his class wouldn't be over until almost noon. I expected I'd be leaving him a voicemail on his cell. So I was surprised when he answered on the first ring.

"Mat! I thought you'd still be in class. Are you cutting?"

"Hey, JC. No. Our regular instructor is out sick, so we have an unassigned period. I'd planned on getting over to you after this class was out. It's supposed to run from 10:00 a.m. until noon. I know we planned for me to be there about 1:00 p.m. this afternoon, so I was just killing time visiting with some classmates about our upcoming test, getting four of us to form a study group for the test. Test questions are given out in advance, which should make passing a breeze. But it doesn't work that way.

"Ms. Becker, our instructor, is devious. Not all the test questions or answers are covered in class. We have to dig and research for each answer. It normally takes about two hours to get the final answer for each of the ten questions. So about twenty hours of study for each test. Our study group splits the questions among us. I have three of the questions to research. We'll all have answers to our questions by tomorrow, then we'll share answers. That gives us the weekend to memorize the answers. Becker expects every answer to be perfect. Perfect spelling and punctuation for every answer. Miss a comma and your answer's wrong. Misspell a word and your answer's wrong. Like I said, she's devious."

"Wow! I'd already forgotten how exacting some of my instructors were. Does this mean you need to skip being here this afternoon? Sounds like you have your hands full."

"No. It's fine. Because I have three questions to research. They're the easier questions. I think I'll be able to find all the answers in about three to four hours. As long as I can start studying by 7:00 p.m. or so, I should be fine. And getting this glimpse into security systems and IT design will be awesome! So if you and your guys are still game, I'm all in."

Sure. We're starting earlier than we'd thought. Paul and Jack are here. Can you get over here now?"

"Sure. I only need a couple minutes to wrap up here, and I'm on my way. I should be there in about twenty minutes at the most."

"Perfect. See you here before eleven." And we disconnected.

"Guys, Mat will be here before eleven. He's out of class for the rest of the day."

"Excellent. Great news! JC, while we wait, why don't you tell us your concerns? We can start discussing them while we wait for Mat. He'll get exposed to our solutions as we design them to satisfy your safety and security concerns. I think Mat's main focus is on the hardware and software, not necessarily the human side of the equation, except how our solutions resolve your needs. Does that make sense?" Seemed Jack was ready to go.

"Sure. Great idea. As we go over this, I'm going to be looking for you two to guide me. Right now, I'm in the 'I don't know what I don't know' arena. Basically, I want what you design and install to be my early warning system. I know it takes either the police or sheriff a minimum average of ten minutes to get here unless they're already in the area. But that's random chance, and I know I can't count on it. Based on recent events, that means I need to be able to survive for a minimum of ten minutes. That means hiding, defending myself, in general preparing to do whatever I need to do to get through ten minutes of deadly threats.

"I know those ten minutes are not my window to prepare. I have to be prepared before any alarm goes off. The security system needs to give me as much warning and protection as it is able, so wherever I am on the property or in the house, I have a solid action plan, one that is second nature to me. I'll need to act based on muscle memory, not reading some notebook or taking the time to look something up in a user's guide. Means I need your help to develop a strong plan of action, then practice those actions until they are as much a part of me as breathing."

We discussed some general ideas and thoughts for the next several minutes.

Hearing a vehicle drive up, I looked out the front window to see Mat's Honda. I walked out to meet him. "Hey, Mat! Glad you're able to be here!"

"What happened? Are you remodeling? Looks like your front door is missing, and the area is really chewed up."

"Yeah. I'll bring you up to speed as we visit with the guys I want you to meet." Saying that, Mat and I walked into the house so I could introduce him to Paul and Jack. "Mateo Betancourt, meet Jack and Paul. They're the two primary guys who will be designing, building, and installing my security system. Jack, Paul, meet Mateo, or Mat."

"Hi, Mat," came from Paul as they shook hands.

"Hi, Mat, glad to meet you," came from Jack as they, too, shook hands.

"So you guys are here to design and install a security system for JC? What's going on with the front door? I see the back door is being reworked as well."

Time for me to jump in. "Mat, there've been some developments since you were here last. In fact, since we really visited last time. I really only want to tell the story once. We're all gathering this Saturday, so is it okay with you if I hold off until then?"

"Sure. I mean, I guess so. It's your story. Speaking of stories, what's up with your left arm? Did you wrestle a cougar or something?" he said with a grin on his face.

"Something like that. Details on Saturday. Okay?"

"Sure. Where are you so far on your security system?"

"We were just going over some of the basic groundwork before you got here. Jack builds all their systems. He and Paul do the design. There's one other team member, Kim. She isn't here today. We hope she can be with us for our Saturday gathering. But she may not be able to make it. Details Saturday."

Jack and Paul brought Mat up to speed on where we were as they began describing the purpose of my security system specifically and systems in general.

"There are two basic types of security systems. The first is designed to defeat intrusion. They are both defensive and offensive in nature. In an extreme example, you'd have a command-and-control center with live-view security cameras, possibly remote-controlled or automated defense measures, like turret-style machine guns that would activate on command or when a particular sensor or set of sensors were tripped. In this scenario, you'd have armed security personnel on patrol, and the list goes on. Think of these, most generally, as military or military-grade systems. They're designed to remove the threat by force. That makes these systems both defensive and offensive.

"The other systems are only defensive in scope. They are designed to alert either a private security company or the police, sometimes both, that there is an intrusion. Their purpose is to get either private security staff or police or both on-site as quickly as possible. Security staff and/or police are the ones who then act to investigate the cause of the alert or alarm. Here's the thing, the police are not charged with protecting any particular individual or business.

"Police uphold law and order. Contrary to what you see on TV and in movies, they don't go running around chasing bad guys and firing their pistols at those who flee. Their job is to protect and serve their community. If somebody is shooting at you when the police arrive, they won't immediately start shooting at the trigger puller. While it usually takes only seconds, they first evaluate what's going on. Then they act to contain the situation. Then they'll act to resolve the conflict by disarming the shooter or shooters. Finally, they'll investigate the incident because events are not always as they first appear.

"Private security, whether an electronic system or live bodyguards or a combination, are designed to protect their principals. My company knows who hired us. We work for that individual or group. For us, they are the good guys. Anybody looking to harm them in any way is considered a bad guy. My company carefully and quietly verifies prospective clients before we make any decision to work with them.

"As an example, JC wanted to hire us. We were referred to him by one of our former clients. Before we committed to working with JC, we did a full background check. We do this every time with every new client request. We now have a contract with JC to design and install a security system and to monitor that system. Our contract with JC also has a bodyguard provision.

"We're designing JC's security system to give him enough time to act in ways that protect him until help arrives. In JC's case, that help will be in the form of responding police and one or more members of my team. We already know it takes an average minimum of ten minutes for law enforcement to respond to this location. We want a margin of safety as well. We've agreed that to be reasonable in protecting JC, we need to plan a twelve-minute response time. That means wherever JC is on his property, it's up to him to protect himself, however he is able, for a minimum of twelve minutes once sensors are tripped or an alarm sounds. In an active-shooter situation, twelve minutes can quite literally be a lifetime.

"Keeping that in mind, JC will be part of his own system. His security system will automatically call for help as soon as its sensors trip. Those sensors will trip when and where an intruder sets off a designated series of sensors. That is the time when his twelve-minute clock starts ticking. At the same time JC's system calls for help, it notifies JC of the alarm. That notification is JC's cue to become an active part of his overall security system."

"I never looked at it that way. I just assumed the system notified the police, and they took care of the problem." Mat had much the same view I had before I was invaded. Now I knew differently.

"Sure. That makes sense. In this case it's wrong, but it makes sense," Jack commented. "Most of the home security systems today are simply monitors. Some sensor trips in a home and the system notifies a central switch board. That switch board operator then either calls the home to verify there is a problem or they notify local police. Police then respond, not knowing whether there is a real problem or if it's a false alarm. There are a lot of false alarms, especially with the less expensive systems we're seeing today. Bad sensors and false positives are a real problem in our industry."

"Outside JC's home, we'll be using infrared sensors, motion sensors, motion-activated cameras with night-vision capabilities, and in-ground pressure pads. All these are wireless and battery operated. They're cutting edge and not yet available to the general public. We're able to purchase them because of our ongoing government contract work. Some of our clients are military or other government agency personnel. Many of those folks are quite high profile and need systems capable of providing very early warning of a threat.

"As I told JC early on, any security system in the world can be defeated. Our job is to make it very time-consuming to defeat his system. That way, my staff and the police can arrive in time to catch the intruder before any harm comes to JC. That's our primary goal, protecting our client." It was easy to tell Jack was passionate about his work.

"How do you eliminate false positives?" Mat was getting drawn in. I liked what I was seeing from him. It was obvious he was anything but bored.

"We work on a three-sensor system design. While there is no perfect security system, ours is designed to virtually eliminate false sensor alarms. Tripping an alarm requires a pressure-pad trip, a motion-sensor trip, and a camera trip. Here's an example. Imagine a motion sensor tripping because a large bird flew in front of the camera at night. Maybe an eagle or owl or even a sparrow. Trips the motion sensor, right?

"But no pressure plate was tripped. Our system knows something other than a human being tripped the motion sensor. If the motion sensor was tripped by somebody creeping in, a pressure pad would have to trip. Imagine Kip running through the forest. He's a hundred-plus pounds of healthy dog. How do we fix Kip not activating the alarm and the police arriving?

"He'll be wearing an IFF tag. That tag tells the system to ignore him. So what if somebody steals Kip's IFF tag? Well, that tag is implanted.

"And our systems are monitored by highly trained humans. As soon as any sensor trips, our human monitors get eyeballs on that sensor and area. The cameras we use give us real-time visuals of every area in JC's forest.

"Or a motion sensor trips. A camera trips, and a pressure pad trips. We already have eyes on, and we see somebody sneaking in. We send a minimum of two operators with any verified intrusion. We'll send more, depending on how many intruders we see. Those operators are on their way to JC within one minute of the sensor tripping. As they are being activated, we're notifying the police and sheriff. They'll act within whatever timetable they have established as protocol. Worst case, our first operators are here within twelve minutes.

"We can do this because our people are scattered throughout the greater Seattle and Tacoma area. We have operators from Everett to Olympia. Our protocol is that there are at least two operators within a maximum of twelve minutes of every one of our clients. Some areas are covered by a minimum of eight of our responders. It depends on the geographic area, the client, and our contract.

"JC is on a heightened alert status for now. He'll explain that if and when he chooses. Our contract with him is for this higher level of security and will remain so until he changes it. So you see, our systems can be quite robust."

"Wow. I had no idea! Pretty cool!" Mat was in all the way.

"JC's home interior setup will be much the same. Motion sensors will go active when he arms the system. It'll be designed to not 'see' Kip due to his implanted IFF tag. There'll be infrared and motion sensors as well as cameras on all entry points, meaning all doors and windows, plus pressure pads.

"JC will wear his own IFF tag, as will Ms. Abreo at JC's request. That way, the three of them will be able to walk throughout any live sensor area without tripping any sensors. This is our best tech advancement in a long time. We're really excited to deploy it, and JC's system will be the first to use it.

"We use sound sensors, sensors designed to detect breaking glass, sensors that detect abnormally loud noises, like a door being kicked in, and sensors to detect smoke, fire, and natural gas.

"We also employ pressure wave sensors. In the event of an explosion, say, from a faulty or tampered natural gas line, the pressure wave created from the explosion can knock out sensors. But ours will trip before going dark. And by including pressure wave sensors, the pressure wave will trip the sensor, letting police and our monitoring team know we need to respond.

"All our sensors are wireless and battery operated. So if the power goes out by accident or design, our monitors and sensors are not affected. If the phone lines go down by accident or design, nothing changes for us. JC's monitoring system is controlled by a notebook computer with an additional uninterruptable power supply. JC's security system is not affected by outside utility interference. All our sensors are tamper-resistant. While they can be defeated, they have to be defeated in such a way that the entire grid goes down at once. In all practical situations, that just does not happen, especially at a residence. You could achieve deactivation with an EMP (electromagnetic pulse), but that is incredibly impractical for a residence. Still, all our sensors are hardened against an EMP strike. So that avenue isn't available to bad actors.

"The obvious solution to defeat our system is to jam the frequency. But as soon as our system components are unable to communicate with home base and/or each other, an alarm is triggered, and we and the police and sheriff are notified.

"All JC's sensors are fed to two locations in real time from two independent sources. We're running fiber optic cable to the house, insuring near instantaneous communications between our center and JC's home. There will be a full-time monitoring station in the house as well as our monitoring center. JC will be able to see his system just as robustly as our monitors every hour of day and night. And his system is broadcasting over a secure wireless node.

"Imagine water flowing through a garden hose. Data is the water. The larger the hose diameter, the more water flow you get. Compare a common garden hose to the hose on a fire truck. See the difference? Fiber optic cabling is relatively new to this area but has been around for a while. Fiber optic is a very large data hose, capable of moving an enormous volume of data nearly instantaneously. The fiber-optic hose serving JC's home and alarm system is the size of four fire hoses. Enormous throughput of data and video images. There won't be any slowdown or bottleneck in the system. JC's data is moving very fast through a very large pipe with no measurable lag time.

"There are only three ways to defeat our alarm system. One is to know JC's alarm code, which he would use to disable his system. But there is no such code. In order to turn off JC's system, he has to call our control center and speak to our center administrator while being viewed from a hidden camera. There is only one place in JC's home where he could make such a call, and that location is covered by three separate hidden video cameras, each with infrared capabilities.

"The second way is to force JC to disarm his system. But there is no disarm code to use. So that track isn't available for use. JC's system is on every hour of every day. There is no off switch. Anybody visiting must wear an IFF tag. No tag and alarms trip and twelve minutes later or sooner, our operators and law enforcement arrive. When JC is expecting guests, he notifies us, and we go into video monitoring, watching who shows up and watching for prearranged visual ques from JC.

"There's a panic button feature. Imagine JC's home and somebody parachutes to his roof or lands a helicopter or in some manner gets to the roof without setting off any perimeter sensors. JC hears the loud noise, so he hits his panic button. We're dispatched, as are the police.

"Or imagine JC is away from home and attacked. His panic button is still available to notify us he needs immediate help. That device has a GPS feature built in. Upon activation, that panic device broadcasts JC's location to within eighteen inches.

"The remaining way to defeat our system is to have enough perimeter guys to take out all our cameras and pressure plates at the same exact time. That is incredibly impractical. Every sensor is tamper resistant, as I've already said. Each sensor type is on their own isolated piece of network, arranged by grid. So if one sensor goes down, that counts as an alarm trip. But nothing happens until a second sensor fails or is tripped. We design each sensor network to interact with every other sensor network within a single system.

"Here's how it works. We assign random sensors to individual networks within each sensor type. Then we mesh each of the outside networks into a whole, separate from the interior network. Like the outside sensors and networks, we design the interior sensors and network them randomly by type, then by networked group, then by inside, then combine everything inside and outside to arrive at a whole system.

"Finally, the entire network is self-monitoring. It pings itself several times every second. If any sensor within the network fails three consecutive pings and this happens, it means a sensor is malfunctioning and needs to be replaced. Our commitment is to get failed sensors replaced within twenty-four hours of failure. Battery life is thirty-six months on average or 26,000 duty hours. All our sensors have a MTBF (mean time between failure) of 25,000 duty hours. However, occasionally, one will bench-test just fine, then fail well before the end of its anticipated life cycle. To mitigate that, we do a system-wide sensor and battery replacement and upgrade every thirty months or at about 22,000 duty hours. This schedule really reduces our equipment failure rate in all our field applications.

"JC, all your equipment is covered under our monitoring plan. Our scope of work for you includes providing personal protective services until your security system is fully installed, tested, and certified by us and your local police department. The system we'll be installing for you is very robust. Your situation is somewhat unusual because of the size of your home and land. Where we mostly work with lots measured in square feet, we're measuring your coverage in acres. More area equals more sensors and more opportunity for bad actors to gain entry. More sensors equal more cost but also more opportunity to catch the bad actors because we've more equipment to detect them."

Chapter 26

Jack continued, "I want to make two suggestions. First, given what's happened so far, I think it would be prudent to create a safe room in your home. This would be a smaller room we can harden to delay and perhaps defeat an intruder. We would use your smallest bedroom and rework every wall, ceiling, and floor against intrusion. We use hardened half-inch steel plates on all outside walls, including your outer hallway wall, on both sides of the hallway.

"We'll use hardened half-inch steel plate on all inner and exterior walls, welded to and held by engineered steel studs and joists. All welds are continuous, edge to edge, top to bottom, in a square groove configuration. Weld strength is 70,000 pounds per square inch and x-rayed to expose any welding defects. We expect none, but any identified will be repaired on-site. All welds are CJP (complete joint penetration) to each steel stud using continuous runs. In short, we'll end up with a solid steel cube for the entire room.

"Some of your safe-room steel will have to be fabricated off-site and brought in. These pieces are lifted in by crane. This means some renovation to your roof. When we're finished, you'll have a completely reshingled roof. We'll insulate all outer walls with spray foam and Rockwool and further support with three inches of quilted Kevlar fabric sandwiched between inner and outer steel sheets, including the underside of your floor in the basement. We'll remove your existing bedroom window and replace it with the same sheet steel, insulation, and Kevlar.

"We use a hardened four-inch solid steel, reinforced bedroom door with six hardened interior door hinges, and contained within a hardened steel doorframe.

"We'll turn that bedroom closet into an interior safe. Every surface will have two additional layers of half-inch steel in staggered layers and staggered double layers of Kevlar with a full industrial-grade safe door for entry. Here too, we'd use solid steel studs. Essentially, you will have a walk-in safe within a safe room.

"The door to your safe room cannot be locked or unlocked from outside. The outside of the door into your bedroom will have a welded-on handle only, no lockset. When finished, it will look much like a smaller version of a handicapped grab handle. The difference with your handle is that it's made of solid, hardened iron and finished to look like antique bronze. There is no penetration from the handset into the steel door itself.

"Inside, there will be a handle and one lever that throws, either opening or closing, eight-inch-and-a-half hardened steel bolts directly into your doorframe. Each bolt has a six-inch throw into both sides of the steel doorframe. Each bolt is formed from cold-rolled steel. For all practical purposes, this is designed like a vault or safe door with all the strength but without the added bulk of an actual bank vault door.

"Once that door is closed and locked, nobody from the outside is getting in in any reasonable amount of time. Breaching with hydraulic jacks or rams require well beyond your twelve-minute time clock. Our best time to breach your first room, from property intrusion detection, is twenty minutes. Breaching your gun safe is an additional nine minutes.

"Breaching your safe room with a plasma torch could be accomplished in about ten minutes in addition to the time from property intrusion detection. So a total of no less than fourteen minutes. Add another ten minutes to breach your inner safe. That gives you twenty-four minutes for help to arrive when we know emergency services arrive within twelve minutes of your alarm.

"The downside to cutting with a plasma torch is power. The electric current required to run one of these portable machines is not typically available from a residential power source. You don't just plug it into a standard wall outlet. Once again, your safe room has caused your intruders extra time and planning. Remember, our job is to make getting at you expensive and time-consuming.

"We'll need to reinforce the load-bearing requirements of your bedroom through your basement by replacing those floor joists with engineered steel beams. Half-inch sheet steel weighs just over twenty pounds per square foot. By the time we're finished replacing your walls, ceiling, and floor, joists and studs, entry door, and adding your closet safe room, the overall weight of your safe room and inner safe will exceed 26,000 pounds, way beyond what you will find in any average home. We'll work with an engineer to verify load requirements.

"JC, this will change part of your home forever. Any future remodeling you contemplate will have to take your safe room into consideration. If we make these alterations, there is no going back. It cannot be undone without some very major demolition to that entire area of your home. Your bedroom walls will be welded to the ceiling and floor. The concrete piering necessary to support this weight will be obvious in your basement.

"We'll have to cut out a bedroom-sized section of the concrete floor in your basement and add concrete piering and more steel beams and joists to support the new weight load. When we finish, your safe room will withstand serious firepower. Your house will likely be totally destroyed before your safe room is breached. We'll give your safe room its own isolated air supply. Help will arrive long before anybody can gain access. We'll build your room so all weld seams are invisible and not where you'd expect them.

"I had no idea, Jack." I was amazed by how much needing to be security conscious intruded in and was going to change my life. And this was before anybody knew about my budding abilities. Seemed to me I needed to take my personal safety and security even more seriously than what Jack was describing, given what I'd been keeping private.

"When you arrived so very few days ago, I really believed any security system would be overkill. I really didn't think I'd need the sort of protection we first discussed. Now I'm convinced I need to take this whole thing seriously. What you described for a safe room is beyond anything I would have imagined. But given what's happened, I'd rather be overprepared than blissfully unaware of what could happen. I do have a question. Won't the interior of this room look industrial? I mean, welded steel?"

"Not at all," Paul chimed in. "We've done this before. The visible walls, floor, and ceiling will all look normal to an uneducated eye. However, if you look closely, you'll notice the room is just a bit smaller than it was. The floor will have the same look and feel as it does now. We'll use Sheetrock on all wall and ceiling surfaces. We'll tape and texture the walls and ceiling to match what you have now and paint the room whatever color you wish. The only difference will be that your Sheetrock is glued to the sheet steel, not screwed into a wood stud. You can still hang pictures and decorate, but your picture hooks will only nail in a half inch, so be careful of the weight of any pictures you might want to hang. You'll have a carpeted floor and pad, just as you do now.

"You'll have electrical outlets only on your inner walls. We'll give you electrical outlets according to code, so no worries. But those boxes are manufactured out of one-inch steel and are welded to a precut hole in your sheet steel wall instead of being screwed or nailed to a wood stud. All you'll see is a typical wall plug receptacle that is anything but typical.

"We will want you to use indirect lighting instead of any overhead fixture. That better protects you and gives another denial of a breach point. The same lighting design will apply to the inside of your walk-in safe. The only industrial look will be the inside of your bedroom and gun-safe doors. The inside of those doors will show the full locking assembly. We could hide that as well. But the inside of those two doors would look extremely odd and not really serve any purpose. It really is better overall to leave those two locking mechanisms fully exposed."

"Okay, guys, I get the picture. I've two remaining questions. First, how long will this take, and second, how much will it cost?"

It was Jack's turn again. "It will take our crew three to four weeks. I don't know the cost yet, but I want you prepared for mid six figures, probably between $350,000 and $450,000."

"Three weeks is faster than I'd thought. That's a nice surprise. From all you described, the price doesn't seem all that much. I'm hearing that once you're finished, nobody will really notice anything from outside or inside. Am I correct?"

"Yes," replied Paul. "One of our intents and purposes is to have you live as normal a life as is manageable. We don't want you to feel like you're living in a prison. We're just making it more difficult for intruders to gain access to you in your home."

Chapter 27

"The last part of the upgrades we're proposing concern the remainder of your home. We want to install steel doors and doorframes to your front door, back patio door, garage access door, and all man doors in your garage. We'll reinforce all three of your garage's oversized vehicle doors. We want to install ballistic glass in all your windows and apply a protective film on the inside and outside of each window. The film we use is under development by DuPont. Again, our government work allows us access to this incredible material."

"I've never heard of that stuff. It sounds amazing," I told Jack.

Paul picked up the narrative. "You won't see this film on the market for a good ten to fifteen years. It really is amazing. We've applied the film to regular window glass, then shot the glass with a .45 caliber round from ten feet. Didn't penetrate. Shattered the glass but didn't penetrate. By installing ballistic glass in all your windows and adding inner and outer layers of this protective film, your windows will be able to withstand 7.62 mm NATO rounds and all pistol ammunition.

"Repeated hits to the same area of glass will get through, but not fast. And if one area of glass is completely penetrated, all the surrounding glass remains intact. Weakened, but intact. Far more resilient than regular window glass." Paul was really impressed with this stuff.

Just then, Jack's phone rang. "Hey! Good to hear from you… so what's up? Yea? That's great! When? Okay, we can work with that. Very good news, I agree! Okay, see you then.

"Wow! That was Kim! They're releasing her tomorrow. Her healing is amazing her doctors. Everything is checking out normal. They do want to keep her tonight just to observe, but if all goes well, and everybody thinks it will, Kim will be back tomorrow by noon!" Jack had a huge smile on his face as he gave us the news.

"That is so great! I'm really happy for Kim and you guys too!" Okay, I was pretty sure this would happen but had to admit I was relieved. Besides, I was supposed to be surprised, right?

"That's great news," Paul chimed in.

"I wonder if she'll feel like being with us this Saturday?" This was something I didn't know and was probably expecting too much too quickly. But I could wonder, right?

"She mentioned she was looking forward to Saturday, so I'd take it as a yes, so long as she keeps improving or at least doesn't slide backward. She's one to always push boundaries, but this time it might be better if she took it a bit easy." Jack was voicing his concern, and I agreed with him.

"Well, we'll most likely be sitting around most of the day anyhow. The only thing I can think is that she might be advised to avoid alcohol for a while just to give her brain time to fully heal from the trauma. Guess we'll see." I couldn't see all of us running around playing tag or any other silly activity. But who knew what we might get up to?

"Okay, Jack. Get me your estimated cost of the whole security package. I'll get in touch with Angus and see how he advises paying the bill. I've some ready cash but don't really want to take the account to zero. I don't think there will be any issue, but I want Angus's blessing before I give you an absolute answer. Fair enough?"

"Of course. This project should not be taken lightly, although, like I said earlier, given what we know at this point and regarding your particular situation, I think it is a reasonable course of action unless you want to relocate. I just don't see you doing that. Your home and this acreage are amazing.

"It doesn't make sense to have a bodyguard joined to your hip every hour of every day. Even then, going through one person, even one of my people, is a pretty easy solution if somebody nasty wants you badly enough. I'd rather you invest in a robust security system where multiple people respond to any threat that might happen."

"I understand, Jack. And I agree." Saying that did make me feel some better. While the overall design of the safe room seemed like it was way over the top, it would certainly be worth it even if I ended up using it only once.

The rest of Thursday involved Paul doing a sketch of our forest and where to place the cameras, motion and infrared sensors, and pressure plates. Jack and his team believed in a robust defense. My system would be monitored by Jack's team every hour of every day. If any sensor tripped, a red light flashed on the monitor screen watched by a human being. Once any alarm tripped, the monitor had a maximum of ten seconds to decide if the trip was a false alarm or an intruder. If it was a false alarm, nothing happened. The incident was logged, and the video tape was stored permanently.

If the alarm was due to an intruder, one of Jack's staff alerted the police immediately and dispatched a team of two of Jack's armed operators.

Every camera and sensor would be camouflaged or placed deep inside ground cover. The cameras were small enough to fit in the palm of your hand and operated on a low-frequency radio band. Repeaters throughout the property assured a strong signal regardless of location.

The final pieces of my security system included an IFF bracelet and necklace for me, an IFF tag implanted in Kip's left flank, undetectable and untraceable, and an IFF bracelet and necklace for Lu as well as several more to give those visiting. Extras would be kept in my gun safe within my safe room. These IFF tags needed to be worn at all times and were tied to my system so I could keep my security system active, and the three of us could wander in the woods without fear of setting off the system.

Our three sets of tags also gave full GPS positioning in the event any of us was away from home when somebody took a run at me or if Kip or Lu were to be kidnapped or dognapped. Our devices were fully waterproof, so no worries showering or swimming. They were even waterproof to a depth of fifty feet! Sheesh! The things the military had that us common folk knew nothing about. It was amazing! The GPS feature constantly broadcast where we were at all times, and the batteries were supposed to last up to nine months. In Kip's case, his chip would last several years before needing to be replaced. I intended playing it safe and changing all the tag batteries on New Year's Day and on Independence Day. That way I'd know the batteries had not failed.

We wrapped up Thursday night by grabbing burgers and fries at our local Bob's Burgers. Bob's an independent, not a chain. And he is very picky about the food he serves. Bob doesn't do fine dining, but I swear his hamburgers and fries are the best you'll ever eat. He uses some combination of spices and grinds his own burger from chuck and boneless, short-rib beef. His standard hamburger is a six-ounce single or a ten-ounce patty for his monster burger with or without cheese, your choice.

Bob uses a coarse burger grind, which causes two things to happen. First, you're eating ground beef, not beef paste. Grocery-store hamburger is ground so fine there isn't any real beef texture, just beef paste that you fry or grill. A coarse grind gives you a much better bite of beef, and your taste buds will thank you forever. Second, a coarse grind allows those chunks of beef patty to better drain while the patty is being grilled. Next, it's fresh, never frozen, all-American, raised in Montana beef. Finally, Bob grills his burgers over an open flame, not on a griddle. The beef fat drips onto open flames, causing the flames to shoot up and sear the patty. Again, more flavor.

When you marry Montana-raised, coarse-ground beef burger with Bob's secret spices and cook the result over an open flame, well, you're in hamburger Nirvana. Of course, Bob cuts his own potatoes for fries. He has two schoolkids who do nothing but cut spuds for french fries. A couple of years ago, I'd asked Bob how many potatoes he cuts for fries on an average day. He told me on a slow day he cuts more than a hundred-pound bag of Idaho's finest for french fries. Wow! That was amazing!

Like his burgers, Bob has his fries down to a science. They're cut, rinsed three times to get rid of excess starch, then blanched. Next, they're deep-fried for about two minutes, then drained and set aside until they're cooked to order for each customer. He has four double fryers going nonstop every hour he's open. His fries go from being fried and drained directly onto the baskets he uses to serve 'em. His final secret is the oil or fat or whatever that he uses to deep-fry. I've never had fries as good as Bob's.

Nothing ever goes under a heat lamp or holding station. That's just Bob's way. And that's why he is so incredibly busy and successful. That, plus he makes his milkshakes using real high fat, ice cream, and fresh fruit, not fruit-flavored syrups.

I ordered Bob's ten-ounce monster—no cheese, thank you very much—fries, and a strawberry milkshake. Mat had the same, except a blueberry shake. Jack had the same monster burger, no fries, and a Coke, and Paul had a regular burger with cheese, fries, and a chocolate shake. We were all stuffed when we finished eating, but it was a happy stuffed thing.

We trooped back to my place and everybody then headed home, except Paul. I made Kip's dinner, cleaned up, then we relaxed…as much as you could relax when your front and patio doors were plywood with plank bars for door locks. But I was healthy and had a full stomach. Kip was fed. I was lying back in my favorite recliner with Kip acting as my lapdog. God was certainly in His heaven, and all was right with the world. At least for tonight.

Kip and I relaxed like that for about an hour and a half, then I decided it was time to get to bed. Tomorrow was Friday, and I imagined it would hold even more surprises of some sort. As usual, while Kip and I relaxed, I'd absently stroked his nose and that area between his eyes up to his noggin. His sighs and groans told me Kip was relaxing just fine and appreciating my undivided attention. Amazing how loving on my dog could calm and center me. I could feel myself relax as I loved on my pup. He protested a bit when I made him move so I could get up and head to bed. Ever the loving companion, Kip padded along after me, and we both settled in for the night.

Events of the prior days and weeks were rolling around my brain as I lay in bed, thinking it was a miracle I was alive, thanking God for His many gifts, both known and not. Next thing I knew, it was morning.

CHAPTER 28

Kip and I woke at our usual seven the next morning, Friday. I lay in bed for a couple minutes, making my mental list for the day. Needed to call Angus and discuss Jack's system cost. Needed to check with Andy at Finholm's to make sure he remembered my steaks and chicken for tomorrow morning. Also, needed to ask Andy if they had any fresh sweet corn on the cob. That'd go great with our steaks and chicken.

Andy never forgot an order as far as I knew, but I wanted him to know we were still on, and I'd not forgotten him. And I needed to make a list of fresh fruit to get while I was there. Also, I needed to check with Olsen's Bakery to be sure we had rolls to go with our steak and chicken.

I'd spend some time today cleaning house and getting ready for tomorrow. There was nothing I could do about the doors, but I sure could clean the floors, the kitchen, and living area and make sure two of the common bathrooms were clean and well supplied.

I wasn't sure about dessert; Kim was going to bring that. Because she'd been injured and in the hospital until sometime today, I was reasonably sure she wouldn't be making or bringing dessert if she was even able and feeling up to coming tomorrow. So I added dessert to my list: pie from Olsen's.

First, I called Andy at Finholm's. "Andy Garcia, please, in your meat department... Andy! JC Merrick. Calling to confirm my order for tomorrow morning. A dozen rib eyes cut one-and-a-half-inch thick and a dozen chicken leg quarters... Yup... Excellent! Do you guys have fresh corn on the cob? Good local stuff? Excellent. I'll get some in the morning. Oh, probably fifteen ears will do... You will? Excellent! I'll be getting some fresh fruit as well but no idea what yet... They are? Hermiston's? Excellent again! You bet. I'll take two. Is that enough for about ten people? Sure. Hey, thanks, Andy! You're the best!" And we disconnected. Andy's an amazing asset for Finholm's.

Well, that part was easy. Andy already had our steaks and chicken cut and ready for tomorrow. He said they just got a delivery of fresh corn on the cob; truck delivered it straight from the field this morning. Came from the valley, a local grower who always supplied and never disappointed, according to Andy. And yesterday they got in a fresh shipment of Hermiston watermelons. You've never had a watermelon until you've had a Hermiston. Best watermelon in the world, and Andy was picking us two! This was shaping up to be a legendary meal!

Next call was Olsen's Bakery. "Olsen's. This is Trudy."

"Hi, Trudy. JC Merrick here. Are you going to be making your famous dinner rolls in the morning?"

"You betcha! How many do you want?"

"I'm feeding ten to twelve hungry adults, so six dozen? That way folks can take some home. Is that about right?"

"Sure, JC. That'll give you extras for sure."

"Trudy, will you have any pies or plans on making any by morning?"

"What would you like? We'll have strawberry, blueberry, apple, cherry, and strawberry rhubarb as well as chocolate cream, banana cream, and lemon meringue."

"Holy cow! I've no clue! What do you recommend?"

"Our cherry is a favorite. We sell a lot of chocolate and lemon meringue too. Twelve people, right?"

"Yea, about that."

"What about one apple, one cherry, and one chocolate? All your sweet bases will be covered!"

"Deal, Trudy. One each of those. Will they be ready by about ten thirty tomorrow morning?"

"JC, unless you reserve them, they'll be gone by then!"

"Okay. Consider them reserved. Thanks, Trudy. Bye."

Life sure is good when a plan comes together. Trudy said they'd be making dinner rolls early in the morning. Just so you can appreciate a real baker, Lars, Trudy's husband and primary baker, gets up at two every morning, Monday through Saturday. He's in the bakery by two thirty and starts baking all their rolls and breads. Trudy is the slacker in the family. She doesn't get in until 4:00 a.m. and makes all the pies, cakes, and pastries. They open at six and are finished baking by 9:00 a.m. and usually sold out before noon when they close for the day. Their only day off is Sunday. They're a young couple, no kids yet, but give 'em time. They'll make exceptional parents.

Angus was next on my list. "Hey, Angus, JC Merrick here."

"Good morning, JC. What can I do for you this fine Friday morning?"

"Two things, Angus. First, I'm confirming you'll still be able to be here tomorrow for our gathering and food?"

"Yes. In fact, my day has loosened some. I will be there close to 1:00 p.m."

"That's great, Angus! Can I lean on you to teach me how to properly grill the steaks and chicken?"

"Happy to share my knowledge, dear boy. Delighted. Now what was the other thing?"

"Jack, Paul, Mat, and I have gone over Jack's security system plan. It's significantly more elaborate than I'd imagined. The way Jack explained it, I understand much more about what's involved. This is turning into a major expense. It's a one-time cost for equipment and installation, then monthly or annual fees for monitoring. However, they take care of all maintenance, upgrades, and parts replacement. Jack says I need to be prepared for about $400,000, plus or minus a bit. Takes about three to four weeks to install and set up everything. As I said, it's robust. What do you think?"

"That's a lot of money, JC. But. I know you, we've already seen the risk or part of it at least, and we know what's at stake. You've been spending significantly less than you earn monthly from interest on the insurance, so you're already ahead by nearly a million five. Minusing out four hundred will put a dent in that reserve. But it's still well within your budget. The money's fine. We know it'll take the police or Jack's team at least ten minutes to get to you once they're notified. I suspect that cost includes a safe room, yes?"

"It does. How did you know?"

"Well, I know your electronic system wouldn't cost nearly that much. I know it'll take at least ten minutes for help to arrive. That tells me in the event of an intrusion or sensor alert, you need to survive for at least ten minutes. That's a long time, especially if there is a gunfight, more so if there are six or eight attackers or more.

"Here's a couple ideas for you. Why don't you have Jack include some hand-to-hand self-defense training for you? And ask him to give you some training and coaching with your pistol. Those two add-ons might not cost you anything if you ask him to include them both as part of your package. I think there's every chance he'll say yes to both. There's also the added benefit that as a customer, you're more likely to survive long-term if you're more capably prepared than you are right now."

"I like that, Angus. I'll do it. Might even ask him while we're gathering tomorrow. Seems like an opportune time, to me."

"I agree, JC. That's it, then. I'll be there at 1:00 p.m., perhaps a couple minutes later. We can discuss as needs present themselves. See you then!" And he was gone.

I'd only just disconnected when my phone rang. I glanced at the clock; it was just a few minutes before 10:00 a.m. "Hello?"

"Hey, JC. It's Kim."

"Kim! How are you? Are you home yet? Still in the hospital? How are you feeling? What have the doctors told you?"

"Whoa! Slow down, Cowboy! I'm fine. I'm home. Jack brought me home a few minutes ago. Wanted you to know, so thought I'd call."

"Excellent, Kim! What do you think about tomorrow? Will you be able to come? Do you even feel like venturing out yet? You've been through a lot! I don't want you pushing yourself, but would sure like you to be here if you feel up to it."

"Sure. I think I'll be fine to come tomorrow. I'll have either Jack or Paul bring me. Probably not a good idea to drive just yet. Maybe by Monday or Tuesday. I also wanted to let you know I'm not up to bringing dessert. I haven't shopped for the ingredients and just don't have the energy yet for that kind of effort."

"No worries at all, Kim. You're covered. I just ordered pie from Olsen's Bakery. They're the best at what they do. I'm picking up three pies in the morning. So don't concern yourself. Okay?"

"Thanks, JC. I really appreciate it. Okay. I'll see you tomorrow about 1:00 p.m. Looking forward to getting together and meeting your friends! Bye."

"Bye, Kim." And she was gone. Things were definitely coming together. *Thank you, God!*

Now to call Jack and confirm the purchase of my security system. "Jack? JC Merrick here."

"JC! What can I do for you this morning?"

"I'm calling to confirm the order for the security system we discussed. Go ahead. Green light on everything we discussed. If you need any sort of prepayment, let me know tomorrow, and I'll give you a check."

"Thanks, JC. No, I don't need any sort of downpayment. I won't bill you until your system is completely installed and we've verified everything works as designed and intended. Don't worry about payment until then. Besides, we know where you live!"

I could hear a bit of mischief in his voice. I'm sure Kim being out of the hospital had a lot to do with it. "I just talked with Kim. She told me you'd just gotten her home. She also said either you or Paul would be bringing her tomorrow."

"Yup. I'll get her and bring her tomorrow. Happy to do it. Except for looking a bit tired, you'd never know Kim was in a coma until yesterday. Brain surgery! It really is a miracle she's healing like this. Just hope there isn't a downside coming."

"Jack, if it helps, I believe Kim is just healing quickly. I don't think there's any downside or bad surprises on the way with this situation."

"Hope you're right, JC. Anything I can do for you until tomorrow?"

"Nope. Paul is around here somewhere. We're just hanging out, getting ready for tomorrow. I saw him earlier this morning prowling around in the woods like he does. Maybe scouting sensor and camera placement. I'm not sure. Just Paul being Paul. I really appreciate him staying like this. Must be the most boring assignment in his life."

"You know, JC, I've seen some operators become addicted to adrenaline. They need the rush of danger. It's like a drug for 'em. I don't want any of those folks on my team. Eventually, they take chances they should never take. That kind of stuff either gets them seriously wounded or killed or it gets the client killed. No thank you. I know Paul is quite content in this assignment. But know beyond any doubt, he's as ready as a coiled rattler. You couldn't be in better hands."

"Thanks, Jack. It's always nice to hear things like that. I feel safe with you or any of your team around. I'll let you go. Just wanted you to know we're good to go on the security system."

"Thanks, JC. See you tomorrow." And Jack was gone.

Chapter 29

With all my calls made, it was time to do some cleaning. I'm not generally a messy person, so the house was still in pretty good shape from my earlier full housecleaning. I made sure the kitchen and main living area were clean, cleaned the two main bathrooms, and went through the refrigerator to clean out anything that was old or gross. I was amazed! The fridge was already clean, nothing disgusting in there at all. Guess I might be getting the hang of this living alone and taking care of myself thing. Maybe there was life after death.

Paul came in the house, looking like he'd just spent some time in the forest. Come to think of it, he had! "Hey, Paul. Good morning!"

"Good morning, JC. Looks like you're busy getting ready for tomorrow."

"Yeah. Cleaning the kitchen, living area, and bathrooms. Just finished checking the fridge to make sure I pulled anything nasty. It's good to go, with room for the steaks and chicken plus all the other goodies needing to be refrigerated."

I'd never paid attention to my folks' kitchen. Why would I? Up until recently, I'd been very much a self-absorbed teenager. Maybe more responsible than some. But still, a teenager. All of a sudden, I'm growing in my appreciation for things most others my age took for granted. Stuff to which you just don't pay any attention. Like my parents' built-in, side-by-side, dual-door stainless-steel refrigerator.

I'd realized only recently just how much this refrigerator held. It had two doors and was huge. Looked like a commercial model. Mom and Dad bought it because…well, actually, I'd no idea why they bought this monster. It's built in, kinda. I mean it's flush to the counter depth with part of the unit going back into a recessed area behind it.

And the freezer! Same double-door style in stainless. Almost the same size of huge. This thing would hold four or five full-grown adults. I think I could store a full-grown steer in it, whole or cut up, and still have room for a case of frozen pizza and who knew what else.

Both the refrigerator and freezer were installed in an alcove constructed specifically for these two units. Mom and Dad also had the foresight to install dual fans behind these two appliances, circulating air to keep the motors and compressors cool, giving them a longer life. Both appliances were on casters, so I could pull them out completely and clean around, behind, and under them with minimal effort. The whole cleaning process took me about five minutes. Easy peasy when your parents planned ahead, right? Hmmm. Lesson learned.

I was feeling like I should be wearing an apron and have my hair in curlers and wearing a scarf. A scarf! Jeez. Domesticated much? I really needed to find some kitchen and cleaning help! Angus had said he had a few prospects. I imagine Jack's team were checking them out. Maybe I'd find out more tomorrow. There's always hope, right?

By the time I'd cleaned everything I wanted to clean and taken care of other chores, it was 4:30 p.m. Once again, I'd skipped lunch. Just focused on other things and wasn't hungry. Maybe I'd make up for it tomorrow during our gathering. I'd an idea we'd be eating and grazing for a few hours. I was starting to get excited about our event and was especially happy that Kim would be able to attend.

Tomorrow morning, first thing, I'd set up our patio and deck. I'd left it to the last minute to do a weather check. Weatherman said partly cloudy, so rain, probably. Or maybe not. I think they all forecast with darts and a map. In our part of the country, wherever the dart tip stuck indicated dry and sunny. Everything surrounding the dart was cloudy with rain. Seemed as good a forecasting tool as anything the experts used.

"Paul!" I thought he was around somewhere. Time to stop for supper. Now that I had a reasonably well-stocked refrigerator, I'd figure out what sounded good to him for food. After all, he'd spent the entire day looking out for me and prowling the forest. Seemed only right I make him a supper he'd enjoy. Or at least I'd try. I figured cooking was an acquired skill, one perhaps taking years to master. At this stage in my life, I'm a novice's apprentice. But I'd not poisoned anybody yet, so there's some hope!

I wandered into the garage, thinking maybe Paul was in there. At a glance, no such luck. Time to check out the back door. Stuck my head out and saw him just at the edge where the yard met the forest. "Paul. What sounds good to you for supper?"

"Hey! Give me a minute and I'll be in." Paul was studying something right at the edge of the lawn. It was apparent something had grabbed his attention.

"No worries. I'm just cleaning and puttering. I'll be on the patio and deck when you're finished." Maybe I'd get a bit ahead on tomorrow's work. I set off toward the patio to clean the area and furniture. Once there, I discovered only dust. Easy enough to fix.

I went back to the garage and grabbed our leaf blower. Changing the setting to high, I grabbed the start button and pulled the cord. Instant hurricane. Maybe tornado. Take your pick. I had a dust cloud that would make a kid dance in the street. Blowing off the concrete and wood deck took only a couple minutes. Then I attacked the furniture. Should have done that stuff first. Just blew furniture dust all over the concrete and wood, so I cleaned 'em all again. Just a few minutes and all was much better. I'd still wipe down all the furniture in the morning, but now I had a bit of a head start.

Paul was walking toward me, so I met him halfway as I walked toward the garage to put away the leaf blower. "Hey, JC. Getting ready for tomorrow, I see. Pretty fancy duster you have there."

"Why wipe when you can blow and eliminate half of what I'd be wiping tomorrow? Call me inventive or lazy, whatever. Just made tomorrow morning much easier as far as I'm concerned."

"Absolutely. I'm all for tools that save time and energy. You have enough property here to keep you busy every day for the next ten years!

"I've been looking around again for clues about the attack on Kim. I have to tell you there isn't much. No footprints, a few broken bush branches. I suppose Kip could have caused them, but I don't think so. There's a pattern to the bent and snapped twigs. Not a trail exactly, but almost. Between the bushes, grass, and ground, there's enough to strongly suggest somebody was through the area. What I can't figure out yet is how they got from the edge of the trees to where Kim was hit without her hearing or seeing anything. It wasn't normal, that's certain.

"There's nothing on the lawn to suggest somebody walked across it. When I looked at your yard after we'd got Kim loaded in the ambulance and on her way, I didn't see any sign of disturbance in your yard. No footprints, no gouges in the grass. Nothing. I didn't expect anything in the grass, but I did expect to see definite disturbances in the area of your trees and forest. What I found isn't nearly as defined as I expected. Putting what I've found since Kim was attacked together with your original creeper, I think we're looking at somebody who knows how to sneak.

"I just can't figure out how that individual or those individuals got from the tree line to Kim without her seeing anything. It makes no sense at all. Yet. I know it wasn't magic, so I know I'll figure it out. Eventually. Maybe the how isn't important, but I think it is. Once we know the how, we can build a defense against it. Until we figure it out, we're just guessing. I hate guessing."

"Paul, remember we all heard a loud thump before you and Kim went to investigate?"

"Sure, I remember."

"Well, what caused that thump? I mean, it shook the house! Had to be something significant. Whatever it was made waves in my coffee. What I'm saying is, it took a lot of force to make those ripples. We've all been so focused on Kim. Maybe we need to change our focus to what caused the thump or bang or whatever you want to call that noise."

"You're right, JC. We were all focused on Kim once we found her down. Why don't we both go to that side of your house right now while we still have good light and see if we notice anything out of place?"

"Deal." And we both went back around the house to where Kim had been attacked. Looking at that area of the side of the house didn't provide any clues. Paul and I walked the length of that side of the house until we came to the other end of the wall. Standing back, looking straight on, neither of us saw anything.

Purely by chance, I moved a few steps away and looked at the wall from an angle. Something was different and not where Paul found Kim. The difference was about where Paul and I were standing. There was a change in the color of the wall, as if the dust and outdoor stuff that gathered on an outside wall was disturbed, missing. The sun was hitting the area just right, or I don't think it would have been visible.

"Paul, come look at this," I said as Paul moved toward me. "Look along the wall from this angle. Tell me what you see."

"I'll be damned. You're right, JC. It's as clear as daylight. Has to be the light right now. I'd looked along this wall after they loaded Kim in the ambulance. Nothing. But the light was different. Different time of day. This shows up as clear as a photograph."

"Yup. And I'll wager what we're seeing now will disappear in about fifteen or twenty minutes and not be visible again until tomorrow at this time."

"I think you're right, JC. In fact, I'm sure of it. What made you think to look from this angle?"

"Pure chance. I just knew I'd not sighted along the wall, so thought I would. Coincidence?" Or was it another hunch that was more than a hunch? Another gift/curse? Thinking quickly, it didn't seem there would be an obvious way to test this one. About all I could do was pay close attention and see if I was really being guided in some way. Not sharing this yet. No way in the world.

"Paul, am I thinking about this in the right way? What I'm seeing suggests that some force of some type hit Kim hard enough to shove her pretty forcefully from where she was walking or standing into the wall. That would account for her bruise and concussion. It seems to me the height of the dust pattern on the wall corresponds fairly closely to Kim's height. But if that's the case, how did Kim get from this area to where you found her? Somebody carried her?"

"That's a great question. It needs an answer and doesn't have one. What else are you thinking?"

"I'm thinking about where else we've not looked. I want to get a ladder and get on the roof and look at this end of the house. See what I can see from the height of the roof." Saying that, I began walking back to the garage to get our extension ladder.

Chapter 30

Paul followed and gave me a hand getting the ladder and carrying it to the front side of the house near where we had seen the disturbed dust pattern.

"JC, let me get on the roof first. There might be nothing to see up there. Then again, who knows. I've had a lot of experience with heights, so let me go first and steady the ladder from the top. That way, it will be stable for you to climb."

"You talked me into it. I've not spent any time on ladders or heights for that matter. Lead on, I'll happily follow!"

We put the ladder against the eave and adjusted the height so the top was about four feet above the edge of the roof about twenty feet above the grass. That would give us both a decent ladder height to grab at the top to provide some balance as we got on and off the roof. Paul went up first, climbing the ladder like a monkey. Looked to me like he was as comfortable climbing a twenty-foot ladder as he was walking across the yard. It was only seconds later, and he was waving me up.

Taking a deep breath, I started up. With Paul holding the top of the ladder steady, I was up the thing and standing on the roof much more quickly than I'd imagined. Together, we walked gingerly toward the western edge of the roof, approximately even with where Kim, assumedly, was thrown into the wall.

"JC, stop. Don't take another step." Paul had obviously seen something.

"What? What did you find?"

"Take a look at the shingles in front of where you're standing. Look at them and compare what you see to the shingles nearby. Tell me what you see."

"Huh. They're different. Well, they're the same shingles. Same color and such, but these in front of us look newer somehow. Just in this area. Everything else looks the same. Why would somebody replace only a few shingles? Doesn't make any sense. Does it?"

"Maybe, JC. Maybe." Kneeling down, Paul got a close-up look at the area where the newer shingles were fastened to the roof. "Kneel down here and take a look." Paul was pointing to where the new and old shingles met.

"What am I supposed to see? You mean where the lower edge of this row of old shingles is curled up a bit?" Looking at the row of shingles where old met newer on the top run, I'd noticed the lower edge of the old shingles were uniformly curled up, but only in this one area. The difference wasn't dramatic, but it sure was noticeable if you were looking for it. I also noticed along the bottom row of new shingles, right in the middle of that row along the lower edge, there was a bald area of shingle. No imbedded gravel in that area at all. In fact, it was smooth to the touch.

"Did you see this, Paul? Why is this area so smooth? There isn't anything normal about this at all. What are we seeing?"

"You and I need to take a trip to a nearby glass shop. If we hurry, we may be able to get there before they close." Saying that, Paul walked back to the ladder and motioned for me to follow. "You go first. Once you're down, hold the ladder steady for me. We'll get this thing back in your garage, then hustle to a glass shop."

It only took a minute for both of us to get off the roof and down the ladder. I grabbed it, with Paul guiding it to the ground. We had it back in the garage, hung where it belonged, in another minute.

I locked up while Paul made his way to his Jeep. Once we were both belted in, Paul started up, turned around, and we were headed to Gig Harbor proper in search of a glass shop. It seemed that Paul had scouted Gig Harbor earlier. He knew his way around better than I did. We arrived at Harbor Glass just before 5:00 p.m. I still didn't know what he was up to. Figured I'd find out soon enough.

We walked inside and were met by a lady behind the counter. No name tag. She was all smiles and sparkly eyes.

"Hi. How can I help you?"

"Hi. My name is Paul. This is JC Merrick. He owns a home just a few minutes from here. We're in need of a couple different sizes of suction cups to hold glass. Do you have any for sale? Or perhaps we could rent one until tomorrow morning?"

"I'm sorry, we don't have any for sale. Ralph! Get in here for a minute!" It wasn't any time later and Ralph came into the customer area.

"Howdy. I'm Ralph. How can I help ya?" Ralph was an older guy, maybe fifty or sixty. Only had one arm. That arm looked like it could wrestle a grizzly. Maybe a birth defect as his missing arm had something there. Not a stump, more like a tapered upper arm. No idea what or why, but I think he had enough left arm to be of some use.

"Hey, Ralph. My name's Paul. This is JC Merrick. JC owns a house just up the road a bit. We need a couple different sizes of suction cups, the kind used to move glass, install windows, and such. I'm familiar with Woods Powr-Grip…suction cups like they make. This young gal here told us you don't sell them. Could we rent one each of a couple different sizes and bring them back in the morning? We're happy to pay a deposit that would cover the loss if we ran away," Paul said with a grin and a face the picture of innocence.

"What sizes are you thinking? We have about twenty different sizes and configurations. What do you need to lift?"

"That's the thing, Ralph. We're not sure of the weight. I don't think the weight will exceed two hundred pounds. But we've not lifted it yet, so no real idea. I'd say the diameter of the area to attach the suction is right at six inches."

"I think we can help. Come on back and take a look. I've a couple ideas for you." Saying that, Ralph proceeded to walk back the way he came, likely back to the shop area. Paul and I dutifully followed.

"Here's what I have in mind." Saying that, Ralph picked up a pair of suction cups with handles attached at the top. They weren't large, but they were each taller than they were around. A lever at the top of the suction piece allowed for activating the suction function, then releasing it when finished lifting whatever. Seemed to me they'd do the job.

"Those look like they'll work, Ralph. Do you know the lifting capacity of one?" Paul had a definite idea, and I'd finally figured it out.

"Sure. As a pair, they'll lift well over two hundred pounds. They're rated at 175 pounds each. You just need one, not a pair?"

"Right. One will do what we need. Can I give you a $100 deposit? I don't want you feeling nervous that you're giving away a valuable tool." Paul reached for his wallet.

"Not necessary. But I'll tell you what. We're closed tomorrow, being Saturday and all. How about you bring it back Monday morning? Will that work?"

"That works. JC and I will bring it back first thing Monday morning. We appreciate your help, Ralph. Thank you." Paul took the suction cup Ralph was offering. The suction part had a diameter of about five inches, maybe a bit more. I'm not very good at estimating inches and sizes. Not enough life experience yet, I suppose.

We made our way back to Paul's Jeep and headed back home. By now it was closing in on five thirty, still enough light to get back on the roof and do whatever Paul had in mind. I thought I'd an idea, but we'd see.

Pulling into our driveway, Paul parked, and we made our way back into the garage and grabbed the extension ladder again. Carried it to the same place as earlier, and I steadied it while Paul climbed up, again like a monkey. Once he was off and had it steadied from the top, I climbed back up as well.

We walked back to where we'd been standing not very long ago. Paul had the suction cup in his hand and looked again at the area where the newer shingles were fastened to the roof. "Okay, JC, let's see if my idea is brilliant or if I'm an idiot." He was grinning, like he knew the world's oldest secret. "JC, once I get this thing placed and anchored, I want you to lift, but from the top, not directly in front of it. Okay?"

"Uh, sure?"

Placing the suction cup in the center of the smooth area on the bottom shingle, Paul fastened it in place, then I moved to lift. There was significant weight, but the suction cup was holding…and that piece of roof swung up like it was on hinges…because it was! What in the world?

I noticed Paul had his pistol out and pointed at the new hole in my roof. What the…?

"Let's just think about this for a minute before we do anything. What you have is a bona fide intrusion setup. Do you have any idea when somebody could have done this, JC?"

"If it's possible, I'm more amazed than you. I have no clue, Paul. You're telling me somebody reworked this area of my roof when nobody was around and managed to install this trapdoor, cover it in similar but newer shingles, and leave undetected?"

"Well, that's about it. Somehow, that person or persons are probably responsible for the attack on Kim. Maybe she saw something, maybe not. Either way, I think I have an explanation of how Kim was attacked with no tracks across your yard or through your trees and forest. I need to call Jack right now." Saying that, Paul pulled his cell phone and began punching in numbers.

"Jack. JC and I found a trapdoor in his roof. This kid has skills, Jack. He's finding ways to look at things I just wasn't seeing. Hell, none of us thought to look at the roof. Except, JC."

"What? Where?"

"Right on top of where Kim was attacked, the opposite end of that outside west wall. In fact, I think Kim was jumped from above. That's why she didn't respond. You know as well as I that sort of attack is nearly perfect. Only a sixth sense will alert to something happening, but then it's almost always too late to make a difference."

"I also think this trapdoor is the source of the noise that drew Kim and me outside to begin with. The trapdoor in JC's roof is heavy, maybe 150 pounds heavy. If somebody was lifting that thing and it slipped, it'd create a hell of a racket when it slammed shut."

I could hear Jack's reply, "What? What in the hell has JC gotten himself into? I don't want him or you to misunderstand. I'm not saying or suggesting this is his fault. I'm certain there is nothing he did or could have done to cause this trouble. I'm just amazed at the amount of determination these idiots are showing. These guys have some serious stones!"

"Yeah. We need to explore what's going on inside the rafters in the attic. I don't want to go in there without outside backup. Who can you send? Oh, have 'em bring plenty of portable lighting. The attic is likely dark as pitch, and we'll need the whole area well lit to see what we can uncover."

"I'm sending Bobby and Taco. They'll be there with rope, two dozen battle lanterns, a high-res camera with night vision, just in case, and some sample carriers, again just in case. Can you think of anything else?"

"I know this sounds a little paranoid, but can you send Teal too? And comms gear for all of us. That should do it."

"Yeah. I think I can round him up. Are you thinking sniper?"

"Hell, I don't know what I'm thinking! All I know is these guys seem to be two steps ahead of us, and I don't like it. I don't like it a lot. It's been a very long time since we've been in an off-foot position. I think we need to expect the unexpected. That's why I want Teal. If anybody is going to find these asshats in JC's forest, it's Teal. Have him bring his night scope with him as well. If these ass clowns are in the forest, I want 'em lit up."

"He'll be there, Paul. Tell JC, good catch. I knew there was a reason you and I hung around here that extra week. Good thing we didn't take that other gig. Besides, that one just didn't feel right to either of us if you'll remember."

"I remember just fine, boss. I'm glad we stayed too. Okay. Gonna go. We'll hang out either on the roof or at the base of the ladder until help arrives. Talk to you again later tonight." With that,

LIFE AFTER DEATH

Paul disconnected and put his cell phone back in his pocket. "JC, can you think of any time you were away from home for a few days or longer? Whoever put this trapdoor in your roof needed some time to accomplish the work. More so because they couldn't afford to be either seen or heard."

"Paul, the only time I was gone for any length of time was when I was in a coma. I was in the hospital for a month, so that must have been when all this was built."

"That makes sense, but they've waited a long time to use this access. Could be because their hard-entry attempt failed. I don't know. All this is just nuts. Whenever your roof access was built, we're shutting it down now.

"As you heard from my end of the conversation, we've some help coming. They'll start getting here in about twenty-five minutes. Teal will take a bit longer. He's our go-to sniper and overwatch specialist. There's a ranking of world-class snipers. Maybe a dozen at any given time in the real-life arena. These folks don't do it for sport or a trophy. They do it because they can and because it needs doing. They get deep satisfaction from putting an enemy in the ground. Acquiring that level of skill takes thousands of hours of practice, tens of thousands of rounds of ammunition fired over those hours. All kinds of skills to learn. Otherwise, you're just another trigger puller.

"Control your breathing and heart rate. Learn to squeeze the trigger in the gap between heartbeats. Attaining focused calm regardless of what's going on around you. A good sniper can hit a target at a half mile all day long in a variety of weather conditions. A world-class sniper can hit that same target from over a mile. The military record is over two miles in active-combat conditions and without any publicity or medal awarded. Teal is in that league. He's at the height of his profession and at the apex of his abilities. Best thing, he's on our team. Soon he'll be in your forest set up for any intrusion.

"Bobby and Taco are also incredibly skilled. Maybe a couple hundred people in the world as good or better. A couple hundred out of 8 billion dirt huggers. Their primary job is to protect, regardless of conditions or adversities. Not only are they good at it, but they also love the challenge. Like the rest of our team, none of these guys are adrenaline junkies. That kind of operator washes out of our team in about three months if they're sneaky enough to get in in the first place. No. Bobby and Taco have been here as long as me. Nobody I'd rather have watching my back anytime anywhere. I know there won't be any surprises with those two guys guarding the two of us."

"You're saying I'm going in our attic with you?"

"Of course. This is your house. Aren't you curious what's in your attic?"

I'd never thought about it. Huh. "Sure, I guess so? Never thought about it before."

"You'll find all sorts of interesting stuff. How much insulation in your attic. What kind. Any evidence of critters nesting. Any moisture leaks from the roof. Any evidence of the intruders. About intruders, I think there is a very strong probability we'll find evidence of somebody setting up camp in some manner once we start exploring. And we want to watch for any evidence of trip wires or alarms. If I went this far to intrude, I'd damn sure protect my hide with multiple trips. I'd always want to be certain I'd not been found out."

Glancing down the driveway, I could see a Suburban pulling in. I pointed it out to Paul. "Yup, Bobby and Taco are here. Won't be long and Teal, Nick, and Toni will be here too. Let's go down and say hi." And Paul started back toward the ladder.

Chapter 31

We moved to the ladder and climbed down, leaving the roof hatch wide-open. We were walking toward the Suburban just as they were getting out.

"Bobby, Taco, say hi to JC Merrick. This is Mr. Merrick's home and land. Area is just at twenty acres of forest, the house and yard you see here. JC is the beneficiary of an uninvited guest accessing his house through a roof trapdoor installed at some point in the not-too-distant past.

"Young Merrick and I didn't want to go exploring until you arrived with lights, rope, and more weapons. Teal is coming too. Expect him in the next ten minutes. We'll relieve you of some of those battle lanterns and start exploring. By the time we've all the lanterns on the roof, I expect Teal, Nick, and Toni to be here as well."

"Hey, JC." Hmmm. Taco or Bobby?

"Mr. Merrick," came from the other. No clues on who was whom. Figured it would get sorted at some point.

Paul and I each grabbed four lanterns in our left hands and made our way back to the ladder. "Let me get up the ladder, JC. Then hand me your lanterns one at a time. When you're finished, Bobby will hand you more to get to me." Ah-ha. Now I knew which one was Bobby. The other was Taco by default.

I'd handed my four lanterns to Paul, stepped down four steps to get more from Bobby, and moved back up and handed that group to Paul as well. We all repeated the process until we had twenty-four battery-operated battle lanterns lined up along the roof near the hole we'd soon go in to begin exploring.

That was when another vehicle pulled up, and two more got out. Both were wearing combat gear and holding rifles. A guy and gal, must be Nick and Toni. Right behind was another pickup, an older Chevy that had seen some hard use.

Guy got out of the pickup in his thirties somewhere. Maybe six feet or a bit better, rugged looking, heavy, but not fat. Shorter, dark hair, piercing brown eyes, and heavily weathered features. Carrying a long rifle, brutal-looking thing. Definitely not your typical deer or elk rifle. I got a closer look as he approached. His rifle looked like an HK MSG-90, sniper rifle, complete with a silencer and scope. This guy must be Teal.

Paul stepped up. "Teal, say hi to JC Merrick. JC seems to be a magnet for bad guys right now. We've discovered a trapdoor in his roof and are going to explore. You know the background of what's going on here, yes?"

"I do. Hi, JC. Good to meet you, though I'd prefer better circumstances."

Shaking hands with Teal...strong grip without crushing my fingers. Guy used his hands a lot. Callouses, very short fingernails. Hard hands. I expected his whole body was hard and ready to go. "Nice to meet you, Teal. Thank you for coming."

"Teal, JC is surrounded by twenty acres of forest. As you know, he's been attacked. Kim was assaulted here, and JC had a creeper several days ago. Do what you do out there in case we've another unexpected visitor. I'd like 'em captured if you can. If not, light 'em up. Everybody is tired of these idiots."

"Got it." And Teal headed into the trees.

Paul and I went back up the ladder to find out what was going on in the attic. Paul went down the hole first and found a ladder built right in the side of the hole. It was anchored to the underside of the roof with a two-by-four and anchored to a floor joist at the bottom. My guests were nothing if not industrious. It was only a couple minutes later, and I'd handed all the lanterns to Paul. He'd spaced them along the closest joist. Just two joists away, I could see a sheet of plywood lay on top the joists, giving a roomy platform.

The ceiling inside the attic was about three feet near the eave, tapering to about a foot. The pitch of the roof was fairly steep, giving ample headroom once we were a few feet from the eave. I could easily stand up once we moved to the piece of plywood. It was thick enough it didn't bow when we walked across it. Looking closely, I could see there were two pieces, each two feet wide and eight feet long. That's how they were able to get the two pieces through the hole they cut. The hole, on the diagonal, was easily two feet across, probably more like thirty inches or a bit better. Paul and I didn't have any trouble climbing through it, and neither of us was small.

Now it was time to explore.

Chapter 32

By the time we were ready to explore, it was getting close to 6:00 p.m. This time of year, we'd have decent outside light until 8:00 p.m. or a bit later, depending on any cloud cover that came along. I figured we'd be able to explore and find whatever there was to find in an hour or less. Imagine my surprise.

Paul grabbed his flashlight and began pointing the beam into and through the dark attic space. Not seeing anything immediately alarming, Paul squatted down and played his flashlight along the floor joists nearby, looking, I assumed, for any trip wires or alarms. It only took seconds to see the first filament line stretched near the plywood sheet. Seemed to me it was only pure luck that neither of us had tripped it already.

"JC. Do you see that filament line right here?" pointing to the line stretched in front of the sheet of plywood.

"Yup. Your light really makes it show up. I imagine, with one here, we're very likely to find more."

"Count on it. Let me get another flashlight for you." Reaching into his back pocket, Paul pulled out a smaller version of his multi-cell flashlight and handed it to me. "What I want you to do is shine your light around the bottom and sides of this trapdoor and along all the surfaces of the ladder. If I were setting trips, I'd be certain to put at least one on a ladder step and another along one of the ladder uprights. Let's see if these clowns did the same. Whether they did or not will tell us something."

I went to work with the light Paul had given me. Smaller it was, but the light it generated was way impressive. The cone of light was ultrabright. It didn't extend as far as Paul's, but it turned darkness into almost daylight in the area where the light shone.

Sure enough, there was a filament along the inside of the bottom step. Looking at it carefully, I could see they'd not done a good job of the installation. You could put your foot on that step all day long and not disturb the thread.

"Paul. I have a trip wire on the bottom step, but I don't think it will ever activate. It's on the backside of the riser and just below parallel. I don't see how it could be accidentally disturbed."

Paul walked over, and I pointed out the wire to him. "You're right, JC. This one isn't a concern. Did you find any along the uprights or directly under the door?"

"No. Nothing. The handrails are clean, and I don't see any kind of trip or sensor anywhere along the opening."

"Okay. Now I want you to look for infrared beams. You'll need these goggles to see 'em." And Paul reached into his bag again and brought out what looked like swimming goggles but tinted. "Put these on and look under and along the hatch again. We want to be sure we've not tripped some infrared beam of some type."

Hearing that, I put on the goggles and began examining the space just under and along the inside of the trapdoor. After giving it a good look twice and from different angles, I was convinced there was nothing to find.

"Paul, I don't see anything on infrared along the underside of the trap or in the immediate area. Do you want me to use this and start expanding the search area?"

"Yes. Parallel what I've lit with the battle lanterns. If they didn't beam the entrance, it's not likely they've used infrared anywhere down here. Still, let's be safe and smart. The combination of your light and goggles will detect any beam or wire so long as you're diligent. Just keep your head and the light on a swivel."

I started where I was, nearest the eave and slope termination point inside the roof. In time, I'd worked my way all along the inner eave perimeter without detecting a beam of any kind. In my examination, I'd been careful enough to look for any regular trip wires or filaments as well.

The only thing I did notice was that it looked to me like the attic insulation had shrunk. I made a mental note to get hold of an insulation company once some of this excitement died down and have them inspect the attic. Seemed to me I'd benefit from more insulation up here. Thinking about it, I hadn't seen any stains that would indicate leaks in the roof. Another thing I suppose I needed to think about at some point. I'd have whomever I hired as my safe-room contractor take a look and add whatever he or she thought was necessary. They could do that when they constructed my safe room and rebuilt my roof.

Paul had worked the inner area of the attic space and seemed keen in the attic area above the main living room. I made my way over to him to see if he'd found anything interesting. He had.

"What did you find, Paul? This looks like some sort of monitoring station!"

"Uh-huh. If we poked a hole in this Sheetrock, we'd find your bedroom directly below. Look here." He pointed to some clear, flexible tubing and what looked like a fair-sized gas cylinder, like what they used for a portable oxygen supply. The tubing was lying right next to the attic side of a ceiling-mounted light fixture. There was an X marked next to one side of that light fixture housing and a small hand drill beside the tubing.

"We'll take this tank with us, JC. I'm pretty certain this tank contains something nasty. This cylinder is most likely filled with some sort of gas designed to either kill or incapacitate you. Given earlier activities, I'm thinking the gas is lethal. And judging by the dent in the truss, this tank won't be exactly light."

I watched Paul's face redden when he lifted the cylinder and carried it to the trapdoor in the roof. "Is that thing as heavy as it looks? I watched your face turn a bit red while you were hauling it… I could have helped, you know."

"I really didn't want you handling this thing, JC. However, let me get on the roof, and you can lift it to me. Be ready for some weight. This thing weighs close to a hundred pounds."

"Sure." Paul climbed up the ladder, and I lifted the heavy cylinder to him. Paul was right…the thing had to weigh a hundred pounds easy.

"Crap! These guys just don't stop! What's going on, Paul? Why me? What have I done to deserve all this attention? I don't know of anybody who could possibly be this angry with me. This is either a huge case of mistaken identity or there is something going on that I do not understand."

"I understand your concern and frustration, JC. I know it doesn't help, but our team is as concerned as you. Some of the actions of these bad guys are very amateurish. Other actions are as professional as it gets. I don't believe there are multiple groups involved. I think there's one small core group of folks, and they've been both directly involved and hired local idiots to act on their behalf.

"Your initial two shooters were contract. I'd bet on it. You and Kim were tailed and shot at by contractors. Kim was taken out, almost permanently, by a principal, I think. What we're looking at here is elaborate enough for me to think the same person or another in the core group is directly involved. It takes a serious commitment to do this to a target's home.

"I can assure you, if I were as committed to your demise as it seems these folks are, I'd just bomb your house. You've a main-line gas feed into your home. If your termination is the goal, just rig an explosive to your gas line. It isn't subtle, but neither were the two guys who were breaching your front and back door. No. I'd just blow your house and call it a day.

"That makes me think. We need to put sensors on all your gas appliances and along your main gas line. Do understand, JC, we're with you on this. Jack and I have talked, and I know he's talked with Kim as well. None of us can figure out why you're a target. You're seventeen! You haven't lived long enough to create this kind of enemy. If you were a drug dealer, even a supplier, they'd hit you in an entirely different manner. Guns in the street. Have eight or ten guys knock your doors down with AKs, maybe a grenade launcher to make a loud statement. Bomb your pickup. Assassinate you when you were out with Lu, or run you off the road on your way home. Any of that would make more sense than this.

"I gotta tell you, JC, this is starting to make me cranky. We're all, in our group, pretty mellow. We've learned to be relaxed and easy until it's time for action, then we go full-on. That's the only way to describe it. We go from mellow to lethal in one move. Whatever is going on here is just stupid, but with purpose.

"I know Jack's working with you to vet some candidates you're considering hiring to help you around here. I think, and I'm going to talk with Jack and Kim about it...I think it would be a good idea to seriously consider recruiting former military for your hires. There's a lot of retired military who are in their midthirties and up who are retired from an injury or just recognized it was time to move on. They could be a good fit for what you're seeking.

"Many are on some sort of pension or disability, full or part, and looking to use their skills in a very different setting, similar to what you're looking for. Some'll have cooking as a hobby and may be pretty good at it. Military life gave them multiple skills besides bringing hell to our enemies.

"Vets tend to be very well organized. They pay attention to detail. They'll be self-disciplined. Depending on their MOS, they'll be capable of self-defense and combat. Some will be extremely capable. A surprising number are unattached, yet crave the stability of a life lived in one location, a home if you will. They seek family but are not marriage and family material, at least not yet. They've seen too much. Done too much. Too many skeletons in their closet. Maybe someday, but that day is not today or in the near future.

"Military life moves you around all the time. In its own way, it's a good thing. You get to see parts of the world you'd never visit as a normal citizen. It's bad because many of those places are cesspools of misery and suffering. But not everybody is assigned to those locations.

"Military police come to mind. As a group, they're pretty level-headed. But they're the guys and gals sent in to break up bar fights between, say, Seals and Delta or Rangers and Green Berets. An MP is a damn tough individual, and their jobs can be unimaginably difficult, fraught with military politics. When that life gets to be more than the individual wants to deal with, they move on."

"Do you see what I mean? That kind of individual might be ideal for you, near and long-term. You may well end up wanting the protection of a bodyguard sort of person, someone with other skills as well, to be here permanently. The more I'm describing this to you, the more I'm convinced if we find a good fit, there are more benefits to you to be had than in hiring a civilian."

"Think I'm agreeing with you, Paul. Let's look in that direction as well. At this point I'm not ready to kick out a normal, but from what you've said, it makes very good sense to look at the pool of former military or regular law enforcement."

Paul continued, "Let's visit with Jack about this during our gathering tomorrow. For now, let's wrap this up. I don't think anybody is going to climb inside your roof tonight. I'll put Taco up here to make sure. And I'll arrange for Teal to stay on overwatch until we're finished with our gathering here tomorrow. In fact, let's keep overwatch until your system is installed and running. We can rotate Teal and Bobby. I've trusted both of 'em to watch my back in the past and never questioned my decision. I want to keep Nick and Toni as rovers and creepers in the forest."

"Hey. I'm game for whatever you suggest. You're the expert, not me. I'd also like you or the best instructor in your group to teach me about pistol and shotgun shooting. You know, techniques and tips, so I'm better than just proficient. And I'd like some serious training on self-defense. Had either of my earlier intruders made it to me, even without a weapon, I'd have been seriously screwed."

"We can teach you shooting, JC. But because it's an acquired skill, it is also a perishable skill. If you want to become very good and keep that edge, you need to be willing to commit to shooting every week and plan on putting a minimum of one thousand rounds downrange every month. If you're shooting a pistol and shotgun, I'd recommend two hundred pistol rounds and fifty shotgun rounds per week."

"Wow! I didn't realize. Takes that much?"

"Yes. You can become skilled with half that amount. And that might be enough. Everybody has a certain aptitude for things. Part of that aptitude is the ability and willingness to participate at a consistent rate every day or every week or every month. But if you shoot fifty rounds of pistol ammunition a month, you'll never be better than competent and maybe borderline at that.

"You'll be amazed at how fast you'll run through a hundred rounds of pistol ammunition. As you become more proficient, you'll find it easier and more enjoyable, and you'll run through your ammunition faster. I've seen shooters go from complete novice to experienced in only a few months. Their ammunition usage jumps from fifty rounds a session to over two hundred or more. Regardless, when your attention starts to wander, it's time to stop pulling the trigger. At that point, you're just wasting ammunition."

"Well, I'm excited to begin learning. I might need to unlearn some habits, and I'm willing to. Mostly, I want to feel secure and know that I can protect myself, regardless of the situation. Right now, I don't have that sense of inner security."

"Got it. We'll need to get you permitted for concealed carry. Not an easy process in this political climate and state. No worries, we'll get you there, JC. There is a justifiable need for you to be armed, based on the attacks on you. Plus, there is a police record of your home invasion. That'll serve you in your application. First, let's get through this weekend. I want to get in your attic from inside your house.

"I'll do that Sunday. Get that thing screwed shut so no suction cup in the world will lift that trapdoor. We'll add sensors in your attic as we install your security system. I'll get to Jack tonight, so he's aware. We'll have folks around your property tomorrow during the gathering. Jack and I will be armed. Kim too, but we're not counting her. All our outside team will be armed and armored. Kim is our last-line person for now, just in case the rest of us fail. Know that's never happened. Ever.

"We'll keep one sniper outside with three of our guys creeping your forest. Two more on the outside perimeter of your home.

Taco on your roof. One in your garage coordinating everybody and the three of us in your home during your gathering. We'll all be on comms until your gathering dissolves. Then we'll cut back and keep one sniper, one outside rover, one inside as coordinator, plus Kim or me, and Taco or Bobby on your roof. That'll stay until we either engage or have your system up and running. We might keep two in your forest until you've hired capable staff and have them on-site."

"Crap! That sounds like war!"

Paul continued, "It is, JC. Right now, we're engaged in a skirmish with an unknown adversary of unknown size and skill. Every one of our people can take on one opposite number of equal skill, and the worst we'd do is a draw. That's enough time for the deputies to arrive. If your opponents are at least one tier below us, we can defeat twice our number, even adding one or two more bad actors. Again, long enough for help to arrive.

"If we're able to add you as one of our shooters, our odds of success go up, as do your odds of survival. You move from a soft target status to hard target status. That's way good for our side. But by the time you get to that level, we'll likely be gone, and your team will consist of you and your staff. That's why I'm thinking of retired military." I was hearing that Paul had given this a lot of thought.

"Yeah. That's coming through more and more. So retired military folks enjoy gardening, clearing brush, cooking, and cleaning, among other tasks?"

"More than you'd think. Most retired military really are normal folks, JC. We'll obviously eliminate those who don't want to do domestic and those addicted to the rush of combat. Not at all good choices for you. Some retired military folks suck at normal life. But there is definitely a group who will thrive in a quasi-domestic setting. Like you, they're willing to learn and have some innate aptitudes and interests. It doesn't take a lot to learn how to get pretty damn good at any domestic skill, especially if you already have an interest. A lot of them will bring skills, even at a hobby level, with them. A hobby level skill set can be sharpened pretty easily if there's a willingness and desire to learn.

"Remember, there's a whole different type of satisfaction to be learned and enjoyed in accomplishing some forestry management skills, cooking skills, and such. People can learn to appreciate the hard work and accomplishment in creating and serving a special meal, in designing and creating a new landscape project, or whatever. The wider the net we cast, the more candidates we'll capture. The more we capture and vet, the better our chances of finding your ideal matches."

"That makes sense, Paul. I'd rather take longer to fill a position and end up with a great fit than fill the position quickly and give up half of what I'm looking for. Does that make sense?"

"Absolutely," Paul replied. "As a bonus for you, Jack, Kim, and I have many contacts in the military, as do others of our team. We'll begin getting in touch with our contacts on Monday. I think we'll have a great pool of folks to begin to vet before the end of the week. This group of folks will be easier to check out as well. We'll be able to gain access to most of their military files, talk with their former COs, and even talk with some of those they served with. Naturally, you'll have the final say, but I'm convinced we'll be able to present some excellent candidates."

Now it was my turn. "I'll want Angus to sit on the personal interviews and I think Jack and Kim if we can. I don't mean any offense, Paul, none at all. My thinking is it might be a bit much for a candidate to sit before Angus, Paul, you, and Kim with me hovering in the background as an unknown observer. If you guys don't think that's too much, then by all means you're included. I figured Jack because he has a definite command presence, and he's black. I wanna see if that throws anybody. If it does, they're out.

"I want Kim because she's a woman, obviously. She's attractive and young. I wanna see if any of the candidates focus on her to the exclusion of Jack and Angus or if they pay attention to whomever is asking the question. I also want Kim, if she's agreeable, to dress to distract if you get my meaning. Nothing obvious or flagrant, just some subtle suggestion. My goal is to find those paying attention to the purpose, not somebody trying to score. Does that make sense?"

"You are devious, do you know that?"

"Maybe. I want our final selection to be right for all the right reasons. I have my own BS detector, but I don't trust it completely. At least not yet. And Angus is a definite must for me. He can smell a turd buried in a two-foot pile of fresh-cut roses. Then I suspect Jack and you and Kim can as well. I want to see how often, if at all, everybody comes to the same decision on any of the candidates.

"Talking with you right now, I'm changing my mind. I want you included if Jack agrees. Let's see if the four of you intimidate any of the candidates. If they're that soft, I'm not interested. Besides, you'll be another set of eyes and ears to gauge the fit of the interviewees into what I'm looking for. Ideally, I want unanimous yes decisions on every hire. I've an idea for three staff, maybe four. I'm kicking an idea around and think it might be a lot of fun for the fourth. We'll just have to watch and see."

During all the talking the two of us had done, we'd gathered the electric lanterns and cylinder of pressurized whatever-it-was and brought all of it to and out of the hole in my roof.

"Hey, Bobby. Will you help us haul all this all down the ladder?" Paul started to hand down our gear as Bobby climbed partway up the ladder.

"You bet." Saying that, Bobby set his weapon on the ground and climbed midway up the ladder. I handed all the items to Paul, and he handed them to Bobby, who in turn handed them to Taco on the ground.

Taco caught each item as Bobby dropped them to him. It only took us about three minutes to have everything off the roof and on the ground.

Paul told Bobby to take special care with the cylinder, acknowledging it might well hold poisonous gas of some sort. Once we were all on the ground, there was the question of what to do with the mysterious cylinder.

"Bobby, will you put this in your ride? Make sure it's secure. I've no idea what's inside, but I suspect it isn't pleasant. Get it to our lab for testing. Make them aware the contents could be particularly nasty, so they need to take every safety precaution. Full biohazard setup in their pressure chamber. If my hunch is right, just one whiff of this stuff might be deadly. Then get some rest tonight. Be back at first light?"

Saying that, Paul handed the cylinder to Bobby, who put it in a hard case with a gasket seal running around the lip. He then latched the six hinge clamps and secured the case against the floor of the pickup bed with three heavy, ratcheted straps, two running across the short front-to-back surface of the case, the other running side to side, all tightly ratcheted down and fastened to inset rings in the bed of the pickup. They'd obviously done this sort of thing before. These guys really were prepared.

"Once you have this to the lab, head home. I'll keep Teal in the forest as well as Nick and Toni as creepers. I'll be here too and spell Taco on the roof about 2:00 a.m. We already have extra comms gear in case we get an extra guy or two. Okay?"

"Paul, why don't you stay inside tonight? I'm fine on the roof until morning. Give me a couple hour break around six, and I'll be good until after the get-together. By then, you and Jack will have a firm game plan. Teal will need a couple hour break by morning as well, then we'll be back on task and set until tomorrow night."

"You're sure, Taco? I'm happy to spell you."

"Naw. There's a nice pitch up there and a hip corner just right for sighting the forest, the one up against the chimney. It'll keep me invisible from the back side in case anybody gets creative, and it'll give me decent cover if I need it. I'll have my NVGs on. Teal and I can signal each other without breaking comms."

"Okay."

"Bobby, get out of here. JC and I are going to take down the ladder."

"Teal, you up?"

"Talk to me, Paul."

"We're taking the ladder down and storing it in the garage. Taco's on the roof tonight. I want you two guys taking care of each other. I've no idea if things'll get interesting tonight or not, but we're done with easy. You need anything before we all settle in?"

"I'm good. Brought my favorite granola and a water bottle. Found an excellent hide. They'd have to step on me before they find me. Even then, they'd get only a maybe before I owned 'em."

"Perfect." Paul continued, "Nick and Toni are creeping the forest. All our guys on-site have their IFF tags on, so you can see who is where. Everybody except Taco is on the ground until daylight. Then either I'll switch with you or somebody else will. Maybe Bobby. I'll talk with Jack in a bit, and we'll figure out a plan for the rest of tonight through the weekend. I'll let you know when I know. Make sure everybody's broadcasting IFF tags. No tag means hostile."

"Perfect. I'm silent until morning." With that, Teal was gone. I assumed his comm was live. He just wasn't talking.

Paul went on, "Toni. Did you get that?"

Toni's reply was a click in my earpiece, already comms silent. One more time, I was impressed with how these guys worked together. It was seamless.

"Nick?"

Same click in my earpiece. Our players were where they needed to be. I was feeling more secure.

"Okay, JC. Let's get this ladder down and get it in the garage." Saying that, we grabbed the ladder and lowered it and carried it back in the garage. I'm certain Teal had a good view of the area. The sun was in the process of going down. Dusk. Almost time for Teal to go to his NVGs. I was already picking up their acronyms. NVGs was military speak for night-vision goggles.

"Alright. That's done. Let's get inside, and I'll let you impress me with your cooking, JC. Let's see just how much help you need!" he said with a grin on his face.

Paul didn't suffer much. I put two potatoes in the oven after I'd washed and poked holes in 'em. Learned the hard way that potatoes explode and create a horrible mess when you bake 'em without poking holes in 'em first. Jeez, what a lesson that was!

I'd bought some pork chops at the store earlier, so I seasoned two with Johnny's salt and put 'em on the grill on our stove.

CHAPTER 33

My kitchen stove was another purchase made by Mom and Dad. The unit had eight burners and a center grill section with a downdraft vent that ran across the entire backside of the stove. That way grease and smoke didn't set off every smoke alarm in the county. I'd set 'em off earlier in my culinary adventures and never wanted a repeat of that experience. Those alarms ringing hurt my ears! Seemed like it took an hour for them to shut up. Probably didn't, but sure seemed like it.

Anyhow, along with the baked potatoes (you can't screw up baked potatoes unless they explode or they're undercooked or exceptionally overcooked; yeah, I'd made all those mistakes too) and the pork chops, I had fresh asparagus and figured that stuff had to be pretty easy to cook. And there were a variety of grocery-store cookies for dessert. I've not tried to bake anything. That'd come, just not likely this year. I had five varieties of cookies, vanilla ice cream, banana popsicles, and fudgesicles. Fudgesicles and banana popsicles are the best!

"Paul, do you know how to cook asparagus? I've never done it but figured it can't be seriously hard."

"Sure. First you soak and rinse the spears really good. Sand likes to hide in the heads of asparagus. Then you snap the butts. The bottom part of an asparagus spear is tough and will never be tender no matter how long you cook it. Some people leave the butts on. I snap 'em off. Give a few of the butts to Kip. See if he likes 'em. Some dogs do, some don't.

"Then get a pot large enough to lay the spears in, horizontal, unless you have a pot designed to cook asparagus. I've seen those pots but never thought it made sense. Those things are a one-use design. Unless you are an asparagus fanatic, just use a regular pot but one big enough you can lay the snapped spears horizontal. It's okay if they lie on top one another.

"Use just enough water to cover the spears. Get your water boiling, then add a couple teaspoons of salt. Then add your asparagus spears and cover the pot. Then you watch the water in the pot until it starts to boil again. Then turn off the heat and let it set covered for two or three minutes, depending on the number and size of spears you're cooking. Your asparagus will turn out al dente or cooked but still a bit crunchy. That's how I like it. If you cook it longer, the spears get very soft, then quickly, slimy. Not good, at least not good for me. Might as well buy the stuff in a can. That's about it."

"Sounds easy enough. Baked potatoes are in the oven. I think they need about forty-five minutes. I set the temperature at 375. Is that about right to get the skin crispy?"

"Sure. Sounds good to me."

"I got out two pork chops. Finholm's had thick-cut ones. Andy said they were really good, so I bought some. I sprinkled Johnny's salt on both sides, so I'll put those on the grill when there's about fifteen minutes left on the potatoes. Sounds like the asparagus doesn't take long, so I'll have the water ready to go at about the five-minute mark. Does that sound okay?"

"Sounds like you have a plan. I'm prepared to be amazed!"

"We'll see. Remember, I'm seventeen. Haven't had much experience cooking. Since Mom and Dad died, I've had to cook for myself. I like to eat... Well, I like food, really. I figured if I wanted to eat decent food, I'd need to learn to cook. Mostly, it's been trial and error. Like exploding a baked potato in the oven and way underbaking them and baking them until they turned into hockey pucks.

Learning curve. But I'm not dead yet, so I must be making some progress, right?"

"Seems like. What did you make for dessert?" he said with a very sly grin.

"Huh. Not me. Finholm's. Cookies, ice cream, fudgesicles, banana popsicles, and that's it. I've got regular pop, diet pop, iced tea, fresh orange juice, and water."

"You're doing fine, JC. I'm impressed! Any beer in the house? Oops, don't answer that. Like you said, you're seventeen."

"Yea, just because I'm emancipated doesn't mean I can buy alcohol. Then again, I've never tried. Can't imagine the amount of paperwork, court dates, and hoops I'd have to jump through to legally buy alcohol! I've never had the stuff, so I don't even know if I'd like it."

"Well, let me tell you, the first time you work hard outside in the summer heat for an entire day, then go inside and have a cold bottle of beer, nothing will ever compare. At the end of a day of hard outside labor, that stuff is nectar of the gods. Hands down. Other than that, meh. Just isn't the same. Still tastes good and all that, but it's not the same. Did your folks drink? Alcohol, I mean?"

"Some. I've never seen my folks overindulge or even get tipsy. Dad liked beer. Mom liked red wine. I've had sips, but that was a few years ago. Nothing since. Couldn't see the big deal. I know kids who drink like a fish. Kids younger than me. They're already hooked and not even out of school. What a waste of a life."

"It can be, JC. It can be. Most of life can be lived extremely well if you remember moderation. Too much of anything isn't good for you. I don't care if it's water. Too much can kill ya. Damage your kidneys and do all sorts of other damage. Mind you, we're talking about an awful lot of water but water just the same."

While we'd been talking, supper was cooking. The oven timer had just chimed, so it was time to add the pork chops to the grill. Already seasoned and the grill hot, each one sizzled as I placed them on the grates. I checked the asparagus water. Looked ready to me; so when I flipped the chops, I'd drop the asparagus in the boiling water.

I was pretty excited to see if this would be an acceptable meal. If not, there was always Bob's, right?

Rummaging around in one of the kitchen drawers, I found our temperature probe, a Thermapen. To make sure the meat I cooked was safe, I'd jab the pen in and get an instant reading on internal temp. Pretty handy gadget. I didn't want to poison Paul, so I'd jab the two chops when I thought they were cooked to verify their internal temp.

Just a few minutes later, I dropped the grass in the boiling water and covered it with a glass lid. Turned the chops and we were almost ready. I watched the pot of water. Took only a couple minutes for the water to boil, so I shut off the heat and let it sit. Poked both chops with my probe. Internal temp showed 162, so I knew they were ready. I'd read somewhere that meat continued to cook for a bit even removed from the pan or fire, heat, whatever.

So I plated the chops, dug butter and sour cream out of the fridge, found part of an onion, and quickly diced it. Another plate for the asparagus to let it drain. Pulled the potatoes from the oven and slit each one so we could add butter, sour cream, diced onion, and salt and pepper. Pulled the asparagus from the pot and plated it, added a wad of melting butter, and we were ready to eat.

Paul and I decided to eat at the island. Pulled out a couple stools, grabbed the salt and pepper, napkins and glasses of ice water, and we were ready to go. "Is this supposed to be finger food?" Paul had a smile as he said it.

"Nuts! Forgot utensils. Sharp knives and forks, right?"

"Yup."

Pulling them out of a kitchen drawer, we were finally ready to eat. "Well, don't hold back, Paul. I'll not learn if you suffer in silence. I need honest feedback if I'm going to learn."

We began eating, first in silence, enjoying our meal. "Remarkable, JC. You did a really good job with everything except the asparagus. It's just a bit overcooked. See how the spear bends under its own weight? Not so crunchy. Like I said earlier, asparagus is tricky. One minute less in the pot, and your asparagus would have been perfect. It's still good, just not al dente.

"Lots of good stuff in asparagus. Only downside I've ever found is it makes your pee stink. No idea what chemical reaction causes it, but the first time you pee after eating asparagus, you'll notice a definite difference in odor. Then it goes away. I like to think its pulling toxins out of your kidneys, making you healthy. Absolutely no idea if there's any truth to it, just something I like to think."

Didn't take us long to clean our plates. "Pretty good, JC. Not bad at all for a seventeen-year-old guy. Did your mom teach you anything about cooking?"

"No. I really didn't show any interest. Both Mom and Dad were good cooks. They traded off some. When Mom knew she'd be later than usual, Dad would cook. Otherwise, Mom was usually home first. She left for work at four thirty every weekday morning, so had long days that normally ended earlier than traditional. She liked to get an early start and be ahead of traffic. Then she could get home for a nice family meal. Dad was more traditional. He was on the way to work a bit before 7:00 a.m. and usually home by five thirty. That was just normal for our family. Sometimes Mom came home early, sometimes pretty late. Dad was the same. But their extralong days didn't happen often, probably less than once a month."

Supper was over, and we'd cleaned up and put the dishes in the dishwasher. Time to run it so it'd be ready for tomorrow's assault.

"I think I have everything organized for tomorrow, Paul. I've written my list of what and from whom. Would you take a look at it and see if I've forgotten anything?"

"Sure. Let me call Jack first and bring him up to speed on what we found today. See if he has any changes to our plan for tomorrow." Saying that, Paul pulled his cell out of his pocket and started punching buttons.

"Jack? Paul. JC and I went exploring. You already know about the trapdoor. Bobby, Taco, and Teal got here pretty quick. Toni and Nick got here just a few minutes later. Teal was and is on overwatch. He'll stay out until after daylight. Didn't see or find anything. Taco and Bobby were on the roof while JC and I explored. Once we were finished in the attic, I sent Bobby home. I've kept Toni and Nick for overnight creeping.

"The cylinder we found is like a small-ish portable oxygen tank. Whoever it was had set up right next to the ceiling light in JC's bedroom. There was a hand drill with a small bit attached, rubber tubing, the portable tank, and that was it. Oh, they'd marked a spot with a red X, probably where they planned to drill the hole. Looked to me and to JC like that tubing would have been mounted flush with the ceiling drywall inside his bedroom. It would have been hidden pretty good by the glass shade of the light, virtually invisible day or night.

"Bobby took the canister to our lab folks. Told him to be sure they take every precaution. I'm pretty certain the tank contents are nasty. We should know by tomorrow. Bobby'll be back in the early morning. Taco's spending the night on the roof. He found a great spot where, when it gets dark, he'll be invisible to everything except infrared. Teal says he's in a perfect hide. Those two guys have line of site on each other. They're in place until daylight tomorrow. Then I'll pull Teal and Taco, get 'em fed and a few hours' sleep.

"Everybody's on comms, but quiet, just in case. We're all broadcasting IFF, so no friendly fire issues involved. Bobby can spell Teal, and I'll spell Taco early. And we'll get Nick and Toni rested when you arrive with more help in the morning.

"This is nuts, Jack. I really want this place locked down for tomorrow's event. I'd be happier if we had two or three more of our team from midmorning through the overnight. Whoever's behind this isn't screwing around. Finally, I'm hoping we'll find out what's in that cylinder by midmorning. I don't have a good feeling about the tank contents.

"Oh. One more thing. JC and I were just running thoughts, and I think we need to monitor the hell out of his gas line. It would be far easier to just blow the house with JC inside. All this sneaking around is dangerous for them. Much easier to just blow the house, right? Easiest way is through a gas line leak. Hell, I've used that trick back in the day, if you'll recall. Makes a mess, but it's effective, and I doubt these guys care about leaving a mess. Whaddaya think?"

I could hear Jack's reply, "You're right, Paul. I added that to our system yesterday, but it's still good the two of you thought the same thing. I don't think we can be overly aggressive with this. We still need to remember to keep the system simple, not overcomplicate it. The best systems are elegant in design, robust in features, and completely reliable. That's our goal with JC's system.

"You did good, Paul. I think you'll all be okay tonight. We both know Taco and Teal are rock solid. Nobody is getting by them without serious consequences. Adding Nick and Toni was a great idea. With that much coverage in the forest, I think you'll all be fine.

"Those extra eyes give you plenty of time to get JC well covered. You two can sleep tonight. Teal, Taco, Nick, and Toni can get a few hours down time in the morning. I'm bringing three additional for the gathering: Dave, Connie, and Belle. I want them on the perimeter of the group during our festivities. I'll introduce them to the group so everybody knows what's going on. Had a brief chat with JC, and he approves. This is too important to keep hidden from those close to him.

"I also want to talk to the group and make them generally aware of what's going on. I suspect the stitches on JC's arm will generate questions from his friends. Perfect opportunity to make them aware. It feels like JC is holding something back, and I suspect tomorrow he'll enlighten us all. At least, I hope so. That kid doesn't need to hold back on serious stuff, and this is about as serious as it gets. Anyhow, I'm hopeful."

"Jack, there is one more thing. Again, while JC and I were talking about all the crap that's come his way of late, maybe we want to expand his search for appropriate help. You know, the folks he's considering hiring. We thought it might be a good idea to check with former military. We all have some strong contacts in that community. We can vet those folks much better than a civilian, and if we pick wisely, we'll find a few who could provide another layer of security. Being a bodyguard would be part of their duties, but certainly not all. Whaddaya think?"

"I like it. You and JC did good. I'll start making calls when we're finished here."

"Okay, this is the last thing for sure tonight. JC wants instruction on self-defense weapons and hand-to-hand combat. Says he's tired of, in his words, waiting for something to happen. I think it's a great idea. He already has a passing acquaintance with pistols. He had good instinct with his shotgun even if it was designed for birds. Told him I'd run it by you, then let him know. Your thoughts?"

"Of course, I think it's a good idea. He's already gone through the trauma of taking a life face-to-face yet. That's not easy, as we both know. The first time you kill a human being, regardless of the circumstance, changes you forever. Some citizens, I've even seen military personnel so changed they never recover. It's almost like they lose a vital piece of themselves.

"It should bother, taking another life. But done to defend yourself or other innocents, it shouldn't incapacitate. But sometimes it does. Regardless, I believe if he's interested, we can certainly accommodate. We might even have Kim be his instructor for everything once she's fully healed and ready. Until then, she could certainly give him some good pistol instruction. Yea, I like it. Let's grab Kim and have 'em both talk at some point. See what the two of 'em think. Kim can keep JC humble if he strays. It's a definite ego bruise when a young guy gets thumped by a woman like Kim."

"You can be a devious bastard, Jack. You know that, right?"

I could hear a grin in his reply, "Yup. If we do this, I don't want JC getting all macho or a swelled head. I don't think there's much danger, but I want to be certain. You know how some guys get when you put a pistol on their belt. They get all John Wayne and Rambo invincible. We know it's a load of crap. But early on, most of us thought we'd grown armor for hide when we had weapons in our hands. Didn't take long to disabuse us of that notion. I want to get that out of JC before it has a chance to germinate."

Paul replied, "Absolutely. I have a hunch it'll be a nonissue with him. He's way more mature than his age suggests. I know lots of fully grown, supposedly mature adults who don't stack up to this kid. Working with him, it's almost like he's a peer. In fact, he is in very many ways."

"You're not wrong. Anyhow, let's put this conversation to bed for tonight. I'll start making some calls to find staff candidates. You guys wind down. Tomorrow's going to be busy. Should be fun, but there'll be some tension too. We need to watch and gauge how his friends, even Angus, act when we tell them all this stuff." And there was the dial tone.

"JC, Jack likes the idea of getting you some training on hand-to-hand combat and weapons. We'll talk about it tomorrow. Between now and then, why don't you think about what you want to accomplish in self-defense and weapons training? There are all sorts of goals you might have. I don't want to plant any seeds here, so I'm not giving you any examples. Just think about what you want as an end result. Keep in mind that both disciplines take dedicated training if you're going to achieve significant results. Okay?"

"Sure. I've already been thinking about it. I'll definitely do more between now and our get-together tomorrow. I'm kinda excited for everybody to be here. This'll be the first gathering or party or whatever I've ever hosted. Didn't do any of this when Mom and Dad were alive. There were birthday parties and holiday gatherings, but those were different, ya know? This is my first, so I'm nervous a bit."

"Relax, kid. I've looked at your list. You've thought of everything. One suggestion, get heavy paper plates, not regular ones. Less likely for the plate to fail. Besides, paper plates make clean up a whole bunch easier. Big plates for the meal, sturdy enough to stand up to a sharp knife. Smaller ones too so people can get chunks of fruit or whatever. That's really the only suggestion I have. Plastic utensils are good too, so long as they're sturdy. That flimsy, cheap stuff cause more frustration than they're worth. They're pretty useless for cutting steak. But they do make sturdy disposable flatware. Let's check Finholm's tomorrow while we're picking up all your goodies."

"Good idea, Paul. Thanks!"

Chapter 34

Paul and I moved to the living area. I was in my favorite chair when I heard Kip's nails clicking on the hardwood floor as he made his way to us. A quick look at me and he hopped up and wiggled into position. Paul sat on the sofa, so we were basically facing each other as we continued talking about one thing and another, just winding down for the night.

Kip was lying across my lap, his head on my chest, his considerable self giving an occasional sigh or grunt of satisfaction. He was such a wonderful companion. I figured with Kip beside me, I could take on the world and gladly suffer whatever the consequences. Just scratching his ears, petting his nose and head, patting his butt, I could feel myself relax and let go of tension I didn't even know I had.

Paul watched us with interest. "Kip's definitely your dog, JC. You two are bonded for life. I've watched him look at you, study you, really. There's complete acceptance and adoration of you from him. He'll lie out there in the forest and watch what you do. A lot of dogs aren't so devoted."

"Well, it's pretty mutual. Even when we brought him home for the first time, he picked me. I mean, he paid attention to Mom and Dad. They were food sources after all. But I think his primary focus was me for some unknown reason. I've never been sure if he's just curious or if he's kinda guarding me, ya know? Especially given what's been going on recently. He's not exactly clingy, but it seems he's paying more attention.

"Would you like me to turn on the TV, Paul? I don't normally watch it. Usually, I'm occupied with a book or magazine or on my computer or phone or just hanging out with Mom and Dad. We didn't spend a lot of time with television, except the local news and an occasional movie. But I'm happy to turn it on and see what's available if you'd like."

"Naw. I really need to go through the house and check all the windows. Look into the yard and see what I can find. Hopefully, and probably, nothing. Still, needs to be done. Feel free to do what you normally do. Don't let me interrupt you. Remember, JC, I'm your employee, not your guest. You're not obligated to entertain me. Don't feel bad not paying attention to me. Remember, my primary function is to protect you, not be entertained by you. Okay?"

"Sure. I get it. Even makes sense. Just feels odd, that's all. I've never been around bodyguards before. It's different. In this case, in a good way. I appreciate what you and everybody else is doing to protect me. Has to be completely boring for you. I know I'm a pretty dull guy. No sparkle or flash in my life. To be honest, I'm feeling a little lost by this whole process, like I'm a spectator in my own life right now. It's odd. Not sure I particularly like it, being not in control."

"JC, I've met a lot of people in my career and life. Thousands. Military, nonmilitary, from all manner of backgrounds. A lot of them, most, are more boring than watching paint dry. You, Mr. Merrick, are far from boring. Whenever I look at you, I see the wheels in your brain turning. It's true you're not the life of the party. Nothing wrong with that. In fact, lotsa folks prefer those not the center of attention. Those around the center of attention get exhausted. People who are always on are tiring. They never stop, never rest, never let another share their ideas and thoughts. They are the center of the universe in their minds. If you don't believe it, just ask 'em. They'll launch a lecture at you, guaranteed to put you to sleep."

Paul continued, "I remember my grandmother. Now there was a very wise woman. I was young, maybe seven or eight thereabouts.

Seems like it was yesterday. A room filled with older adults, but who isn't old to a seven-year-old? Anyhow, I was running my mouth for no good reason. I'd interrupted some conversation, and my grandmother reached and got hold of my arm and pulled me to her. She said, 'Hush, child. You don't learn anything when you talk. God gave you two ears and one mouth for a reason.'

"I've always remembered that lesson. You've learned it too, JC. I've watched you. There are so many reasons it's hard, challenging, really, to remember you're seventeen, not forty. Don't go getting all cocky on me. I'm not telling you this so you'll get a big head. I just want you to know you're a hell of a distance from boring."

"You've nothing to worry about, Paul. I've nothing to get ego-y about. We've already talked about my inheritance. Right now, it's a burden if you want the truth. I mean, what in the world am I going to do with all that money? I could give it away, and I've thought about it. There's a ton of causes, organizations who would benefit from that size of gift. But that idea doesn't feel right. Just like it doesn't feel right to go out and buy a dozen Ferraris. That just isn't me. I like cars, and I've an idea on that. Probably talk to Angus about it tomorrow in really general terms. Get his thoughts. For now, I'm still thinking.

"There's a ton of people and kids who are way smarter than me. Lu is one of 'em. Mat and Kyle too. Lu is wicked smart in hard sciences. She challenges her instructors pretty regularly, and what she says is right. Not opinions but hard facts. Like I said, off-the-charts smart. Mat's gifted with computers. That kid'll end up inventing, writing, or developing multiple things in the next few years and earn a truckload of money doing it. I expect by the time he's thirty, he'll have more money in the bank than I do. And I'll be happy for him. I'm blessed to have him in my life.

"And there's Kyle. The guy's a complete brain. Quiet. I don't think he ever stops thinking and examining. He's interested in studying law, and I know he and Angus have had a few conversations. I believe Kyle's going to get his law degree and do equally amazing things in his own career.

"As far as money's concerned, it's just a tool. I've heard some folks say it's a way of keeping score. I don't see the need. Those people are so busy comparing their wealth to that of others. It's just stupid. Their focus is wealth and how to get more. Their focus should be how they can serve humanity.

"It's easy for me to say this, I have more money than I'll ever spend. It's what can be done to help others that's the source of joy, not money. It's just a tool, like a hammer or screwdriver. People don't go around bragging about their hammers and screwdrivers, right?"

I was definitely on some sort of roll. "You know, stupid is a choice. It's deliberate. Dumb is a condition, not a choice. Dumb can sometimes be fixed by introducing knowledge. Stupid is knowing better but doing or acting poorly anyhow. Stupid. I'm dumb about all the things I don't yet know. But I can learn. Learning makes me less dumb. I have a fair degree of common sense. Common sense. That stuff can't be taught, at least not much. It's learned, maybe more an idea about learning.

"I'm in no danger of growing an unhealthy ego. I'm barely hanging on to what little ego I have now. I'm overwhelmed by all the stuff I don't know. Now in the situation I find myself, the stuff I don't know could get me hurt or dead. All because I don't know stuff. Makes me very humble."

Paul was staring at me. "Wow. Think it's time for me to go and check windows, locks, and gander outside for a while. Why don't you relax with some easy reading? Get your mind closer to neutral for a while. Unwind."

"Kip is doing that for me right now. He's my source for relaxation, and he's an expert at it. Thanks for listening to me rattle, Paul. I appreciate it. If you need me, I'll either be here or in my bedroom."

"Thanks, JC. Sleep well." And Paul got up and walked toward the hallway and bedrooms.

Kip and I sat there, in the quiet. Kip was asleep, his soft, occasional snores telling me he was utterly relaxed. My mind, as usual, was going about a hundred miles an hour. All sorts of thoughts. I wanted everybody to have fun tomorrow, enjoy the day and our gathering. I was a bit nervous having this event, hosting it. There was some pressure, self-imposed, to have this be smooth and enjoyable. There were the conversations I hoped to have with Jack and Kim. I wanted that to go well and not sound like an idiot. That was on my mind. I wondered how Kyle, Mat, and Lu would react to my being shot, to having an intruder, to killing two people. That would be a shock to them, and I had no idea how they'd react or what they'd think of what I'd done.

Most of all, I wondered what they'd make of my ability to heal others. Would I even tell them? I thought so, but my resolve was a little shaky. I'd already gone over this in my head. I'd already decided sharing would be selfish on my part, then changed my mind. Countless times already. I was still unsettled about the whole thing.

I glanced at the clock and saw it was past 11:00 p.m. I'd been riding my indecision merry-go-round for over two hours. All I'd really accomplished was to put a knot in my stomach. Time would tell soon whether I'd even sleep tonight. Sleep had become a sometimes event. Kip and I would see what this night brought.

Gently shaking Kip, I said, "Hey, buddy. Time for bed." I got a groan for my effort. Gently got hold of the ruff of his neck and shook it a bit. "Hey, buddy, time to go outside and pee. Then let's go to bed. Okay?" Kip raised his head and looked at me as if to say, "You woke me up to tell me to go to bed? You are sooo human." But he roused himself.

I let him out to answer nature's call and sniff around. He was back in a few minutes. I let him in and locked up, and we made our way to the bedroom. I got undressed and in bed, and Kip hopped up and lay beside me. Wow. He rarely got up on the bed at bedtime. He's usually by my side but on the floor or wandered to a different area of the house. This was unusual for him. I didn't mind, that was for sure. Only thing, he lay so his head was pointed at the door with his butt more toward my head. Never slept with a dog's butt before. Hmmm.

I'd always slept with my bedroom door open. With all this security stuff going on, I might have to rethink that. Maybe I'd ask tomorrow.

That's the thought I had when I fell asleep. Next thing I knew, the sun was up. Kip was gone. Time for me to get up too. I looked at my watch and saw it was already 7:00 a.m. Big day today.

Chapter 35

Saturday morning, just past 7:00 a.m. Time to shower and get ready for the day. Got dressed, worked on my hair, without much success, and headed down the hall to begin what I hoped would be an excellent day. Kip was sprawled out on the floor by the sofa, one of his favorite places. Raising his head to see I was up and moving around, he stood, gave himself a good shake, and ambled toward me in the kitchen.

Teal was sacked out on one couch; Taco was slumped in my recliner, and Toni was sleeping on the other sofa in the living area, near Kip. From Paul's side of the phone conversation with Jack last night, I expected more of Jack's people would arrive this morning, likely in a while. For now, I'd let these guys sleep. I suspected they'd had a long night.

I'd just made coffee when I heard somebody stirring. Teal had his head up, then up popped Taco and Toni. So much for my being quiet. Then again, maybe it was the coffee. "Scrambled eggs, bacon, and toast? Coffee?" A chorus of yeses. "Give me about fifteen minutes, longer if you need it. Bathrooms are down the hall if you want showers. You know where the powder room is." Time to crack some eggs.

Right on schedule, fifteen minutes later, I had an audience of three hungry bodyguards and a platter of eighteen scrambled eggs with tomato, sour cream and onion, bacon, a pile of toast, and a pot of coffee ready for 'em.

Each grabbed a plate and fork and started shoveling food from the platters. I had placed strawberry jam and grape jelly on the island too, and each made short work of loading up. Minutes later, I was making a second pot of coffee, this time including a cup for myself. Helped myself to the remaining egg, a couple slices of bacon, and some toast, and I, too, was ready to go.

"Thanks, guys, for being here last night. Kip and I had a good night thanks to your keeping us safe."

I was met with nods from everyone, mouths still chewing the last of their breakfast. "Happy to do it, JC," this, from Taco.

"Good breakfast," was Toni's comment. And a grunt from Teal's full mouth.

Time to prep more food for those still outside. Another eighteen eggs, more bacon, and toast. The inside crew went out, and in came the rest of the team. "Good morning! Help yourselves to eggs, bacon, toast, and coffee."

"What a guy! And he cooks too!" Nick said as he, Paul, and Bobby came inside, while Teal, Taco, and Toni went out and carried on. This last group loaded their plates for breakfast and grabbed cups of hot coffee.

"I need to head out in a bit to pick up the food for today's get-together. I stopped my pain meds yesterday, so I'm good to drive. No sense disturbing you. I'll leave about 9:00 a.m. Should be back in an hour or so."

"Not gonna happen, JC. We're here to protect you, not your house, right?" This came from Nick. "Paul will drive you to pick up your food."

"This really is hard to get used to. I'm feeling like an invalid."

"No, you should be feeling protected. Safe. That's our job, and we can't do it if you're out driving around by yourself. We'll get you knuckled up in no time, then you'll be much more prepared to be on your own." This was Bobby this time. I was feeling tag-teamed but in a good way, I suppose.

"Okay. I can see I'm outnumbered. What you're saying makes sense, Bobby. It's just there's this part of me that feels invulnerable, you know? Like I'll live forever regardless. The rational side of my brain knows better, but that indestructability is still there."

This time it was Nick. "Sure, kid. Everybody feels that way, and in part it's a good thing. Let's us do things we'd not otherwise do. But you have to know your limits, or you can die quick. Right now, and this isn't picking on you, you're a very soft target. Luck's been on your side so far, but never trust luck.

"Skill counts, and right now you don't have any. We'll fix that. Paul talked with us last night and this morning. You're a smart kid, JC. We all think you'll catch on quick. We need to plan and develop your skill set. We're all glad you're willing to learn, and we think you have a certain aptitude for what we're going to be teaching you. Give yourself some credit. Be patient, and listen to what we teach. You'll do fine, probably much better than that, truth be told."

"Paul, you're planning on driving me this morning? Only two stops to pick up food, Finholm's and Olsen's Bakery. That's it. Should be quick. How about we leave in a half hour, say, right at 10:00 a.m.?"

"Sure. Jack might get here before we're back, but that's okay. He knows what's going on and can brief everybody whether we're back here by then or not."

I set about cleaning up after breakfast. Stuffed the dishwasher and turned it on and wiped down the counters and island. Put things away. Seemed like only minutes later and it was time to go.

Paul and I took off in his Jeep. I figured the back of that thing would be stuffed with food in no time. First stop, Finholm's.

We went inside, and I found Andy. True to his word, he wheeled out a grocery cart filled with two Hermiston watermelons, a dozen beautiful rib-eye steaks, twelve chicken leg quarters, eighteen ears of sweet corn, a stack of thick paper plates, and heavy-duty plastic forks. "Here you go, JC. Everything's there. The knives I've included will cut the steak and chicken just fine. I've already put everything on your account, so you're ready to go."

"Thanks, Andy. I need to get more eggs, and we'll be out of here. Thanks again!"

"Nuts! Ice, Paul. We need ice!" I grabbed another grocery cart and piled two twenty-pound bags of ice in it. Along with the eight dozen eggs we'd just picked up, we were now ready to check out and get to Trudy's. Just a couple minutes later, we were loading everything in the back seat of the Jeep.

"Now to Olsen's Bakery! Best part of the whole meal coming up!" We climbed in the Jeep, and Paul headed to Olsen's.

Trudy greeted us and had a small grocery cart loaded for us. "Everything's here, JC. I put in eight dozen of your favorite dinner rolls, two loaves of white bread, three of whole grain, a dozen cinnamon rolls for tomorrow morning, and the three pies you ordered. Lars says those pies are the best he's ever made, and you know Lars. Let me know what your guests think, okay?"

"You bet, Trudy. We'll have this cart back to you in just a shake." I pushed the cart to Paul's Jeep and found space in the back seat. That area was now officially stuffed. I took the cart back to Trudy, paid the bill, and headed back to Paul's Jeep. Climbing in, I heard a distinctive nearby whine, like a ricochet.

Paul shouted, "Get in!" And we were headed out the lot before I had my door closed. Paul didn't drive straight across the parking lot but drove erratically, then exited toward home. We were both hunched down as Paul raced along the street. Glancing at his rearview mirrors, Paul sat up straighter but didn't slow down. We approached the turnoff to my road, and Paul took the corner as fast as he dared in the Jeep, and it seemed, seconds later, he was pulling in the driveway. He parked as close to the house as he could get.

Pulling in the drive, I saw Jack's H1. Good. Jack and Kim were here, maybe others. Paul hustled me in the house, leaving the groceries in his Jeep. "Jack! We've had a sniper. Olsen's Bakery. Maybe three minutes ago. Nobody hit."

"These guys are ridiculous! You okay, JC?" Jack had worry lines showing in his face.

"I'm fine. Happy their sniper is a lousy shot. The shot hit the pavement about a foot from me. Had to be at a side angle 'cause the bullet didn't come my way after it hit the pavement. This crap is getting old."

"At least you two are okay. Are you having second thoughts about your gathering today?" I could see Jack was watching me closely.

"No. We might eat inside. That'll reduce our exposure to these jerks. Other than that, I'm not willing to change my life. I know I have to think of the safety of my friends, and I am, and I will. But I won't be intimidated or live my life like a hermit. Right now, I'm going out to the Jeep and bring in the food for our event today." Saying that, I headed back toward the front door and Paul's Jeep. I was as mad as I'd ever been, and I swore that I'd become a warrior, one extremely capable of defending myself and those important in my life.

Walking out to the Jeep, I thought Kim looked good. She had staples in her scalp above her hairline, where they'd had to cut a hole to relieve the pressure from her brain swelling, but I could see it healing, not red or swollen. I was still amazed she was here, given how recently she was attacked and in the ICU. Her color was almost normal, and her smile was as radiant as ever. She didn't look as tired as I'd expected. Back to her vibrant self, or almost.

Bringing the groceries in held no drama. Nothing happened, and I was grateful. Once all the goodies were inside and put away, Jack introduced me to more of his team. "JC, here are the folks who'll be here today keeping you and your guests safe. Meet Dave, Connie, and Belle. Guys, meet JC Merrick. His folks died several months back. No siblings or other living relatives. We're in JC's home and forest."

"Hi, Dave, Connie, Belle. Good to have you here, though I apologize for the need." Dave was about forty and had short light-brown hair and brown eyes. He was about six feet tall and slender, like a runner. His face was neutral, neither friendly nor otherwise. I got the sense he held all his emotions in a very tight rein. His handshake was firm but not crushing. He'd nothing to prove, and he knew it. I liked him instantly.

Connie looked a bit younger. She had short medium-brown hair and brown eyes. Connie was a little shorter than me, about five feet, eight inches slender, and had a smile that went all the way to her eyes. Her smile said friendly, but her eyes said folks tended to underestimate her abilities. Connie exuded casual confidence. Just the girl-next-door type, you'd think. I believed you'd be wrong. In the presence of a bad actor, they'd be dead wrong, or so my hunch told me.

Belle was altogether different. She was about Connie's age and had almost black hair and pale-blue eyes. Her hair was worn in a ponytail. Belle was a bit shorter than Connie, about five feet, six inches or so. She was stockier than Connie. I was pretty certain Belle's stockiness was muscle. I could tell by the way her clothing fit and the way she moved and held herself, she'd spent serious time in some form of martial arts discipline. It was obvious she'd dedicated thousands of hours to her training. Like Jack, she moved like a predatory cat. Belle exuded raw, deliberately focused power.

It was obvious why they were part of Jack's team. I had nothing to fear with this many folks protecting us today. Didn't realize I'd been so tense about this event, but seeing the rest of the team Jack brought, I could feel tension easing away.

Of course, Kip was right with us, making his introductions as well. He gave each of the three a polite but focused sniff. They all passed, and Kip sauntered over to me and promptly lay down on my feet, his signal all was well with him, and he approved of our new guests.

It was closing in on noon, so I went to the kitchen area and began prepping the food. Seasoned the chicken and steak, separating steak and chicken on their own sheet pans, covered the pans with plastic film, then back in the refrigerator. Cut the butts off the corn so they'd be easier to peel when cooked. Washed the watermelon, dried 'em off, then proceeded to cut off the rind and cut up the melon meat in fork-sized chunks, putting the peeled chunks in two large stainless-steel bowls and returning 'em to the fridge.

I set out the paper plates, a tall pile of paper napkins, four sets of salt and pepper, butter for the corn, and the heavy-duty plastic knives and forks. I'd set everything along the long outside edge of the kitchen island. The island was big, twelve feet long and just over four feet wide, lots of room to place the food and set it up like a buffet line. I'd found an extralarge steel bowl able to hold all ears of our cooked and shucked corn, a couple platters where I could stack the grilled chicken and steak, and a large cloth-covered basket for maybe eighteen of Lars's dinner rolls. The rest of the rolls would find their way home with some of my guests and friends.

There was plenty of room for each of the pies. I'd noticed Trudy had already cut each pie into eight slices, saving me the trouble and mess I'd doubtlessly cause. I found three pie-serving spatulas and placed one beside each of the three pies. Everything was ready, waiting for my friends to arrive, and I was a bit ahead. It was a quarter 'til one. Paul would be here soon with his green salad. There was plenty of island room for it.

I'd brought a portable cooler in from the garage and washed it earlier. And I'd already cleaned all the patio furniture. I grabbed the two bags of ice from the freezer and dumped both into the cooler. As I was getting bags of ice cubes from the freezer and dumping them in the cooler, Jack and Dave went out to the H1 and began bringing in cases of pop.

"Holy crap! How much pop did you bring?" It looked to me he bought out the store.

Jack grinned. "Well, I didn't know what everybody likes, so I brought some of each. Coke, Diet Coke, Pepsi, Diet Pepsi, ginger ale, orange soda, and root beer. Figured that'd cover all the bases except water. I know you already have that."

Jack and I got busy, and soon there were six cans of each pop flavor nestled in the cooler of ice. I knew we'd be refilling both the ice and pop. Should've put this outside so I could drain the melted ice water more easily. "Jack, will you help me move this to the side of the patio? That way, I can drain the water and add more ice as it's needed."

"Good thought. I should've thought of that too." We each took an end of the cooler and carried it outside, where draining it wouldn't bother anything.

Walking back inside, I heard another car pull up. I saw an older-model beige Toyota. Lu was here, and my heart beat just a little faster. I was walking toward her when Mat drove up with Kyle in the passenger seat.

"Hey, guys! Thanks for coming! Welcome to our gathering. Almost everybody's here. This is great! Lu, what are you getting out of your car? Can I help?"

"It's nothing, JC. I just thought everybody might appreciate some vegetables, so I made a veggie platter and ranch dip to go with it." Saying that, Lu brought out a huge platter filled with fresh mushrooms, radishes, broccoli, cauliflower, a couple different sliced summer squash, asparagus, and a couple things I'd never seen before, all nestled around a large center bowl of dip. "Let's get this inside, JC. Then I can get rid of the plastic film, and we can snack!"

"Thanks for bringing this, Lu. I really appreciate it. This goes perfect with what we're having." I moved ahead of Lu and held open my plywood door.

"What's this, JC?" Lu asked, looking at the destruction of my front door.

"One of my new fashion statements, Lu. Seriously. Along with the broken pane of glass on the side here, I'm trying to give the house more of a distressed look. Whaddaya think?" It was all I could do to keep a grin off my face.

"It does not suit you, Sailor. Does not suit you at all. What's really going on? And what happened to your arm? Are you okay?"

"All will become as clear as mud in just a bit. Patience, grasshopper, patience."

Just as we were walking in the front door, two more cars arrived. I knew from the large Lincoln land yacht Angus was here, all attired in his grilling apron! I didn't know the owner of the Porsche 911 Turbo that pulled up right behind Angus. Interesting. Ohhh. Ah-ha! I knew Dr. Church had style, just not this kind! She had evidently followed Angus here. I imagined separate cars just in case Doc got called away on some emergency.

Excellent! Everybody was here, and I introduced everybody to everybody. Interesting that none of my friends mentioned Taco on the roof. Then again, maybe not so much of a surprise.

"Everybody! Make yourselves at home. Grab a plate and help yourselves to anything except the pies! They're for dessert later on. We'll be grilling steaks and chicken. Well, Angus will be doing the grilling. I don't want to tempt the food-poisoning gods. We're likely to eat within the next hour or so."

I remembered that earlier I had picked up a variety of crackers, and there was still a good bit of summer sausage in the fridge. Seemed like a good idea to get those out as well. I went in the pantry and found four varieties of snacking crackers, poured each of them in their own bowls, and put them on the island.

Then I looked through the fridge and found the summer sausage and a couple of chunks of different cheeses. Got those out and sliced up a good bit of each on another platter I'd found and added them to what was already there. Amazingly, the island was about to get crowded!

"Let me introduce everybody to everybody! When I call out your name, just raise your hand." I proceeded to call out everybody's name. That way everybody could associate a name with a face or at least close.

Once all the introductions were made, Angus came up to me. "JC, let's get those steaks out of your refrigerator. Put them on the counter just here, and let them start to come to room temperature. Doesn't do to burn the outside of a good steak, any steak, before the inside gets warm."

I pulled the covered steaks out of the fridge and put them where Angus indicated. "Chicken too or just the steaks?"

"Just the steaks, JC. Raw chicken has more bacteria. No. Raw chicken can turn quickly. Wouldn't do to give everybody food poisoning, would it? You had the steaks cut just right. Two inches is more challenging to grill. Lots of distance before you reach the center. One-inch thickness gets easily overcooked. Inch and a half is just right. Easy to cook to order without making the outside dried out and tough."

I could see our gathering was off to a good start. It looked like everybody was making themselves comfortable and engaged in conversation with my friends. I could also tell that Lu, Mat, and Kyle knew something was up, as did Angus and the doc. They didn't know what yet, but they'd find out in a couple minutes.

"How about everybody that wants something to munch or drink gets it now? I have a short story to tell and some things to share. Then I'll want us all to discuss if you're willing. Basically, I'm looking for some help and guidance from you all. Just don't be too disappointed if I don't take the advice you offer!" I said with a smile on my face and in my voice. Once all the plates had goodies piled, I began.

CHAPTER 36

"Thank you all for being here. Kyle, Mat, Lu, I'm not sure you've met Angus Dunbar. He's my attorney and friend. Angus is also my mentor and confidant. He introduced me to Jack and his cast of characters. I know you've not met my doctor. Phyllis Church has been my doc since before I was born. I'm privileged to count Dr. Church among my close friends."

"Please, JC, when we're away from a medical setting, call me Phyllis, or Phyl...with a *y*."

"Uhhh, that doesn't feel right. At least not yet. Would it be okay if I keep it to Doc? I mean this in the most complimentary way... Hope you know that."

"Okay. We all have a deal, right, everybody?"

A chorus of "Sure," "You bet," and "Absolutely" followed.

"Jack, Paul, and Kim are, for lack of a better description, my bodyguards. Lu picked up on the stitches in my left arm. I've learned I have an enemy or two. I've no idea why or how this happened. Summary, I've been shot at a few times and recently had my home invaded. That's how I got all these lovely stitches in my left arm. You've noticed my fashion statement front and back doors. What you see is the result of that same home invasion, as are the stitches in my left arm. Replacement doors are being made now. With the help of Jack and his team, I'll be turning this house into a fortress in the next month or so. Not to worry, everybody here is always welcome, although I suggest you call first to make sure I'm not under siege when you get here… I'm joking!

"Seriously, you're about as safe here right now as I can make it. There are bodyguards in the woods on patrol, a sniper in the forest, another on the roof, and three prowling the backyard and forest in that direction. I'm determined to keep us all safe today and beyond. Any questions so far?"

Of course, Lu was first, "When did this all start, JC?"

"Seems a lifetime ago, but truthfully, it's only been about a week."

"What do these people want from you?" Kyle asked.

"Kyle, I have absolutely no idea. I've been thinking on it since this whole thing began, and I haven't one clue."

"How long do you intend keeping your security force?"

"Mat, they'll be here at least until my security system is installed and tested. Then we'll take another look and reevaluate what's going on."

"JC, why don't you tell them your plans about bringing on staff?" Good of Angus to think of this and keep us moving forward.

"Yes. I've decided this place is just too much for me to manage alone. I love this house, forest, and overall location. I've no intention of selling or moving. Ever. As of now, I have to assume the people who are determined to do me harm have no intent of quitting. That's why I've hired Jack and his company to install a security system.

"However, even the best security system available today leaves me pretty isolated until help arrives. We've measured the response time for the police. It averages ten minutes. That can easily be a lifetime when people are shooting at you.

"This is the first time Angus is hearing about this part, so, Angus, please feel free to jump in anytime. Jack and some of his team and I have discussed hiring former military to come on staff in domestic positions. Basically, one person for cooking, cleaning, and helping me be more organized, like a *major domo*. Another hire will help with the outside work and probably add one more. Managing a twenty-acre forest is not all that easy, especially if I want it to become more park-like and less wild. There's landscaping, upkeep on the exterior of this house, managing the forest and other trees, and so on.

"Rather than train a cook and gardener to be semibodyguards as well as domestic help, I thought it made more sense to find former military who also enjoyed the domestic tasks I have in mind. I might not find anybody who fits, but I think it's a good place to begin. I can always change if needed."

"JC, this is a good idea you and Jack have." I could see Angus already buying into this thought. "I think it's an excellent place to start."

"Why are you telling us this, JC?" As usual, Kyle was asking a great question.

"Two reasons, Kyle. First, you, Lu, and Mat are my closest friends. I didn't want any of you to just stop over, see all the demolition and construction, and have to tell each of you individually what was going on. It feels like I've already told this story more often than it needs. You should all know you are welcome here at any time.

"Second, everybody in this room right now is as close to family as I'll likely ever have. I'm tired of rattling around in this house. I do intend hiring. The sooner the better. I wanted you three to know first, so if I have somebody on staff and you come over, you'll already be aware, and it won't be strange or awkward. Make sense?"

"What's the demolition you mentioned?" Lu was a curious one, and I appreciated that about her.

"Part of my security system will include, for lack of a better term, a safe room. A place where I can go to survive until the police and/or Jack's team get here. As I just said, ten minutes is a long time in a gunfight. Sometimes, it's a lifetime."

Then I took a deep breath. Here we go. "I had to kill two men when they attacked me in this house about a week ago. It was that or let them kill me. I hate that it happened, but I didn't create or invite the situation. All I did was protect myself and Kip. I have to live with taking those two lives for the rest of my life. I regret what I had to do, and I never want to do it again. I hope that situation never happens again, but I need to be prepared, just in case. And I'm grateful to be alive."

"Jesus, JC!" Kyle looked really surprised. "You must feel awful."

"Surprisingly, not a lot, Kyle. I'm grateful I survived. I'm grateful I had my wits about me, and I'm just plain lucky the two guys weren't pros, or I'd be dead."

I glanced at Lu, afraid this would really bother her, that she'd think less of me for what I'd done. All I could see from her, in this moment, was sadness. Not quite sure what to make of that, but I was concerned.

"There's something else. Something I've not told any of you. I'm not sure I should tell any of you. Part of me thinks that by telling you, I'll be putting you in danger. But I also think you're in some danger whether you know or not. However, knowledge is better than ignorance, right? So here we go."

My audience consisted of Jack, Kim, Paul, Angus, Doc, Kyle, Mat, and Lu. All of them very precious to me.

"Most of you know me well enough to know I don't do dramatics or thrive on drama. Quite openly, I don't like it. But…if I share what's happening to me, I have to know you'll keep it to yourselves, that you'll keep my secret.

"If this gets out in the world, my life will never be the same. I'll be forced to move, never see any of you again, and live on some mountain or on some island, spending my days gazing at my navel lint. I'm serious! This is as serious as anything you've ever experienced in your lives or likely ever will. You can't tell your parents, spouses, kids, or workmates. Nobody.

"With that as a condition and knowing I need a unanimous decision before I tell anybody, what do you say? If anybody isn't comfortable keeping this secret or just can't keep a secret anyway, say so now. I'll keep quiet, and life will go on. I'll not think less of anybody if they want out. Seriously. What do you say?"

Angus looked at Doc, then Jack, and the three of them looked at one another and at my friends. Kim looked around, as did Paul, reading the room. Then one by one, each of them looked at me and nodded. That was my signal to proceed.

"Are you sure? Absolutely sure? Don't take this lightly, ever. There is more riding on your decision than you know, especially right now. If you've any doubts, now's the time to say so."

"Jeez, JC! We're your friends already! Except for Jack and his crew, we've known you for years! We knew you and your parents. We knew you when they died, and we stood by you. We were there when you died and never gave up hope! You think whatever this is will deter us? Keep us from being friends? Okay, we're more than friends, yes? You said it yourself. We're family. That goes both ways, Sailor. Remember that. Get over yourself and get on with it already!" Lu did have a way.

"Anybody else?" Had to say it that way, didn't I?

Chapter 37

Taking a deep breath, I began again, "This is going to sound like I'm making it up. I assure each of you, I am not." And I proceeded to tell everybody in the room about my ability to heal. I told 'em about the robin, the foxes, and the Danvers family. They just looked at me, didn't say a word, so I thought I'd drop the final bomb.

"Jack, Paul, you remember Kim being hurt and being in the hospital, right? You remember my insisting that I go see Kim just a couple nights ago when she was in ICU. How we had to practically threaten Nurse Ratched to let me in for five measly minutes? Kim, do you remember me visiting you while you were in ICU?"

"No, I don't, JC. You were there?"

"Yup," came from Jack. "Paul and I took him to see you. JC was adamant that he see you. Hmm, that would have been this past Wednesday night."

"This past Wednesday? Like, three days ago?" An astonished look was on Kim's face.

"Yes. Right, Paul?"

"Yup."

I jumped back in. "Well, I did visit, Kim. I held your hand for about a minute. Told you that you were going to be alright. As I was holding your hand, I knew everything would be good. I knew as certainly as I know anything this would be so. With Karen Danvers, I hoped, suspected. All I had was a strong theory at that time, formed by a robin and foxes. Karen, too, didn't remember me or anybody with her. You don't remember. There's a pattern here."

"Jesus, JC! What are you saying, really? Are you saying you heal people by just touching them? This is crazy!" Kim was getting upset.

"I'm sorry, Kim. I didn't mean to upset you. That's the last thing I want to do to anybody. I can understand how this might be upsetting, but I had to do something, didn't I?"

"I'm not mad at you, JC. I'm just feeling a little, well, kinda violated. Okay? Like something was taken away from me. It's stupid, I know. Give me a couple minutes to digest this."

"Of course. Here's where I need your input. Think about this for a bit. Apparently, I can heal animals and people by just touching them. The two times I've done it with people, they don't remember me being there. Karen Danvers didn't remember. Kim doesn't remember. But it happened. Paul and Jack can attest to me being with Kim. I deliberately shielded holding Kim's hand, kept my body in front of touching her so the nurse wouldn't see. But Kim doesn't remember.

"I've spent days obsessing over this. Maybe this has something to do with the people trying to kill me. Just for a minute, imagine you have this ability. How do you pick whom you're going to heal? How do you pick one and not another? How many ill, suffering, and deserving folks do you walk by to help somebody else? What makes one person more deserving than another? This could give anybody a god complex, right? How do you choose?

"While you're thinking about that, think about this getting out in the world. Just for a bit, think about an evil old man or woman. Sick, frail, but evil. Say, a drug kingpin. Or a mob boss. Or a cruel dictator. Lots of money, lots of resources, a small army at his or her command. Then they learn about me and my ability. What would they do to capture and use me for their own selfish ends? What would they be capable of doing? When would they stop pursuing me?

"Think about all the families with loved ones dying. Their children or spouses. What wouldn't they do to gain my help? How far would they go? How far would you go? Now imagine a world full of those people needing, wanting, seeking.

"Just a bit ago, I told you if this gets out in the world, I'll have to move. Live on a mountain as a recluse. Cut all ties with everybody I know. Live my life completely unattached. The alternative is to run and keep running or be a slave to bad people or become little more than an animal, poked and prodded by some government's secret lab, until I die.

"Right now, all I know is I have this gift or curse, if you prefer. So far, I've been able to use it at will. There doesn't seem to be any time required to recharge this ability. No reset of any kind. It's just part of me. I healed Karen Danvers just to see if I could. She was dying of a rare, incurable cancer. She had weeks to live, days maybe. Now she gets to live a longer life. I have no idea how long her cure will last, maybe months or weeks, maybe the rest of a normal life. But it seems she has more time now than she had before I visited her.

"Kim, you were looking at a month's time for a full recovery, maybe longer. They didn't know about any permanent brain damage. By rights, you should still be in the ICU. Yet here you are, nearly fully healed. I confess I was selfish in healing you, Kim. First, because you were injured protecting me. I felt obligated to help. You were looking out for me, protecting me. I didn't think it fair that you were hurt just doing your job. Second, I believed I could help, so I tried. You're only the second person I've helped. I wasn't 100 percent sure I could do it. Didn't know if there were conditions to my ability. Now I believe there are none, at least none that I know. Besides, who else is going to give me a ride in a classic Vette?" Things were getting really serious, and I needed to lighten the mood a bit.

"Now you all know. I'll ask again, how am I supposed to use this ability? I admit here and now I do not have one clue."

I was met with silence. Nobody said anything for what seemed like an hour. In reality, it was likely less than a minute but the longest minute of my life so far.

"Wow. This is a lot to take in, Sailor. I really don't know what to say. I need some time to think about this. If you think you've scared me away, just stop it. Okay? I'm not going anywhere, and your secret is safe with me. No worries on those two things. I'm just not sure how to answer your question, and I can see it really does need an answer." What a relief that Lu was still on my side, that I hadn't pushed her away.

Kyle looked at Mat, and Angus looked at Doc, then everybody in the group looked at everybody else in the group. Then Angus spoke, "This is a lot to take in, JC. Coming from anybody else, I'd say bullshit. However, I've never known you to lie or bend the truth to fit any particular circumstance. Your friends and I believe you. We've really no choice. It's either believe you or believe you've lived a lie every moment of your entire life. None of us believe that. In particular, I've known your parents as long as I've known you. Longer, really. I've watched you since you were a baby in your mother's arms. I've watched you grow into a young man, in many ways wise beyond your years.

"I've watched and am watching you bear burdens that would crush lesser men. I've watched you handle your life with purpose and dignity. You've kept both feet on the ground where the temptation to do otherwise would overwhelm many. I could not be prouder of you if you were my own son." Angus's little speech made my eyes moist.

"JC, I'm with Angus. I was your mother's doctor while she was carrying you. I was your mom and dad's doctor before you were conceived. I've watched you since before you were born and every year thereafter. I've been a physician longer than you've been alive. Along the way, I've seen some amazing and inexplicable stuff. What you're saying easily falls into the amazing and inexplicable column.

"I've never known you to lie or shade the truth to fit your circumstance. On the contrary, I've known you to be truthful even when stating that truth was not in your best interest. I'm afraid that's my long-winded way of saying I believe you. And this brings up something I need to divulge.

"I'm aware of Catherine's research. I'm aware of many of her experiments. She confided in me about the work she was doing and her hopes for you. This is going to be difficult to hear, JC, but your mom experimented with you before you were born. She did some alterations of your DNA. Neither she nor I knew the outcome of her manipulations, but we suspected a few things.

"First, we suspected you would gain in physical abilities. In short, I don't think you're finished growing. By that I mean growing taller, heavier, more muscled, and with enhanced reflexes. If we were right in our earliest beliefs, your bones will become more dense, able to take more stress and abuse before fracturing or breaking. Your muscles should grow more dense, heavier, perhaps by as much as a quarter more.

"Your brain and mental capabilities should improve as well. That may be the source of your ability to heal others. Of course, I'm not certain of this, but I strongly suspect it. I don't think your brain has stopped developing. I suspect you'll notice ongoing improvements for some time to come.

"I have additional suspicions as well. Knowing what's happening to you right now, I suspect other abilities will manifest. These may take months or years or may not occur at all. At this point, all you and I can do is observe and wait. Frankly, I'm still amazed that you have this ability to heal. That came straight out of nowhere and was not any focus of what your mom researched or manipulated in your DNA. I suppose stranger things have happened. If they have, I've never read any credible evidence to support the claim."

Jack was next, and I was still trying to come to terms with what Phyl had just dropped on me. "Out of all the things you might have said, this certainly wasn't what I imagined. This gives us another angle to think about, JC. It's another reason why people may be pursuing you. You've said nobody knew anything about this until you just told us now. So I'm not sure this revelation fits with you being in danger." I could tell Jack was still mulling this over. Probably would be doing it for days, if not longer.

"Add to this what your doctor has just revealed, and I'm getting the idea that there is a force of folks out there determined to destroy what your mom's research and experiments achieved in you. I dare say your entire situation is much bigger than any of us imagined."

"JC, what you've said makes sense. I hadn't had time to think about what kind of impact your healing touch would have on your life. I apologize. I spoke before thinking things through. I am grateful for your help, for healing me. I'm humbled, and I'm embarrassed.

I've always taken care of myself. Depended on myself. Prided myself on not needing anybody. Jack and Paul can tell you I don't ask for help. I find a way. I make do. In the work we do, being self-contained and self-reliant is as much an asset as liability. It balances out over time. Accepting help, even when it's needed, isn't easy for me. That you did it, the way you did it, is humbling. Thank you." I could see Kim was getting a bit emotional.

"Hearing from your doc, I agree with Jack. This takes your risk to an entirely new level. I don't think we can be cautious enough when it comes to protecting you. We're already going back to the freeway wreck that took your parents from you. I've a hunch there is more information there to be had. We just need to look more closely and do our own investigation.

"Regardless, I'm in. Whatever you have going on is just another helping of crazy, JC. Drowning. Dying. Being attacked in your home. Getting shot. You and Kim in a running gun battle in downtown Tacoma. Getting sniped at the bakery. Invaders in your roof. Nuts! It's all nuts. For you, this is turning out to be just another life event. Seems to me like you're going to have many of them in your life. I wanna be around to see how this comes out!" Paul had an interesting way of looking at life, that's for sure.

"Wait! What? You were in a gunfight in downtown Tacoma? Somebody snuck in your attic? Sailor, your life is nuts!"

"It is, Lu. That's why we're taking steps to be proactive instead of reactive. I have one request with all this. Let's keep this limited to the people here right now. Jack, I'm sure all your people are trustworthy. But I think the more people who know, well, the more people who know, right? I really like Taco, Bobby, and Teal and everybody else, but let's keep this in a tighter circle, okay?"

"Sure. No problem. I understand completely, JC. And I agree. Your circle of knowledge is plenty big as it is. We're all on the same page here. Let's keep this tight." I was glad Jack wasn't offended.

"Okay. Enough serious stuff for one day. Angus, how about you and I go fire up the grill, and you teach me everything you know about grilling steaks and chicken? I think it's time to start cooking!"

Chapter 38

Angus and I got up and moved to the patio, uncovered the built-in grill, and began poking, lifting, and studying. The grill was gas fired, stainless steel, and huge. You could put a side of beef on those grates, almost. Plenty of room for a dozen chicken quarters and twelve steaks. The top rack would easily hold the sweet corn.

Pushing the ignite button on the grill, the gas caught, and we had fire. Angus adjusted the ten burners to medium and lowered the lid. "We'll let this heat up for a few minutes, then start cooking. We'll start with the chicken quarters, give them about twelve minutes, then add the steaks and corn to the top grate. Everything should be ready in a bit less than a half hour."

There was a smaller reefer beside the grill along the base of the built-in. I didn't see any need to use it but could see its value if I were to use it for three or four people. Built-in shelving with stainless doors was opposite the reefer unit with additional storage below the grill. All in all, plenty of room for storage out here. And a very nice landing area on top. Both sides of the grill had countertops, looked like quartz or some other cultured stone, swirled gray veins running through white, about twelve feet in length overall and about two feet deep. I was really looking forward to learning how to use this thing.

"How many for steak and how many for chicken? Jack, don't forget your outside crew." When I finished counting, I had eight chicken halves taken, and the rest wanted steak. Everybody wanted their steaks bloody and their chicken not. Thought that would make Angus's job easier. Might as well cook all the protein now.

Angus and I got busy with the meat and grill. "JC, did your folks have any sort of temperature probes to use while grilling meat?"

"I have no idea. Let me look." I prowled around the kitchen drawers and didn't find anything resembling any sort of temperature probe, so I went to the grill area. When I opened the area right below the grill, I saw some stainless-steel organizer bins. One had several colored, stubby prongs inside. There were red, yellow, orange, and black. Each had a small, probe-like affair sticking out about a half-inch. "Are these what you're looking for, Angus?"

"Yes. Red is for bloody inside, yellow for red inside, orange is for pink inside, and black is for well done, no color at all inside. We'll use the red for the steaks and add a couple minutes. Orange is for the chicken, adding four minutes after the probe lights up. We'll probably plate the steaks first as they'll cook a bit even off the grill."

"Hey, this isn't so bad. Those probe things help a lot, don't they?"

"They do. Good probes take the guesswork out of cooking meat or just about anything really. The only trick is to know which probe color signals what. Once you have that down, the rest is straightforward. This kind of grill even takes away the flare-ups you get using coal or charcoal. That can really play havoc with cooking."

Time was up, so I got the chicken out of the reefer and on the grill. We set the burners to low and the timer for twelve minutes. Steaks and corn would go on when we turned to chicken. Once everything was cooked and off the grill, everybody loaded up and started enjoying food.

The next three hours were spent eating, visiting, and getting to know everybody. Our outside guys and gals rotated through too, so everybody was able to enjoy all the food and assorted goodies. It was a group effort for sure, but we did manage to eat nearly everything on the island. I was glad we'd gone ahead with this event. The more the day progressed, the better I was feeling about everything, including sharing my secret.

It was now about 7:00 p.m. Kyle and Mat were getting ready to head out. I visited with them a bit, then we said our goodbyes, and they left. Angus appeared to be next. "I've loaded your dishwasher, JC. Your trash is filled with paper plates and plastic cups. All you need do is put some plastic wrap over the remaining chicken and pieces of pie. I combined the leftover pie slices on one pie tin. I think Trudy reuses those tins, so maybe you'll want to move all of them to a plate. Then you can wash the tins and get them back to her.

"Jack and I have visited about your candidates, and we've agreed. I'm sure he'll go over them with you yet tonight. It hasn't been long, but I think we've found you some interesting folks. Listen to Jack and see what you think. If you agree, we can begin proper personal interviews by mid next week. That's it for me, then, JC. I'm headed home. I know you won't hesitate to call if you have a need. It was a very nice gathering. You did well." Angus gave me a smile and walked out to his car. He seemed tired. Some of his age showed through tonight. I guess none of us live forever. I heard Angus start his Continental, then pull out of the driveway.

Doc Church was right behind Angus. "Nice event, JC. Thank you for inviting me. I want to apologize again for not telling you about keeping an eye on you and some of the reasons behind my actions. I'm sorry Ben, my husband, couldn't be here this evening, a prior commitment. Regardless, JC, know you are very dear to us both. We considered your folks close friends and were devastated by their deaths. You already know to contact me if you have any questions or needs, right?"

"I do, Doc. No worries about the history. I'm not worried or bothered in any way and want you and Ben to be the same. Okay?"

"Thank you, JC. Don't be a stranger." And she headed to her Porsche to drive home.

Lu was next. "Nice party, JC. I'm impressed. It seemed everybody had a good time. Mat and Kyle told me they enjoyed themselves, so I think you nailed it. What's next on your list?"

"I need to work with Jack and his folks on getting the security system installed. We need to discuss the candidates he has for the positions I'm considering. I need to get some training scheduled for weapons and self-defense, and I'm thinking of another project entirely. I'm happy to share it with you, really want to get your input, when and if I decide I'm interested enough in it to consider moving forward."

"Not fair, Sailor! Not fair at all. What's this you're thinking about? Give me a hint?"

"Sure. I mean, I'm happy to talk about it. I'm just not sure yet whether or not I'm going to do anything with what I'm considering, that's all. I don't want to waste your time or anybody's for that matter. This might not lead to anything at all."

"Enough. What's going on in that handsome head of yours?"

"Well, here's the thing, Lu. Mom and Dad left me three cars. Mom's Lexus is one of them. So far, I haven't been able to let it go. I don't drive it. Start it about once a month just to keep the oil moving around and the battery charged, but that's it. Just can't seem to let go, ya know? Then there are two others. Why don't I take you to the garage and show you? I think showing is much better than telling, especially right now." Saying that, I reached for Lu's hand, and together we made our way through the door leading to the garage.

Stepping in the garage, I turned on the overhead lights. Lu glanced around and saw the Mustang. Her eyebrows went up. "That's yours? I mean, really?"

"Yup. There's another surprise under the tarp." We walked toward it; Lu's eyes fastened to the Mustang.

"This Mustang is beautiful, JC! Stunning comes to mind. Did your dad do this?"

"Honestly, I have no idea. These have all been here since before they died."

Lu opened the door, reached in, and looked inside. "This is amazing, Sailor! All you have left to do is put the seats in, reinstall the hood, and do the headliner?"

"Yup."

She moved to the car under the tarp, and I pulled it off. First thing I heard was Lu's sharp intake of breath.

"Oh my! It's beautiful! Incredible, JC. I can see us driving in the country, the wind in my hair, and both of us laughing. Oh, this is crazy!"

"Mom and Dad left a graduation letter here on the driver's seat."

Lu picked up the envelope, then began reading the letter. I watched as she read the brief note, tears running down her cheeks. "My god, Sailor. This is beautiful. The most beautiful thing I've ever read. So like your parents. So very much." Then she just stood there, tears continuing to make their way down her flushed cheeks.

"Hey." It was almost a whisper. My throat was suddenly thick, my voice soft. "I didn't mean to upset you, Lu. Why don't we go back in the house?"

"No." Her voice was as soft as mine. "I'm fine. I'm just remembering your folks, JC. They were both such wonderful people. You are blessed in so many ways to have had them for your parents. They will have an influence on you for the rest of your life. They were such a gift, JC, to you, to all of us who knew them. I know you're still hurting from their loss, but I see so much of them in you. You're a good man, Sailor. How do these two beautiful cars relate to whatever you have floating around that handsome head of yours?"

"Well, I've plenty of room here in the garage and on the land as far as that goes. I thought I might want to hire a master mechanic, somebody who loves cars as much as my folks did, and have them rebuild and restore modern classics like these two, Corvettes, and whatever else defined the era of sixties muscle cars. Honestly, I'd probably end up keeping a few, but the rest I'd sell to those who appreciate the era. Maybe auction off or raffle off some for charitable causes. I don't need the money, so I've no profit motive."

"Your brain just doesn't stop, does it? I think it's a wonderful idea! Where will you find your mechanic?"

"Jack might have an idea or two, or Paul. Maybe Kim. I'm thinking there has to be a retired or former military gearhead somewhere who'd enjoy the work. All any craftsman needs are the right tools and the ability to afford them and pockets deep enough to fund the project. I've plenty of money for something like this. I'm not thinking of this as a profit-motive project. It would be more of a means to an end. I'd like to use it as a way to support fundraising efforts for worthwhile causes, I'm thinking veteran related.

"I've even thought of setting the business up as a mentoring program. You know, have one master mechanic on staff, then work with one of the trade schools or community college and mentor some of their students. That would be another way to help young kids like me learn a valuable trade and get a leg up in life.

"Alternately, I've thought about using it as a training site for disabled veterans. Retrain them with marketable skills so they can become productive members of society. Nothing worse than somebody who used to be productive and capable and all of a sudden no longer able to function the same way. Has to do a real number on their confidence and self-worth."

"This is going to work out, JC. You'll have your shop up and running before the end of this year! I know you, Sailor. You're not only handsome. You're smart. I have every confidence in you."

"Okay? Now I suppose I have to live up to that!" I was smiling when I said it. "Let's get back inside. I still need to visit with Jack, Paul, and Kim."

"Sure. But I need to have some more time with you this evening. Alone time. There're some things I need to tell you."

Chapter 39

"Lu, you're sounding...serious. Is it?"

"It is. It'll all become clear as I explain it to you. Okay?"

"Okay. What's on your wonderful mind?"

"JC, I'm not sure where to start, so I'm just going to dive in, and we can address any gaps as they come up. Is that all right?"

"Of course. Now you have me really intrigued."

Lu began, "You know I was born in France, right?"

"Yes. And I know you moved here from Montreal when you were in the sixth grade. That's when we met at Kings Academy. And we've known each other since. And I know you have dual citizenship here and in Canada, right?"

"Of course. It's time I told you the rest of my story. What I am about to tell you has been told to me by both my parents. I've talked with Mom and Papa, and they agree. With part of what's going on in your life, it's time for you to know my history. My folks know we're friends... Okay, something more. That's for another time. My point is that you're not the only one with a secret. Both my parents know I'm telling you this, so no secrets between you and me, and you and my folks. Okay?"

"Of course."

"When we lived in Paris, France, Papa was a biochemical engineer. He was employed by an agency within the French government, doing research on improving the human condition. His area of expertise was very focused and specialized. In some ways he and his team of researchers were doing what your mom and her team were doing but from a different point of reference.

"Papa and his team were focused on the chemistry of human biology, even the chemistry of DNA and how those individual strands communicated as well as what they did. Papa's mandate was to find organic means and methods to improve the human condition. Ways to remove or lessen certain birth defects through organic chemistry. Techniques to use to correct birth defects *in vitro*. Methods to control or eliminate conditions such as epilepsy, multiple sclerosis, certain cancers, and heart disease...all through the use of organic chemistry combined with the body's own chemistry. This all sounds wonderful and worthwhile until you understand the ways and means this 'innocent' research can be taken in darker directions.

"Papa had a team of thirty-five researchers and analysts who reported directly to him. They were all PhD-level scientists, each at or near the top of their particular discipline. His project was very secret, and he had all the proper clearances, as did each of his team members. Papa told me everything was progressing normally for the first three years. Then Papa got a new director, somebody from the outside...not from within the company or his group. This is unusual but not outside normalcy within that community.

"The new director, Ali Khan, was different, or so Papa believed. It was only after his first year as the new director that Ali Khan started to institute changes. A few of Papa's most productive and talented scientists were forced to quit or were removed by Director Khan. Everything appeared normal and open, but Papa suspected some deeper agenda. The replacements for those who left seemed to be of similar descent, perhaps Muslim in nature or something related. Still within normal expectations, but less centrist.

"Then the focus of their research had subtle changes. There were side projects that Papa learned were focused on enhancing certain traits. Creating medical procedures and combining chemical cocktails to enhance a person's endurance, speed, resistance to pain…those sorts of things. There was even a project to enhance vision, including night vision, using some concoction of eyedrops. All of a sudden, the research seemed more focused on creating better warriors. Super soldiers. According to Papa, they had some success with the program, but at a cost.

"The next thing to show up was reduced activity on their legacy research. There was a measurable drop in results and progress. Everybody was working. They seemed diligent in their disciplines, but there were meager results to show for all their efforts.

"Within two years of Ali Khan's directorship, half of Papa's original team had left, all for seemingly normal reasons. But staff changes in that field specialty are far less frequent than that. Papa went to the DGSI, the general directorate of internal security. Their head at the time was General Jules Aubert. He was the guy ultimately responsible for the security of Papa's division.

"General Aubert asked Papa to be his watchful eyes and ears within the division and especially within Papa's department, and Papa agreed. Things settled for about a year, then another wave of staff changes took place. JC, Papa's team of researchers all had PhDs. They were leading thinkers in their specific fields. Papa had recruited and created a cutting-edge team that Ali Khan destroyed in four years.

"There were a few incidents of sabotage, and four scientists, each a group leader, died under less than normal circumstances. One died as the result of a mugging. Two died in car wrecks, and one committed suicide. The last straw was when Director Khan sent one of his supposedly private security officers to Papa's office. Papa was told to leave France in forty-eight hours or his wife and child would be butchered. That's the word the messenger used, *butchered*.

"Papa went home immediately, packed two suitcases, put Mama and me in the car, and drove away. Just before leaving, Papa called General Aubert and told him what happened. The general told Papa he was doing the right thing and to go immediately to Le Meurice Hotel. Aubert told Papa reservations waited in the name of Paul Cenac.

"We arrived at the hotel and were getting out of Papa's car when a man jumped in and told Papa to leave as quickly as possible. At that very moment, two people standing in front of the hotel were shot, and the car directly behind us was riddled with bullets.

"Papa drove like a crazy man while the guy who had jumped in directed Papa through Paris. Papa said he drove for miles while the guy in the back seat watched for anybody following. This man had us change cars three times. Each car change was the result of this stranger stealing a random car from various parts of the city. Finally, nearing dawn the next day, he directed Papa to an abandoned farmhouse several miles outside Paris.

"That's where we all met the general. He gave us new identities, complete with passports for all of us, and driver's licenses and credit cards for Mama and Papa. The other man had left… We never learned his name. General Aubert drove us to a private airfield, and we were flown by private jet along with eight more adults and four little girls, first to Vancouver, BC, then on to Calgary, Edmonton, and finally Montreal. At each stop, a man and woman, together with a little girl, would leave the flight. Then we were off at the last stop, Montreal.

"We lived in Montreal for six years. Papa became a mechanical engineer, and Mama was a nurse. General Aubert contacted Papa three or four times a year, sometimes in person, sometimes by telephone. General Aubert kept Papa updated on Ali Khan and his activities.

"We had resumed an almost normal life when we received a call from the general. I remember it was late at night and cold outside. Papa was only on the phone for a minute, then we were all running for our car. I remember we didn't even take time to grab our winter coats. We were all in our pajamas. The garage door was going up, and Papa was driving down the driveway like a madman. Our car hit somebody… I remember seeing a body flying off to the side of the street, and we were gone. Before we were around the first turn, there was a huge explosion. I turned around in the back seat and saw our home go up in flames.

"Papa drove us around until he was sure nobody was following us. General Aubert and Papa had prepared for some disaster like this since we arrived in Montreal. The trunk of our car had one suitcase for each of us, new identities for all of us, complete with passports, driver's licenses for my folks, and credit cards with histories of use. Papa also had a small bag containing $20,000, all in used $10 and $20 bills. General Aubert had been generous to us and had become more accomplished in establishing deep histories for us and, I suppose, others.

"We changed clothes behind an abandoned warehouse, throwing away everything that was not kept in the car. The next day we abandoned our car. Papa bought an older Toyota he found in an ad in some local paper. Paid cash for it, and we drove straight down to Manchester, New Hampshire. Papa called General Aubert and told him where we were. The general told us to drive straight through to Seattle and call him once we were there or sooner if we had trouble. Papa drove for five days before we arrived in the Seattle area. We bought a different car in Chicago and again in a little town in Montana. There seemed no way to track our trip to Seattle. We slept in our car every night and only ate at drive-through restaurants, paying cash for every purchase.

"By the time we were in Issaquah, we were all tired, dirty, stinky, and cranky. We stopped at a very forgettable motel for the first time since leaving New Hampshire. Papa paid cash for one night, and we all took long hot showers and brought food back from a local restaurant.

"Papa contacted the general that first night in Issaquah. Aubert told Papa that we needed to live in that motel for a month while he set up a new life for us. Three weeks later, the general found a great job for Papa in Tacoma, and we moved here the following week. We've been here since, and are still in touch with General Aubert. We still keep suitcases in the trunk of each of our cars as well as what Papa calls running money. We still live a life of 'ready to run' with a minute's notice."

"Lu, I had no idea! This must still be making you crazy!" I was beyond shocked that Lu had lived through such an ordeal.

"That's not the end of things, JC. This is the hardest part. What your mom did with you, manipulating your DNA, well, my father did the same with me. Remember, he came at what you and I share from a completely different angle. Where your mom used technology to splice in your DNA, Papa used chemistry. So far as we know, the only enhancement or gift, whatever you want to call it, for me is that it's only my brain and mental functions that seem to be affected.

"This is embarrassing, JC, but I'm way smarter than I let on. I do have an eidetic memory. I have total recall of everything I've seen and heard. Believe me, this is not a gift. I've worked with Papa and others to learn how to filter what I see and hear. When this first manifested, it was like living with a thousand voices screaming at me all at the same time. I've mostly learned to filter that chaos but still have challenges every so often.

"The only part I've not said yet is that Papa collaborated with your mom. They knew each other. They'd meet at conferences and had discussions over the phone. I didn't know about your mom and Papa until very recently. Papa and Mom decided not to tell me until they knew we were dating. They could see for themselves that there is a certain something between us. Not the genetics thing but a real attraction. They asked me to not tell you any of this until I was certain of who you were inside as well as my attraction to you and feelings about you. And here we are. Now you know all my secrets."

I'd thought I had a tough life. Huh. "I had no idea, Lu. No idea at all. I'm at a loss for words."

"There is one small, final piece. I was not born Lucienne Abreo. I had a different name in France and another one in Montreal. But I'm Lucienne Abreo now and will remain so going forward. Mama and Papa are tired of running, of always looking over their shoulders. Life is good here. We're living a life similar to what we had in Paris but with a reduced risk of immediate discovery."

"What I don't understand, Lu, is why this Khan guy was so relentless in tracking you down. Do you or your parents have any idea?"

"We think so. Papa thinks Ali Khan found out about me and wanted to capture me so he could see what and how Papa had enhanced my brain. Papa thinks Khan wants to do it to others. It was something that General Aubert said that makes Papa think this is the reason. Even if that part is accurate, it doesn't explain why we were pursued to Montreal. That piece remains a mystery."

"Would it be okay with you and your parents if I asked Jack and his team to do some very quiet digging into the life of Ali Khan?"

"I don't know, JC. We have a good life here. The last thing I want to do is shine a light on Mom or Papa or me and cause us to have to abandon our lives once again."

"I understand. How about if we do this, let's you and me approach Jack very quietly. Nobody but Jack. Lu, I trust Jack with my life. Same goes for Angus and Doc. And Kim and Paul. But I want to keep this to Jack only. With you there, I'd ask him how much exposure there is in researching somebody out of country. No specific country, no specific target name. Let's find out if there is an acceptable way to check out this Khan guy through a fourth party, somebody Jack trusts with his life.

"That would give us two degrees of separation, actually, three. A researcher outside Jack's group, Jack, me, then you. If everybody agrees to do this, we have to have as much of a guarantee as can be that nothing done traces back more than one step. That gives you and your parents two additional degrees of separation. Whaddaya think?"

"Before we do anything, I'd have to ask Mom and Papa, get their thoughts and permission. I know they trust you, JC. That's never been an issue. Never. But I think you can see from our point of view this presents risk. And risk is something we've lived to avoid at all costs for nearly two decades. Do you see what I'm saying?"

"Sure. I understand. I guess I'm just as curious to find the bad guys in your life as I am to finding them in my own. Truly, I do understand. You have my word, if your parents say no, I'll drop it and say nothing to Jack or anybody else. Okay?"

"Of course. This isn't a matter of trust, Sailor. It's all about risk, not trust. Okay?"

"No worries, Lu. Your secret is safe with me."

"Now it really is time for me to go, JC. I told Mom and Papa I'd be home a bit later because of our talk, but I need to go. I'll just go out your garage door here." Saying that, she took my hand and pulled me to her, went up on her toes, and kissed me. A full lip-to-lip kiss. Longer than our first. My arms were around her waist, not wanting to let go. Ever. Not wanting to come up for air. Not wanting this moment to end. All too quickly, it did.

Another lightning storm was in her eyes, accompanied by a warm, yet teasing smile. "You have great tonsils, Sailor. Good night. Call me soon, okay?" And she was out the door.

I stood there for a moment, savoring the afterglow of her kiss. That woman knew how to kiss. I don't know how or where or from whom she learned, but my, oh my, Lucienne has terrific lips! Every dream in the world was in her kiss. It promised forever. For once in my life, something was going incredibly right. Almost made me afraid to breathe. Almost. Time to get both my feet back on the ground.

Walking back into the house, I could see the only people still inside were Jack, Paul, Kim, and Taco. They were all together and talking in low tones as I approached. "Hi, guys. Did you have a good time today? Get enough to eat?"

Taco spoke for the group, "It was great, JC. Everybody had a great time. Plenty of good food, great company, and a low-key afternoon for a change. I know you four have things to discuss, so I'm headed out. I'll relieve Bobby on the roof."

Jack was next. "I think we can let Dave, Connie, and Belle leave too. That will keep Teal on overwatch, Bobby on patrol with Taco on the roof, and Paul will be inside. When we're finished here, I'll get Kim home, then we'll start on your system tomorrow."

"Jack, tomorrow's Sunday." I had to say something. These guys were working day and night to protect me. Seemed they should be taking a day off.

"It is. I want us to get a jump on the week. There's going to be enough construction time for us to take a breather, JC. Right now, I want to get this moving forward. There's a lot to do, and I want it done sooner rather than later."

"Don't hate me yet, but I've another idea for you all to consider. I've given this some thought, really should have brought it up while Angus was still here. But I didn't. I'm thinking of finding and hiring a master mechanic or somebody who wants to be one and has a mechanical aptitude way above average. I'm thinking about starting a business of restoring modern classic cars—sixties Vettes, Mustangs, Dodges, Chevys, and the rest. My idea is to buy all the tools and gear needed. Run it out of my existing garage or build a separate building here. Maybe set it up as a mentoring program. Work with injured vets or young folks who want to learn a marketable skill and get a leg up on life. I kinda like the vet rehab focus. Whaddaya think?

"Part of the purpose would be to use the restorations as charity auction donations to raise money for area nonprofits and veterans groups. I'd also use any revenue generated through regular builds or contract builds to donate to the same groups. I don't need the money. I have more than I'll ever spend."

Paul was first. "How much thought have you given this, JC? What you're talking about isn't cheap. If you build a separate shop next door, even a pole building, I'd think you'd want it to match your house or at least compliment it. You don't want some ugly eyesore next door. Water line, electrical, fully insulated, heated, cooled, seal the floor, hydraulic lifts…you're going to run a couple hundred thousand or better once you add a master set of tools. Include a paint booth and metal fab and it adds more."

Jack was next. "Paul's right, you know. He's maybe a bit light. I'd think for all you'd end up doing to a vehicle, from getting it in the door to having it ready to sell, it takes several skill sets. Master mechanic, metal fabricator, welder, upholstery, paint, frame straightening, detail. I don't think one person is going to have all the skills you need. Maybe, but doubtful. Still, you're young. Your whole life is ahead. I'm thinking you're not wanting or needing to build a car every month, right?"

"No. I'd only get impatient if there wasn't any visible progress. Maybe have two or three in process, so when we had to wait for something on one, we could move to a second or third. Somehow, that sounds right. The more I'm talking about it, the more I'm liking it. Hire a master mechanic, work out the details for the other skill sets, rehab interested vets, and grow it, but always keep it manageable."

"Well, I think it's a great idea!" I've never known Kim to be shy. "Like Jack said, you're young. You'll figure it out as you go. Yes, I expect you'll spend some money unnecessarily. You have the luxury of being able to afford it. Very few people can say that. There's no debt to service, no overhead or payroll to meet from work accomplished. It might be easier to find your mechanic than you think."

"Hey!" from Jack. "I didn't say it was a bad idea. Just that it's going to get expensive, fast. I think it's a great idea. I can see the benefits too. Nice tax write-off, building for charity auctions and raffles is a terrific idea. No, I like it. And you're not suggesting you'd do it by yourself. I like that part best. Get your elbows greasy when you want, but leave the build to the pro or pros you hire."

"I'm in as well, guys. I was just thinking out loud. Of course, it's a great idea. Sounds like fun even. Just remember, your attached garage will only hold six cars comfortably. Okay?"

"Alright. I want to fund this without touching my principal. I've accumulated extra funds from saved interest. I think I can get everything needed from what I'll have left after the security setup. Might take a couple extra months. And I suspect it'll take time to find my mechanic. Now I just need to run this by Angus. I'm sure he'll agree with me. Even if he doesn't, I think I'll go ahead. I need a project. Something I can get my hands on, physically and metaphorically. Jack, add robust security to the new building too. Do any of you know a good, reliable contractor? Seems I'm in need of one! I'd also like each of you to keep your ears open for a master mechanic."

"Can't think of a contractor off the top of my head, JC, but I'll bet Angus knows somebody or knows somebody who knows somebody. He has connections all over the place." Jack was right.

"How about this? While you're scouting for military hire candidates, see if anybody knows a retired military contractor. They'll have to know their stuff and be honest. All the same ground rules apply. But as long as I need a general contractor, I might as well work with a military guy or gal. In fact, I'd prefer. They served this country, time we gave back where we can. And I can, so let's find one. Okay?"

All three in chorus said, "Deal!"

"Tell me about who you found for the other two positions. I'm curious to hear who you found and why you like 'em."

"We have three prime candidates, six altogether. They're all subject to background checks coming back clean," Jack offered. "First good one, of the three great ones we found, is Toby Randall. Toby is forty-two, five feet eleven inches, 190, brown and blue, disabled vet, but no worries there. He has a leg prosthesis but gets around as good as any of us. He had his twenty years in, so retirement. He lost his leg while on active duty, so has some disability income as well. Was a master sergeant. What I have on file says he's tougher than an old boot. No disciplinary actions. No blemishes at all. He'd be your outdoor guy. Enjoys manual labor and just wants to work. Employers shy away because of his leg. This is all paper on him. I've not looked in his eyes. A Monday interview works for Toby.

"Next one is Patricia Osteen, Patti to friends. Thirty-eight. Five feet, ten inches, 150, brown and brown. Combat vet. Has serious hearing loss resulting from a combat injury. Took up cooking as a hobby. I hear she enjoys it. Early reports say she has an attitude, can't stand those who question her ability at anything. I visited with two of her squad buddies, and both said she was fair and hard as a nail. Focused. Driven. Said she could back 'em up any day anywhere. So I have two references and some paper on Patti. I'm waiting on a call from her former CO and more paper. We can interview her this Monday.

"Last primary is Dawn Sperling. Dawn is thirty-nine. Five feet, six inches, brown and green, 130. Holds black belts in four disciplines and rates an expert in small arms. She's a leftie. Missing two fingers on her right hand from a direct action. Loves the outdoors and has become an avid gardener. Studying for her master gardener license. Waiting for more paper on Dawn, a call from her last CO, and our interview. She's slotted for this Monday as well."

Jack continued, "We do have three additional that we'll interview. They're what I would call second tier. Still, there may be a diamond or two in the rough with these three. I don't want to dismiss them out of hand."

This sounded great to me. "Let's do all six on Monday, as scheduled, then wait and see who else pops up. Does that sound like a reasonable plan?" I was curious about all six and thought there might be at least two winners.

"You bet, JC. I'll set it up for Angus's office. You've been there, yes?"

"Yeah. Several times. If it's okay with you, I'd like you, Kim, and Paul there, Jack. And Angus. I want to sit in but just as an observer for this first interview. That work?"

"You bet."

Jack left with Kim, leaving Paul with me. We still had Taco on the roof, Teal in the trees, and Bobby prowling. Things should be good. I'd had a good day, full and busy but filled with friends and purpose. It was good to be social again. The highlight was Lu, of course, as I thought and hoped it would be. That she and I shared such unique circumstances was beyond amazing. That our parents actually worked and collaborated, together? Unbelievable. What a very small world we lived in.

Seemed like it got late faster than I'd realized. Kip was sleeping on the sofa. Seemed like a good idea, sleep. "Kip! Let's go to bed, buddy."

"Paul, we're going to call it a night. Anything you need or anything I can do before I head to bed?"

"Nothing, JC. It's been a good day. Thanks for putting everything together and for all the food! See you in the morning." With that, Kip and I made our way to bed. Tomorrow was going to be another busy day.

Chapter 40

Sunday came quickly. It seemed that I'd just put my head down, and it was already time to get up. I smelled coffee, so somebody was already ahead of me. I noticed Kip already gone. Maybe I'd overslept? Glanced at the clock; nope. Just 7:00 a.m. now. Huh. Time to get ready for the day.

I headed to the bathroom to do what needed doing. Got myself cleaned up, then headed toward the kitchen. Paul and Teal were talking in low tones when I walked in. Looking up, "Good morning, sunshine! From Paul." I could see they were already in fine form.

"Good morning, Paul, Teal. How'd you guys do last night? Any issues?"

"Quiet night," Teal said. "Nothing but squirrels, rabbits, and birds. Jack will be here about nine. We'll get started on securing your roof, then start marking specific trees and installing sensors. We won't start on pressure plates until tomorrow if the weather cooperates. There's a chance of a storm coming in later today, so we'll see."

"Okay. Everybody good with scrambled eggs again? That's one thing I'm not likely to screw up. We have Trudy's cinnamon rolls and some watermelon chunks too. Whaddaya think? Will that work for breakfast for everybody?"

"Sure. You bet," Paul chimed in. "Bobby and Taco aren't picky. None of us are. In fact, don't feel like you have to feed us, JC. That's not necessary or expected. Very few of our former clients ever bothered and none of 'em like last night. That was above and beyond."

"I'm glad you enjoyed yourselves last night. Cooking, even just breakfast for y'all gives me valuable practice, and I know I need the experience. Maybe tomorrow I'll make a big batch of oatmeal with fresh strawberries and blueberries. I've not screwed that up for quite a while, so it should be another safe breakfast!"

I set about the kitchen and made breakfast for everybody. Once Paul and Teal were finished, they relieved Taco and Bobby. Those two came in and cleaned up the eggs and toast, and we visited a bit. They gave me a hand cleaning up, and by the time we had things put away, I heard the familiar sound of Jack's pickup. I watched him park in the driveway, then walk to the back of his truck and begin unloading boxes.

Bobby, Taco, and I went out to see if we could help. "Good morning, Jack," was our chorus of three voices.

"Good morning. Everything quiet last night?" Jack had unloaded the last box from the back of his truck.

"No surprises, boss. How do you want us to work this setup?" Bobby had knelt down, opening one of the boxes.

"Let's do sensors first. I want uppers and lowers, overlapping fields. Use what natural camouflage you can for each. I want everybody on comms all the time from now on. That includes you, JC. Let's not take any chances. Make sure each camera has a clean line of sight to at least one other, again, overlapping fields of coverage. Ideally, I'd like every spot covered by a minimum of two cameras.

"Perimeter will be pressure plates and cameras. We want to 'see' anybody parked out beyond JC's property. We want to capture anybody setting up for anything. Set all the plates for sixty pounds. Kip is indoor at night but has his IFF tag regardless, so no issues there at all.

"When the exterior system goes live, I want us capturing any motion or pressure. Once we've dealt with the current threat, we can always reconfigure. Until then, I want as much advance notice as we can get. We'll route all alarms to our monitors and notify authorities, if necessary, from there. That eliminates false positives getting to authorities. For now, our monitoring team will be kept pretty busy on this system. That's okay. We'll adjust. I'm more concerned about nailing these bastards than dealing with a few inconvenient false trips.

"All outside cameras will have night vision and infrared capabilities. They autoswitch according to available lighting conditions. That should give us good viewing regardless of weather or available light. They're weatherproof, so no issues there, and they're camouflaged, so that base is covered. They're EMP hardened and tamper-proof, so those bases are covered.

"We're also installing infrared sensors throughout the forest. These will give us direction of travel for any intruders as well as number of intruders and near exact location on your property. Combined with your cameras, we'll have an excellent idea of number of intruders. We'll also get a clear idea of their direction and speed of travel.

"When we've finished installing your system, JC, every square foot of your forest and yard will be covered by infrared motion sensors and motion sensitive cameras. The result to you is full coverage every hour of the day in any weather conditions. What you're getting right now is state of the art. As time goes by and equipment improvements become available, we'll change out and upgrade your system. That's part of our service to you.

"Pressure pads are the final component. Randomized, but tight. Only a couple steps between pads. Blanket from the perimeter to twenty feet in, then randomized. Nothing gets by unless it's flying above the trees. We're not using anything offensive, defensive only.

"Let's set this up so it takes at least two infrared sensor trips to activate the nearest duo of cameras. Let's program the alarm to activate only after we get at least one infrared plus a duo of cameras and at least one pressure pad tripped. That will eliminate some false alarms. Once it's up, we'll run it in test along with guys on overwatch and see what we get after a few days of operation.

"Pressure pads will be hidden inside below all windows and doors, plus infrared-capable ceiling cameras and discreet motion sensors. We'll want cameras covering all the windows, doors, hallways, and this open area. Glass-break sensors will also cover all the windows. All this gets hidden so nothing is obvious inside.

"We'll set one master control in JC's emergency room. The other will be in our ops center. For here, we'll use a tower computer with an independent backup power supply that can keep the system-monitoring computer running for twelve hours. Shouldn't be a big deal to set up. We'll set up the computer for wireless broadcast as well as being hardwired through your fiber optic, JC. This is going to be one hell of a security setup, probably more robust than anything we've done to date. We'll mount a wireless repeater in your forest, one with enough boost to easily acquire your local cell tower.

"Same as your exterior system, everything inside will be hardened against an EMP, and we'll install a whole home surge protector and power conditioner. We'll also add an additional surge protector to the power that gets to your computer and backup power. That protects you and your interior system against power spikes from area lightning and other spike sources. The power conditioner assures your power arrives clean and free from large power fluctuations. Right now, that's the best equipment available to ensure stable power to your home and interior system.

"I heard back from a contractor this morning. Former Seabee, been out for ten years. Name's Dan Hastings. Has a ton of references. He'll be here tomorrow to look at our safe room proposal and JC's shop project. By then, I'll have more background on him too. This is coming together nicely."

Jack finished up, "Bobby, why don't you relieve Teal? I'll go tell Paul we're ready to start on sensors. Then I want to get out a ways and watch. Make sure we don't have any remote observers or over-curious neighbors."

And that's how Sunday went. Kip and I prowled and watched. Paul and Teal worked on sensors and cameras, with Jack giving them both a hand and spending some time in the house. It was slow work. However, by the time they quit for the day, they had thirty cameras up and fifty-two sensors installed, all on a closed network. If you didn't know exactly where to look, you'd miss 'em all, even in the light of day. Seeing them at night would be impossible unless you were wearing infrared goggles to see the beams shining. At this stage, nothing was activated, just installed.

It looked like they'd be finished with everything except the pressure plates by tomorrow night, maybe Tuesday morning. Amazing how much gets done when a group of people work together as a team.

Paul took the night off but stayed on-site just in case. Connie and Belle came back for a night in the forest, giving Bobby and Taco a break, although they, too, stayed on-site. Teal stayed on overwatch but would be gone in the morning.

We had an intruder Sunday night. It was about 3:00 a.m. when all the outside lights snapped on, and some alarm gave one short, shrill blast. I had my Beretta on the nightstand, grabbed it, and headed to the living area. Paul was up and had his earpiece in and his Beretta in low ready.

"What's happening?" I'd had just about enough of these surprises.

"Unknown. Belle saw movement in the trees. She hit the button. That's what turned on all the outside lights and triggered the alarm chirp. She and Connie are scouting to see what they can find. Teal's on NVGs doing a sweep as well. We should hear something in a bit."

Then we heard gunshots. Sounded like several pistol shots and the bark of a rifle, twice, three times. And one more. Then quiet.

"Everybody, check in!" Paul had me on the floor in front of the island. My pistol was in hand, and my Mossberg was within easy reach.

"I got nothing, boss," said Taco on the roof.

"Two shots after I was fired on. Nothing," Teal was whispering. If he didn't hit anything, this was a pretty serious situation.

"What about Connie and Belle?"

"I don't know, boss. All is quiet. I'm on infrared and don't see 'em. Searching." Again, it was from Teal.

"Taco. Get down and help Teal. I want to know where Belle and Connie are."

Paul turned to me. "Belle and Connie are dark. You heard our conversations in your ear. Either something's happened or they're dark for a reason. Either hunting or being hunted. Either way, this isn't good."

"Do you need to go out there? I'm fine. I have Kip and both guns. Kip will alert before any surprise. Go see what's going on."

"We don't normally work this way, JC. But this situation sure as hell ain't normal. Stay here. I mean it. Right here. Your back door is a formidable barrier, so pay attention to other noises in the house. We're all on comms, so if that front door starts to open, be ready. Nobody will enter without letting you know who it is first. You're in shadow, so that's good. Now hunker down and stay put." And Paul was out the door.

A pistol barked twice. Distant. And a rifle. One shot. Again, distant. No close shots, so no bad guys near the front. Then it was quiet. Kip and I stayed where we were. I had my Mossberg on the floor with the barrel pointed at the front door. All I had to do was grab it and pull the trigger. My Beretta was in my right hand, trigger finger on the guard, pointed toward the front door but in as low ready a position as you can get while sitting on the floor.

I wanted to activate my comm and ask what was going on but knew that was about the dumbest idea ever. These people were working. There seemed an active threat, and two people hadn't checked in. I was getting worried.

Kip had turned his head toward the front door and started growling low in his throat. Somebody was right outside. That was when I noticed the front door move ever so slightly. I put my left hand on Kip's muzzle, signaling him to be quiet. Both hands back on my pistol, I watched the door. My mind was racing with a thousand thoughts. My pulse was up. I knew anybody protecting me wouldn't open my front door like this. I knew it. Still...

My earpiece came alive, "Connie's gone." Sounded like Teal.

Adrenaline was pouring in my body. I was both tense and calm at the same time. I'd been through this before and recently. In less than a second, I knew I'd do whatever I had to do again. I also knew

I'd let my front door intruder backlight himself before I shot him or her.

Now the door was open several inches. Kip was behaving, his hackles straight up, but he was quiet. Kip was a very quick learner. He was staring holes in the front-door plywood, his legs gathered under him, ready to launch. Ready to tear the head off whomever was paying us a visit.

I didn't want Kip involved. I didn't want him hurt in any way. He was my lifeline. Waiting these seconds while my front door continued to creep open, I realized Kip was infinitely more important to me than I'd thought. He was all that was left of my earlier life, life with Mom and Dad when everything was normal. I now knew with certainty my former life was gone forever.

The front door was almost open enough for an adult to slide in. My Beretta was steady in my hand, pointed exactly at the edge of the plywood, about four feet from the ground. I could easily move the barrel up or down quickly if I needed to adjust.

First, a hand grasped the edge of the door, then a leg slowly pushing against the edge of the plywood and a body starting to show. Standing, not crouching. Big. Probably a guy. Maybe more than one. Something over his head. A baclava or nylon, something. Looked like an assault rifle in his hand. Pointed at the ground? Was this guy nuts?

I watched as he began raising his gun. I had my Beretta at center mass and squeezed the trigger. Once, twice, three times. He jerked as each bullet hit him.

Still on his feet? Body armor!

Shifted my aim for his head. Pulled the trigger again and again. Next one hit his throat, another his nose, and he began to fall. I was focused on his hand that held his weapon. His finger was on the trigger, the barrel pointed in my direction. I shot him again, hitting his leg. Again, this time his right arm and his finger spasmed on the trigger. The bullet hit the kitchen island about an inch from the side of my head.

His hand was no longer holding his weapon. I sat there waiting. Wondering. Who would be next through the door? Anybody? My question didn't wait long for an answer.

Another figure rushed the door, diving through and came up about ten feet in front of me. His weapon, a similar AR type, was swinging toward me. I shot at him three times. Two slugs penetrated his head. The third was a clean miss. His finger pulled the trigger, and a spray of bullets flew into the kitchen, all missing both Kip and me.

My Beretta held fifteen rounds, and I'd just used ten. I sat there, waiting. Listening. Nothing more in my ear, no update. Nothing. I ejected the magazine and inserted a new one, just in case. I decided I'd sit where I was, waiting for another intruder or one of my guards showed up. It seemed like forever until I heard Paul's voice.

"JC. I'm approaching the house. I see your front door is open. I heard ten pistol shots and several AR rounds. Are you hurt?"

"No, Kip and I are both okay. Two dead guys in my living room."

"Coming in."

When Paul told me he was approaching my front door, I laid my pistol in my lap. When Paul walked in, my hands were empty and in plain sight.

"Jesus! Who are these guys?" Paul was more upset than either Kip or me. My nerves would likely hit in a bit, right as the adrenaline stopped flowing like a river.

"What about Connie and Belle? Are they okay?"

"Connie's gone. We've called Jack and an ambulance. And the sheriff's deputies should be here in a few. Jack's about fifteen out now. We can't find Belle."

"Gone? Where did sh... Oh. She's dead?"

"Yea. Sniper round. Never had a chance. Her pistol was still in her hand, several rounds fired. We heard Belle fire two shots. She's still out there somewhere. Teal's looking for their transportation. Bobby and Taco are hunting and looking for Belle. We know there were at least three of them. Two here and whoever shot Connie. These two have ARs. No pistols. Connie was shot with a long gun.

There's a sniper rifle out there that isn't Teal. Shit. Shit. Shit. I hate this part of my work. Hate it!"

I called Angus. Three rings and came, "Angus, JC. We've had another attack. Connie, you met her at the party yesterday? She's gone. Bobby and Taco are hunting for Belle. I've shot two more. They're in the house and untouched. Jack knows, now you. Jack said he'd be here in fifteen minutes. Paul called the sheriff. They'll probably be here in eight or so. What do you want me to do before you get here?"

"I'll be there in less than twenty minutes. Doubtless we'll be dealing with Sheriff's Detective Winslow again at some point. Be ready for him. Tell him I'm on the way and don't say anything until I'm there with you. Maybe he'll be in better humor this time." And with that Angus was gone.

It seemed only a minute later and the first squad car was pulling up. Paul and I were outside in plain view of the driveway. All our exterior lights were on, so he and I were perfectly viewable. My hands were empty and at my sides. Paul had his pistol in his holster, holding his ID and concealed carry permit open and in plain view.

The two deputies opened the doors of their squad car, keeping themselves behind the doors. Both had their pistols drawn and pointed in our general direction.

"Put your weapons on the ground and approach slowly."

Paul emptied his holster and placed his pistol on the ground. We both maintained eye contact with the officers as we slowly approached.

The sheriff's deputy on the passenger side spoke, pointing his pistol more in my direction, "Who are you, and what's going on here?"

"My name is JC Merrick. The man next to me is Paul. This is my home. We were attacked earlier by multiple intruders. Paul is one of my bodyguards. One of his team was shot and killed. Connie is back in the woods. An armed team member is with her. Two more guards are in the woods looking for a missing member. Her name is Belle. I've shot and killed two armed intruders. They're in my front living area. I've called my attorney, Angus Dunbar. Paul called his boss, Jack. Both are on the way here. Jack is about seven minutes out. Angus will be here in about twelve minutes."

"Okay. You two can put your hands down, but keep your pistols where they are on the ground. Show us what's inside."

Paul and I headed toward the house. I led the way with Paul about two steps behind me. We walked inside, and the two officers following us stopped just inside the doorway.

"Stop here." The older officer seemed to be in charge. "How do you know both these guys are dead? Did you check for a pulse?"

"Officer, I shot them both. They're dead. Haven't moved since they went down."

Nonetheless, the younger officer moved and checked each for a carotid pulse. He shook his head as he examined each.

I heard another vehicle approach. Kip had been behaving, pacing back and forth from the kitchen to the living area just shy of where the two dead guys rested. I could see he was upset but was handling it better than most humans would.

Just then, my favorite person walked in, Detective Archibald Winslow. Oh joy.

"Merrick! I knew you'd be involved. Who did you kill this time?" he started yelling at me before he even got to the house let alone where we were inside. His two patrol officers walked outside, not wanting to become the focal point of Winslow's ire.

Now standing in my living area, it seemed the detective sergeant was winding up for another verbal barrage. Thought I'd deprive him of the pleasure.

"My attorney is on the way. Mr. Dunbar will be here in less than five minutes. I'll wait for his arrival to answer any of your questions."

Winslow was opening his mouth to say something when we all heard another vehicle approach. This time, a red Ford pickup. Good. Jack was here, and it looked like he was ready for action. Once out of his pickup, he began walking toward the forest. Paul moved to walk outside and have a word with Jack. Both of them were headed into the wooded area of my property.

"Wait a minute! Jack, isn't it? Where do you think you're going?" Winslow was in full bluster.

Jack continued ignoring the detective, as did Paul, and they both made their way into the woods with Kip following beside them.

Winslow looked like he was about to bust a blood vessel. This guy had to be on blood pressure meds, or he was headed for an early stroke. He turned back to me.

"What's going on here, Merrick? I'm looking at two more dead bodies here. Did you kill 'em?"

I just looked at the detective sergeant, staring at him, really. Not with hostility, I'd schooled my face to remain neutral and passive. This guy had hostility boiling inside. I could tell with certainty that he did not like me even a little bit. I could feel his resentment toward me. No idea why, but it was certainly there and clearly on full display. My intuition again. A good ability to have and cultivate, it seemed. I was determined to keep my mouth shut until Angus arrived.

"Start talking, Merrick." Sarcasm was dripping as he spoke.

My only response was to slightly cock my head to the left as I looked at him. Not a huge gesture but enough for Winslow to notice.

"Just what the hell is that supposed to mean? What are you hiding? You know whatever it is, we're going to find it. Might as well save us all some grief and talk, Merrick." Again, sarcasm dripped from the use of my last name.

We both heard another vehicle approach. I figured it was Angus this time, and I was right. Another car, this one a Corvette, parked just behind Angus. An ambulance pulled up behind the Corvette.

"Detective Winslow. How delightful. JC, how are you doing?"

"I'll be okay. This one's worse than the last, Angus. They killed Connie. Everybody's there with her now. Let me point the paramedics to where Connie is. There's no rush." Saying that, I walked outside and toward the ambulance, walking past Kim. Giving her a nod, I continued toward the ambulance crew and pointed them in the direction of Connie. Told them she was gone; no gurney was necessary. Still, they took their gear minus the gurney and headed into the woods.

Kim had stopped and waited for me, then we both made our way back to the house. I suspected Kim was here to support Jack and the team. Maybe to help hunt for Belle as well.

Kim and I made our way back inside. Winslow was as red-faced as ever, having words with Angus. "Why is it when something happens here, you're the first one this kid calls?"

Ignoring the detective completely, Angus looked directly at me. "JC, have you given anybody here your statement yet?"

"No. I was waiting for your arrival."

"Good. Why don't you and I along with the detective sergeant move to the dining table, and you can tell him what transpired here?"

"Sure." We all moved to the dining table, me at the head of the table and Angus sitting directly across from the detective.

"As you know, Mr. Winslow…"

"That's Detective Winslow to you, boy."

"Kip and I were sound asleep when we heard the alarm, and all the outside lights came on. This was about 3:00 a.m. I pulled my jeans on, grabbed my tee shirt and shoes, and Kip and I ran in here. Paul was here already. He'd been sleeping on the sofa. We heard shots. Paul made sure I was armed and out of sight. We kept the inside lights off, but the outside lights were all on.

"Back door was locked and barred, as you see it now. Paul went out the front door and closed it. Oh, we'd heard in our ear comms that Connie was gone. I knew, without anybody explaining, she had been killed."

"How did you know that, Mr. Merrick?" Again with the sarcasm dripping from him using my last name.

"If she had been wounded, they would have said hit or injured or shot. They didn't use any of those words. Instead, they said, 'Gone.' To me, it meant she was dead, and unfortunately, I was right."

"So while all this was going on, you were here in the house?"

"Yes."

"Then what happened? And I want the whole story, kid. Why did you end up shooting these two people?"

"Detective." This time I let some sarcasm drip from my use of his title. "They came in my home, armed with the weapons you see there on the floor. They both shot at me. This guy here"—I pointed to the first guy I'd shot—"was very furtive in his entry. It took him at least a minute to open the front door enough for him to slip in. I saw his left hand first, then his leg, then his right hand holding the rifle you see beside him. You'll notice he's wearing a head covering, masking his face. "If you check his weapon, you'll find one round missing. If you look a bit, you'll find the casing and the slug, somewhere near here." I pointed to the hole near where my head had been. "It was just three in the morning. I didn't think it was a social call.

"I shot him three times center mass, and he was still on his feet. So I shifted aim and hit him in the throat and head. That's when he went down. He managed just the one shot, a reflex, I think.

"The second guy was coming in hard before the first guy was on the ground. I was still on the floor right there in front of the island. Second guy was moving his assault rifle in my direction when I shot him. He managed to fire five or six rounds before he went down. I'd hit him twice in the head, and one of my shots was wild, missing him completely.

"I stayed right here, watching, just in case either remained a threat or somebody else came in. It was only a minute or two, and Paul came back in the house, letting me know what was going on. I learned from Paul that Connie had been killed, and Belle was missing. As far as I know, they're still out there looking for Belle. That's everything I know."

"Something's going on here, Merrick. You've become a one-kid crime wave. In less than a month, you've killed four people, and you say another has been killed on your property. What's going on, Merrick? Drugs? That's it, isn't it? You're selling drugs."

"Detective Sergeant, don't be an ass." Angus was getting wound up. I could feel it. "Why would Mr. Merrick be involved in the drug trade? He certainly doesn't need the money. There isn't a drug kingpin in Washington state who has the finances of Mr. Merrick. So what's his motive for getting involved in that lifestyle?

"You can clearly see, Detective Sergeant, that both these intruders are well inside Mr. Merrick's home. You can see they've obscured their identity with masks. They are both wearing body armor. Both have rifles and have fired their weapons in the general direction of Mr. Merrick.

"In fear of his life, Mr. Merrick did the only thing he could do. He defended himself, successfully. He didn't run out the back door. We know now there was another hostile somewhere else on the property as that person or another accomplice shot young Connie. Why don't you focus your energy on figuring out who is behind these deadly assaults on my client instead of treating him as a suspect? Why do you insist on trying to belittle him? All you're doing is antagonizing somebody who is in a position, if he so chooses, to make your current career choice very uncomfortable and difficult."

Angus continued, "I recognize you dislike my client. Your reasoning baffles me. Regardless, Mr. Merrick and I expect you to begin treating him with the same respect you treat other residents and citizens of this area. I have created a file of your dealings with my client, Detective. There are ample reasons to file a complaint. If you continue your current behavior, I will advise Mr. Merrick to pursue a formal complaint. Do you understand?"

Detective Winslow was seemingly not taking this in a constructive manner. Veins were bulging out of his face and head. He'd turned an interesting shade of deep red, and again I feared for his health. Truly.

Angus and I just stood there, watching the detective. He said nothing, then after a couple minutes, turned on his heel and strode out the front door.

"We'll see if he takes that to heart or not. I'd say our odds are not good."

"It's okay. Really. I should thank him. He doesn't know it, but he's giving me a great opportunity to learn how to hold my tongue and mind my manners even when confronted by a verbal bully. Quite honestly, I'm grateful for the opportunity to practice this while under pressure. I'm not angry with him, not really. I realize he can't help it. He's just being who he is. I doubt his life is very happy. I feel a bit sorry for him, truth be told. He's a pretty insecure guy overall."

Angus and I walked outside. It was still dark but seemed to be lightening up a bit in the east. The crime scene van had just pulled up. Big ole high cube box on the back of a truck cab, dual wheels in back. They were packing a lot of gear in that rig.

Winslow approached the truck and talked with the occupants for a bit, then moved toward the woods. I assumed he saw lights through the trees and was headed to where Connie was lying.

Just then I heard some static in my earpiece, then Teal talking in my ear, "We've found Belle. Get paramedics here quick."

Angus and I looked at each other. I hurried to the two ambulance paramedics and told them to follow me and hurry. Each grabbed a heavy-looking bag and kept up with me as we hustled into the woods. Teal was guiding me, describing where they were with Belle.

The three of us continued hustling through the trees. We could now see a couple flashlights moving around just ahead, so we moved in that direction.

Teal's voice was in my ear again, "I can see you, JC. Keep coming toward our flashlights."

I hustled a bit faster, and the two paramedics kept up. It was just another minute, and we arrived where Teal and Taco were knelt beside Belle. She had a huge bruise forming along the right side of her head, had cuts on her face, and the knuckles of both hands were bloody. She'd evidently been taken by surprise and only had time to fight, no time to call for help. It was pretty clear she'd given some accounting of herself. From her hands and knuckles, it looked like she at least did some damage.

The lighting was lousy, but I could still see that Belle's coloring wasn't good. It looked like whoever had done this to her thought she was down for good. They'd piled leaves and brush over her, thinking to obscure her for a time. It had almost worked.

While the paramedics were working on Belle, I was able to grasp her foot. She was missing both her boots and wasn't wearing any socks. How in the world did that happen?

At least I had direct skin contact. I just mumbled, no louder than a very soft whisper, "You're going to be okay, Belle. Don't worry. Everything will be fine." Then I moved away so the paramedics could continue their work.

I hadn't been in their way but still didn't want to crowd them. Nobody had noticed me touching Belle or mumbling. They were occupied with other thoughts and actions.

Over my earbud, I learned that Kip had found Belle covered in dead leaves, brush, and other forest detritus. He went to Teal and guided him back to where he'd found Belle. Teal got Taco to come to him, and they uncovered Belle.

I'd learned the paramedics told both Teal and Taco that had they not found Belle until morning, she'd not have made it. As it was, they said she might survive but was in grave condition. I saw Bobby hustle toward the aid truck. He was back in view in no time with a collapsible gurney under his left arm.

Two more squad cars arrived, thankfully with no sirens. I'd left Belle to the paramedics. My work there was finished, and I didn't want to slow down the process of treating and transporting Belle to the ambulance and Tacoma General. I was headed back to the house and emerged from the forest as officers got out of their squad cars.

Four more deputies had arrived and were walking up to where Winslow was in hushed conversation with the first two responding officers. They were together for just a minute or two, then the officers who had just arrived returned to their cars and drove off.

There were four crime scene technicians. All were carrying hand luggage and had white Tyvek-like clothing under their left arms. Splitting up, two went into the forest toward where Connie had died. The other two toward the front door of my house, stopping and set down their cases. These two proceeded to climb into their crime scene garments, then slip white booties over their shoes. Looked like the booties were made of the same stuff as their onesies. They picked up their cases again and stepped inside. I figured this might take a while.

Angus had been listening to Winslow, watching the crime-scene folks, and now walked up to me. "Your whole property is now an active crime scene, JC. They'll bring in a full team at first light and go through your forest with a sieve. Winslow doesn't want anything disturbed in your home in the living area. You can still stay here and move about, but stay out of the living area and your lawn.

"Jack will likely make arrangements to pull more of his people to you. They need to get the upper hand on your safety. Whoever is involved is determined. It would be nice to have a motive, but right now we can only guess. How are you? This has been another rough night for you."

"Right now, I'm pretty numb. Part of me doesn't think this is real. Feels like I should wake up and all this will have been a bad dream. I mean, I know better, but still…"

"I understand, JC. This is tough. I'm very saddened to have lost Connie. Jack will likely be devastated. First, Kim's attacked, now Connie's death, and Belle's in grave condition. A suggestion. I'd not use the kitchen at all until the crime scene folks are finished. This is a pretty straightforward scene. I think they'll be wrapped up by 9:00 a.m. or 10:00 a.m. Then they'll release the house back to you. I know you didn't get much sleep last night. Why don't you and Kip go back to bed? That way, the detective sergeant will leave you alone and can't gripe about you or Kip disturbing his crime scene."

I saw Jack coming out of the forest as Angus and I were wrapping up.

"I'm going with Belle. I'll call from the hospital." Jack jumped in his pickup and seconds later was gone.

Angus said he'd be in touch later in the morning, and he was gone. Paul was still here, as were Teal, Taco, Bobby and Kim. I left them to make their own arrangements. I'd been riding my adrenaline high and was in the process of crashing; needed my bed badly.

I knew Paul and Kim would watch the crime scene crew as well as be on alert to any more attacks or events. I was back to feeling confident the rest of the night would hold no surprises but was just beginning to deal with losing Connie.

I called Kip, and we headed in the house and to bed. I could feel Winslow's eyes following my every step, making sure I didn't screw up his precious crime scene. Kim was watching the detective closely, and I could tell he didn't like it much. Kip was right beside me, so I knew we'd not disturb anything.

Once the two of us were back in my bedroom, I closed the door. Kip looked at me like I'd lost my mind. How's a dog supposed to prowl around the house when he's confined to a room, his stare seemed to say. "It's okay, Kip, you can stay in with me for a while."

I didn't even bother changing clothes. I just lay on top the bed and pulled the bedspread over me. Figured I could sleep for a week like this. Kip was feeling chummy as he hopped on the bed and lay down with his butt almost in my face, his head facing my bedroom door. And I was gone, like spitting in a hurricane. Next thing I knew, it was morning.

CHAPTER 41

Monday. Supposed to be a busy day. There was a pall in the air. Then again, maybe it was just me. Getting myself cleaned up, I made my way to the kitchen. Kim was already up. Coffee in the pot. She was sitting at the island deep in thought as I approached. I noticed her pistol resting near her hand. I guess we all needed to have our weapons in easy reach. I went back to my room and grabbed my Beretta from the nightstand. Checked it to be certain the magazine was full with one chambered and the safety was engaged. I shoved my Beretta and the holster inside the back of my jean's waistband and slid another full magazine in my pocket. Clipped the holster on and made my way back to the kitchen.

Approaching Kim, I said, "How's everybody doing this morning, Kim?" Looked like she was feeling the loss of Connie too.

"It's quiet." Kim was staring off in the distance, likely not seeing anything in particular.

"How about oatmeal this morning? I can make a good-sized batch. Promise I won't screw it up. We've fresh berries to add and toast if you'd like."

"Fine." I didn't know Kim well, but in the time I'd known her, she'd not been a one-word person. It seemed she was really down.

I'd noticed her coffee cup was nearly empty. I walked to the coffee maker, got the pot, and refilled Kim's mug. Went back in the kitchen and started another pot, then set about making oatmeal, cleaning berries, and toasting some multigrain bread.

Oatmeal was just ready when Paul came in. He looked like Kim sounded. Withdrawn and tense. He, too, had his pistol on his hip and determination in his eyes.

"Hey, Paul. Any word on Belle? Have you heard from Jack yet this morning?"

"No." And that was it from Paul. Wow. Things were really tense around here.

"Fresh oatmeal on the stove. Berries, brown sugar, milk, toast on the island. Coffee's fresh. Help yourself."

Paul moved to the kitchen while I busied myself pouring my first cup of coffee of the day. Then I grabbed a bowl, scooped some oatmeal, added strawberries and blueberries, brown sugar, and a bit of milk, picked up a couple slices of toast and a spoon, and sat a couple seats away from Kim. I wanted to give her space; seemed she'd prefer the distance right now.

Paul had loaded up on breakfast and sat beside me. "So how does this healing thing of yours work? You used it on Belle last night, yeah?"

"I did. Honestly, I have no idea how it works or why. It's like I said Saturday night. I've not had this, whatever it is, long. Belle is the third human I've touched using it. I don't know if I'm doing it right or wrong. Don't even know if there is a right or wrong. Don't know if it is always available or only sometimes. I've no hint whatsoever of why I seem to be able to do this. Why?" Paul didn't answer, just looked at me. Something was definitely off. "What's going on? Something's up. I can see it in both of you. What is it?"

"We heard from the hospital last night. Belle didn't make it."

"What?! How can that be? She was conscious when we found her. I didn't see any gunshot wound. She made eye contact with me while I was touching her foot. I did the same thing with her that I did with Kim and Karen Danvers. They're both fine. I don't understand."

"Neither do we. All I know is Belle seemed to be holding on when they got her to the hospital. They had her in the emergency room examining her when she started to fade. Doctors and nurses couldn't get her stable, and she was gone."

Now I was down to single-word responses. "No." My appetite had been a bit shaky already. Now it deserted me completely. I pushed my bowl of oatmeal and berries away. Same with the toast. Picked up the dishes and scooped the uneaten food in the garbage. Put my dishes in the dishwasher, then walked out the front door.

I needed some undisturbed quiet, a place where I could go and just sit and think. Kip would find me if he wanted. Right now, I needed to figure out what was going on. This wasn't right. Something was messed up and messed up good.

Evidently, I'd walked fairly deep into the trees. I was sitting there, back leaning against a majestic old cedar, thinking, when I heard somebody approaching. Nothing registered, and I just didn't care. Bobby walked up and sat down beside me. "Hey."

Just kept staring at the trees. I wasn't trying to be rude; I just didn't want to talk. We sat like that, I really don't know how long, and I realized I was crying. Tears making their way down my cheeks and dripping on the ground. Huh.

I was feeling lower than a snake's belly. I'd failed. My supposed gift had failed me. Now I couldn't trust it if I ever could. Were Karen and Kim accidents? Coincidences? Had I ever had the ability to heal? Maybe the robin and foxes really were only stunned. Both things couldn't be true. One of 'em had to be a lie. I was afraid the lie was me. It felt like God betrayed me, and right now I was starting to get pretty upset with Him. He let a nice person die.

Well, I certainly wasn't the hot stuff I'd thought. Just a kid with too much money. Amazing how fast we can accept wonderous events in our lives. I'd helped or been a conduit to help two people. Maybe. Probably not. It had felt good to help, amazingly good. I'd assumed my new ability would be with me forever. In my hubris, I hadn't realized it wasn't me at all. Not in any way. An accident of fate. Nothing more. Nothing else. Another lesson learned…don't get full of yourself even if only to yourself. And never ever tell anybody else. It just is not worth the pain. It's a sure path to failure and worse. *Lord, please forgive my folly.*

Somewhere along the way, Bobby had left. I was still sitting there, a thousand thoughts running through my head and heart. None of them good or constructive. I was lost in my own emotional forest, trying to figure out where I was, trying to figure out if I'd ever find my way back to who I'm supposed to be. I figured finding my way was going to take some time, longer than I intended to sit here lost in my thoughts.

That's when I realized somebody was standing nearby watching me. It was Lu. It was also late afternoon.

"Hey." Lu did have a way with words.

"Hey. What are you doing here? Aren't you in academy today?"

"This is more important. You are more important. Angus called and filled me in a while ago. It seemed to me it was a good idea to come see you. Standing here, watching, I was right."

"Belle's dead."

"I know. Angus told me."

"I don't understand. I knew she was going to be okay. But she died. All that crap I spewed Saturday was a lie. I don't have any gift. If I did, Belle would be here. She'd still be with us. Losing Connie was bad enough. Belle is impossible. I'm lost, Lu. Completely and utterly lost."

"Why, JC? Why are you lost?"

"I thought I had this ability. But I don't. What happened with Karen Danvers and Kim were accidents. Coincidences. Nothing to do with me. It was all a false belief. I bought into that ability with everything. Guess I'm too young and naive to have known better. I know now. I've always believed everything happens for a reason. We don't have to understand the reason, and most of the time we don't. Nevertheless, there's a reason.

"This. This defies my belief system. There is no logic here. It doesn't make sense of any kind. Connie's loss was terrible. I'm feeling guilty because if she hadn't been here, she'd still be alive. So I'm responsible. It's my fault. Belle is even worse. I believed I could help her. I believed I had a power, a touch, that could save her life. I lied to myself. I lied to Belle. And I lied to all of you Saturday night. I'm a fraud of the first order."

"You really don't like yourself very much right now, do you? I've never seen you like this. Not even when you lost your parents."

"I wasn't responsible for my parents' death. I had no hand in that, so it wasn't my fault. See the difference? I'm glad for Karen Danvers. Most especially glad she doesn't remember me being with her. What a fake I am. Kim knows. I told her Saturday. Now she knows I'm a fraud. Angus, Jack, and all these people know I'm a fraud. You and Mat and Kyle know too. All I had to do was keep my mouth shut, but no. I had to 'share my wonderous secret.' How am I supposed to live this down? Tell me that."

Her voice was a soft reply, "Self-loathing doesn't suit you, Sailor. Back up and listen to me. You were who you were before you ever even thought about having any sort of ability, right? Don't answer that. Your folks raised an incredible young man. You have shown that to everybody with whom you've interacted if they were paying attention. Before your ability, you were generous, funny, talented, smart, caring, and kinda cute.

"Then this ability of yours gets discovered. You test it, and it seems valid. You use it, and it works. Then it doesn't. How does that ability, when it disappeared or perhaps was never there, how does that change you?

"When you had the gift or whatever you want to call it, you were still generous, funny, talented, smart, and caring. Right now, cute is off the table. That ability, whether you had it or not, appears to be gone. Maybe it was never there, as you said. Maybe it was coincidence. Doesn't matter. You were you, with a bit of added spice, that's all. Great spice, to be sure. But it was only the cherry top of the whipping cream on top of the sundae. You, Mr. Merrick, are the whole sundae. Or you were. You have exactly what you had before your ability showed up. Except now you doubt yourself, and you're wallowing in self-loathing. That's not the JC Merrick I've known, not my classmate, and sure isn't the guy who took me to the Mariners game.

"This new guy I'm talking to? I don't think much of him. He's depressing. He's focused on his own misery. He isn't funny or generous. He's squandering his talent, acting anything other than smart and isn't caring in any way. It's given him an ugly personality, one I don't care to be around. Let me know if you find the other guy. I liked him. I liked him a lot."

With that, Lu got up and walked away. Great. Just what I need. Another person leaving my life. Probably for the best anyhow. She was always outta my league. Time for me to get used to it. I continued sitting there, thinking about absolutely nothing.

The shadows were getting longer in the trees. Evening. A lost day. Maybe I needed to get used to these too. I got up and made my way back to the house. Walking back, I realized Kip hadn't visited me. Smart dog. I wasn't fit company for man or beast.

I was just walking out of the trees, headed toward the house, when I saw Lu get in her car and head out the drive. Huh. She'd stayed longer than I'd thought. Wonder what that's all about? Didn't really matter.

I saw Paul, Angus, and Jack standing near where Lu had been visiting with them. Whatever.

"How are you doing, JC?" this came from Angus.

"Not good. I'm headed to bed." I'd looked at my watch; it was exactly six thirty in the evening. I didn't care.

Nobody said anything as I made my way into the house and to my bedroom. I left the bedroom door open, didn't bother getting undressed, just put my pistol and holster on the nightstand, kicked off my shoes, and lay down on the bed. I pulled the quilt over me and closed my eyes.

Chapter 42

Sometime during the night, Kip had jumped on the bed and was lying beside me. This time, his head was by mine. I could feel his warm breath on my neck. Kip was the constant in my life. He always understood. He could sense when things weren't right. Today had been one of those times. I was almost afraid to see what tomorrow would bring.

I didn't get up Tuesday morning. Just stayed in bed and felt depressed. Part of my brain knew this was silly. I'd hardly met Connie or Belle. They seemed like nice people, but I wasn't close to either of them. I'd known them a couple of days. That was it. Now this. That part of my brain knew I needed to snap out of it. Right. I just wasn't interested enough to try. I was locked in sadness, grieving the loss of two human beings who had died protecting me, grieving the loss of an ability to heal others, to make a positive impact in the lives of so many who just needed a break. Now I couldn't even do that.

It was dark outside now. Another day lost. First yesterday, now today. I needed help. I dug in my jeans pocket for the card Dr. Church had given me. It was 8:00 p.m. I hadn't eaten since yesterday morning; still wasn't hungry. Definitely needed help. I called Dr. Church.

Two rings, then came, "Phyllis Church."

"Hi, Dr. Church. This is JC Merrick. I need your help."

I could hear concern in her voice. "What's going on, JC? Are you okay?"

"No. Two of my bodyguards were killed Sunday night. All this stuff has caught up with me, and I'm not handling it well at all."

"Do you need me to meet you at the hospital?"

"No. I'm not suicidal. I'm just in a really deep hole where it's dark with no way out. I need you to throw me some sort of ladder so I can climb out of here."

"Frankly, I'm amazed this hasn't happened sooner. I've been waiting for this for months, JC. You've had to deal with more tragedy in two years than most people face in a lifetime. Will you be okay until tomorrow morning?"

"Sure."

"I want you in my office at 7:00 a.m. Can you be there then?"

"Yes."

"Alright. I'll see you then. Do you have someone with you now?"

"I've had bodyguards staying since before Saturday's party. I assume there's somebody in the house."

"Okay. I want you to be very mindful of yourself, JC. If anything changes or you feel worse, I want you to go to whomever is in the house with you and have them drive you to the hospital. Have them call me right away. Do you understand?"

"Sure." And I hung up.

Lying back down on the bed, I saw Kip was gone. He'd had enough too. Didn't blame him at all. He could come and go as he pleased. Good for him.

I set my alarm for 6:15 a.m. and closed my eyes. My brain was on a hamster wheel. I don't think I slept more than an hour all night. I looked at the clock for the umpteenth time and saw it was just after six in the morning. I thought about not seeing Dr. Church. Why bother? Didn't make any difference. But some small part of me knew I was in trouble and had to do something, or I'd get stuck here maybe for a long time.

Getting up, I got cleaned up, put on clean jeans and tee shirt and a clean pair of socks, found my tennis shoes, and was putting them on when I heard Kim enter the room.

"How you doing, Cowboy?"

"Not good. I'm headed out to see Dr. Church. Probably be back before nine this morning."

"Okay. Let's go."

"No. I know how to drive there."

"Of course, you do. That's not the point, is it?"

"I'll be okay."

"Well, you aren't now, are you? And that still isn't the point."

"Fine." And I walked around Kim and down the hall.

Jack was there with Angus. Paul and Teal were in the kitchen, drinking coffee.

"I'm glad to see you up, JC," came from Angus. "I imagine you're hungry. I'm hearing you've not eaten for two days."

"I'm going to see Dr. Church. Kim insists on taking me. Should be back before nine." And I walked out the front door to Kim's Corvette. Somewhere along the line, she'd gone home and brought her car back. I heard her footsteps approach and climbed in the passenger side.

"Buckle up, Cowboy. We've a doctor to see." And we were off to see Dr. Church.

Traffic was heavy this time of morning. We were already in the first minutes of the morning commute. It took about twenty-five minutes to get to Dr. Church's office. We ended up only a few minutes early.

I noticed LeAnn had just pulled into the parking area. She got out of her car, locked it, and walked up to us. Leaning down on the passenger window of the Vette, LeAnn said, "C'mon in, JC. Dr. Church is waiting for you." Huh.

Kim and I got out of her car and followed LeAnn into the office. She had me follow her back to the patient exam area and took me to Dr. Church's office. I'd never been in a doctor's office before. Not what I expected. Her office was neat and well organized with a couple original art paintings on the walls. Real plants. Overall, comforting.

"Good morning, JC. How are you this morning? Any change since we spoke last night?"

"No change. Still in the bottom of a hole." Tears were running down my face. I was just so damn sad. About everything.

"Okay. We're going to do a couple things this morning. First, LeAnn is going to pull your stitches out. It won't hurt. A couple might sting a little bit, but nothing worse than that. I'm prescribing you amitriptyline. It's a TCA drug or tricyclic. It works well and has been prescribed for thirty years. I'm giving you a prescription for a thirty-day supply and two refills. You'll take the full ninety-day course. I'm prescribing 25 mg tablets. Take one with breakfast... You will be eating breakfast this morning, one with lunch and one at bedtime. I want you to keep this up for a full ninety days, regardless of how much better you're feeling. Okay? It can take up to ninety days for these drugs to be fully effective. It's obvious to me your blood chemistry is out of balance. This is what's most likely causing your symptoms.

"JC, these things happen. What you're experiencing is happening because you've been through a ringer. Most people can handle one tragedy. They'll be blue for a week, maybe two, but then they'll start climbing out of it and get on with their lives. In a little over a year, you've lived through the loss of both your parents. That life event will throw anybody. You died. I don't even know how to suggest you deal with that. You were forced to kill two human beings, and life just caught up with you."

"There's more. We were attacked again this past Sunday night, early Monday morning. I had to kill two more guys who were determined to kill me. During that attack, two of my bodyguards were killed. Belle was alive when she was taken to Tacoma General. I'd touched her, and we had eye contact. She got to the emergency room, then died. Whatever ability I thought I had doesn't exist. What I told you all Saturday evening was a lie. I don't have any special talent or ability. Otherwise, Belle would be recovering instead of being dead."

"Good Lord! No wonder you're here! This explains everything."

"Only almost. I was pretty messed up Monday. Lu came to help cheer me up, and it didn't work. She's out of my life now. So another loss."

"JC. Don't think for a minute your Lu has given up on you. If she is who I think she is, she's just giving you time to recover. If she's worthy of you, she's giving you space to heal before coming back in your life. She probably hoped that a stern talk from her would snap you out of it. Well, it didn't and frankly couldn't. What you're experiencing is chemical, not emotional. Your brain chemistry is, I strongly suspect, way out of balance. LeAnn will be drawing blood to verify what I suspect. We'll let you know either later today or tomorrow morning.

"I want you to be prepared for the side effects of this drug. It's going to make you sleepy. That's because your body needs time to heal, and sleep allows your body to heal at a deep level. Your extreme sleepiness will probably last about a week, perhaps a bit less, but maybe as long as two weeks. As those days go by, you'll notice you're not as sleepy as you were a few short days earlier.

"You'll also notice you're not as down and not feeling as depressed. That should start somewhere in the next week or so. I think your emotions won't feel so raw by the end of this coming weekend. You'll be amazed at how much better you feel. I think, given a couple weeks, you won't even recognize yourself. I'm pretty sure you'll feel better than you've felt in quite a while.

"Remember, JC, it isn't the drug that's making you feel better. You aren't getting addicted to something that'll give you a false sense of euphoria. The drug is only restoring your brain's chemistry, putting it back in balance. That's it. Balance is a wonderful thing, my friend, and you're going to get there rather quickly, I suspect. Regardless, this process is going to take as long as it's going to take. There is no rushing it. Not if you want your emotions resolved and returned to your version of normal. This is not a course in taking short cuts. Alright?"

"Sure. Any other side effects?"

"Yes. Very minor. You might have a dry mouth. Just drink water or whatever. Sip on it throughout the day, and it won't bother you. Eat healthy meals. Have you been eating?"

"I'd been getting better at it until Sunday night. I've not eaten since then."

"This is Wednesday, JC. Wednesday. You must eat. Force yourself if you have to. As the drug begins to work in your system, and the time varies for everybody, your appetite will come back. I expect you'll be eating like a horse within a week. Now anything else?"

"How long do I need to take this stuff?"

"I want you to take it for a full ninety days. I think you'll feel completely normal in less than half that time. But we need your brain chemistry to stay in balance. If we stop your med early, you can slide back, and we don't want that. I think ninety days will do just fine. We'll still reevaluate in six weeks. I want you back then. LeAnne will schedule your follow-up now."

"Okay. At least now I have some hope. For a couple days, even that had left me."

"You're going to be fine, JC. And you're going to notice positive changes very quickly. Now wait here. LeAnn will be in for a blood draw. She'll remove your stitches and get you scheduled for a follow-up. She'll call you with the results as soon as we have them. Okay?"

One of the reasons I liked Dr. Church so much was her positive outlook on life. Her smile lit up the room, and it was directed at me. I had always trusted her before; I was going to trust her now. She patted me on the shoulder then got up and left the room.

It was only a minute later and LeAnn was with me. Tweezers, a scalpel-looking knife, and stuff to draw some blood. "Which do you want first, JC? Stitches out or blood draw?"

"Whatever works best for you, LeAnn. Doesn't matter."

"Blood draw it is." A minute later, she'd drawn two vials of my blood, put a cotton ball over the needle site, and taped it in place.

"Okay, now for those stitches. Have they been itching?"

"Not yet."

"Well, let's get 'em out. We're a bit early on this, but they look ready. A few of these might sting a tad, but nothing painful, I promise." LeAnn set to work grabbing stitches with the tweezers and gently pulling them out, the scalpel neatly slicing every now and then to let the suture release enough to grab with the tweezer. A couple stitches pulled, but nothing really bothered. It was the work of only a minute or two, and they were all out.

"There may be one or two hiding in there, JC. Don't worry. They'll work themselves out. It'll itch and look like a pimple or ingrown hair. Next thing you know, out comes a stitch! This sometimes happens three or four years later. Anyhow, nothing to worry about.

"I'll call you on your bloodwork as soon as the lab sends their report. Shouldn't be later than tomorrow. I'll send you a reminder in the mail for your follow-up. Any questions for me?"

"No. Thanks, LeAnn."

"We're always here for you, JC. Whenever you need us. Keep that in your mind and heart, okay?" She picked up all her stuff and was gone.

I followed LeAnn out with my prescription in hand. Kim saw me coming, and we walked to the front door. As usual, Kim was out first, and I followed. We got in her car and headed out the parking lot. It was 7:40 a.m.

The drugstore wouldn't open until at least eight, probably nine. "Do you know of a twenty-four-hour pharmacy, Kim?"

"I think there's a Walgreens close to the hospital that opens early, like, about six in the morning. Do you want to check there?"

"Please."

We made our way to Tacoma General. Sure enough, just down the street was a Walgreens with a few cars in the parking lot. "I'll just be a minute. Need to get this filled, then I'll be right back out." I opened the door and climbed out. Kim was waiting on the sidewalk.

"We have a deal, remember?"

"Sure." And we both walked into Walgreens. Their pharmacy was open. There were a few customers in the store, but I was first in line at the pharmacy. I handed my prescription to the druggist behind the counter and was told I needed to wait a few minutes.

Five or six minutes later and my prescription was filled. Kim and I headed back to her car, got in, and were ready to go. "Remember the last time we got a prescription for you, JC? That was exciting!"

"Yeah."

"You're no fun at all this morning. Hang on, Cowboy!" And we were out of the parking lot headed down the street toward the Narrows Bridge and home.

No surprises all the way home. It did feel kinda dull, but I was still feeling numb and disengaged. Time to put something in my stomach and take my first med.

There were some scrambled eggs on a platter. Bacon and toast too. I put a couple spoons of cold eggs on a plate and microwaved 'em for a minute. Warm was okay. I poured a glass of orange juice and grabbed a slice of bacon and toast. Sat at the island and picked at what was in front of me, tasting nothing, then took my med.

I'd noticed some people by the garage when Kim and I drove up. I slowly walked outside to where they had gathered to see what was going on.

Jack was there with Paul, Teal, and Angus. A new face and a new vehicle in the driveway. Bobby was looking toward the forest. I figured Dave would be around somewhere, or maybe he was off today. Kim had joined Jack and the others.

This must be Dan Hastings. The side of the new pickup, a heavy-duty one-ton Ford with dual rear wheels, had a graphic on the driver's door, Hastings Construction, with two phone numbers.

I could tell by looking that this guy was hands-on. He was wearing heavy trousers that had seen a lot of hard use, a flannel shirt, unbuttoned, with a blue crewneck tee shirt underneath, and heavy work boots that had seen a lot of miles. All his clothing was clean but obviously tools of his trade.

Dan's face was weathered and lined. I'd guess him to be around fifty-five or sixty. Hard miles, but he was animated and smiled easily enough. He and Jack were deep in a conversation.

"Sure. You can do that. But it's going to cost. I'd prefer an engineering study to make sure your foundation and soil can handle the load. It's probably nothing, but I like to make sure. This house looks well constructed. I think I remember when it was built. I'm not remembering the builder, but they did a lot of ground prep before they started on the foundation.

"Is there anybody you recommend for the engineering study?" Jack was pursuing his original line of thinking when he described what he wanted to do for a safe room.

"There're three or four names I can give you. People I've worked with before. I don't recommend anybody. That way you know I'm being straight with you. I don't have deals with anybody. I do my job, others do theirs. I can tell you what to look for, some questions to ask. I just don't want any responsibility for work I haven't controlled. Saw that happen to others. A couple went broke trying to make an extra buck. No thank you."

"That's about right. Okay, Dan. You're hired. Tell us what you need from us. Get me the names of the engineers, and we'll get started. What do you need to know about the second building?" This came from Angus.

"Give me a rough sketch, dimensions, and what you're going to do with it. I'll write up some thoughts, and we can go from there. I'd like to do this room first. Get that completely finished so you can see my work before we dive into building the shop. I'm capable and confident, but you don't know that yet. I want you satisfied with the remod before we move onto the shop. Okay?"

"You've got a deal. What kind of deposit do you need on the remodel?" Angus was still in attorney mode.

"No deposit. I'll buy all the material, submit original invoices to you for reimbursement. I'd like to be reimbursed within thirty days of original invoice dates. We'll settle the labor end when you've signed off on the completed job. Sound fair?"

"Yes. That works for us just fine." Jack and Angus shook hands with Dan, who then wrote on a piece of paper and handed it to Angus. He then walked back to his pickup, climbed in, and drove away.

"He checked out, Angus. No complaints. Happy customers. Builders Association says he knows his stuff. They said he quit a couple jobs when they pressured him to cut some corners. My kind of guy." This came from Jack.

"Same thing I heard, Angus. He's been out of the service for quite a while, but I did track down a couple guys who served with him. They said Dan was usually given the tough stuff because he always came through. Quality work every time, even on the tinker toy crap that's all precut and just bolts together. No. I'm satisfied," came from Paul.

They, Teal and Kim, seemed to notice me for the first time. Amazingly, I managed a small grin. "Seems I'm in good hands."

"You are that, JC. You are that." Angus was watching me closely. "How are you this morning?"

"Lousy. But I think I'm about to get better." Then I turned around and made my way back inside. I was placing a lot of hope on this medication, but at least I had some hope now. I'd see what the next few days held.

Going inside, I found Kip snoozing on the sofa. Seemed a fine idea, so I sat in the recliner, put my feet up, and lay back. Next thing I knew, somebody was talking to me.

"Hey, sleepyhead. Time to wake up. Time for food and your noon med." Kim was standing beside me, smiling. Seemed I'd fallen asleep and had a couple-hour nap.

"Sure." I made my way to the kitchen, grabbed a couple slices of bread, some ham from the fridge, mustard from the pantry, and a Coke, built my sandwich, ate it, and washed it down with the Coke, saving the last couple swallows for my med. These things did make me sleepy. Time for another nap.

I walked back to the recliner, climbed in, and lay back. Kip decided it was time to cuddle. He jumped up alongside me, laid his head and paws across my chest and lap, let out a couple soft sighs, and closed his eyes. I followed his example, and I was gone.

Somebody was shaking me gently again. This time it was Dave. "JC. Time for supper. I warmed one of your chicken quarters. There's some salad and watermelon. Your med is beside your plate."

"I'm not supposed to take the last one today until bedtime."

"The way you're going, this is your bedtime, buddy. I don't think it'll matter. I'd rather not have to wake you up just to swallow a pill, then have you work to get back to sleep. Just eat something, take your med, and you're finished for the day. Okay?"

"Sure." Again, I climbed out of the recliner and made my way to the island. Just as Dave said, I had some of the cooked chicken quarter, a plate with salad on it, and a bowl of watermelon chunks. A full glass of water was beside it all.

I nibbled at the chicken and salad but ate some of each. Worked through most of the watermelon and drank the water taking my med. I put everything away where it belonged. Noticed there were a couple more cooked chicken quarters in the fridge along with a big bowl of watermelon that was almost full. No bowl with salad in it; I wonder who made that for me. Dave?

Anyhow, I wandered outside. Saw Paul and Jack over in the grassy area near the house, right where I'd thought of building the garage. They had bright-orange string tied on stakes they'd driven in the ground. Looked like they were marking the perimeter of the shop. These guys were more involved than I was right now. Time for me to help at least.

I walked over to them and watched as they tied the string on the last stake. "This looks good."

"Well, we talked about it. We figured you needed space to store future builds, space to work on at least two, so we figured three. Space for tools and chests, three hydraulic lifts, paint and metal work rooms, and space for a small office. You know, where you go to order parts, make lists, do things other than wrenching on cars. You'll notice we added areas for paint and metal fabrication.

"Altogether we figured about 6,500 square feet, so we spent some more of your money and made it 7,500 feet, just in case. No matter how big we build this, you're going to run out of room. Just a question of time. We figured this size would last you a couple of years, and we want the build and plan to allow for an addition of whatever size. That means we have to plan the building orientation and where we put the lifts and any other things that are very expensive to relocate."

"How about we push it out to ten thousand square feet and call it good? We'll add a small showroom area for three or four completed cars before they're sold or donated, whatever. And there'll be space for me to keep and store a couple too. I'll just manage the growth and not exceed the size of the building. I really don't care."

"Let's think about that. We've a month at least until this will break ground. I think you're going to care, just as you always have. Let's give it a couple weeks. Okay?" I knew Jack was being gentle with me, guiding me without telling me what to do. I appreciated that about him.

"Sure. I'm beat, guys. Heading to bed. Maybe I'll have more energy tomorrow." And I walked back to the house, down the hall into my bedroom. Left the door open again. Fell in bed with my clothes on again. Tomorrow I'd take a shower.

Chapter 43

Sleep wouldn't come. My brain was going round and round with Belle's death. It didn't make sense. I'd healed Karen and Kim, most probably a robin, and a fox and her kits. What had happened with Belle? No matter how I tried, I just couldn't put this square peg in any of the round holes. Nothing about her death fit. Nothing.

My brain chased shadows all night long. No matter how I looked at the situation and circumstances surrounding Belle's death, I couldn't settle it. The situation with Belle was an outlier. Everything else fit together. The prior events made sense of a sort. There was a certain logic even if that logic was nuts. Supernatural? Maybe. Extrasensory perception? Again, maybe. An ability given by God? Made as much sense as anything else, probably more.

Finally, around four in the morning, I figured out the only circumstance that made any sense at all, regarding Belle. Whatever gift or ability I had had been temporary. It had to have been a short-term thing. I could get my head around that. Nothing else came close. Satisfied I'd solved the unsolvable, I was finally able to drift off to sleep.

Seven in the morning came, well, at seven in the morning. I'd had a very short night's sleep. It would have to be enough. Lots to get done today. I needed to find the energy and motivation somewhere.

It was Thursday already. Have you ever noticed how sometimes the days just fly by? And how other times the days drag? Well, I was dragging today, not time. Meds had really kicked in. Looked like I'd be a temporary charter member of the WBNS (We Be Napping Society). I was hoping for a very temporary membership.

Got myself cleaned up and headed to the kitchen to make some breakfast. Walking into the kitchen, I noticed Kim already there along with Paul. "Good morning."

"Hey, Cowboy. How are you doing this morning?" Kim had that sparkle in her eyes. She had great eyes. Very expressive. Reminded me of Lu. Ah, Lu. I'd call her later today to apologize.

"Hey, Kim. I'm okayer than I was yesterday, I think. Didn't sleep much last night despite the meds supposing to make me sleepy. My brain wouldn't shut off thinking about Belle. Sometime late last night or early this morning, I figured out why she died."

"What do you mean?" Paul was looking directly at me.

"Nothing else makes sense. Whatever I had was a temporary thing. I know, sure as I'm standing here, that something about my touching Karen Danvers caused her to go into remission and recover from her cancer. I know holding Kim's hand while she was in the ICU caused her to heal far more quickly than is considered normal. And I know when I touched Belle as the paramedics were arriving, her eyes fluttered some, and she smiled. I know she was getting better at that point.

"What I think is, whatever caused the others to heal was missing with Belle. It wasn't full strength if you understand what I'm meaning. She got half a jolt or whatever. The ability or gift or curse, whatever you want to call it, was leaving or diminished. Maybe I didn't touch her long enough. Either which way, I ended up unable to help Belle like I thought I could or did. That's the only thing that makes sense."

"None of us thought that, JC. Look. It wasn't your job to heal Belle, okay? Not your responsibility, regardless of you having or not having any healing gift or touch. What happened happened. Risks come with this job. We all know it. Our group has been riding a long string of good fortune. That string was bound to break at some point. With Belle and Connie, it did. None of us like the outcome, especially losing two of our team at the same time. These things just happen, regardless of how good we are or how hard we train. We never want to lose a team member, but shit happens.

"Be very clear, JC. You are not to blame. None of this is your fault. Their deaths were caused by the people out to do you harm. Period. Healing Kim or Belle or anybody is not your responsibility. You can't be held accountable for stuff over which you have no control. And you have absolutely no control over whatever was going on when you helped others get well and recover. Okay?" Paul was looking very intense and serious as he said this to me.

"Sure. Intellectually, I almost buy what you said. Emotionally? Not so much. I know emotionally what I had and what I lost. No, it doesn't make sense. No, I didn't have any control over it apparently. Yes, it appears whatever gift or ability I had is gone. But while I had that ability, I truly believe I had a responsibility to help others. How could I not? The dilemmas were there, but still. How could I turn my back on everybody when I knew—knew, mind you—that I could help? Regardless, we are where we are, and it appears there is absolutely nothing I can do about it. I apologize to you and everybody for thinking and offering myself as some sort of healer. I certainly am not."

"JC, we've already said none of this is on you. None of it. You're seventeen! Nobody of any age should have the world on their shoulders, especially at your tender age!" Kim had a bit of fire in her eyes now. "Let's put the blame if we must assign it on those trying to do you harm. That's where the blame rests. Besides, I think we'll learn more today or tomorrow. Jack is having a full autopsy on Belle. We're all wanting to know what happened. We want to know what killed her not why you didn't save her. Do you see the difference?"

"Sure. Change of topic, have you heard when Dan is going to be starting on the remodel?"

"Nothing firm. From yesterday's conversation, it sounded like he was on it as of yesterday, like he was going to start ordering supplies right away. I know he gave names of engineering firms to Angus and Jack yesterday. I'd think they would be calling and picking a good firm to do the study right away. We might have one or more firms out here yet this week to get a look and do their thing."

"Okay. Guess I'm just anxious to get this process started. Sooner it's started, the sooner my life can return to some version of normal. It's great having you here and all, but this has to be tedious for you. Nobody wants to babysit a seventeen-year-old."

"Hey, Cowboy. There's a huge difference between babysitting and protecting. I think Jack told you in the beginning. If you were some snot-nosed, spoiled rich kid, he'd not have taken the contract. No. This is not babysitting. Babysitting doesn't involve guns, getting shot at and shot, people dying, and multiple attempts to kill you. Definitely not babysitting." Kim's eyes had some serious heat in 'em.

"Why don't you go take a nap, JC? You're getting grouchy. Best thing for you now is sleep. Tilting at windmills doesn't serve anybody's best interest, right?" Teal seemed to be another voice of reason. In fact, all Jack's team were pretty good at deescalating situations. Must be part of their training.

"Sure." And I went to my favorite recliner and lay back for a nap.

Next thing I knew, it was noon. Kip had curled up on the sofa and lay there with his head on his front paws looking at me with his big, soulful green eyes. Looked like he was sad. Or maybe it was my imagination.

Several days went by with little interaction from me. I slept, got up and ate, took my meds, and took naps. Rinse and repeat for the rest of the week and well into the next. It was the following Friday, late afternoon, before I realized I'd not yet called Lu. Time to remedy the situation. I'd been on my sleep marathon for nearly two weeks. Maybe I was feeling better.

I dug out my cell phone and called Lu. Second ring... "Lu? JC Merrick here."

"Hey, Sailor! I'd about given up on you. How are you?"

"Think I'm getting better. My doc gave me some meds to take. They really took my legs out from under me. All I've done is sleep for the past couple weeks!"

"This is your Dr. Church, right?"

"Yup. One and the same. They ran some tests, and my brain chemistry was messed up. Meds to fix a chemical imbalance. Side effects of the medication are extreme sleepiness for a week or two and a dry mouth. That's about it."

"But you're getting better, right?"

"I think I am. Today's the first day I've not slept throughout the entire day and night. Up until today it's been a struggle just to wake up and eat, take my meds, and get back to sleep. Not a way to live life for sure."

"Well, I'm glad to hear you're doing better. Have they started on your remodel yet? You know, building your escape room or whatever it's called."

"The engineering study is finished. The contractor starts Monday. Then it'll be about four weeks of noise from seven in the morning until it's too dark to work. It's a good thing I'm getting this sleepiness behind me. I doubt I'll be able to nap at home while the remodel is in process."

"What do you think about coming over to my house for supper tomorrow night? I know Mom and Papa would enjoy seeing you and catching up."

"Thanks, Lu! That means a lot. Can we put it back a week? I'd like to get more on top of my meds than I am right now. Another week should do the trick."

"You mean I have to wait another week before I see you?"

"Not at all. You're welcome to come over anytime. I just don't think my stamina is going to be normal for another week or two. I'd hate falling asleep at your dinner table! Don't think that'd make a good impression on your folks, right?"

"No, I suppose you're right. How about this? Why don't I come visit you tomorrow afternoon? You can show me what they're doing with your safe room, and we can play Scrabble or chess or some board game? I promise to leave before you fall asleep!" I could hear the grin in her voice.

"That's a great idea. You're incredible, Lu, you know that?"

"Flattery alone only gets you to first base, Sailor." I could hear the mischief in her voice.

"Lu, I'm not counting bases. Not with you. Not ever. Regardless, you are incredible, and it's past time I said so."

"JC, you say the nicest things. Gotta go. I'll see you tomorrow afternoon." And with that, Lu was gone.

The rest of the day floated by. I was less sleepy. I was also feeling better about life in general. Still bugged about Belle, but that sharp edge was gone. My drive to answer the question remained, but it didn't consume me. I was starting to feel less a failure in trying to heal her.

Late in the day, Jack drove up. Bobby, Dave, and Taco were here. Bobby inside with me. Taco was on overwatch, and Dave was prowling. All in all, I was feeling secure, and life had found some balance.

I watched Jack approach. He didn't look particularly happy. "Hey, Jack. Good to see you."

"JC. How are you doing?"

"Think I'm improving. Not so desperate to sleep all day and night. I think the med is definitely helping."

"That's good. I thought I'd drive over and give you and everybody an update. I know Bobby's in with you. Dave and Taco are on their way in. I've called Kim, Teal, and Paul. They should be here in just a few minutes. I'll get into everything once everybody is here."

Hmmm. Now I was a bit curious. "Sure. Sounds good. Would you like something while we wait? There's cold pop in the fridge. And there's lemonade and fresh orange juice."

"Lemonade sounds good, JC. Thanks."

So I walked into the house and poured Jack a tall glass of iced lemonade. I'd check with the others when they arrived.

Kim, Teal, and Paul all drove up about two minutes after Dave and Taco walked back to the house. Everybody helped themselves to cold drinks and found seats. Seems we were all curious about what Jack had to share.

"Thanks to you all for coming. There are a few updates, and I want to tell you all at the same time. JC, I've told Angus you'll give him the details of what we'll cover here. He's expecting your call either yet today or tomorrow. Let's get started."

Chapter 44

"First, the engineering study is complete, JC. Dan will be doing a small excavation in your basement, then placing precast, rebar-reinforced concrete piers below your existing basement concrete floor. Once those piers are placed, he'll backfill with sand and gravel, then pour new concrete to bring that part of your basement floor level with the rest. Each pier will have exposed rebar so he'll know the exact placement of reinforced steel floor joists and concrete columns. That solves the weight load of your safe room. The piering and reinforcing process will take ten days, again starting Monday. While the concrete cures, he'll begin demolition of your existing bedroom and frame out the remod using steel studs to replace your existing wood two-by-fours. He's still on target for an overall time frame of thirty days but is hopeful of shortening the timeline, perhaps by as much as a week.

"Next. We've finished installing all your perimeter security. At your convenience, we'll walk your forest and show you what's set up and where. Overall, your sensor network will be invisible to you and everybody else unless you know exactly where to look. That's by design, not accident. We'll start installing your inside sensors this week, doing some coordinating with Dan as he starts demolition on your designated safe room.

"Except for waiting for the completion of your safe room, we'll have your entire security system installed and in beta before the end of next week. We'll beta the entire system within a couple days of Dan's completing your safe room. We've already set the system to accommodate your shop, whatever the size and configuration you decide. Your entire security system is robust and scalable. No worries on expansion or reconfiguration at any time.

"We're staying with your current bodyguards throughout your remodel and construction process. I'm not comfortable with any fewer team members. I suspect you're already thinking about your shop. You and Dan can go over it whenever you like. Always feel free to ask any of us for ideas or suggestions. Other than that, we're out of your way on the shop. It's your baby, and you're in excellent hands with Dan. He's already proven himself as far as Angus and I are concerned.

"I've saved the most difficult topic for last. I commissioned a private autopsy for Belle. JC, I was as baffled as you regarding her passing. Nothing about her death made any sense. That's why I decided to do our own autopsy after the coroner completed his. The coroner found nothing suspicious. His official finding was death caused by heart failure. In other words, natural causes.

"Our people were much more thorough. They did the normal tox screens, then moved to exotic screenings when they found the normal screenings in the normal range but with a few elevated values. However, initial findings did not exceed the normal limits. Upon further testing and screenings, they found evidence of poisoning.

"In this case, Belle was poisoned with batrachotoxin. It is an exceedingly rare neurotoxin produced by a poisonous frog from Columbia. I'll spare you the details. The summary is this. We know from the paramedics that Belle was lucid when she arrived at the hospital. She was taken to the ER for a thorough check. While there, she died of heart failure.

"This particular neurotoxin opens the sodium channels in nerve cells and prevents them from closing. This causes paralysis and, very quickly, death. The usual cause of death is attributed to heart failure, though not exclusively. Belle died quickly, as in very few minutes.

There is no antidote or cure. I believe, based on what we now know, Belle was poisoned in the ER. We don't yet know by whom. The paramedics brought Belle to the ER and put her in an exam room.

"She was transferred to an ER gurney and helped in that transfer process. At that time, she had yet to be poisoned. We believe she was alone for only a minute or two before being seen by an ER nurse, Emily Rittenhaus. Emily has been an ER nurse at Tacoma General for nine years. Excellent employment record. No history of suspicious deaths in connection with her. As far as we can tell, Emily is clean.

"The ER doctor, James Sutton, has been an ER doc for three years. He rotated in from general surgery and has been employed by the hospital for eight years. Again, nothing to suggest he caused Belle's death. His employment history is clean, no record of suspicious deaths or substance abuse. No financial issues, no history of gambling or anything untoward.

"We watched the security footage of Belle's treatment room from the time the paramedics brought her in until she was found deceased. There is one twenty-second spot where the camera is filled with static. Three minutes and twelve seconds later, Belle is found dead. That's all we have. I'm satisfied it's enough to know Belle was murdered by a person or persons unknown.

"My thinking is that Belle got a look at who attacked her and Connie. Whoever it was gave her something that was supposed to kill her. For some unknown reason, it didn't or hadn't had time to act. JC entered the picture, and Belle was saved. By all accounts she was recovering on her way to the hospital. The paramedics, ER doc, and nurse confirm this. Then suddenly, she is dead of a heart attack, which we later learned was caused by an administered neurotoxin.

"The toxin was not injected. It was merely administered on her skin. One drop from a vial would have done it. One swipe from a contaminated cotton swab would do it. The smallest amount placed anywhere on her exposed skin would do it. It leaves no outward trace. Nonetheless, our people are examining every inch of her skin for any tell. I don't know if we'll find anything or not. We'll see. Any questions?"

"Why would somebody go after Belle while she was in the hospital? That had to be high risk for them." I was stumped.

"JC, the only thing we can think is she saw something she wasn't supposed to see. So she had to be eliminated. Nothing else makes sense. As you say, this was very high risk for them. We've questioned the relevant hospital staff, and nobody saw anything suspicious, except for the security camera misbehaving for those few seconds. We've timed it, and it works. That's likely when they killed Belle."

"Do we have any idea yet why whoever it is is after JC?" Paul was asking what we were all wondering.

"Not yet. However, we may be getting closer to a reason. I've assigned one researcher and one analyst to this on a full-time basis, and they're looking into everything. If there is anything to learn, I expect we'll learn it in the next few weeks. We're going all the way back to the time your parents died, JC. Might as well start there and see if something goes off the rails, and if it does, when and what."

"Is there anything I can do to help?" I still felt responsible for Belle's death. However, now it seemed I'd not lost my ability to heal others. Maybe. Seemed to me another test was needed to confirm this ability of mine one way or the other. I'd find somebody needing healing and see what happened.

"There isn't right now. Just keep your guard up. Let me restate that. Yes. There is something you can do, a couple things. I'd like you to coordinate with Teal for some pistol training. Once you're both comfortable with your pistol proficiency, we'll move you on to long guns. The second thing, work with Kim on self-defense. Let's start next week, if that works for you. There is one more item. We missed our job interviews, JC. Are you okay if we do them on Monday?"

"Yes. I want to move forward with this. Have you completed the backgrounds?"

"We have. Six have passed initial screening. All are as clean as we can determine. Three of them seem, again on paper, to be excellent fits. Of course, this is all on paper. If there is anything dark, it's exceptionally well hidden. It may be tough picking only two."

"Well, if it's that tough and three of 'em are as good as we hope, I'll just hire all three. That'll solve that little issue. I have enough cash flow to absorb three domestics and add a mechanic or two later. Besides, I want to help these folks if they are who they say they are. This is something I can do and am more than willing to do. And they'll be helping me too. Goes both ways, so this isn't charity. I think they'd resent that. Know I would. Yeah. Let's get 'em done Monday. Have you mentioned this to Angus at all?"

"No. Thought I'd let you do that."

"Okay. Let me give him a quick call, see if we can do them all in the morning. Then he'll have his afternoon free from us. Give me a minute." I walked down the hallway and called Angus.

"Angus, JC here."

"JC! How are you doing, my boy?"

"Getting better, Angus. I'm home working with Jack and his team. He and I would like to set employment interviews for Monday morning. I want to include you if you're available. Does this work for you?"

"JC, Monday morning is horrid. I'm nonstop until nearly 1:00 p.m. Can we do it in the afternoon?"

"Let me find out." Covering the phone… "Jack, can we do Monday afternoon?"

"Sure."

"Angus? We're good for Monday afternoon. Wanna do 'em at your office?"

"Works for me."

"Okay. Let's give you a cushion, just in case. We'll start at 1:30 p.m. and run until we're finished, probably around 4:30 p.m. Will that work?"

"I'll be ready. I'll make arrangements for Ms. Penrose to stay as well. You never know what a receptionist will learn from loose lips."

"Excellent. Thanks, Angus. I owe you."

"Nonsense. You already pay me handsomely." I could hear the smile in his voice. In fact, I had paid him handsomely. No joke at all. I had Angus on retainer, probably had burned through most of the annual allotment already, or so I assumed. I'd sent him another hundred thousand right after all this drama started. Angus was a polished diamond, and I intended keeping our relationship in top condition.

"Okay. See you Monday." And I was gone this time.

"Alright. Jack, we're set for interviews Monday afternoon, starting at 1:30 p.m. Whoever fits wherever in those times... Kim, you can drive me and participate?" I definitely wanted a woman on my side in this process.

"Absolutely. You forget, Cowboy. We're nearly joined at the hip for now, right?"

"Yup. I'm glad we're moving forward with this. It feels good getting back in action."

"Okay. I think that's it for now," said Jack. "Thanks, JC, for being so flexible and accommodating. You have remarkable patience for one so young."

"No, thank you, Jack. I appreciate you picking up the balls I've been dropping recently. I've been pretty useless these past couple weeks. Today's the first day I'm beginning to feel I have something besides a nap to contribute."

Jack gave us all a nod, then went back to his truck, climbed in, and drove away. Teal and Bobby went into the trees and Kim stayed inside. Taco and Paul headed home for the night. All sure seemed well in hand. I was definitely on the mend. Tomorrow was Saturday, and I was looking forward to sharing time with Lu. She would certainly be the highlight of this week!

CHAPTER 45

Saturday turned out to be wet and soggy. I was up at my usual time, went through my morning cleaning ritual, and headed to the kitchen for breakfast. Kip had deserted me at some point in the night. In the living room, I found him sprawled out on the sofa, taking up the entire three cushions. When Kip stretched out, he stretched out.

Teal was making coffee, and Kim was sitting at the island. I imagined Bobby and Dave were outside and probably miserable with the drizzle.

"Good morning. What a beautifully soggy day." I had to try to inject some humor somewhere, right?

"Ah, welcome to Gig Harbor. Where it's always green because it almost always rains!" Teal was in good form as well this morning.

"Hey, JC. How'd you sleep last night?" Kim had a permanent grin this morning. She likely knew Lu was coming over and wanted to tease me if only just a bit.

"I slept like a baby. Got up every two hours, peed, and went back to sleep." Two could tease. "What's everybody want for breakfast? Eggs? Oatmeal? Pop Tarts? Okay, I don't have any Pop Tarts. But I could run to Olsen's and see what they have for pastries. Interested?"

"You know, that sounds good. Why don't I go and bring back an assortment? Trudy and I are practically on a first-name basis anyhow." Teal liked the idea. Excellent.

"Great! Gives me a bit to get something cooking. Anybody hate oatmeal this morning?"

"Sounds good. I'll be back in fifteen." And Teal was gone.

In the meantime, Kim had made coffee. Now she got busy breaking pecans into small pieces for oatmeal. I made a large batch: three heaping cups of raw oats. In about twelve minutes, it'd be perfect.

Kim dumped in two cups of pecan bits along with the thick-cut rolled oats and water. I stirred 'em in, put the lid on, and moved the stove dial to simmer. Between us, we got cinnamon and brown sugar ready. Kim grabbed some fresh blueberries to wash, and I grabbed the strawberries.

I had just finished cleaning and cutting the strawberries when I heard Teal drive up. I watched him walk up to the house with a closed box of pastries from Olsen's. The oatmeal needed another couple minutes, then we could eat and rotate so Bobby and Dave could come in, get dry, and have a hot breakfast. Today was shaping up to be an excellent day, regardless of the drizzle.

I heard a vehicle in the driveway, then the sound of a car door closing. The crunch of feet on the driveway. Looking out the remaining front room window, I saw Dan walking up to the door. Then his knock came.

Opening the door, I said, "Good morning, Dan. What brings you out on this wet Saturday?"

"Good morning, Mr. Merrick. Jack and I talked earlier. We both thought you'd be sick of your plywood front and back doors by now. Probably more than sick. I made a few inquiries with some suppliers and was able to score three high-security steel doors for you. I have them in the trailer I'm pulling. If it's okay with you, and I can get a couple of your guys to help with lifting, I can get them all installed today. Will that work?"

"Dan, just call me JC, please. All my friends do. And yes, getting the two plywood doors replaced and a hardened door to the garage installed is just fine with me."

"Excellent. We got lucky with your new doors, JC. My one concern was what color to paint 'em. However, they're already grained and painted solid steel, made to look like real wood. So that's solved. There's no wood involved. I'm going to reinforce your two-by-six outer wood frames on all your exterior doors, adding an additional two studs per side per door. That means I'm going to have to cut some of your interior sheet rock to get at those studs.

"When I'm finished with these three doors tomorrow, you'll never know any alterations were made. Your doors will look very natural, like true hardwood doors. But they'll be able to withstand a four-man hand ram, most likely for six hits. Jack and I agree. That gives you ample time to get secure in your safe room."

"Sounds good to me. How can I help? Oh, one thing. A friend is coming over this afternoon. No worries on your working at all, just want you to know I'm having a friend over."

"No worries, JC. If I can borrow a couple of your guys for a bit, that'll be all the help I'll need for a while."

"Great! Teal? Who can help Dan?"

"Dave and I are happy to give a hand." Teal got on comms and asked Dave to come in for a few minutes, telling him what was going on.

It was only a couple minutes, and Dave was walking up the driveway. Teal and Dan walked out to meet him at the trailer. It was only a minute later, and the three of them were carrying what appeared to be a very heavy door and frame to the front of the house. Leaning it against the outside wall, they went back to the trailer and started carrying the second door around back.

I opened the garage door so they could bring the third door inside the garage.

The whole process took only a few minutes, maybe five, and all three doors were staged. Dave walked back toward the trees, and Teal came inside.

"I'm going to eat, then get out there so those guys can grab some hot food too. Paul and Taco will be here about ten this morning. They'll spell Dave and Bobby and spend the next twenty-four hours here while we get some rest and ready for tomorrow. I don't know if Jack will be here at all today."

"Either way works for me, Teal. Thanks for helping Dan. Looks like he's serious about getting on with this project."

"It does, and you're welcome. Always." Teal moved to the kitchen and helped himself to oatmeal and extras, grabbed a large cinnamon roll, and poured his coffee.

Seemed like only a couple minutes later and Teal and Kim were walking toward the forest. Only a bit later and Dave and Bobby were walking up to the house, both of them dripping wet from being out in the drizzle all night. They were both wearing hooded ponchos, but I suspect that didn't really keep the drizzle from finding its way to skin.

"Hey, guys," I said as I handed large towels to each of them. They climbed out of their ponchos and did what they could to dry off as they moved to the kitchen and breakfast. I had two blankets, single-bed size, sitting on one of the island stools ready for them.

"Why don't you get out of your wet clothes and wrap up in these blankets? I can put your clothes in the dryer while you eat. If you slow down on gulping your food, your clothes will be dry before you're finished with your second cup of coffee. Okay?"

Dave and Bobby looked at each other, grinned, and had a race to see who could strip out of their wet clothes first. They didn't bother with the blankets until their bowls and plates were loaded and coffee cups filled. As they were loading up for breakfast, I took their clothing to the washer, set it for a quick cycle, and started it. They'd be a captive audience until their clothes were dry about an hour and a half from now.

Telling them what I'd done, they both slowed their eating and coffee consumption. It was just ninety minutes later and their clothes were washed and dried. I pulled their clothing out as soon as the cycle finished, shook 'em out, and most of the wrinkles disappeared.

"Here you go, guys. Nice, dry, warm clothes." I handed the outfits to them and let 'em figure out who was going to wear what. Didn't take them any time to get dressed and ready.

Bobby continued, "We're going to hang out with you here until Paul and Taco show up, probably an hour or two. Then, Dave and I will rotate home until tomorrow. You'll have Paul in the house with Kim, and Taco will be outside. They'll bring rain gear, so we'll all end up some dryer even if it does this for the next couple days. They'll probably bring dry clothes as well." Bobby was letting me know who would be where.

"Thanks for the hot breakfast, JC, and for our clean and dry clothes. Not necessary, but we do appreciate it. We're used to being cold and wet, but it's much nicer to be warm and dry," Dave said with a chuckle.

"No reason for anybody to be any more uncomfortable than necessary. Not as far as I'm concerned, is there anything more I can get you for breakfast?"

"I think we're good. Bobby, anything more?"

"No, boss. I'm warm, dry, and stuffed. What more can life offer?"

"Good. I'm going to check with Dan, see if I can get him anything. Be right back." And I walked to the front porch, where Dan had finished assembling the tools he'd need today and tomorrow and was in the process of removing the front plywood door, hinges, and brackets.

"Hey, Dan, you hungry? I made oatmeal this morning if you're interested. There's some fruit, pastries from Olsen's, and hot coffee."

"Thanks anyway, JC. I think I'll get on this. Maybe coffee in a couple hours and see if anybody left a pastry."

"You're sure?"

"Yup. I came here to work today, not eat. I do appreciate the offer."

"You're welcome. I'll make sure to have fresh, hot coffee whenever you want it. If I can help with anything, just let me know, okay?"

"Deal. Thanks again, Mr. Merrick." I really didn't want to correct him again, so I let the "Mister" slide for now.

This really wasn't the atmosphere I wanted for this afternoon with Lu. But I figured she'd understand. Besides, there were other rooms in the house we could move to if construction noise became a bother.

It was just after ten when Paul showed up. Taco was only a few minutes behind him. They greeted Dan, then visited with Bobby and Dave. Comparing notes, I suspected. They were huddled, talking in quiet tones for maybe fifteen minutes, then broke up. Bobby and Dave came over where I was sitting with Kip's head on my lap.

"We're heading out, JC. Paul, Taco, Kim, and Teal are with you until tomorrow. Kim will be your primary, glued to your hip, as usual. Any issues, they all know what to do. Have a safe day, yeah?"

"Thanks, guys. I appreciate you being here." And both Bobby and Dave were out the door. They'd be back at some point tomorrow. Paul and Kim remained inside, while Taco and Teal would be outside for several hours yet.

Amongst a life now filled with curious events, there was another to add. Since the last attack where Connie and Belle died, everybody had added to their arsenal. They were all now also carrying Colt M4s, the one with the shorter fourteen-inch barrel. They were carried on single-point slings, currently hung on their backs, barrels pointed down. I'd asked Teal about it earlier. The Colt M4 variant they used held thirty-round magazines plus one (if you carried it hot), used .223 caliber rounds, and was as reliable as anything on the market.

Teal explained that while there was a ban on so-called assault weapons, the status of Jack and his team doing protection work for the military and government in general allowed them to be licensed to own and use this particular weapon. Now each of the team members protecting me had added combat vests complete with four extra thirty-round magazines for their Colts plus two extra fifteen-round magazines for their Beretta pistols. When everybody gathered, it looked like they could start a small war and win.

Come to think of it, I'd noticed Dan had a pistol on his hip too. It looked like a revolver and big enough to fill his large hands. Looked to me, one more time, like everybody was prepared, just in case.

I'd cleaned up from breakfast, loaded the dishwasher, and turned it on. More dishes than I wanted to wash by hand. I busied myself cleaning up the counters and island, straightening things a bit, then went to the sofa and sat with Kip. He seemed fascinated by Dan and the work he was doing.

Dan had hauled some two-by-six studs from his trailer and piled those beside each of the doors and frames. With all the tools he'd lined up, it looked like he could almost build an entire home, not just replace three doors.

Kip and I watched as he cut and removed some inner Sheetrock, moved some wiring, and trimmed four two-by-six studs to fit along each side of the new front doorframe. The new steel doors came prehung, meaning the door and frame were already assembled as a single unit, ready to install and use. The outside walls of the frame on both sides had six three-quarter-inch holes predrilled, each one equidistant from the others. There was an included template to use to mark the location of each of the predrilled holes along the outer two-by-six wood studs.

That meant Dan could, using the provided template, drill holes from the wood stud side through the four studs, and those holes would line up with the predrilled holes in the outer wall of the steel doorframe. I'd learned a few construction tips from Dad when he did a home repair or modification. One of the things I learned was that the right glue used to bind pieces of wood together was stronger than any nail or screw. I was watching to see how Dan secured the doorframe to the wooden studs. He'd added the extra studs to each side of the outer doorframe and glued them to the existing wood studs, then clamped them in place. Those uprights would never come apart, not in my lifetime.

He marked and drilled holes in the wood studs, used some glue, and pushed heavy bolts through the holes. The bolts had broad heads with L9 stamped on them and self-locking nuts with that same stamp. He added a drop of thread lock on the threads. No way were these things loosening.

I'd asked Dan about the L9 stamp. He said they were significantly stronger and tougher than common bolts and nuts of that size. Once each side of the frame was complete and bolted in place, the clamps were removed, and Dan reattached the inside face of the doorframe. The edges of the removable frame pieces fit well inside the doorframe itself, completely invisible once reattached. Made the entire bolt-securing action easier, faster, and more secure.

Before I knew it, 1:00 p.m. rolled around, and I saw Lu drive up. While the day was still overcast and dripping water, Lu made the sun shine, and my day was definitely brighter with her here. I thought it amusing that Paul and Kim made themselves scarce as soon as Lu drove up. Still, I appreciated it.

Lu stepped around Dan and his work, came inside, and treated me to a huge smile. "Hey, Sailor. How's your day? Where is everybody?"

"Well, it was good. Now you're here, and it's terrific! Paul and Kim are in the house somewhere. Taco and Teal are outside on overwatch." Lu walked up to me and gave me a quick kiss on the cheek, then dropped the bag she was carrying, putting it on the island counter.

"Figured we could enjoy a treat in a while. Looks like you're finally getting your doors replaced. Are those doors what I think they are?"

"Don't know. What do you think they are?"

"They look like wood, but somehow that doesn't fit with all the extra studs he's using. Sooo steel? Or steel clad?"

"When did you learn about steel doors and construction?"

"You'd be surprised what I know, Sailor. You'd be surprised."

"Fair enough. Would you like to sit with Kip and visit for a while? Or I can dig out Scrabble or chess. What's your preference?"

"Why don't we start with Kip and go from there? Is that okay?"

"You bet!"

Lu and I moved to the sofa, currently occupied by Kip. He looked at us both, probably wondering why we were invading one of his favorite spots. I sat on one end of the sofa and turned toward the other end with Kip's head and paws in my lap. Lu sat on the opposite end and turned toward me with Kip's butt and tail near her thigh. Kip seemed pleased with this arrangement and showed no intention of rousing himself or moving anywhere. Worked for me. It just felt right for Lu to be here, ya know?

"How is your remodel coming? Looks like the process is just beginning, but you'll soon have good doors, right?"

"Yup. Oops! Manners!" I raised my voice a bit. "Dan Hastings, say hi to Lucienne Abreo. Lu, this is Dan Hastings, owner of Hastings Construction. Dan's doing the build on the safe room. His project after that is to build the shop I'll need for rebuilding classic muscle cars."

Lu rose from the sofa and walked to Dan. Sticking out her hand, she shook with Dan's. "Hi, Mr. Hastings. Nice to meet you."

"Thank you, Ms. Abreo. It's nice to meet you too."

"Please, Mr. Hastings, call me Lu. All my friends do."

"Thank you. It'll be my pleasure. Please call me Dan, okay?"

"Sure, Mr. Hast...oops, Dan," she said with a full-wattage smile.

Lu walked back to the sofa and sat. Kip wiggled his butt a bit, wagged his tail, and resituated himself so his hind quarters were pressed against Lu's thigh. Kip was one classy dog.

"You decided to go ahead and build your shop? I thought you were going to think about it."

"I did, both. I thought about it, and I decided to go ahead. The only thing I need to decide is how big to build it. I don't want it cramped, and I don't want to waste space either. And I don't want to have to do an add-on ever. I'm thinking of about nine thousand square feet of workspace."

"That sounds big. How many lifts will you have?"

"Probably three. That way the mechanic can switch to a second vehicle if he or she gets hung up waiting for parts. I've included room for a paint booth, an area for metal fabrication, and an office to do planning and managing. Also adding three enlarged bathrooms. Two are for customers, his and hers. One for staff, complete with separate his and hers shower rooms and lockers in each for changing clothing.

"The garage will have a twenty-foot wide, sixteen-foot tall overhead door at each end. One end brings in the project car or bits and pieces. The other overhead door opens up from showroom end and allows completed cars to exit. The more I think about it, the more the nine thousand square feet seems to fit. But I still want input from Angus and Jack and, of course, Dan. Especially Dan, who knows more about construction than I ever will, so I'll give considerable weight to his opinion and input."

"Sounds like you've thought about this a lot in just the last couple days!"

"I have. This feels like something I can do to help others in a different way. And I think I'll get a lot of enjoyment from the process."

"Good for you, JC. I'm proud of you all over again!"

Just then, we heard a vehicle drive up. I could tell from the sound of the motor it was Jack. He walked up in full combat gear, like the others. It seemed to surprise Lu a bit.

"Hey, Jack. Welcome! Thanks for working with Dan on the doors. Just think, in a couple days, the house will have real doors again!"

"Hi, JC, Lu. Look, I hate to spoil your day, but we've uncovered some disturbing information. I've notified Teal and Taco. Kim and Paul are already here. I'd like them to run interference, so you and I are undisturbed."

"Jack, would you prefer me to leave? It's okay. Whatever you've learned sounds important."

"Lu, that's up to JC. I'm good either way."

"If you're okay with it, I'd like you to stay, Lu. I'm sure there's no earth-shattering news coming, no nuclear codes being divulged or state secrets shared. We're only dealing with the drama that's come up in my life. I for one could really do with less drama. A lot less."

"Thanks, Sailor. I admit being curious about what's going on. I know Kyle and Mat are as well. You have my word, I can and will keep secret whatever you wish. Just want you all to know that."

"Let's move to the atrium? It's quiet, and we'll have enough privacy for whatever's going on. Do I need to call Angus? What about my doc? Should she be in on this as well?"

"That's probably a good idea, JC. I think you'll want them to know what's going on."

I pulled my cell phone out of my pocket and called Angus. Second ring… "Angus? JC calling."

"JC! What can I do for you this fine day?"

"Jack's dug up some disturbing information, to use his words. I'd like you here to hear what he's learned. I think this is some of the information having to do with people trying to kill me."

"Say no more. I'm on my way."

I punched in a second number, and the phone rang twice. "JC. What can I do for you?" Dr. Church was part of my inner circle, so she should be here too if she was available.

"Jack has learned something important. I'd like you here to hear what he has to say if you're available. He just arrived. I apologize for such short notice."

"Angus is coming as well?"

"Yes. He'll be here in about twenty minutes."

"I'll see you then. Thanks for letting me know, JC." And I was listening to a disconnected line.

"Jack, Angus, and Doc are on the way. Should be here in minutes. Until they arrive, can I get you anything to drink? Pop? Water? Orange juice? Lemonade?"

"Just ice water, JC. Please."

"Lu? What can I get you?"

"Do you still have some Diet Pepsi?"

"One Diet Pepsi on ice coming right up."

Drinks in hand, the three of us moved into our atrium. Well, it wasn't exactly an atrium, but that was better than calling it a sunroom. A larger room, with a glass southern and eastern wall, it had dozens of plants and indoor trees, some of them fruit bearing. During the summer months, I could remove the southern wall, and the entire space was transformed to an outdoor living area.

Anyhow, there was comfortable outdoor-like lounging furniture, a very old solid oak table with six chairs, and an older but very comfortable sofa. It was my favorite room. I'd done a ton of studying in this room while I attended Kings Academy. Now I used it, somewhat frequently, when I needed to think about some important thing or other.

Kip decided to attend too. Seems his curiosity was up as well.

It was only minutes, and I heard Angus calling my name. "JC! Where are you?"

"In the atrium, Angus! Grab a soda and meet us here." And a minute later, Angus and Doc were with us in the atrium. They each pulled up a chair and gave Jack and me an expectant look.

With us moved to the atrium, we'd have the privacy we needed without interrupting Dan's work. He was making great progress on the three doors.

Jack looked at each of us as seriously as I'd ever seen him. That included when he'd lost Connie, then Belle. Something was definitely up.

"Thank you for indulging me. I'm sorry to have interrupted your day, but this is important. There are things I need to discuss with JC, and now you as well, Lu, and Angus and Dr. Church. It'll be up to JC whether he tells anybody else what's going on. For now, we need to keep this knowledge very tight.

"Please, Jack, and everybody else present, I think it's time for you all to drop the doctor title and call me Phyllis or Phyl, whichever is more comfortable to each of you. Doctor is great in a medical setting, but this is anything but, okay?" And a round of agreement followed.

"You already know the shit that's surrounded JC these past weeks..." This must be something. I'd only heard Jack swear one time before. He'd always seemed more in control.

"One of our analysists has come across some very disturbing information. Bear with me, please, because this is going to sound completely nuts. However, what we've uncovered explains a lot, all the way back to JC's parents dying in their car wreck nearly two years ago. I'm warning you in advance, this is going to sound like science fiction, but given JC's life these past couple of years, it all seems to fit."

Huh. Seemed to me normal was not going to be how I'd describe my life, at least from this point forward. No matter what I did in the future, I'd have to deal with whatever Jack had discovered. It also seemed that there was some possibility bad actors would continue to pursue me and mine. With these two things in mind plus whatever Jack was about to share, the first thing I needed to do was build some sort of foundation that would address those things I wanted to do with my life as well as take whatever action was required to keep me and those close to me as safe as possible.

But that, of course, is an entirely different story.

What comes next? Watch for JC's next book, Foundation*!*

Author's Note

Two of my primary motives for writing *Life After Death* were real-life events. The first happened in the late spring of 1971 in Portland, Oregon. Emery and his roommate lived near the Banfield Freeway and were enjoying a quiet evening. Without warning, there was a tremendous crash, and the whole house shook.

Running outside to see what happened, they could both see a cloud of dirt and debris rising right over the nearby freeway. Running to the guardrail, they both witnessed a car wreck involving at least four vehicles. One of the wrecked cars was upside down at the very entrance of a freeway on-ramp.

Emory had an instant, compelling urge to cross the multiple freeway lanes and get to the occupants of the upside-down car. Freeway traffic is very unforgiving. There was no practical way for him to make his way across multiple lanes of cars to get to the car resting upside-down. Nevertheless, he began climbing the guardrail to make his way down the embankment and across the busy traffic.

Luckily or not, his roommate stopped him from performing a dangerous run toward and across lanes of cars and trucks not even bothering to slow down.

Reading the local paper the next day, Emory and his roommate learned the driver of the upside-down car was a pregnant woman who was driving herself to the hospital to give birth to the daughter she was carrying. Neither the mother nor the soon-to-be-born child survived, both dying at the scene.

Fast-forward thirteen years, Emory was again at the scene of a traffic accident. A car had lost its brakes while traveling down a steep, dead-end residential hill. Unable to stop or even slow down, the car attempted a sharp left-hand turn at the intersection. Unsuccessful, the car slid across the street and T-boned itself into a power pole while traveling about forty miles per hour.

Not this time ran through Emory's mind as he watched this tragedy unfold. Traveling slowly down the same hill as the now-wrecked car, he put his car in neutral, applied the emergency brake, and ran toward the wreck. Dodging a few cars that were completely unaware of the unfolding drama, Emory was first on the scene of the wreck.

The front passenger door had sprung open. The driver, the only occupant, appeared to be a young woman. She had been thrown into the front passenger seat, her upper body and right arm dangling outside the car.

In the background, Emory could hear others approaching. "Don't move her! Don't move her!" came a loud voice as its owner hurried toward the car. Some unknown force, some urge that was not to be ignored commanded Emory to touch the young woman's right hand. At the touch of his hand, she opened her eyes, smiled, and then lost consciousness once again.

"What happened? What'd you do?" An off-duty sheriff's deputy was next on the scene.

"Nothing. I didn't do anything."

"You sure did something. I've seen a lot of car wrecks and more dead bodies than I care to remember. That girl was dead. I could tell by the way she lay in the car. She was dead."

"No," I replied. "I think she'll be fine."

As the deputy bent down for a closer look at the victim, a paramedic was next to arrive, only several seconds later. He, too, just "happened" to be nearby and witnessed the wreck.

"Did that guy move her? I saw it all from our truck. This girl was dead."

Backing away slowly, Emory walked back to his car. The following day, he was able to read about the accident and get in touch with the girl's mother. The mom related that her daughter would be fine. She was bruised and sore and had no memory of the accident.

Where Emory had failed to act once, his actions this second time may have saved a young woman's life.

About the Author

Emory Douglas Lynn was born in a very small town along the highline in the state of Montana. He attended nineteen schools throughout Montana, Wyoming, and Idaho before graduating high school, a testimony to his early and varied life of travel.

Emory has been employed as a mechanic, hard-rock miner, welder for a heavy equipment manufacturer, truck driver, midlevel business manager, small business owner, regional manager for a specialty food manufacturer, and regional director of an international legacy nonprofit organization.

Emory has traveled extensively throughout the western United States for work and pleasure. His life adventures have taken him to every state west of the Mississippi and several on the east side. He has traveled internationally to Canada and Mexico as well.

An avid reader for decades, Mr. Lynn reads an average of three books weekly and has done so for years. He enjoys reading historical fiction, biographies, mysteries, works of fiction, and the history of our great nation.

Emory and the great love of his life, Lucienne (strange but true), have five grown children and continue their life adventures with Buck Kip, their Goldendoodle, from their home base in Montana.

Printed in the USA
CPSIA information can be obtained
at www.ICGtesting.com
LVHW040001251124
797341LV00001B/134